THE WEDDING FATALITY

BY

A. TRAURING

AJ Press

This edition published in 2015 by AT Press, Atlanta, Georgia

ISBN 978-0-9915291-4-8

© 2015 AT Press, Atlanta, Georgia
v 5.3

This is a work of fiction. Names, characters, and incidents are products of the author's dubious imagination; all persons and events depicted are fictional. Any resemblance to actual persons living or dead is an unintended coincidence.

While some places depicted exist in what some refer to as the real world, they are used fictitiously.

Other books by A. Trauring in the Amy & Paul Saga:

A Different Kind Of Twin

The Beaded Necklace

The Rothschild Jewels (soon!)

Available at Amazon.com at
http://www.amazon.com/A.-
Trauring/e/B00JCC9RCO/ref=sr_ntt_srch_lnk_3?qid=1442354247
&sr=1-3

Cover photography by Syda Productions
Licensed from Shutterstock

This one's for Cindy. I can barely remember a time before we were friends.

Thanks to Sue Sandell for editorial support. Once again, she has made my work into a better book.

Thanks to the EPC Book Club for fellowship, good reading, and wonderful support.

Amy and Paul live at http://atrauring.weebly.com

✄ PROLOGUE ᘐ

In June 2015, the Supreme Court ruled that same-sex marriage was the law of the land in the United States.

Before the next year ended, 41 state legislatures had passed bills to convene an 'Article five' convention of the states to propose a Constitutional amendment reversing the court decision.

The result of the convention was a seventeen-word proposal: "The definition of matrimony is to be determined by the legislatures and/or voters of each state."

One can imagine the turmoil that followed. Nothing–not Iran's test of a nuclear bomb over Baghdad, not the Chicago Cubs winning the National League pennant, not even a presidential candidate's indictment on nine counts of RICO violations–wrested the headlines from nonstop discussion, ranting, and demagoguery over the 'Marriage Freedom Amendment.'

It took two years for the measure to make its way to the states. The first to take a stand was California; in a rare combined session, the state senate and assembly voted 109 to 10 to defeat it. Two weeks later, the Louisiana Senate approved the measure 81 to 24, and the next day the state house voiced its consent 36 to 2.

Some states put the proposed amendment on a general ballot, where large majorities approved it in the Dakotas, in Nebraska, and Georgia; only New York state voters turned it down.

In January 2018, New Mexico's legislature was the 38th state to approve the Marriage Freedom Amendment. The Supreme Court took expedited action on the inevitable court challenge, and ruled unanimously that the amendment had been lawfully adopted. On the first of May that year it came into force as the 28th Amendment to the US Constitution.

The surprise is that, after all that fuss and political theatre, only four states passed laws to restrict marriage to one man and one woman. The first to do so was Louisiana.

ॐ SUNDAY, August 13, 2034 ॐ

The bright sunlight through the windows was shining in her face, making it difficult to see details. As Amy's eyes adjusted, the black shape at the desk resolved into Pastor Riley Tibbs, head down, slumped over her desk.

Amy heard Christine gasp behind her. Then there was a cry from Associate Pastor Drew Malone; the woman rushed to Tibbs, babbling, and tried to remove the huge knife sticking out of her back.

"Stop!" Amy commanded, "Don't touch anything!" She took the three steps to reach Malone and put her hand on the associate pastor's shoulder. With her other hand she snaked two fingers over the carotid artery on the left side of Tibbs' neck. There was no pulse.

"No emergency anymore," she announced. "Christine, can you call 911? Ask them for Rampart Street PD."

While Christine tried not to drop the phone from her shaking hands, Amy turned to Malone. "I wish you hadn't done that, Preacher," she shook her head. "The handle of a murder weapon still in place ought to be prime evidence. Now Jermaine will have to see if there are any prints underneath yours."

Drew hung her head. "I just–I just–Riley, it's just too much." She looked up, into Amy's eyes. "Can't we do anything?"

Pointing to Christine, she said, "My friend is doing it. We're calling the police. I'm only a private investigator these days."

Along with the sunlight, loud voices and chants came through the window from the demonstration outside the building.

The upset associate slowly walked around the room, looking at books and figurines on the bookshelves and at piles of reports on a credenza. Paul thought, *I feel bad for the lady, but she's messing up the crime scene.*

Amy nodded, then called to Drew. "I need you to leave this room. It's a crime scene and the police will be here shortly." She turned. "Christine?"

The woman nodded silently at her phone, then handed it to Amy, whispering, "It's a Sergeant Francks."

"Walter!" Amy said into the phone, "How the hell are you?"

"Hey, Sugar," he drawled back. "I miss you to death at the station house. What's up?"

"Homicide at the MCC on St. Charles. We need a crew and a meat wagon." Amy turned to Malone and said, "Sorry." Then back to the sergeant, "Body discovered about five minutes ago. Tell the crew to come around to the office entrance. There's a wedding going on, and there's no need to alarm all those folks."

"Slow down, Sugar. What's an MCC?"

"Metropolitan Community Church, you heathen."

"Yep," he laughed, "I was raised by wolves."

"I'll secure the scene, but hurry–I don't want to miss the wedding."

Francks chuckled, "Wedding? I didn't know you were engaged."

"Oh, Walter. You know you're the only man for me."

"Sure thing. I'll send, uhh, Duke Cranston. You know him?"

She thought: a burly black man with a shaved head. "He came in just before I left the force. I know who he is, but we never talked. And Walter? Let the Commander know I was involved. I'm available if he wants to bring me in for the case."

"Yeah, he usually checks in every few hours. I'll tell him. Let me get Cranston moving. You take care, Sugar."

When Amy ended the call, she realized the associate pastor was still standing in front of her. "Please, Drew–out!" She started to point to the doorway like an airline stewardess showing the escape doors, then said, "What are you doing? Nerve pills?"

Malone had poured five or six little pills into her hand, different shades of pink. "Tic-Tacs," the woman said, and she put them in her mouth. "I use them a lot. Especially when I'm upset."

"I can understand upset," Amy said, "but I need you out of this room."

"Paulette, what's next?"

Paul took the lead to hug Christine. "Amy's going to wait on the cops, then we're going back downstairs to watch Gina and Shawna tie the knot." Amy added, "I need you out of the room, too. Keep Drew occupied for a couple of minutes."

When Christine went into the hallway, Amy closed the door behind her by grabbing the side of the lock stile rather than the doorknob, as high up as she could reach to lessen the chance of messing up possible fingerprint or fiber clues. Paul said aloud, "When the cops get here, they're going to want to call you Amy. That won't work."

She smiled and thought back, *I hope that's the biggest thing I have to worry about today.* Then, out loud, "Let's see what we've got."

It's complicated. Paul–as the name implies–is a man. He is 81 years old. However, only 58 of those years were spent in his male body. On a business trip to New Orleans in 2008, he was robbed by street thugs who beat him into a coma and left him for dead on the levee of the Mississippi River. After more than two years as a comatose John Doe, fluid from a bedsore splashed on a little girl while he was being wheeled to the Intensive Care Unit, where his body promptly died. But the next morning Paul woke up in that eleven-year-old girl's body, terrified and angry.

The little girl is thirty-four now. Since that Saturday long ago, Amy Clear has shared her head and her body with Paul. They became friends. They became mutual fans. They wish they could be lovers. Amy has been a market researcher, a police detective, and now a private investigator, with Paul as her constant companion.

How do they live? As Paul once said, he didn't arrive in Amy with an owner's manual. When Amy got to college, Paul had to learn to endure her romances. It was painful for all concerned. Painful, that is, until Amy let Paul lead one night, calling himself Paulette, and visiting the Sappho Rising club. Christine Hodges thought their bent front tooth–mirroring her own–was adorable, and introduced herself. In the years since that meeting, Christine and Paul have been lovers. She understands that he thinks of himself as male, but he is encased in Amy's female body. Christine calls him Paulette. And Amy and Paul reached an agreement: if he wanted Amy to allow him to continue his physical relationship with Christine (he was using her body, after all), he had to put up with her physical dalliances with men.

Amy has demonstrated terrible taste in men, falling for married detectives, itinerant musicians, prime suspects and murderers. Even she acknowledges her consistently bad judgment. She teases Paul that, if she ever gives up entirely on men, she'll let him marry Christine. She's come close, but hasn't gotten that depressed yet.

Amy stood in front of the pastor's desk, trying to ignore the noise of the hubbub coming from outside the church. The desk was made of a light-colored wood, heavily varnished. There was an oversized desk calendar in the middle, partially obscured by the pastor's head and some blood drops; Paul thought to her, *Jermaine is a whiz with blood-spatter patterns.* There was a Tiffany-style desk lamp on the left, the green glass shade glowing. On the right was a pile of file folders. She spotted a mug, handle broken off, leaning against the wall on the right. It read, 'Jesus, Give me Wisdom, Give me Strength, Give me COFFEE.' A few ounces remained inside, but the angle indicated there would be a brown puddle on the floor under the desk.

"Do you see anything out of the ordinary?" Amy whispered to Paul.

The mug, he thought back. *And I could be wrong, but I think there's a dead person leaning on the desk.*

"Really?" Amy countered aloud, "You see dead people? Are you prone to hallucinations? Or is this the first one?" She walked behind the pastor's chair to get an overall sense of the body's position. The desk was no more than three feet away from the office door, which opened out. A muted rust and mustard plaid rug reached the wall with the door, but it ended at the desk chair. Amy muttered to Paul "It would drive me crazy to work at a desk where the chair is always falling off the edge of a rug or getting hung up on it."

"Maybe she used to be a Catholic. I think they believe suffering is good."

Amy snorted, "Ooh, Sister Francis would give you such a whack."

The pastor's chair was pulled in as if the woman had been writing at the desk. Tibbs' right arm was under her chest, but Amy resisted the urge to move the body to see what the pastor had been working on. "I hope Cranston and them get here soon. I want to know what she was up to."

The room itself was a cluttered ten-by-twelve. A window punctuated the rear wall, which otherwise was covered in posters of church events. Bookcases filled another wall. There was a small loveseat opposite the desk, and two worn upholstered wing chairs behind it. You would have to move things to make enough room to lie down on the floor.

Amy scanned the room but did not see anything striking–no overturned furniture, no dumped drawer contents, no open window, no bloody handprints. "Let me look at the door," she mused to Paul. To open it she pulled her hand inside her sleeve so fabric was against the knob when she turned it. Drew came up expectantly but said nothing. Paul thought to Christine, *Amy's looking for clues. Are you doing okay?* He was the only one to notice the woman's weak nod.

Examining the door, Amy saw no scrapes or nicks on the door lock. There were no marks on the door frame near the jamb. *No forced entry,* she thought to Paul; *I wonder if she knew her killer.*

"Can you solve it?" Drew asked. Amy blinked and turned to the associate pastor. "Oh, sure," she answered. "But not yet. Look, I need your help. Put your hands in your pockets, and come inside with me. Tell me if anything looks out of place. Or missing. But don't touch anything. Okay?"

Sheepishly the woman nodded and followed Amy back inside. A metallic smell had begun to seep into the air from the dead pastor's spilled blood. As Drew slowly turned to look at the room, Amy kept a close eye on her. *She probably ruined the knife for forensics,* she thought to Paul. *I'm not going to let her mess up more of the investigation.*

Finally Drew turned back to Amy and shook her head. "I don't see anything missing. Riley was not exactly a neat-freak."

"Okay. Thanks." With a hand on her back Amy ushered the associate pastor out of the room, back into the hallway. Christine was clearly troubled; she whispered, "Paulette, what do we do?"

Paul led, sounding exactly like Amy, and asked Malone, "Can you do a wedding ceremony?"

"Of course!"

"Good. As soon as the police get here to take over the crime scene, there are some friends of mine in the bride's room who are waiting to get married." Then, turning to Christine, he said, "Why don't you tell Gina and Shawna there's been a delay, but they're still going to walk down the aisle."

Christine began, "Should–should I tell them...?"

Paul shook their head. "Not yet. Let's not ruin their day." Christine nodded with relief and scurried off to her friends downstairs, where the air wouldn't smell like death.

"So, now what?" Drew held the plastic Tic-Tac container to her lips and poured more of the little pink pills into her mouth.

Amy said, "We wait. Or I wait here. Do you want to hang out at the office door? That's where the police are–"

A racket interrupted, louder and closer than the street demonstrations. Christine was walking back toward them, hands over her ears, as Lieutenant Duke Cranston, Medical Examiner Doctor Jermaine Tallant, and two uniformed officers followed, all talking at once. "Paulette!" she cried, "The police are here!"

Paul sang silently to Amy and to Christine, *With cat-like tread, upon our prey we steal.* Neither recognized the bit of Gilbert & Sullivan.

"Lieutenant Cranston? Please call me Paulette," Amy said, hoping to prevent confusion. She held out her hand, and the uniformed officer shook it. "Paulette? Wait, I remember you from the station house. I thought your name was–"

"Here, please call me Paulette," Amy interrupted; she attempted to wink at the man.

"Paulette? Ohhh-kay, Paulette."

She pointed into the office, at the late Reverend Riley Tibbs. "Dead right there," Amy said. "Discovered maybe fifteen minutes ago. I didn't see anything obvious. But it's your problem now, Duke. We've got a wedding to attend."

"Wait," the Lieutenant said, holding up one hand. "What the hell is going on out there?" He pointed back down the hall.

"Two lady friends of mine are getting married today," Amy said. "Some of the people outside like it. Some don't."

"Could someone have gotten in to do this?" He was reaching for the notebook on his inside jacket pocket.

"Umm . . . talk to Drew about that; she's the associate pastor. But first she's marrying my friends." She held one hand out to Malone, and the other to Christine. "Shall we?"

The three women walked downstairs to where the wedding participants were waiting in the bride's room. Gina Gales was a tall, slender woman with a professional hair style, midway between blonde and brown. She was wearing a rented tuxedo. With her was Shawna Mallory, in an enormous white bride's dress. Shawna was short, with black hair done up in an uncharacteristic but attractive bun. The woman was cursed with an unfortunate face, marred by two large, hairy moles and uneven eyes, but it struck Paul that today, in that dress, Shawna was the closest he had ever seen to pretty.

"I'm getting worried," Gina said, standing up. "We are getting married, right?"

"Yes, you are," Paul answered, sounding just like Amy. "This is Associate Pastor Drew Malone," he said, and introduced her to the bride and bridess.

"We thought Riley wath going to do the thervice," Shawna said. She had a slight lisp from a recently installed tongue stud.

Drew said, "She's been called away. Was there anything special she was going to do? Vows?"

Shawna shook her head. "Just, you know, no 'he' and 'him' thtuff."

"Understood," she smiled, as she pulled a stole out of an inside pocket and began to arrange it over her robe. "We've kept your friends waiting long enough. I'm going up to the altar. It'll just be a few minutes now. Wait by the archway until you're called." Then she held up her right hand, palm out and facing the women, and said, "May the risen Lord bless you today and always."

Christine hugged Gina and then Shawna. "I'm going to get a good seat. See you at the reception."

Amy turned to leave with her. "Break a leg," she called over their shoulder.

The sanctuary was crowded with some family members, lots of friends from the Sappho Rising club Amy and Paul frequented, Gina's job, from Shawna's art community, and some brave activists who wanted to see Louisiana's first new same-sex marriage with their own eyes. The organ music drowned out most of the chants from the outside demonstrations, although the occasional bullhorn feedback broke through.

Gina was standing in front of Associate Pastor Malone, her father beside her as best man. An odd collection of bridesmaids came down the aisle–six women in six different dresses in six different colors; one of them walked in time to the organ music, while another was chewing gum. They lined up to the side of the altar, facing all the guests.

Someone's adorable little niece came down the center aisle, practically obscured by billows of white chiffon and crinolines as she tossed flower petals from her basket. Some of the guests in the pews snapped pictures with their phones.

Amy and Christine sat halfway back on the left, on the aisle. Next to Christine was Ashley, a waitress at Sappho Rising who once, and maybe still, had a crush on Paulette. "Isn't this great?" Ashley whispered, mouth open in awe at the ritual and the historical importance of the event.

Finally the organist began the familiar music of Mendelssohn's *Wedding March*. Shawna, accompanied by her older sister, slowly walked from the back of the sanctuary to join the clot of people at the altar. Paul glanced at his lover and was touched to see a tear running down her happy face. Then Amy looked up at the altar and saw how excited Gina was as her partner slowly approached.

"Dearly beloved," the pastor intoned, "we are gathered here in the sight of God, and in the presence of these witnesses, to join together these persons in holy matrimony."

Drew went on with the familiar ceremony, occasionally fighting street noises from the demonstrations outside. Gina's father, also serving as ring bearer, stepped forward. "If any person here can show just cause why these two should not be married," the pastor said, "speak now or forever hold your peace."

From the back of the sanctuary came three loud thuds. Standing in full regalia, Archbishop Francis Rouxel Laval of the New Orleans Archdiocese slammed his staff down on the church's tile floor. "In the name of St. Paul of Tarsus, this ceremony is blasphemy!" he shouted. A cowled friar in a black cloak lurked behind him.

Murmurs came from those in the pews, punctuated by shouts from the outside demonstrations. Shawna grabbed Gina's hand in fright.

"You are lost, Archbishop!" Drew shouted back. "The Holy Name of Jesus Church is over at the university. You have no authority here. Bell, book, and candle, go from this place!" She and the prelate locked glares for a few seconds, until the Archbishop banged his staff on the floor again; he and his acolyte left and slammed the church door shut behind them.

After a few seconds of silence, a roar of applause broke out across the congregation. Pastor Malone said something softly to Gina and Shawna, then stepped back, head bowed, and waited for the clapping to stop. When it did she said, "Hearing no objection, who presents Shawna Mallory to be wed to Gina Gales?"

Shawna's sister, dabbing at her eyes with a handkerchief, whispered, "I do."

"And who presents Gina Gales to be wed to Shawna Mallory?"

Gina's father, beaming with a wide smile, answered firmly, "I do."

Drew led Gina and Shawna in simple vows. At the appropriate time, Gina's father gave rings to each of the women to exchange. Finally, the pastor said, "By the authority vested in me by the Council of Elders of the Universal Fellowship of Metropolitan

Community Churches, I pronounce you united by God and married. You may kiss each other." Gina took Shawna by the waist and leaned her back to plant an enthusiastic kiss on the surprised and happy woman. The congregation let out hoots and applause at the sight.

Amy and Christine stood up and eagerly joined the tumult. "I'm so happy for Gina," Christine said of her former lover. "Shawna's a lucky girl."

"Yay for them," Paul said. Christine, who somehow always could tell whether it was him or Amy leading, grabbed their arm and hugged it.

"We're not in the wedding party," Amy said, "but I want to go with them when they leave the church. That's an ugly gauntlet they're going to run. Are you up for it?"

"Sure, Amy. Maybe I'll get to congratulate them before everyone else does."

They made their way to the main entrance. As guests opened the doors to leave, the sounds of the demonstrations pulsed in volume. They could hear slogans shouted from both sides of the issue of same-sex marriage, from "Adam and Eve, not Adam and Steve!" to "Marriage is a human right!"

"This is scary, Paulette. Do they really hate us because we love each other?" Her arms were wrapped around herself as she leaned against them.

"A few of them do, Honey. Most of 'em don't mind the love, but they don't want Gina and Shawna to be able to get married."

Christine tried to bury her head in their chest. It was a childlike search for security. Amy said, "Stick with me, we'll be alright. Won't we, Paul?" He added, "Yeah, we'll all be alright." Christine smiled, but continued to lean against them.

When they saw the newlyweds getting close to the entrance, Amy pushed the doors open and stepped into the hot and loud afternoon. Different groups of people noticed her and Christine as new faces; they waved placards and shouted slogans at them. Paul kept his left arm around the cringing Christine as he pushed their way slowly through the endless crowd.

Only a few steps down the walkway stood Archbishop Laval, surrounded by several parish priests, monks, and concerned laity. He was an imposing figure this close: a tall man, his red and gold mitre added another eighteen inches to his height. He was wearing his crimson chasuble with brocade gold center stripe over a white alb, topped with his cream-colored pallium dangling front and back, and a long crimson stole. In his hands was his heavy staff, taller even than his headdress. Although the prelate was silent, his grim expression, his size, and his colorful vestments were intimidating. The friar who had shadowed him in the church was talking non-stop, quoting Bible passages as he sidled left and right, trying to make eye contact with every person leaving the wedding.

Across the walkway was a mob even more colorful in its dress– and lack thereof. About a hundred people, ranging from 'normal'-looking people in business attire, to men in tutus with wings attached, to bare-breasted women, and all of them either holding picket signs or shouting slogans: "We're here, we're queer, get used to it!" "Lesbian and Christian!" "Did I vote on your marriage?" "Love, not hate!" "Jesus had two dads!" "I'm a woman's woman!" even "Corduroy skirts are a sin!" although Paul couldn't figure out why anyone would think that. The volume, the colors, the constant movement frightened Christine, and she put her arm around Amy to make sure they stayed together in the tumult.

Ahead on the city sidewalk they saw several people holding up a wide plastic banner that read 'Partnership of African-American Clergy.' Behind them was a group of maybe twenty-five African-Americans of all ages, most dressed as if for Sunday church. The exceptions were two tall men dressed for a Saturday night: one in a double-breasted suit with wide gray and black stripes, one size too large, the other in a shiny green suit whose jacket reached his knees. Both men wore bright red bow-ties. They did not hold signs, nor did they participate in the chanting and shouting. Behind big mirrored sunglasses they observed the crowd closely.

With her experience from three years as a detective on the Orleans Parish police department, Amy scanned the nearby people, making sure she was prepared for any threat that might materialize. The only alarming things she noticed were a handful of men, always alone amongst the other groups, wearing camouflage and holding inflammatory signs: "God hates fags," "A woman's place is in the kitchen," "AIDS cures queers," and "Make me a sandwich." These were the red flag people, the sort that the NOPD profilers had taught her were dangerous. She thought to Paul, *Watch out for the lone gunmen. The others aren't a threat.* On hearing it, Paul held Christine tighter.

Finally Gina and Shawna emerged from the church with relatives and friends in tow. Immediately the throng's noise surged and the crowds pushed closer. Amy stopped to let the wedding party catch up to her, intending to be a buffer between her friends and the demonstrators. Cheers broke out from the LGBT segment, with acquaintances and strangers reaching out to shake hands or slap high-fives. On the other side of the walkway, the monk who was shadowing the Archbishop shouted a Bible verse and then spit at Shawna, leaving a nasty white gob on the side of her face. The supporters booed and railed.

It angered Paul so much that he took the lead and stepped off the walkway in front of the Archbishop. "Your pet is off his leash, Your Grace. Apologize to my friends." There was silence from the Archdiocesan group, and even the people supporting same-sex marriage quieted down.

"Well?" Paul prodded, tapping their foot; Christine kept her grip on Paul but slid behind them to hide.

Laval turned to the monk. "We must not sink to their level, Friar Transom. Jesus teaches us to love the sinner while we hate the sin. Apologize."

Friar Ned Transom shuffled to Paul, head down and red-faced with the humiliation of being disciplined in public. He seemed to shrink into his cassock. Shifting his weight back and forth from one foot the other, he finally mumbled, "'m sorry."

"You're a big man to say that," Paul said. "But not to me. Apologize to Shawna."

His face got even redder as he turned to face the woman. "'m sorry," he repeated.

Quietly Paul said, "I hope your day improves, Your Grace," as cheers and hollering erupted from the wedding's supporters. Gina reached out to grab Paul by the arm; not knowing of Amy's existence, she said, "I will never forget what you just did, Paulette." She leaned forward and kissed them on the mouth. "Take good care of Christine," she added about her former girlfriend. Then she turned back to her bride to resume the trek to the waiting limousine.

Christine stepped out from behind Amy and said, "Wait!" When Gina turned to her, Christine said, "Congratulations. I'm happy for you and Shawna," and she leaned forward to hug and kiss the woman.

"A little part of me will always love you. You know that."

Christine broke the hug and said, "Me, too." She was smiling.

Paul thought to her, *Do you miss her?* They were walking a step ahead of the wedding party, still intending to run interference in case of unruly protesters.

"No," Christine said aloud; it made Amy realize that Paul had thought something private to the woman. "I see her and Shawna often enough. But you know I still like her."

"You know you were in love with a good person if you stay friends with them afterwards."

She hugged Paul and Amy's arm as they walked.

The people at the Partnership of African-American Clergy area were bearing silent witness, with a few picket signs saying "God loves you anyway" and "Marriage = ♂+♀." Most of them wore scowls or other looks of disapproval, although the two men dressed for Saturday night were impassive behind their mirrored sunglasses.

As Gina and Shawna reached the sidewalk, a loud woman with a microphone approached them, followed by a man in jeans and T-shirt with a shoulder-mounted camera. "And here are the women behind today's historic challenge to Louisiana lawmakers, Gina Mallory and Shawn Gales. Girls, Eyewitness News viewers want to know how you feel, being at the center of this hurricane."

It was dangerous to be between Shawna and a camera. As an aspiring artist, she had learned how to milk publicity. She stopped, swathed in her beautiful white wedding dress, and stuck out her right hand. "Hi, I'm Shawna Mallory. Who are you again?"

Startled and annoyed that there was anyone in New Orleans who didn't know, the interviewer said, "Sofia Babbleton, Channel

Four Eyewitness News. How do you feel, Ms. Gales? Or should I say, Mrs. Gales?" The demonstrators in the immediate vicinity quieted down so they could watch the television event happening in front of them.

"I'm fine, Thofia, thanks for athking. I'm Ms. Mallory. She–" pointing to Gina "–she is Ms. Gales. We haven't thought about the Ms. and Mrs. thing yet. What do you think we should do?" Despite her unfortunate face, Shawna was relaxed in front of camera and microphone, and came across as energetic and likeable.

"Uh, what our Eyewitness News viewers want to know is how you feel about breaking state law by getting married when the legislature has repeatedly voted down bills that would legalize what you've done?" She was prompting for a political response.

"Getting married is againtht the law?" Shawna said, looking innocent. "How–but–they can do that?"

Shawna's responses were not what the interviewer was expecting, and it was forcing the woman to improvise on camera. Her News Director would criticize her performance in her next air-check session at the TV station.

"You are a woman. You married a woman. That's the part that's against the law."

"Huh!" Shawna said as if it were the first she was hearing of it. "Well, that's a thtupid law, isn't it?"

"How do you feel?" Sofia Babbleton hissed through clenched teeth framed by her best artificial smile.

"I feel great. I just got married. Oh, we have to go now." She took Gina's hand, and glanced up at her smiling face. Then a final look at Sofia Babbleton, Eyewitness News, "Tell everyone to look at my website, shawnamallory.art. Bye."

The quiet group of demonstrators watched as the reporter looked at her camera and said, "There you have it. The first new same-sex wedding in Louisiana, and the bride is a moron. Maybe next time–uh–" she shook her head, patted the sprayed hair over her left ear, and tried again. "An historic first here in the Crescent City, but the principals are too busy getting married to notice how special they are. Now it's up to Baton Rouge to respond to this, to this–" she stopped and shook her head again. "Wrap it up, Larry," she told the cameraman. "Let's stop at the Seven Seas and get a drink, okay? God, this is so fucked."

The demonstrators who were watching broke out laughing. Sofia Babbleton, Eyewitness News, was blushing with embarrassment as she shouted at her cameraman, "Can't you pack it any faster? Go, go, go, you jerk! Oh, Christ, I'll wait for you in the news van." Still holding the microphone, now connected to nothing, she pushed her way through the picket signs toward the place where the van was double-parked.

"Was that live?" Christine asked. "That was, uh, a little strange."

Amy was laughing and said, "Yes, just a bit." Then Paul led to add, "We have got to watch the ten o'clock news."

They hurried to catch up with the wedding party as Gina and Shawna were getting in the waiting limousine. "Gina!" Christine shouted. "Congratulations! You too, Shawna!" The two women waved from the back seat; Gina blew her a kiss. Then their driver whisked them off to the reception.

With the principals–and Sofia Babbleton, Eyewitness News–gone, all the demonstrations folded. A different TV crew was interviewing a man and woman standing in front of the Partnership of African-American Clergy banner, while other members of the group were collecting the picket signs and telling everyone where the recap meeting would be in the morning. The man, dressed elegantly in a three-piece suit, was explaining, "African-American culture has always held a low opinion of homosexuality. Now, as a pastor, I believe God's grace is available to everyone, no matter what their sexual orientation. But the overwhelming opinion of black Christians in America is that marriage is for a man and a woman, period. That is why the Partnership of African-American Clergy is here today, to bear witness to the traditional marriage values of the black community. We hold out love and the possibility of God's mercy to everyone, but there is a bright red line at holy wedlock."

"Thank you, Doctor Bridges," the interviewer said. Then, turning to the woman beside him, he continued, "What is your perspective, Reverend Rutter?"

She was dressed in a gray and brown print dress, skirt falling below the knee. The pastor put a hand to the string of pearls around her neck. "My flock is a rural one. They certainly agree with Chauncey that same-sex marriage is beyond the pale. I hope I don't alarm him–" she looked at him as her hand touched his arm "–when I say I am still trying to convince them that even a homosexual is a child of God and can receive His grace."

"Wait," Amy said, stopping Christine from heading for her car. "I want to see..." and she looked around at the other groups. The Archbishop and his friar and the people who had demonstrated on behalf of the Archdiocese were in a small circle, holding hands or with arms around the next person; heads were bowed, and Amy imagined Laval was leading them in prayer.

As for the supporters, many had decamped, and only a few signs were visible, mostly people talking to friends, holding the picket signs casually because they were taking them home as a souvenir of an exciting day's activity.

Where are the lone gunmen? Paul thought to Amy. She swiveled to see all the grounds around the church, but the handful of camo-dressed bigots were gone.

"Can we go?" Christine pleaded. "It's going to be a great party at The Deauxcent. Aren't you hungry?"

Amy thought to Paul, *I want to run back inside to see what Pastor Malone has told the police.* She paused, then laughed out loud and said, "It's too bad you can't go while I stay."

Christine said, "Why can't I go? We're big girls, we can survive on our own. Well, for a little while."

Paul spoke up. "Amy was talking to me. I have to stay with her while she checks up on the pastor. We'll catch up with you at the reception, okay?"

With a big smile on her face, Christine leaned in and kissed her lover. "Don't let Amy keep you away too long or the cake will be all gone. I can't promise I won't eat your share." She waved and walked off toward her ancient Smart car.

Amy returned to the church, and walked up the dozen steps to the second floor. Lieutenant Cranston was in the hall outside Pastor Riley Tibbs' office, talking with the Medical Examiner, Doctor

Jermaine Tallant. She heard Jermaine say, "...time of death couldn't be more than an hour before I got here."

"Hey, Doctor Tallant," she called to the medical examiner. He was wearing a wrinkled light-gray suit, and his tie, as customary, was pulled to one side. She was very fond of the fatherly man.

"Ah! Good afternoon, Miss. We didn't get to speak earlier."

They exchanged a few pleasantries, mostly about the grandchild Jermaine doted on. Finally Amy asked, "What do we have?"

The lieutenant answered, "A dead body and no clues except the murder weapon."

"About that," Amy said. "When we first found the body, the associate pastor freaked out and grabbed it, like she was going to pull it out."

"Oh, dear," Jermaine said. "So the trick is to find fingerprints that aren't his?"

"'Hers,' Jermaine," Cranston interjected. "That woman who brought us here. She's a she."

"This modern world," he said, shaking his head. "Fingerprints that aren't HERS."

Amy smiled. "It's good to see you, Doctor Tallant." Of all the police and auxiliary the medical examiner dealt with on a regular basis, only Amy Clear liked to use his title and last name. He quite liked it, even as he said, "Please. Everyone calls me Jermaine."

"Am I everyone, Doc? Haven't you figured that out by now?"

He nodded with pleasure.

She turned to the lieutenant. "Is Malone cooperating?"

"I guess. She really isn't much help. She seems to know as much about this as we do."

Paul led to ask, "Have you released this to the press yet?" even though neither Cranston nor Jermaine knew of his existence.

"Still trying to locate next of kin," the officer said, shaking his hand. "Might be morning before the news goes out."

"What would have happened to the demonstration today if those people knew?"

Duke shrugged. "Probably a riot. You know, it's possible someone out there did know. Someone out there may well have been the killer."

"Yeah," Paul replied, sounding exactly like Amy, "that occurred to us, too."

"Us?" Cranston raised his eyebrows.

Amy silently swore at Paul, then said aloud, "Royal we. Bad habit, I know." Then she announced, "I RSVPed for the wedding reception, so I'm out of here. I don't want to miss the wedding cake." She started to turn away, then looked back at Cranston. "Look. My P. I. business is slow right now, so call me if you need some help. Uh, paid help, that is." She waved and left for her car and the drive to the reception.

The Deauxcent Restaurant was two-and-a-half miles from the church. The drive was through the well-to-do Uptown section–first along one of its main roads, St. Charles Avenue, with its grand old houses and converted apartment buildings; then up the quiet Soniat Street, with its smaller, tree-shrouded homes. The roadway was narrow, barely wide enough to allow a car to pass when vehicles were parked on both sides of the one-way street. As Amy neared Deauxcent, the road was increasingly clogged with parked cars; there was no lot at the restaurant.

Paul cried aloud, "There's Christine's car!"–a yellow Smart car that was fifteen years old but in excellent condition. Amy stayed in first gear, looking for a piece of sidewalk large enough for her old Benz, but every gap proved to be at a residential driveway or a fire hydrant. "Are you sure you want to go to this reception?" Amy asked, frustrated.

Yes, I am, he thought back. *Isn't that arts center around the corner? We can park there.*

Amy grumbled, but she threaded the one-way streets and found a place in a small lot by the Fine Arts building of the Newman School, with its red and tan bricks. "I hope we don't get booted," Amy groused.

As they walked to Deauxcent, Paul tried to improve her mood. *There's going to be cake. And beer. And bubbly*, he thought to her. *And everyone will be so happy for Gina and Shawna.*

"And only you and I and Christine know the first pastor was murdered. That news would be a buzz kill."

Silently, Paul asked, *So, who done it?*

Amy frowned, thinking. *That creepy little friar, he's not all there,* she thought back. *Did you notice the two men at the black clergy sign? They looked like enforcers. One of them had a suit that was too big, I'm sure he had a shoulder rig.*

She felt Paul nod as they turned the corner to Soniat, just up from the restaurant. *And the lone gunmen,* he thought to her. *Did anyone from the good guys look like a possible slasher?*

"The good guys?" she said out loud; then, silently, *Oh, the supporters. No. No, they just looked like the usual lovable goofballs. Mardi Gras or not, I am not used to women walking around with no shirts.*

"I hope I have the chance to get used to it," Paul replied aloud.

A clot of people stood outside the entrance to Deauxcent. It showed four large windows to the street, almost entirely blocked by purple swags. A modest sign in the door was the only indication of the business within. Paul recognized Linda and Joni from Sappho Rising, and hailed them. Each of the women hugged the person they knew as Paulette. "Wasn't that a marvelous ceremony?" Joni said, sloshing the drink in her hand. "I thought I'd die when the pastor chased the Archbishop out of the church." Linda was nodding, then added, "And the kiss Gina put on Shawna, that was great. Really, I'm so happy for them."

"Agreed," Paul said, sounding exactly like Amy, uh, like Paulette. "Christine is over the moon. I love how she's still so fond of Gina, that they're still friends."

Linda glanced at her lover and looked down. "That would bother some people," she said softly.

"Linda! Don't!" Joni cried.

"I hear my momma calling me," Paul said, and he left the women on the sidewalk to finish their spat.

The restaurant was not too crowded, but the wedding reception was in the large upstairs room. Halfway up the stairs the racket from the party-goers was deafening. *Just for once,* Amy thought, *I wish other people could think to us.*

Paul thought back, *What?* and snickered.

He led to wind their way from the stairs to the inside of the room, threading between groups of drinking, laughing, drinking, singing, and drinking people. He hailed Lowell Howell, a bartender from a nearby club. "You're looking good tonight, Paulette," he said.

Paul smiled and said, "It's so nice that a manly man like you would notice a girly girl like me. How's things?" He heard Amy think, *He just made a pass at me.*

Silently Paul replied, *Nope. At me. And everyone here knows I'm a lesbian.*

That's my point, she thought. *What a waste!*

"My wife didn't want to come," Lowell said. "She says dykes make her itch. I convinced her I'm only here because Shawna is a customer." He took a sip of whatever was in his clear plastic cup. "Gina is a looker. Almost as pretty as you are."

"You blarney-tongued devil. If I ever wake up straight I'll give you a call." They laughed and parted.

As he walked on, Paul thought to Amy, *There. You can hit on him sometime. Of course, he's going to call you Paulette.*

Why do I ever let you lead? she thought, but she was laughing.

For a while, the crowd was too thick to penetrate. Paul and Amy got to hear five or six gay men, friends of Gina's, talk about the wedding. A tall man, young but with prematurely thinning hair, offered, "They just did it. Louisiana has a law against it, they found a preacher who didn't care, and they did it. What–"

Another man, in a red and black print shirt and a weird upswept hair style like a neo-Mohawk, interrupted, "You know, if we all did that, they'd be stuck with us. What are they going to do, arrest thousands of us?"

Yet another said, "I'm having too much fun to get married." The other men slapped him on the back with "Good for you!" and "I remember the days!"

Finally they heard the last man in the group, dressed in black but for the bright green tennis shoes. "We're queer," he shook his head. "Why do we want to be just like all those straight people who hate us? Call me heterophobic if you must, but I'd rather just live with Marko and give them all the finger."

"Booo!" the man with the odd hairstyle said. "Equality! I want Lance's social security when he dies. I want alimony if he divorces me. You bet I want to be just like everybody else."

Amy thought, *I had a girlfriend at UNO who was like that. Do you remember Angela? She wanted to get married so she could get a divorce and alimony.* Paul felt her shake their head.

The crowd thinned out a bit, and Paul was able to elbow their way to the big table where Gina and Shawna were holding court. There was a huge pile of shopping bags and boxes in gift wrap, wedding presents from their friends and family. Paul laughed to Amy, "When I married Mary Pat, we got, I think it was four toasters."

"Crap!" Amy spoke. Then silently, *That's what I got for them.*

The women were still in their wedding clothes; Gina in her rented black tuxedo, and Shawna in her huge white dress. With them were Gina's father and brother, Shawna's sister, and a few of their closest friends. That included Paul's lover Christine. A stream of well-wishers slowly worked its way past them to shake hands, exchange hugs and kisses, and even shed a tear or two.

When Gina saw Paulette she stood and waved Paul over. "You are my shero!" she shouted, raising her wine glass. Shawna stayed seated but applauded. *You've got fans,* Amy thought to him.

"Listen, everybody!" Gina called to the room at large, and the noise level dropped from ruckus to mere clamor. She stepped to Paul and put her arm around them. "This is Paulette, and she is amazing. For those of you who didn't see it, when Shawna and I left the church, a monk spit on Shawna." Boos and catcalls erupted. "And this woman here," she turned to look at Paul, "this amazing, brave, and beautiful woman, she walked up to the Archbishop of New Orleans and told him to apologize." Applause and shouts of support came from around the room. "And then–" she held up the hand with her wine glass to try to quiet people to hear the rest "–and then, the Archbishop told his monk to apologize." There were louder shouts.

"And then–wait, listen to this! And then, when the dufus did mumble that he was sorry, Paulette told him to apologize to Shawna." The room was cheering as Gina shouted over the din, "And he did! He did! Paulette made the Archbishop back down!" Gina kissed Paul on the cheek, then grabbed one hand and lifted it up like a prizefighter who just won a match.

Paul was excited by the recognition. He had been so angry at the creepy monk that he hadn't thought twice about challenging the prelate. The shouts and compliments, from many strangers as well as some of his friends, filled him with pride. It was for him–well, for Paulette–not for Amy. It was an acknowledgment of his individual existence, such as it was inside Amy, a rare thing since he had lost his body and taken up residence inside Amy Clear's head so many years before.

Paul hugged Gina, then crouched next to Shawna. "Are you all right, love?"

"I am fine. I'm married to my thweetie, all my friends are here, I've had two bottles of wine, and you rethcued me from that dwarf at the church. I am thuper-fine." She opened her arms, and Paul leaned forward to hug the woman.

While they embraced, Shawna whispered, "I hope Christine forgives me for thtealing Gina."

"Yeah. What she tells me is she's very happy for the both of you."

"Oh, good." Shawna pushed Paul back, but still held them by the shoulders. Her inebriated eyes, uneven to begin with, were looking in different directions. "Right now I love everyone. I love Christine. And I love you, Paulette." She pulled Paul to her and kissed them on the mouth, a serious, boundary-defying kiss.

Paul heard Amy laugh inside and think to him, singing like a child on the school yard, *I'm gonna tell Christine!*

Intoxicated, Shawna prolonged the kiss, her tongue teasing for Paul to open their mouth. He thought to Christine, *Help! Rescue me!*

A moment later Christine was standing by them, saying to Shawna, "Can I have my girlfriend back, please?" Shawna let go of Paul, but then grabbed Christine and pulled her close; she continued the kiss on her. People at the table hooted and shouted, while Gina beamed with pride.

An annoyed Paul put one hand on Shawna's shoulder and the other on Christine's, and pried them apart. He heard Amy think, *Relax. Shawna's drunk, and this may as well be her bachelorette party. If she remembers this tomorrow, she'll be mortified.*

"Yeah, I guess so," he mumbled aloud. Christine put her mouth to their ear and whispered, "Thanks!" while Shawna leaned back in her chair and shouted, arms outstretched, "I love everybody!"

The table was crowded, so Christine and Paul shared her chair. "I saved some cake for you," Christine said. She dipped her index finger in the icing, then held it up for her Paulette to lick; Paul was happy to oblige.

Christine used her fork to cut off a piece of cake and was about to hold it out when Amy's phone rang. "I've got to take this," she said; Christine put the piece of cake in her own mouth.

"Detective Clear?"

"Commander Ramirez! What a pleasure to hear from you. Uh, sorry about the noise, I'm at a wedding reception."

"I hear you were at the wedding, too," he said. Amy had known the Commander since she was eleven and he was an eager sergeant on the New Orleans Police force. While she never took his advice to apply to the state Police Academy, she had spent three years as a plainclothes detective under his command, and even now sometimes worked for him as a consultant. "Cranston said you were fishing for a job," he laughed, "and you got it. Be in around nine o'clock tomorrow to get with him and Jermaine. I don't care how, uh, unusual a church is, I don't like preachers getting killed. Got me?"

"Loud and clear," Amy replied. She had their right index finger in their right ear to try to cut down on the room noise as he spoke. "The, uh, the usual rate?"

"Of course. But you better solve this case. You and Cranston."

When Amy closed her phone, Christine–who somehow always knew which one of them was leading–said, "Is everything okay, Amy?"

She nodded. "Just got hired to work that murder–" suddenly Paul was shouting silently, *These people don't know about it!* "–uh, you know, that case you stumbled on today."

Christine's eyes grew big and round. "You're so good at this. You'll find the bad guy, I know you will. Only..."

"Hmmm?"

"Be careful. I don't want Paulette to get hurt. Or you. Just, just be careful."

Amy patted the back of Christine's hand. "You know I will. Paul would kill me if I let anything happen to me." Christine laughed, and Amy, flustered, said. "Uh, that came out strange. You know what I mean."

"Paulette? Are you ready for some cake now?" She was holding a forkful in mid-air.

"Cake *à la* Christine. You bet!"

ॐ MONDAY, August 14, 2034 ॐ

It was 1:30 in the morning when Christine followed Amy and Paul to their house in the Carrollton section. Once inside, Amy clicked on the television while everyone washed up and prepared for bed. The lead item was Tropical Storm Olaf, which had formed in the Atlantic and was on a course for the Gulf of Mexico. Amy was brushing her teeth when Christine called from the living room, "It's all over the news! That preacher getting killed." In a cost-saving measure, the TV station was rebroadcasting its ten o'clock newscast.

Still brushing, Amy walked out to watch the TV. Christine put a hand on Amy's leg only because it was nearby and Amy's hands were occupied; there was no sensual intention, just connection between the two women who, after years of Paul's affair with Christine, felt like sisters. "There's the lady who did the wedding," Christine said, pointing at Associate Pastor Drew Malone on the screen.

After a few moments, Duke Cranston's face filled the video monitor. "We are pursuing several lines of inquiry," he said. Paul translated, "That's official police talk for 'we don't have a clue yet'." Finally the voice of Sofia Babbleton, Eyewitness News came from the speakers, asking Shawna about getting married in a state that didn't permit such things. They watched their friend say, "Getting married is againtht the law? How–but–they can do that?" Christine squealed with pleasure, and Amy held one hand under their mouth to catch the toothpaste her own laughter was letting escape.

Back in the bathroom, Amy finished her nighttime rituals. "Forgive me for being crude," she said aloud to Paul, "but you and

Christine hurry up with what you're going to do. I have to be at the cop shop at nine."

Paul laughed and replied, "You just go to sleep. I promise Christine and I will clean up when we're done."

"I don't want to know," she said, and flipped the light switch off.

When the alarm clock rang at seven, Amy had to pull her body out from under Christine's. *Paul?* she thought, *Did you have a good time?*

She heard him inside their head, *Wha? Why are you getting up? Oh, Christ, what's that light?*

Haven't you heard? It's called the sun, my friend. Welcome back to my world. How late did you two stay up? She rubbed her face, then sat up on their side of the bed.

I think I went to sleep about ten minutes ago.

She slapped their thighs and stood up. "Time for a shower, sleeping beauty." She looked down and saw Christine was still asleep. "Did my body have a good time?"

Silently, Paul yawned. *Oh, yeah. Didn't you have a hot dream or anything?*

"I wish. You owe me, Pal." She was making faces at themself in the bathroom mirror, checking for zits and wrinkles.

"Yeah. Soon as I wake up. After I go back to sleep. Shake me if you need me, but please, not before noon."

Amy enjoyed Paul's silent scream when she stepped under the showerhead.

She left a note for Christine. Unknown to her, the woman had arranged to take the day off from work as a real estate agent. Amy got to the police station on North Rampart Street, on the northwest edge of the Vieux Carré, at ten before nine. She drove into the parking entrance that led to the underground lot, then went up the dank concrete stairway to the main floor of the five-story complex. She flashed her consultant ID badge at the unknown officer in the reception area, and walked to the uniformed officers' bullpen to look for Duke Cranston and start work.

A handful of officers, sergeants, and lieutenants were in the large room, either chatting, or using the computers to write up case notes. The only one Amy knew was Walter Francks, the Weapons Sergeant. He was in undercover dress, although he rarely left the building on police work. His gray, thinning hair was pulled into a ponytail that was strictly against the rules. The man was browsing dirty pictures on one of the computers.

"Hard at work, I see," Amy said to him.

Without looking up, he answered, "That's why I'm sitting down." Slowly he turned his head in the direction of the voice, and a smile spread across his face. "Sugar!" he called, standing up to hug Amy; he did not hide his computer viewing. "What are you doing here? Is today the day we're eloping?"

"Not today, no. I've got a play date with Cranston. We're working on that church homicide."

Francks swung his head around to scan the room, "He was here a minute ago."

Amy sat in the chair next to his. She pointed to one of the more outrageous pictures on the screen and said, "You think she's hot?"

"Huh! Next to you, Sugar, they're all the second pressing of the grape." He shrank the browser to the taskbar. "Your call yesterday–you're the one who found the body?"

"A friend did, a civilian. She came and got me to check it out."

"What's it look like?" The sergeant had turned in his chair to face Amy, to give all his attention to their conversation.

"Wide open," Amy shook her head. "No sign of a struggle or a break-in, but just about anyone could have walked in and gotten to the office where she was killed."

"'She?'" Walter said in surprise. "They let women lead churches?"

"You are such a pagan. When were you born? Nineteenth century?"

"Eighteenth, I think," he smiled. "I love yanking your chain, Sugar."

"And I love playing with you. But as far as the investigation, I'm hoping Cranston knows something I don't. It could happen, you know."

"There you are, Detective." It was a deep, mellow voice from the six-feet-eight-inches of Duke Cranston, standing on the other side of the table. "Are you ready to get to work?"

Amy stood up and reached their right hand across the table to shake Duke's. "It's a pleasure, Lieutenant. Where shall we set up?" The sergeant went back to his web browsing.

"Let's visit Jermaine. I hope he can tell us something."

She tugged gently on Francks' ponytail, then walked to the doorway to join the lieutenant. "I'm looking forward to working with you," she said. "You're big." She glanced at his tall, two-hundred-fifty pound frame. "I feel safe with you."

"I hear you're pretty good at taking care of yourself," he returned. They walked down the hall, then down one flight of stairs to where the Medical Examiner's office was. "You brought down some scum-suckers when the force figured you were dead meat." He opened Jermaine's office door. "I feel pretty safe with you, too."

"Doctor Tallant!" Amy shouted. The anteroom was painted white and brightly lit, but it also was empty.

They heard Jermaine's voice say, "That has to be Detective Clear," coming from the autopsy room. A few moments later the Medical Examiner appeared, wearing blue scrubs, blue gloves, goggles, and a face mask.

Amy said, "Doctor Frankenstein, have you seen Jermaine?"

In an attempt at a comic voice, the Medical Examiner said, "Parts of him are on my work bench."

"What in hell?" Cranston said.

Amy asked, "How icky are your scrubs?"

"Very, as you say, Miss, 'icky'."

"Okay, then," and she waved at him. "Hi."

Cranston said, "Detective Clear and me are working that church murder. Have you finished your analysis?"

"Ah. Mostly, yes." He began removing his protective mask and goggles. "Follow me and we can go over it." By the time the three of them were in Jermaine's lab, the medical examiner had tossed gear and scrubs into various trash cans, and was left in a gray business suit...and blue plastic footies. He motioned to some wheeled stools for Amy and Duke, then settled at a long work bench and opened a manila folder. They studiously avoided looking at the autopsy table, where something large was under a stained blue sheet.

"Autopsy shows the cause of death was one stab wound. A knife penetrated between the 5th and 6th ribs and entered the heart. Considering where the puncture and cut were, death ensued within eight seconds." He took out an autopsy photograph to show the investigators. "See the fishtail on the top of the wound? That is consistent with the recovered weapon, a kitchen knife–sharp on one side, blunt on the other."

Amy nodded at the photograph. "Were you able to get any fingerprints from the handle?"

"Oh, lots and lots and lots. And every single one of them belonged to the associate pastor. I believe you told the lieutenant here that you witnessed that person contaminate the crime scene?"

"Yes," she said, defensive. "It was so unexpected, and she moved so fast, I think I did great to keep her from pulling the knife out of the body." She thought a moment. "Yes." Her defensiveness was replaced with anger at herself for not having prevented the incident.

The lieutenant observed, "So no clues at all."

Jermaine shrugged. "That's about the size of it. No indication the victim put up any resistance, so no skin or hair under the fingernails. No convenient cigarette butt or bloody footprint. What few prints you lifted from the doorknobs belonged to the victim and to the weekly janitor. Just an enormous amount of nothing."

"What kind of gloves was the killer wearing?" Amy asked.

Jermaine turned to smile at her. "You are a wonderful student," he said. "However, no prints that might be glove texture. Looks like the killer wiped the handle clean after stabbing our victim."

Even as Cranston stood up, Amy asked, "Just for my own education, what might a killer have wrapped around the handle before stabbing Riley that would have the same profile?"

"Hmm. Glossy printer paper, I should think. Newspaper would leave ink residue. Even a plastic bag would show wrinkles and maybe ink transfer." Turning to the lieutenant he said, "She is a clever one."

Silently she said, *Did you hear that, Paul?* No, he didn't; he was still asleep.

"Glad to hear it," the lieutenant said, "'cause we're starting from nowhere. Thanks, Jermaine."

Amy put a hand on the medical examiner's arm and said, "Thanks, Doctor Tallant. I hope we have more for you soon."

Back upstairs in the uniformed officers' bullpen, Cranston commandeered a table with one of the computers. "I've got DVDs from NBC, ABC, and Fox," he said, dropping the white envelopes on the table and reaching for the computer's DVD drive. "For some reason the CBS affiliate didn't respond to my request."

"CBS? Is that the one with Earwitness News?"

"Eyewitness News. Yeah. Why?"

Amy laughed, "I enjoyed Sofia Bobblehead's coverage. I'm not surprised they didn't send you anything."

"Isn't her name Babbleton? It's not like I got a subpoena; these are just their ten and eleven o'clock newscasts from last night."

"Couldn't you have gotten a romantic comedy instead?"

"I don't understand you," Cranston frowned. "This is serious shit here."

"Yes, sir. I have a peculiar sense of humor, I know, but it's how I cope. I saw the body before you did; I know this is serious. So first, why the newscasts?"

"Jermaine doesn't have anything. Common sense says the killer was in sympathy with the anti protesters, and might be one of them. The newscasts should show us the organizations and some names. We'll start interviewing them."

Amy nodded. "I see that. Yes, okay. One thing—you're probably right, but there is the possibility that one of the same-sex marriage supporters is behind this. Make a martyr, give their movement a moral high-ground."

"So you think one of the hippies did it?" Disbelief was all over his voice and his face.

"I have no idea who the murderer is, Duke. I'm just saying one of the hippies could have done it."

Cranston put both palms on the table and spread his fingers wide. His hands were enormous, the size of dinner plates. "Shit."

He looked up at her. "You're right, of course. Shit. I would like very much for the hippies to be responsible."

"You got a dog in this fight?"

In a low voice the lieutenant said, "Where I come from, we don't think much of faggots. The idea of two ladies getting married, or two guys–" he shook his head. "It ain't right. It's not natural."

"Where do you come from?" Amy asked. "A cave? Mars? The eighth century?"

"North Vacherie, know where it is?" he challenged her. "It ain't poor, but it ain't rich, either. My father still works at the aluminum refinery. The few white men there may run the politics, but it's the black women who run the people. Lots of church. Lots of 'yes, m'am' and 'no, sir'. And you won't get anywhere talking about gay marriage." Staring at her, he finished, "You want to insult me, fine. But don't you dare say anything bad about my mother."

She felt her face turning red. Amy held her hands up, palms out, and said, "I'm sorry, Duke. I didn't mean to insult anyone." She parked her hands in her armpits. "You assume everyone thinks like you, which is mistake number one. And then you wonder how anyone can think different, and that's mistake number two. Then there's opening your mouth. I was wrong, Duke. I apologize."

He continued to stare at her, not having expected to hear contrition. "Okay," he said. "We have to get used to each other if we're going to work together worth a damn."

She hung her head. "I'll be more careful. And now I think I understand why you think that wedding yesterday was wrong." Looking back up at him, she said, "We don't have to agree. We just have to let each other be."

"Be what?"

"Be whoever we are. Some people like strawberry, some like butter pecan. It's all good."

Cranston rolled his eyes. "Why did the Commander stick me with a wacko?"

"Because I'm a wacko who solves crimes," Amy replied with a smile. She liked it when people thought of her as weird, odd, eccentric, bizarre, or even wacko. "Just like you're a normal person who solves crimes. Between us, we should be able to cover all the possibilities."

The lieutenant considered standing up and walking to Commander Ramirez' office to request a different partner. But that would use up political capital he wasn't sure he had, and Detective Clear's reputation around the station house was stellar. So he said, "Okay. The black guy's normal and the white gal's wacko. I can deal with that."

"Peachy. So we have newscasts. Let's check 'em out." She and Cranston took out legal pads while he inserted the NBC video.

Gale and Shawna's wedding was the last item of the cast, the soft, feel-good piece. The reporter, a young man with meticulously styled hair, interviewed Father Lloyd Johnson, the press secretary for the archdiocese. Amy pointed at the creepy friar standing next to Johnson, his eyes darting in all directions like a spooked animal. "We respect the rights of other faiths to have their own rules, but as the mother of all Christianity, the Catholic Church is unequivocal in its belief in the sanctity of the holy sacrament of marriage as being between one man and one woman."

"Damn right," Cranston muttered.

"He doesn't look like a killer," Amy offered, "but that little monk made my skin crawl."

They each wrote notes.

The lieutenant replaced the DVD with the one from the local ABC affiliate. Here too, the TV station treated the wedding as the final item, the fluff piece to leave viewers feeling good. It was the interview Amy and Christine watched taking place with the Partnership of African-American Clergy. The super-slide identified the elegantly dressed spokesman as organization President the Reverend Doctor Chauncey Bridges. When she heard him say, "African-American culture has always held a low opinion of homosexuality," she touched the pause button on the player. "Where have I heard that before?" she asked.

"See? I'm not the lone bigot," Cranston said with a smile, and he hit the play button. Bridges went on to explain that the church was open to homosexuals, but that marriage remained a sacrament for men and women. Next, the female pastor who was Vice-

President of the Partnership of African-American Clergy, Pastor Anita Rutter, reiterated the point.

"Back it up!" Amy called. Cranston hit the back search button until Amy said, "There. Freeze it." He played the DVD until Amy mashed the pause button. "These guys," she pointed to the two men in mirrored sunglasses. "They look like muscle. They didn't chant, they didn't hold signs, they didn't talk to the other demonstrators in that area. They just watched."

Cranston wrote something on his pad, and sent a print screen command to the color printer. Then he said, "What did the Fox station have?" He traded out DVDs.

This newscast took up the wedding as the lead item. There were camera pan shots of the overall demonstration, but all the interviews were with what the lieutenant had referred to as the hippies–the colorful collection of people supporting Gina and Shawna's wedding.

Amy laughed when the screen showed a person, identified by a super-slide as Sunchild, wearing dangerously short cut-off jeans, no shirt, and huge multicolored wings taped to his back. Cranston was shaking his head. "Love is beautiful," Sunchild was saying, waving a glitter-encrusted cheerleader's baton with a red star glued to the head. "We need more love in the world. That's why these ladies should be able to marry."

"Sunchild," Amy laughed. "And his parents could have sworn they named him something like Joe Smith."

The camera panned, passing a tall woman in a polka dotted yellow dress with color so intense that it might blind people within fifty feet, and then cutting to three shirtless women; being shown on broadcast television, their nipples were pixilated out. Written in black Magic Marker on one woman's abdomen was the censored statement, "Make your own f****** sandwich!" Magic Marker woman, in her twenties, was ranting about feminism and lesbianism. An edit led to the second one, with a man's GI haircut, saying, "I'm having a blast, a (bleep)ing blast. This is so much fun! Look at all these freaks!" Finally the third woman was on camera, explaining, "So what if a woman marries another woman. Does that interfere with some man marrying a woman? So why is there a problem?"

"What's so funny?" Cranston asked.

"Street theatre, I guess," Amy said, trying to hide her smile. "When's the last time you heard anyone saying these things?"

He hit the pause button. "Do you think these people are the killer?"

"Sunchild? And these women? God, no." Then her smile faded. "If I thought they might be, they wouldn't be funny."

"And they're not funny to me," Cranston added as he let the DVD resume.

Next the reporter found two men with the most theatrical stereotypical homosexual mannerisms and speech patterns. "We've been partners for months and months," one said, "and seeing how brave these girls are, well, we want to do that, too." His lover said, "We're going to register at Bed, Bath And Beyond; they have some delicious arrangements." Amy snickered, but she could tell Cranston was getting wound up tighter and tighter.

The reporter did a brief stand-up where the eye-gouging yellow polka dot dress was in the background; some B-roll ran as he finished his piece, and the producer cut to what the super-slide identified as two area college women. They were dressed as if for an office job, in modest dresses, each highlighted with a string of pearls. "What would Captain Mal Reynolds do?" one asked. "I think he'd say, 'Mind your own God-damned business,' I really do."

When the camera angle swung to isolate the reporter, Amy shouted, "Stop! Lone gunman!"

Cranston's right hand went to his pistol grip, and he looked in the direction he thought Amy's eyes were aimed. "What?" he said, confused. "There's no one there."

"On the DVD," she said, pointing at the screen. "Back it up."

The lieutenant hit reverse search until he saw the college women, then pressed play and hovered over the pause button.

"...business,' I really do." As the camera panned, Amy cried, "Freeze it!"

On the right side of the screen, in the middle distance between the collegians and the reporter, was one of the people Amy had noticed the day before. It was a man, maybe 35 or 40 years old. He had a few inches of thin, scraggly beard. He was dressed in green, brown, and tan camouflage shirt and pants, topped with a 'CAT' baseball cap. His hands were on a picket, but the sign he carried was not visible.

Amy began tapping their right index finger on the table. "That's one of the lone gunmen," she said. "There were four or five guys there that didn't belong to any of the other groups. They didn't act as if they knew each other." Cranston began a drawn-out "Well..." and she went on, "I think this is the guy with the sign that said 'AIDS cures fags.'"

"Man, I may not like queers, but that's downright cruel."

She placed the backs of their hands against their back and did some twists in the chair. "The ones who bothered me were the monk, the muscle, and those lone gunmen. I didn't notice any of the, uh, the hippies looking dangerous."

Cranston slid his legal pad in front of himself. "How many of those–what did you call them? Lone gunmen?"

"Five. I'm pretty sure."

"I'm going to call the *Times Picayune*, see if they have any stills that show them. And there's this." The lieutenant pulled a sheet of neon pink paper from the manila folder. "It's a flyer aimed at the hippies. We should contact the what, the three organizations listed."

Amy looked over the flyer. 'We Love Shawna And Gina!' was the heading, followed by date and time and the location of the Metropolitan Christian Church. The groups taking credit were the Community Coalition, the Equality Forum, and Advancement Trust NOLA. "Any of these groups have a profile?"

Without looking up from his legal pad, Cranston said, "Yeah. Community Coalition and the Equality Forum are pretty mainstream. I think they're wrong, but they lobby in Baton Rouge, they hook up, you know, gay kids and families that need a lawyer, who get in trouble. What dealings NOPD has had with both of them, I have to say they're professional. I never heard of that last one, though."

"You're the cop," Amy said, "I'm just the consultant. How do you want to divide this up?"

Cranston was tapping his pen against his lower lip, thinking. "You and me will do separate interviews. You start with the hippies, 'cause I'm afraid I might beat them with a baton just for the hell of it." He wrote notes on his pad, then continued, "I'll talk to the black clergy group, and see if I can get ID on those two guys you pointed out."

"What about the archdiocese?" Amy asked.

"What kind of luck do you think you'd have with them?"

Amy laughed. "Twelve years of Catholic school, but, uh, I, uh, I had a spat with the archbishop at the demonstration." Since Paul was still asleep, he wouldn't know she was taking credit for his courageous action.

Duke paused in gathering up his notes, and silently raised one eyebrow.

"That creepy monk spit on one of the women who got married. I told the Archbishop to make him apologize."

"That's ballsy."

"Well, I guess. And he told the monk to say he was sorry."

"Start with the PR priest that was on the news." He handed the DVDs to Amy. "Get the hippies' names from these newscasts, then go to the newsrooms and get the contact information. You do have a badge, right?"

"I don't need no stinkin' badge. I've got a PI license and a gun."

He rolled his eyes. "Oh, brother. If the Commander really hired you, stop at HR and have them give you some police ID. You'll need it."

Realizing that the meeting was over, Amy stood up and asked, "What's your schedule? What time do you get here?"

"Roll call is seven-thirty. Be here by eight. Got it?"

"Got it."

They stood looking at each other in the quiet bullpen room. Finally the lieutenant said, "I hope this works, Amy."

"Call me Clear," she said with a smile. "Uh, except when we're around those, uh, hippies. I told you some of them think my name is Paulette."

"And what do you think your name is?" He was smiling.

"I'm kind of partial to Queen Bitch."

Cranston shook his head and said, "See you tomorrow, Little Queenie. Right now I've got a robbery case in Tremé waiting for me."

Amy nodded and watched Cranston leave for his other duties. She sat back down with her legal pad and began writing out coherent instructions for herself.

1) Archdiocese - Press Priest - Father ?

She opened a Bing window on the computer to get the address and website for the archdiocese. The webpage reminded her that the headquarters was in Broadmoor/Uptown, between Notre Dame Seminary and St. Mary's Dominican High School. Amy vaguely remembered it from when she was thirteen years old and her father had taken her there to resolve an argument he had with St. Giles Academy, where Amy was in, what, seventh grade? She made notes that the press relations contact was Father Lloyd Johnson, the priest that was interviewed on the NBC affiliate newscast. Checking on the rest of Archdiocese hierarchy, she wrote down the name of the Auxiliary Bishop, Patrick Walsh Villavasso. While she was at it, she got the spelling for the big man: Archbishop Francis Rouxel Laval. "What kind of name is Rouxel?" she asked herself aloud, pronouncing it ROO-ull, as would any Crescent City native. As an afterthought she wrote down 'creepy monk - ?'

2) Hippies
   A) Fox affiliate - Fox 8, WVUE.

A web search for the address put the station in the Zion City area, south of I-10 and Bayou St. John. She wrote down the station's business phone number, and the names of the News Director–Buddy Simpson–and the Program Director–Candy Blaze.

Below that, she noted the people interviewed at the demonstration, but whose real names weren't revealed.

    i)   Sunchild
    ii) Three topless women
    iii) Two hilarious gay men
    iv) Two college girl lesbians

Since Duke Cranston was going to follow up on the Partnership of African-American Clergy, Amy skipped further in her notes. He had assigned the hippies to her, so she wanted to visit the organizations named on the flyer that supported Gina and Shawna's marriage.

    B)   The Community Coalition
    C)   The Equality Forum
    D)   Advancement Trust NOLA

Her search engine got contact information for the Coalition in Faubourg Marigny, and the Forum in the Central Business District, as well as names of the groups' leaders. But the internet was silent about Advancement Trust NOLA. Thinking that the NOLA designation might mean it was a multi-city organization, she changed her search term to Advancement Trust.

She got more than three million hits, mostly for estate tax planning. Near the top, though, was Advancement Trust Official Site. She found that it was a gay respect project primarily concerned with helping bullied gays and lesbians through episodes of depression, and guiding them past suicidal thoughts. It was based in San Francisco. Amy made notes on the address and contact phone number and email. It disturbed her that she could not find the name of anyone in the project. Maybe the Coalition and the Forum could steer her to a local coordinator.

Amy left the deserted bullpen and went to the Human Resources department to get the badge and ID that Cranston had told her she'd need. After she resigned from the police force two years earlier, Commander Ramirez left Amy on the payroll (no pay for no hours worked) to accommodate their arrangement to use her here and there for specific investigations. The Commander still hoped Amy would return to the force full-time, while Amy appreciated the opportunity to earn money while she built her private detective business. She was learning that she was a better investigator than business developer.

"I'm back," Amy told LaToya Winston, the HR administrator. Amy sat in the rolling chair on the customer side of LaToya's desk.

The HR woman was middle-aged, almost as wide as she was tall. While she always sported a smile, she dealt with almost everyone in the most colorful and vulgar language.

"Well, ain't you the proverbial bad penny," LaToya bantered. "What does the Commander want you for this time? Jaywalking in the French Quarter? No, no," holding up one hand, palm outward, "let me guess. That damn Waldo got lost again? Oh, I know, there's a cat in a tree in Bywater, that's it."

"Good to see you, LaToya," Amy grinned. "Actually, there's a gang of fourth graders selling contraband chewing gum on playgrounds in the West Bank."

"Oh, serious stuff," she said, opening a file drawer to pull out the W4 forms, "felony stuff. You watch yourself out there, honey. Them fourth graders will bite your knees if you're not careful."

Amy filled out the tax forms while LaToya printed and laminated a new ID card, and found Amy's old metal badge. "See Walter for a sidearm," she said.

"What are we using these days? Glocks?"

"Shit, I don't know. Blunderbusses, maybe. Or zip guns. That's Walter's business."

"I'm happy with my Ruger 9mm," Amy said, "but it's always fun to yank Walter's chain. Or his ponytail."

LaToya leaned forward and spoke softly, conspiratorially. "How does that sergeant get away with it? I've never seen him in a uniform, and that Godawful hair."

Amy leaned in and answered in a whisper, "He told me that he and the Commander were in Desert Storm together, and he saved Ramirez' life."

The woman leaned back, eyes wide. "No shit?"

"My lips to your ears."

"Well, I'll be fucked. So if I save the Commander's life, he'll let me wear shorts and a halter top to work?"

For a moment Amy envisioned the morbidly obese woman dressed that way. Then she said, "Maybe. Tell him you saved his life by not killing him and see what happens."

The woman slid the ID and badge across the desk to Amy with her left hand, and with her right she extended her middle finger. "Have a day, Detective," she smiled.

"You've always been my BFF," Amy said as she stood up and waved, "Bye-bye."

She retrieved her old yellow Benz from the underground parking and drove across town to the archdiocese office. With her new police ID, she figured she did not have to make an appointment to speak with Father Johnson. Even though the priest was hardly a suspect, it was standard police thinking that an unexpected interview was more likely to solicit honest information, or, at least, expose discomfort, guilt, or lies.

Amy parked on the side of the archdiocese building, an ugly three-story gray rectangle. It harbored a central courtyard and took up a third of a city block.

A private guard at the security desk directed her to the administrative offices. Amy was holding up her ID and badge and telling a clerk what she wanted when suddenly the receptionist saw the plainclothes police detective jerk upright and say, "Whoa! Where the fuck are we?"

Paul was awake.

Amy grabbed control back to say, "I'm sorry, my Tourette's is acting up. The ladies' room...?"

The receptionist's face was a picture of surprise and shock, eyes wide and mouth open; she managed to point down the hall. Amy nodded with a smile and headed for the rest room to have a discussion with her co-pilot.

Do you have any idea where we are? she hissed silently at Paul from the safety of a closed stall.

Actually, no. That's why I asked.

Well, good morning to you, Sonny Jim. You just said 'fuck' to the receptionist at the archdiocese office.

Paul snickered aloud, "You don't say 'fuck' in front of Jesus."

Amy slapped the left side of their head. *I'm on the job,* she thought. *I'm going to interview the PR flack about the demonstration.*

He was finally awake enough to understand. "Oh, shit," he muttered aloud, "I didn't know."

"It's bad enough that Archbishop Laval thinks I'm a rude troublemaker–"

No, no, Paul thought to her, interrupting; *He thinks you have a better grasp of Christian ethics than he does.*

"As if anyone says 'thank you' for that."

"Look, I'm sorry," Paul said aloud. "I expected to see our bedroom, maybe Christine, and instead we were in an office with an old lady at the desk. I was, uh, disoriented."

Amy smoothed her hair as she stood in the stall. "Well, orient yourself. Behave!"

Really, I'm sorry, he thought to her. *What's the mission–you know I'll help if I can.*

Amy tried to hide the smile she felt coming over her face. She understood that Paul's unfortunate garbage mouth vocabulary spilled out in innocence, and she believed he really was sorry about it. "The press guy for the Archdiocese is Father Lloyd Johnson. He doesn't know I'm here to talk to him about the demonstration."

"He killed the pastor?"

Amy laughed. "Well, I see you're not one hundred percent awake yet. I want to know if he noticed anything that can give us a clue."

"Okay," Paul thought, "got it. Did you eat breakfast?"

"What? No, I was in a hurry this morning."

"Breakfast will help. Huddle House? White Castle? Café Du Monde?"

"If you don't behave," Amy said, "I'll eat a steak in front of you and I won't let you have even a bite." She undid the stall latch and retraced her steps to the administrative office.

"I am so sorry. Let's try this again," Amy said when she returned to the receptionist's desk. She unfurled her ID and badge, and said, "I need to speak with Father Johnson on police business."

The woman studied Amy's ID card. "Do you have an appointment?"

"Ah. Did I say this was police business?" Amy tried on the smile that always made her father melt.

"Yes, you did. And I asked if you have an appointment."

Amy heard Paul think, *She looks like a lump but she acts like a rock.*

"I am investigating a murder that happened yesterday within fifty feet of Father Johnson. It is a felony to interfere with a police investigation, and I need to ask him some questions."

They were locked in a staring contest for ten very long seconds. Finally Amy reached under her skirt to a holster and withdrew a set of metal handcuffs. She dropped them noisily on the desk.

"Let me see if he's available," the woman said. Amy smiled and responded, "If you'd be so kind."

Good thing you weren't mud-wrestling, Paul thought to her, *she outweighs us by a hundred pounds.*

Amy looked around the lobby and saw two men in monk's cassocks seated apart. One had a *Times-Picayune* open across his lap. The other one, she noticed, was jiggling his legs and looking everywhere at once with darting eyes. She thought, *Do you see who I see?*

Fuckola, he thought back. *It's Friar Sputum.*

Thank you for not announcing that out loud, you profane blackguard.

Sheepishly he said softly, "I'm more awake now."

Amy heard a new noise and she turned to see Father Johnson striding toward her with the receptionist trailing behind. As in the TV newscast, he was medium height, in a black suit that showed his white collar in front. Clean-shaven, tidy business haircut, with a youthful smile, he was holding out his right hand. "How can I help you?"

"Detective Amy Clear, NOPD," she said, shaking his offered hand. "Also St. Giles Academy class of 2017."

"All twelve years?" Amy nodded. "That's super. Now, what's this about a murder?" The receptionist was standing behind him, head held out to try to catch anything they said.

"This is a police inquiry, Father. Can we go somewhere to discuss it?"

He turned and saw the receptionist mere inches away. "Grace, why don't you go back to the phones?" Then, to Amy, "The conference room is empty right now." He led her around a corner to a large room that held a huge table and at least a dozen chairs. "We'll have some privacy here," he said as he flipped the light switch.

Amy sat at the first chair on the long side of the table and turned toward the short side, which led the polite priest to sit at a ninety-degree angle. She heard Paul think, *Right, that interview technique. You don't want to be opposite someone you're interviewing.*

She thought back, *And I don't know him well enough to want to sit next to him.*

"Father Johnson, you were at the demonstration yesterday at the Metropolitan Community Church. I wonder–"

He snapped his fingers. "That's why you look familiar. You nearly ruined the archbishop's day."

"We're even. He nearly ruined my friends' wedding. His monk spit on one of the ladies."

"Friar Transom means well," shaking his head, "but he's, oh, what is the expression? He's special. But he's a loyal soldier of Christ."

It was Paul who responded, Ah. As in the parable of Jesus spitting on the lepers?"

Amy took the lead back and said, "I think I saw him in the lobby just now."

"Bless his heart, he likes to be here. It seems to help his self-esteem."

Amy felt Paul rolling his inside eyes. Still leading, she went on, "Never mind that. The pastor of the MCC church was found murdered in her office while the demonstration was going on.

That's what I want to talk to you about. Did you know Riley Tibbs?"

"I did not," he said, thoughtfully. "The priest who heads up the Family Life Apostolate Mission probably does. Our outreach to gays and lesbians might not please the Equality Forum, but Deacon Benedetti does what he can within our theology."

"My medical examiner thinks Pastor Tibbs was killed around eleven AM. I want to know who may have been entering or leaving the church through the office entrance. When did you arrive?"

"Let's see," he was drumming his fingers on the table top as he thought. "Bishop Villavasso and I got there with some parish priests and some interns around nine-thirty, maybe nine-forty-five. His Grace arrived a little after eleven with Friar Transom."

"I realize you probably were occupied with other things, but did you notice anyone using the office doorway?" Amy was trying not to be distracted by the contorted face of Jesus on the huge crucifix mounted on the wall behind Johnson.

"Where is that entrance? I was–"

Paul jumped to interrupt. "From where your group was set up, it was on the left side of the sanctuary building, down half-way."

A smile spread across the priest's face. "Actually, I went in there to use the rest room."

"What time?" Paul barked.

"I don't know, maybe a little after ten. Two cups of coffee that morning."

Thanks, Paul, Amy thought; then, aloud, she asked, "What did you see in the hallway? Was there much traffic? Anyone who looked like they didn't belong there?"

"I wasn't paying attention, but let me think." Amy heard Paul think, *I smell smoke.* Finally Johnson went on, "Another man was in the rest room. I didn't see him, he was in a stall, but he was rehearsing a hymn. He kept going over the same phrase." He paused. "I saw two women in the hallway. I assumed they were pastors–both of them were in black robes. They were talking while they walked to the stairwell, then they went upstairs."

"What did they look like?" Amy prompted.

"One was very thin, short gray hair, looked to be, oh, sixty or so–" Paul thought to Amy, *Riley!* "–and the other woman was, uh, ample. Short hair. Round face."

Amy asked, "'Ample?'"

"One tries not to be judgmental," he stammered. "She was fat. Really fat. She had a fat face, too. I'm sorry." He looked down, while Amy heard Paul think, *Drew!*

"No one here but us skinny folks," Amy said, "it's okay. So a little after ten, you may have seen Pastor Tibbs and Associate Pastor Malone talking together, in vestments, and heading to the stairs. An hour later Tibbs was dead in her office up that staircase." She was thinking of how this might be useful information. Finally she asked, "Anyone else?"

Shaking his head, he said, "I went back to our area of the demonstration and didn't pay any more attention to that part of the grounds."

"Any of your people use that entrance?"

"Detective, are you suggesting one of the archdiocese people killed the pastor?"

Amy smiled. "All I'm suggesting is that one of your people may have responded to the call of nature, like you did. If that's the case, I'd like to talk to them like I'm talking to you, to find out if they saw anything significant."

He was silent but contrite. Amy handed him her business card and said, "If you think of anyone, call and let me know."

The priest started to stand up, but Paul took the lead and put their hand on his arm. "There's something else I want to ask you," he said, sounding exactly like Amy. When Johnson sat back down, he went on, "Did you interact at all with the black clergy demonstrators?"

"The Archbishop and I introduced ourselves to their leaders as a courtesy." A sigh, "I'm afraid I don't remember their names. We were there for just a minute or two. They were bearing silent witness, so there wasn't much opportunity for conversation."

"There were two men in particular with them. Tall, big men, mirrored sunglasses, red bowties, and flashy clothes. Did you see them?"

"Now that you mention them, yes. They were kind of intimidating."

"Really?" Amy raised an eyebrow. "Did they say or do anything?"

"No. They just didn't quite fit at the demonstration. They looked–they looked malevolent."

"But did you see them do anything suspicious? Did they accost anyone? Wave guns around?"

"No, no," shaking his head, "it was just their expressions. Just standing by themselves. They looked unfriendly. Hostile. Mean."

"Tell me about the hippies," Amy said.

"I don't understand," Johnson said.

It was Paul who clarified, "The freaks. The weirdos. The men in tutus and the girls *al fresco*."

"Oh. They were a colorful bunch, weren't they?" He laughed at the memory. "They certainly were entertaining. And noisy. They looked like they were having fun."

Paul responded, "Did you get to deal with any of them? Did anyone seem to be belligerent, or drugged out?"

He was tapping his fingers on the table again. "Actually, it wasn't any of them. There were, I don't know, maybe three different men on our side of the walkway. The, uh, the traditional marriage side. They had especially nasty signs. They were dressed in camouflage, like a hunter or a soldier? They didn't look like they were having a good time, like those, uh, hippies did. Kind of out of place, you know?"

Paul said, "The lone gunmen."

"The what?"

"I'm sorry," Amy said. "I noticed those people also. That's what I called them. It's police talk." Silently she said to Paul, *Please stop. Please?*

"Was that pastor shot?"

"No. She was stabbed."

"We have a lot of policy differences with the Metropolitan Community Church. Obviously, or we wouldn't have been demonstrating there yesterday. But we are all brothers and sisters in

Christ. The death of any clergyman is a threat to all of us. You have brought me troubling news."

"Father Johnson, I wonder if you know anything about an organization called Advancement Trust NOLA."

"I don't think so. Should I?" He looked genuinely puzzled.

"That's one of the groups that organized the, uh, the hippies' end of the demonstration, and I can't find anything about them. There was a flyer that said they were involved with the Equality Forum and the Community Coalition."

"Ah. I know about those people."

Amy raised an eyebrow, silently prodding Johnson to volunteer more.

"The Equality Forum holds vigils outside some of our churches because we don't permit women to be priests," he said. "Their officers are professional and civil, but some of their members–well, they can be rude. Rowdy and rude."

"How rowdy? Violent?"

He squeezed his face, "Kind of borderline. The worst of them get right up on you and yell gross things. But it's never devolved into a fist fight."

"For which we are grateful," Paul said. Then silently, *Amy? Anything else? Can we get lunch now?*

Amy closed her notebook, although she had not written a single word during their conversation. "I gave you my card," she said. "If you remember anything else from the demonstration, call me. It may seem like something little to you, but it just might be what we need to solve this case."

They stood up, and Amy finished, "And if any of your people say they went inside the church, call me with their phone number. Don't depend on them to contact me, they might not do it. Okay?"

"Please find the killer, Detective. There isn't a clergyman in New Orleans who will relax until you do."

The public relations priest led them back to the reception area. Amy stood in front of the clerk, finally clearing her throat to get the woman's attention.

"Yes? What?"

"I'm impressed with how you try to protect your boss," Amy said. "But when the Parish police show their ID, it's a good idea to cooperate."

The receptionist pursed her lips but said nothing. Instead, she looked back down at her work. It was Paul who said "Yeah. Well, have a nice day, Grace."

"Why were you such a pill in there?" Amy said out loud once they were in the parking lot outside the archdiocese office. "I may start calling you Tourette instead of Paulette."

I'm sorry, I'm sorry, I'm sorry, he thought back. *I woke up and didn't know where I was and–I'm sorry.*

"And did you have to challenge the priest? I wanted answers to my questions."

We got them, Paul thought back as Amy unlocked the yellow Benz. *Maybe it's ego, but yes, I had to challenge him. Excusing that monk just because he's some kind of mental?*

She pressed the glow plug and waited ten seconds before cranking the diesel engine. "I have to admit, I liked your parable. Where did you learn to talk religionese?"

He laughed and answered, "St. Giles Academy, class of 2017. Didn't I see you there?"

Amy looked at her clipboard on the passenger seat. "Next stop is WVUE. I need to–"

Whoa! he shouted silently. *Lunch, damn it. How do you keep going on no food?*

She backed out of the parking space and headed to the exit. Three quick right turns later she was on South Carrollton Avenue, driving toward the commercial Earhart Boulevard, where she was likely to find someplace to eat.

Taking advantage of the privacy of her car, Amy and Paul spoke out loud to each other. She asked, "What did you think about the PR priest?"

"Young. Eager. Forthcoming. I don't think he killed Riley."

"Oh, you maroon! Of course he didn't do it!"

Paul laughed, "Just checking. I like to state the obvious sometimes."

Amy turned into the parking lot for Ye Olde College Inn. "Will this work, Mister Owens?"

"Indubitably, Miss Clear."

The building was a stand-alone storefront on the corner of the block. It was brick, painted a light green-beige, with huge windows showing the homey dining room. At two in the afternoon it wasn't crowded.

Amy took a table by the windows facing the residential side street, with a view of a community garden. A young waiter brought a menu, and Amy asked him for a Barq's.

That shrimp po-boy looks tasty, Paul thought to her. *Or the cheeseburger.*

Amy thought back, *I love a shrimp loaf, but I'm feeling fat. I'm going for a salad.*

"Salad?" Paul said aloud; then silently, *You can't live on salad. You need protein. And carbs. And vitamin Q, I'm sure it's only in shrimp loafs and burgers.*

What is vitamin Q? she thought to him, smiling as she went over the menu.

It's—It's—Why, vitamin Q is the substance that makes young women beautiful and skinny and sexy. It makes them look even younger. It makes their skin feel like a baby's bottom. It—

Where can I get a bottle of it? she thought, laughing out loud.

No need, he continued. *There's a ton of it in a shrimp loaf. It's a scientific fact. Nine out of eight doctors recommend it.*

Very entertaining, she thought, and signaled to the waiter. When Paul heard her order the Farm House salad with citrus-herb vinaigrette dressing, he moaned silently. *Nooo! Salad is the anti-vitamin Q. It makes people old and fat and ugly. And hungry.*

"I guess I'm doomed, then," she whispered. "Sad. She was still a young little thing..."

If the waiter or the only other customer had been paying attention, they would have seen Amy moving the fork from right hand to left hand and back with every bite. Whoever was leading got the most taste from the food, and the most satiation of hunger, and so they alternated. While right-handed Amy and left-handed Paul didn't always agree on the menu, Amy had made it clear since she was eleven years old: it was her body, and she had the final say. She would try to be considerate and accommodating, but if push came to shove, what Amy wanted was what mattered.

You wouldn't want me to be fat, Amy thought, as they moved the fork back and forth; she blew her cheeks out as if to demonstrate. *You wouldn't want me to be complaining all the time about being fat.*

I was kind of fat when I had my own body, he thought back. *I got used to it. I was married; Mary Pat and I liked to eat. She was a better cook.*

Amy held the fork out in her right hand. "A better cook than me?" She was teasing because she had learned that Paul was the one who knew his way around a kitchen.

"No. A better cook than me."

Since he had slept through Amy's morning meeting with Lieutenant Cranston, Paul thought to her, *Did you and Duke come up with a plan?*

She pushed a crouton aside, even though she knew Paul would eat it next time he wielded the fork. "Yes and no. I hope we can get along well enough to work together. He doesn't have any sense of humor. He thinks I'm a wacko."

But a great wacko, Paul thought. Indeed, he stabbed the crouton with the fork. *You think outside the box, you see things other people don't.*

"That's what I told him! I'm not so sure he agrees."

It was Paul's turn, and he took a long drought of root beer before spearing a piece of lettuce, a hunk of tomato, and something that looked like a back yard weed off their plate.

Amy continued silently, *He's checking up on the Partnership of African-American Clergy. Maybe he can ID those enforcer-looking guys.* She took her bite of salad. *And he's contacting the newspaper to see if they have photos showing the lone gunmen.*

"What's our brief?"

"The archdiocese, which you contributed to, and the hippies. That's why our next stop is Channel 8. They had interviews with some of the pro-demonstrators on the news last night, and I'm going to get them to tell me names and phone numbers so I can interview them."

"Will the station cooperate?" Paul asked. He laid down the fork and took the final crouton between the thumb and index finger of their left hand. "I mean, confidentiality of sources and all." He popped the crouton into their mouth and sucked the garlic out of it.

"We'll see. Oh, and we have to be back at Rampart Street by eight tomorrow morning."

The waiter came to remove the empty salad plate. When he asked if there would be anything else, she heard Paul think, *Aren't you the least bit curious what a fried bread pudding po-boy[3] is?*

I'll look it up on Wikipedia, she thought as she stood and went to the cashier to pay for their meal.

As they drove up South Carrollton toward the television station, Amy sighed, "I'm stuffed. That was a good salad. They raise greens on their own farm."

"Stuffed?" Paul said aloud in disbelief. "How do you survive on rabbit food? I could eat our left foot. Except it would hurt."

"And I'd be kicking you with my right foot. After all these years, you still haven't learned to eat for a 109-pound body?"

He mumbled, "My body was twice the size of yours. More." He felt their face turning red.

"Poor boy. It's okay, we both want me to be skinny. Right?" No response. "Right?" she repeated.

"Oh. Yeah. Right. Right, we both want you to remain just as luscious as you are."

"Do you want to drive?"

Paul's inside eyes lit up. He loved to drive, and from the day he showed up in eleven-year-old Amy until she got her driver's license seven years later, he felt deprived. Ever since, he responded like a teenager with a learner's permit, offering to drive any car, anywhere, for any reason. Out loud, he said, "Please, B'rer Amy, don't throw me in that briar patch."

At the next red light Amy stepped back internally to let Paul lead to drive. The first thing he said was, "Where are we going?"

"Keep going, but turn right at Earhart," Amy explained. "Then make a left on Jeff Davis. If we get to I-10 we've gone too far." She felt him nod their head.

"Who are we looking for?"

"First, the News Director, Buddy somebody, I've got his name on the clipboard." She started to reach for it until Paul shouted, "Eyes front! I can't drive if you're looking over there."

"Oh. Sorry. And if I can't coax him into helping, I've got the name of the General Manager. She's a woman."

He turned onto South Jefferson Davis Parkway, and they began crossing the remaining Muses streets–Thalia, Erato, and Calliope, pronounced by all true New Orleanians as CAL-ee-ope. Clio didn't extend as far as Jeff Davis, which was just as well; on seeing the street sign CLIO, the locals call it C-L-ten. And you thought your town was strange.

Just past Euphrosine–the name inspired by a French opera when France still owned *La Louisiane* in the eighteenth century– they noticed the monument sign saying 'Fox 8 News.' "That's a TV station?" Amy asked. The sign marked a short driveway that led to a gated parking deck, two stories, white brick, set off by four rather peaked palm trees. The only thing that looked at all technological was the cluster of satellite antennas.

Paul turned down the next street, Drexel, and stayed in first gear to reconnoiter. On their left was what he imagined was a seven-story hotel, until he reached South Clark and saw the Loyola University logo over the main entrance; it was a college dormitory. He made a left, and when he had gotten past the dorm, Amy said, "News trucks." There were several in a fence-and-razor-wire enclosed lot, as well as more of the huge round antennas. "Must be the place," she added.

Once they were back on Jeff Davis, Paul passed the sign and pulled into a diagonal space for visitor parking. Amy took up the clipboard, and, leading again, she leafed through her notes. "Buddy Simpson is the News Director," she said, although Paul was looking at the papers with the same eyes Amy was using.

Paul sang, "His name was always BUDDY! And he'd shrug and ask to stay..."[4]

Amy interrupted, thinking, *Is this another one of your Paleozoic-Era songs that no one my age has ever heard of?*

It brought Paul up short. "David Bowie was hot damn shit, I'll have you know."

"I'm supposed to know that name?" She was walking along the cast iron fence, looking for a way into the TV station complex.

Deflated, Paul thought to her, *I'm old and in the way. Push me out on an ice floe and let me die an honorable death.*

"Don't die. Just don't sing me songs that you learned from Thomas Jefferson. How do you get into this place?" She stood still, frowning. "It's all fenced in."

Paul started paying attention to their surroundings. The parking deck was closed off by a sliding gate. The wrought iron fence, spikes up, went across the grassy area between buildings, and then up to the next corner, where he knew it protected the long axis of the Xavier University dorm up to its main entrance. "Can we climb this fence in a skirt?"

She thought back, *Not unless somebody's trying to kill me. There has to be a way in.* Amy walked a short way up the pavement and noticed a gap. There was a pathway–also fenced in–that led all the way to a concrete staircase up to the second floor of the complex. "Hah!" she cried, "Open sesame!"

She ran part of the way, then slowed to take the cement stairs safely. At the top was a glass door, and behind it, a sumptuous lobby. Amy heard Paul think, *Air conditioning, yum,* as she pushed open the door.

She smoothed her skirt so it didn't show a bump from the butt of her pistol in her thigh holster. "I'd like to speak to Buddy Simpson," she told the receptionist.

The young woman behind the desk was chewing gum. "I'm sorry, he's in production."

"Will he be long?"

A shrug.

"Look," Paul said, sounding exactly like Amy. He reached under their skirt for her badge case. "Tell him an impatient New Orleans cop is waiting for him. Will you do that for me?"

The receptionist, maybe nineteen years old, looked around the lobby to see if there was anyone, anyone at all, who could tell her what to do. "Just pick up the phone," Paul coaxed, "call his department. You can do it, I know you can."

Hesitantly, she took the telephone handset. Looking up at Amy, she punched an extension number. "There's a police woman here to see Buddy?" She listened for a moment, then said, "How should I know? Wait–" then, to Amy, "What's this about?"

"Murder," Paul said. They did not smile.

"She–she says it's about a murder." Hearing the reply, she said, "Uh-huh. Yeah. Uh-huh. Okay, wait." To Amy she relayed the message, "Buddy hasn't been murdered. He's in studio 2 filming a promo."

Silently, Paul thought to Amy, *I'd love to say, 'If he's not out here in thirty seconds he will be murdered.' Probably shouldn't do that, huh?*

Aloud, she intoned, "Probably not." Amy put a big smile on their face, then reached over the desk and took the telephone handset from the receptionist, who looked on in horror. "This is Detective Clear with the New Orleans Police. I need to talk to Buddy Simpson about police business. We are investigating someone else's murder. How long before Buddy gets his butt out of studio 2?"

She enjoyed hearing coughs and sputters on the other end. Finally a male voice said, "I'll, uh, I'll get him."

"If you'd be so kind."

Amy handed the phone back to the receptionist, who had neither blinked nor closed her mouth since Amy had taken it away from her. It was Paul who said, "Thanks, kid."

Amy continued to stand in front of the receptionist's desk. First she took in the walls: yellow and gray painted cinder block, with dozens and dozens of plaques and framed awards for various news shows. One big photograph momentarily got her attention: a little league baseball team, seated in their uniforms, with bats and balls and gloves in the foreground. She could read the caption from across the lobby: "The WVUE NewsPups 2031 Greater New Orleans Little League."

She turned her attention to her clipboard and went over her notes again. Amy heard Paul think, *What if the guy goes all 'confidential sources' on you?*

It's happened before, she answered silently. *I call the stationhouse and get Legal to request a warrant. It just takes time.* They were looking at her to-do list: Sunchild, three topless women, two funny homosexuals, and two college lesbians. *All I need is names and addresses. Phone numbers. Emails. I want to—"*

"It must be you," a man said. Buddy Simpson was about six-two. He was wearing a blue pinstriped dress shirt with a diagonally striped necktie, and dark gray slacks. He appeared to be about fifty, with a bald spot in back and an overlarge forehead that had seen its last hair follicles close up shop years earlier.

"Mister Simpson," Amy said. "I'm Detective Clear. Can we—"

"This had better be important," he interrupted. "I was in the middle of making news promos that have to be on the air by four o'clock."

"Murder always is important, Mister Simpson. Where can we discuss this?"

"How about right here? I'm in a hurry."

"I am, too, but I still want to give you some privacy while we're talking. Hmm?"

The News Director seemed to be looking for an excuse to be angry. "Privacy? For me? What are you talking about?"

Paul grew impatient and took the lead. "I'm talking about you and me in a room where the mouth of the south—" he pointed at the receptionist "—won't be broadcasting our discussion. If you like, it can be at the police station on Rampart Street."

"Jesus Christ on a pogo stick," the man muttered. "Okay. The conference room. Let's get this over with." He turned his back and strode to the door that led to the inner workings of the television complex. He swiped an ID card but didn't hold the door open for Amy; she ran the last few steps to catch the door before it locked her out.

Amy caught up to the newsman and had to keep walking fast to stay alongside him. She heard him muttering, but couldn't make out the words. Two turns down a hallway, and finally he opened the door to a small conference room.

Paul thought, *Round table. We're going to have to sit next to him.*

Like hell, she thought back. Without waiting on the man, she took a seat, placed her clipboard on an adjoining chair, and faced in that direction. Simpson sat two seats away, at a forty-five degree angle from her.

"Is this about that weird priest?" he asked.

"Nothing weird about her," Amy answered, levelly, "except that someone stabbed her. And–" she held up one hand "–no, I don't think you did it."

"Whew!" with a wipe of his hand across his forehead, "Glad I'm off the hook."

"Your newscast last night ran a long segment about the demonstration. I want to compliment you for being the only station in town that had any sympathy for the supporters."

"It's August," he said, sounding serious for the first time, "I thought it would make some colorful footage, like during Mardi Gras."

"NOPD has no opinion about the demonstration. No laws were broken and no one was hurt during the, uh, the festivities. All I care about is solving the murder that no one knew about while the demonstration was going on." She took her clipboard from the seat next to her. "I figure whatever it was about the people you interviewed that made you choose to put them on the air is the same thing that tells me they may have seen something. What I need is the names and contact information of–" she dropped the clipboard noisily on the table top "–Sunchild, the three topless women with things written on their bodies, those two delightful gay men, and those college lesbians who were dressed out of an old Martha Stewart catalogue." She looked up at Simpson. "So, what do you say?"

"I'd love to help you," he said, his hands palms up on the table, "but we don't collect that information."

"You have a future in PR," Paul broke in, "but maybe not a good one. You need their contact information for implied consent to broadcast your video of them. So," tapping the clipboard, "let's have the names."

Simpson stared at Amy for several seconds, then took an obvious look at his wristwatch. "Do you have a warrant?"

"If you think I need one, I'll get one."

"Do that," he said, and he began to stand up.

Amy waved at him to sit back down as she used her other hand to retrieve her phone from a holster under her skirt. She pressed a speed dial key, and said, "Walter? It's Detective Clear. We talked about how I might need a warrant? Yes. Yes, he got all huffy. Can I speak to the Commander?"

Paul thought to her, *What the hell? You're talking to your extension voice mail.*

She thought back, *He doesn't know that.* Aloud, "He's playing golf? What kind of officer plays golf in the middle of a work day? Oh, he's playing golf with Judge Noe? Great. So you'll call–that's the ticket! What, fifteen minutes? Yes. Ye–ye–Walter, I hear you. Call me back after the judge signs it, okay?"

As she put the phone back, she said to Simpson, "Got a deck of cards?" She smiled broadly.

"God damn it," he barked. Standing, he said, "Let's go to the news room, see what I have."

As they walked down another hall and a cinder brick staircase, Amy asked, "Were you on site for the demonstration?"

"Yeah. My one weekend a month. I thought it would be fun. Actually, it was." He held open the door for Amy as they left the stairs for a break room, and then the huge news room.

In one corner was the WVUE-TV on-camera news set–bathed in light, but unpopulated, waiting for the 4:30 news. Four large cameras were arranged around it, each on a heavy-duty dolly. Two of them had teleprompter screens, now dark. Around the room were desks, chairs, and maybe ten men and women toiling away at computer screens or bringing scripts to other people. A large section to one side was empty but for another four cameras pointed at a blue scrim.

"I've never been in a TV studio," Paul said, with wonder in their voice.

Simpson chuckled. "It's exciting. It's glamorous. It's crazy. The deadlines will crush your soul." He opened the door to his office, a twelve-by-twelve cubicle with four TV screens flashing soundlessly. He motioned to a chair for Amy, then took his seat at his computer. "What are we looking for?"

"Sunchild."

"A grade-A crazy, but harmless." He scrolled through some scans, and then said, "Larry Weisberg," followed by a phone number and an address in Faubourg Marigny. Amy added the information to her notes.

"Why did you put him in the newscast?"

"Are you kidding? A practically naked man with fucking wings taped to his back? And his home-made magic wand? Anyone who didn't laugh at that was watching another channel."

Nodding, she asked, "You said he didn't seem dangerous. Did you notice what group he was with at the protest?"

A shrug. "One more loony in a sea of loony. Who else?"

Amy began to describe the three topless women, but Simpson interrupted, saying, "The General Manager gave me shit about that. 'We're Fox-8, not Porno-8,' he said. But an excuse to get tits on TV? Oh–" an afterthought, "–uh, excuse me."

He dictated names and contact information, singling out the woman who had taken a Sharpie pen to her stomach. "I wish I'd known girls like that thirty years ago. Oh, wait–I did." He shook his head.

Paul asked, "That delicious gay couple?"

"Jerks," he said. "I don't even know if they were gay."

Simpson didn't notice their raised eyebrow, so Paul said, "How were they jerks?" He was holding their pen in their left hand.

"They were very camp, like a caricature of being gay. Lisping, limp wrists, fondling each other." He found their contact information on his screen so he turned his attention to Amy. "As soon as we had their segment in the can, they started laughing and talking normally. Bastards. But good television footage." He dictated their names and contact details, and Paul dutifully transcribed them to their pad.

"Huh. Weren't you writing with your other hand before?"

Paul smiled. "I don't know what you're talking about," he answered. "How about the clean-cut lesbians?"

"Well..." He stared at Amy for a few seconds, then shrugged and went back to his computer screen. Paul put their pen in their right hand for Amy to take notes. He heard her think, *You're enjoying this way too much.*

More names. The women were students at Sophie Newcomb College, which had finally been reestablished in 2027 after having been absorbed within Tulane University for twenty years. "They seemed very normal," Simpson said.

"Why?" Paul asked, "What are lesbians usually like?" He was curious, since his girlfriend of many years was a lesbian.

"Hmm. I don't know. I mean, these girls were wearing pearls, for God's sake. And dresses."

"Ah. No Sharpie writing on exposed skin," Paul observed.

"But they looked good on camera," he observed. "After three weird supporters, I thought normal-looking people would appeal to our 25-to-44 female demographic. I've scheduled the tape for a dial research study to see–"

"With joysticks?" Amy asked. "I've got a Masters in statistics. I spent a few years doing projects like that."

"So you understand about demographic segmentation and appeal. It's the dirty little secret behind television news."

She leaned back in her chair, now that she had gotten the information she wanted from the News Director. "You were there," she said. "Did you see anyone or anything that you thought might be dangerous? Bullying? Screaming? Foaming at the mouth?"

"There was lots of screaming," he laughed. "And I spent a lot of time looking at the mammarial scenery. I'll tell you, though–there were a couple of guys who were pretty creepy."

Lone gunmen? Paul thought to Amy.

"Tell me about them."

"They had particularly nasty signs. They were wearing camouflage. And, I don't know, they just looked a little unhinged."

She thought to Paul, *Bingo!* Then to Simpson, "How many of them? Were they together?"

"I think I saw three of them. They were here and there; they didn't seem like they were part of the same contingent. They were on the anti-marriage side."

"And which side are you on?"

"Definitely anti-marriage. I'm paying alimony to two ex-wives."

"That's what I get for asking," she laughed. "Something else: did you notice anyone going into or out of the side door on the church?"

It was Simpson's turn to raise his eyebrows. "There's a side door? I was working, Officer. Aside from scantily clad women, I wasn't looking around a lot."

"Detective," Amy corrected. "You were covering the pro-marriage side in your news. Did you talk to any of the organizers?"

"That was organized?"

Amy took the pink neon paper out from behind the pad on her clipboard. "The Community Coalition, the Equality Forum, and Advancement Trust NOLA. Did you talk to anyone from those groups?"

Shaking his head, he said, "I've heard of some of them, but– look, I was just after colorful video that would make viewers watch Fox-8 again the next day. Sorry."

Amy said, "I appreciate your time and your help, Mister Simpson," as she stood up. "If you think of anything–" she held out a business card "–anything at all that might be helpful, please call me."

The News Director heard he was being dismissed, so he stood up. "About the warrant?" he said.

"What warrant?"

He frowned. "The one the judge was going to sign in fifteen minutes?"

"I'll fax it to you when I get it," she said. "Thanks again, Mister Simpson."

When they were back in Amy's old yellow Benz, she said, "You want to drive to–"

YES! he silently shouted. Then, aloud, "Where are we going?" He mashed the glow plug button and started counting to ten.

"The Community Coalition," Amy said. "It's in Faubourg Marginy. Go up to Elysian Fields and then head for the river."

Paul cranked the engine and carefully backed out of their diagonal parking space. "You totally buffaloed that News Director," he said out loud. "Now I know why you have your phone number on speed-dial."

She responded, "You didn't let him get away with that 'we don't collect that information' routine. Between us we make a decent detective."

"Yeah, I guess," Paul said. He was pleased with Amy's unexpected praise. "Do we have to interview all of those people?"

"Yes, but not until tomorrow. Duke is running this investigation, not me. We'll go over it at the station house in the morning. But today it's those groups on the hot pink flyer."

He snorted. "That would be a great name for a rock band." Affecting the voice of a boxing announcer he went on, "Ladies and Gentlemen, put your hands together for Hot! Pink!! FLYYYYYYYER!!!"

"Playing their hit single," Amy added, "'Who Killed the Pastor?' You can play guitar, and I'll sing, and Christine, she'd look awesome playing bass. And we'll get Duke to play drums. He's so big, I'm sure he'd be great. This will be a great Plan B, if I never join the circus."

"Ah, circus is Plan A," Paul laughed. "Weren't we going to become traveling groupies for SpongeBob SquarePants? I thought that was Plan B."

"Fun, but no money in it. If you turn right up there we'll be halfway to Community Coalition."

Part of the Faubourg Marginy is a young, trendy, offbeat mecca, with music clubs, art galleries, and dozens of coffee houses. Although it sits just north of the French Quarter, rents are nowhere near as high as in its famous neighbor. Then, the closer one gets to the Mississippi River, the more warehouses appear; slightly dingy souvenirs of the city's industrial and maritime history. As Paul drove east on one of the border streets, Elysian Fields Avenue, they passed typical single-story bungalows, the occasional two-story jobs, and the odd Baptist Friendship House and mental health center. A hair salon in a loud, red bungalow, and a Wash-Dry-Fold in a converted single-family house. Empty parking lots. Low office buildings with "For Sale or Lease" signs. A hardware store in a low brick building from the 1950s, a three-story apartment with an uncharacteristic bland facade, a nursery and outdoor furniture outlet, and a funky converted warehouse now housing a pricey art gallery. Just past that, next to the WPA-era New Orleans Public Service power plant was a low industrial building with window shutters tightly closed. The paint was mottled from someone trying to stay ahead of the spray-paint taggers and vandals.

"This is Community Coalition?" Paul asked. From the car they could see an enormous fastened padlock on the only door.

She glanced at her clipboard. "Number 501, but I don't know," Amy mused. "Drive around the corner."

He turned up Decatur Street. More mottled wall greeted them. There was a truck entrance, closed and gated. There was a sealed door. And near the rear corner of the building, by the driveway to the huge deserted parking lot, was a door that appeared possibly to have been used within living memory.

Paul pulled into the parking lot. The back of the building had unshuttered sash windows and siding in desperate need of repair. The roof line sagged in the middle, where a short piece of gutter was swinging slowly off a nail. "I think we ought to park on the street," he said. He turned the car around.

Amy led to walk from where Paul parked on Elysian Fields to what they hoped was a functioning door on the side street. "The woman I talked to was–" she leafed through the pad on her clipboard "–here, Jess Rodgers." She knocked on the door but got no response. She knocked louder, and shouted, "Jess? Are you there?"

Silence reigned. Paul led to try the doorknob, and it turned. He walked them in to a pitch black room. *Wait,* Amy thought to him; she fished her LED flashlight out of one of the thigh holsters under her skirt and clicked it on. Swinging the light around, they could tell they were in a mostly deserted office, about fifteen feet square, housing a few dirty folding chairs and not a little crumbled plaster dust from deteriorating walls. As they stepped toward an inside door, they saw it open.

Suddenly the room was brightly lit from overhead bulbs. Amy held their hand up to block the light that was making them squint and flinch. It took a moment to realize she was looking at the business end of the barrel of a revolver, held in a woman's shaking hands.

"Don't you move," the woman said, tentatively, "or I'll–I'll–I'll shoot, I'm sure I will."

"Jess?"

"How do you know my name?" she asked. Her hands were shaking more, and Paul thought that actually increased the chance a bullet would hit them.

"I'm Detective Amy Clear. We talked on the phone a little while ago?"

"Oh. Thank God." the woman said. Then, as if she were just noticing that there was a gun in her hand, "Oh, I'm sorry." She pointed it at the floor and pulled the trigger with a quiet click. "Anyway, it's not loaded."

Amy's jaw dropped at the implications of the woman's foolish behavior, even as she heard Paul think to her, *She was going to confront a bad guy with an unloaded gun? That's a sure way to get killed.*

"You might want to rethink your security strategy for the future," Amy said. "Like locking the door?"

"I couldn't do that. I knew you were on your way, and I can't hear anyone knock from my office."

Amy reached under her skirt and took out her badge case. "Here," she said, handing it to the woman. "I really am the detective." Then she turned to the door they had entered and locked it.

"Of course you are," the woman said, returning the ID. "Come on back to my office and let's see if I can help you."

Jess Rodgers was a few inches taller than Amy, and a few pounds heavier. About 23 years old, she wore her blonde hair in a medium bob. She was wearing a blue denim jumper over a white shirt, an outfit that made her appear even younger. Paul thought her soft, round face was particularly attractive.

The woman turned off the overhead lights as they left the room, then took them through two other disused spaces before entering a meagerly outfitted office. There was an old, bulky computer monitor and a combination printer-copier-fax on the main desk. Amy noticed half a dozen filing cabinets, and several organization posters on the walls. "Just push that stuff off the chair and sit down," Jess told her.

A copy of the hot pink flyer was lying on her desk. Pointing at it, Amy asked, "Did you attend the demonstration?"

"Oh, yeah. Were you there?" When Amy nodded, Jess went on, "Wasn't it fun? All those people there to support those women getting married. Really inspirational." She was silent, her right hand pressed against her chest. "I thought it was so moving."

Amy ran through her litany of questions. Jess told her she had not entered the church, nor had she noticed anyone using the side door. She ignored most of the protesters because she knew so many people on the same-sex marriage side of the grounds. No, she didn't notice the muscle, but she did spot some of the lone gunmen– "hateful assholes" is how she described them. "Their signs were so ugly. Disgusting. I hope they're happy living under a rock somewhere."

Amy let Paul lead to ask, "Did you talk with any of the other organizers? The Equality Forum, or Advancement Trust NOLA?"

"Oh, sure. I talk to Dakota Phillips at Equality Forum a couple times a week. We specialize in practical assistance, like food or a place to stay, and they've got the lawyers to beat up on the bigots. We try to coordinate."

"That's my next stop," Paul said, sounding exactly like Amy. "What about Advancement Trust NOLA?"

Jess stuck out her lower lip as she drummed her fingers on the desk. Choosing her words carefully, she said, "Sam Atkins. That woman is not very organized."

Paul put their left ankle on top of their right knee, until Amy moved both feet to the floor and adjusted their skirt. *Ooops,* he thought; then, to Jess, he asked, "How did she show off her stellar organizational skill?"

"The flyer. I must have gotten two dozen emails from her in two days. Each time she suggested something different about it; some of her ideas were way out." Jess shook her head. "Dakota and I had to tell her to stop, that we were going to send it out like it was. She sent us emails in all capitals, just shouting crazy stuff."

"Did you see–"

"She came here one time, before the flyer craziness. You know she smokes? Cigarettes, I mean. Who smokes in 2034?"

"Euw," Paul said. "Thanks for the warning. Do you think she's sincere? I mean, isn't Advancement Trust a social services organization? Like yours?"

"I can't figure out what they do. Part of me thinks it's just the Sam Advancement Trust. But she's as gay as I am, so that part's sincere."

Paul looked puzzled. Jess said, "It's not just men who have gaydar, you know." She pointed at Amy and went on, "But I can't tell about you. You send out some mixed signals."

He thought to Amy, *You want to handle this?* He heard her think back, *God, no,* but he felt her step forward to lead. "Yes," she said aloud. "We're complicated." She and Paul both were heterosexual, but, of course, Paul was a heterosexual male.

"It's okay," said the woman ten years younger than Amy, "you'll figure it out."

Amy thought to Paul, *If she only knew.* Then aloud, "Did Sam ever mention an idea she had about the church pastor?"

"That time she was here, fumigating the office, she said something strange. She said she thought the pastor was a phony. I was trying to get rid of her, so I didn't ask what she meant." Jess stabbed at the air with her index finger and added, "She was at the demonstration. God, she was wearing the yellowest dress ever made–"

"With polka dots?" Amy interrupted

"You saw her! Me, I made sure to stay far away from her." The woman shook her head. "I don't want to have to deal with her again."

Amy slapped their hands on their thighs and stood up, saying, "Okay, I'm done. If you think of anything, anything at all, that might help us, call me." She held out her business card.

Jess stood as well. "I didn't know Reverend Tibbs," she said, "I'm a Wiccan. But she was helping gay rights, and it's a double shame what happened." She slipped the business card into the pocket of her jumper. "I feel better that you and the police are investigating."

Amy smiled, then let the woman lead their way back to the functioning door. Standing in the well-lit but deserted room, Paul said, "What's the story on this place? It's huge, but you've got a little office. And from the back it looks like it's falling apart."

"It is falling apart. I'm in the only room that doesn't leak." She put her weight on her right leg, and held both her hands on her left hip. "The owner is some hotshot who wanted to build a high-rise apartment, but the city council turned him down."

"So, why hasn't he sold it?"

"Nobody wants it. The only reason I have the Community Coalition here is I can't beat fifty-dollar rent."

Their eyebrows shot up. "Fifty dollars–a day?"

"A month. And he pays the utilities. He's a sweetheart. Well, for a hotshot. Maybe he thinks the zoning board will change its mind. I just say 'thank you' each month."

Amy unlocked the door to the street. "Make sure you lock this when I'm gone," she offered. "And buy some bullets for that revolver."

"I'll be all right," she said. "People like me."

Amy let Paul lead to drive to Equality Forum in the Central Business District. She waved as they passed the police station on Rampart Street. In the privacy of the car, Paul spoke aloud: "Is there anyone who likes that Sam character?"

"I'm trying to keep an open mind," Amy replied. "She's last on my list for today."

Paul turned left when they reached Poydras, headed toward the Mississippi and the touristy Riverwalk. When Amy saw the seventeen tan stories of the Staybridge Hotel she said, "This is Tchoupitoulas. Turn right." As he drove, they passed the

Ambassador Hotel on one side, the bizarre Piazza d'Italia and the Lowes Hotel on the other; looming beyond them was the enormous Harrah's complex.

"Crap!" he blurted out. "Lafayette's one way the wrong way. We want to go over there," pointing out the driver's side window.

Amy thought to him, *Go straight. There's a parking deck a little ways on the right. It's–there! There it is.*

"I remember this place," Paul said. "We parked here when you were investigating for the Goode At Law firm."

As he turned into the entrance to press the button to get a parking ticket, Amy said, "Eleven dollars? That's a French Quarter price. When did–" She stopped when Paul hit the brakes. He thought to her, *Are we going in or not?*

"Crap. Yes, go ahead. Crap and a half!"

He found a space on the fourth floor of the huge deck. As they walked toward the elevator, Paul said, "In the words of Captain Kirk, 'everyone remember where we parked.'"

Eleven dollars! she thought to him. *I'm not made out of money.*

Keep the receipt, he thought back. *The Commander might reimburse us.*

I don't get it, Amy thought as they took the elevator down to the street. *The Community Coalition is in a little room in a derelict building in a warehouse section, and the Equality Forum is in the Central Business District. How does this work?*

"Maybe it's because the Coalition is a charity, but the Forum is made of lawyers who lobby in Baton Rouge."

That's not fair, Amy thought as they walked out onto Tchoupitoulas Street. Paul went to the side of the parking deck and stopped.

What do you mean, 'not fair'? he thought to her.

If the world was fair, she thought back, *the people helping hungry people would have all the money, and the lawyers would be stuck in a leaky building that's one council meeting away from being demolished.*

Paul blinked. *And to you that's fair?*

"Yes," she said out loud, startling a woman walking past; then, silently, *I don't like lawyers. They make a policeman's life hell.*

Paul smiled inside as he thought back, *You know I don't think much of police. I guess a person's view of what's fair depends on their prejudices.*

Hey, she barked silently. *I'm not prejudiced.*

We all are, one way or another. You said you don't like lawyers. You know I don't like cops. We have different ideas of what's fair.

Amy and Paul had been a dyad for more than twenty years. She knew–and she was grateful–that Paul wasn't being critical with his observation; but more than once she had told him what she repeated now: "Sometimes I hate it when you're right. Can we go now?"

Paul stepped back internally and let Amy resume control of their body. *The Forum should be around the corner,* she thought.

The organization was based in a three-story red brick building, with typical full-length windows that often confused tourists into thinking they were doors. They passed a shuttered entrance with a For Lease notice, then came to a door with a brass plate beside it that said 'Scheister & Hsu, Attorneys at Law.'

Amy opened the door and stepped inside to a lobby. The walls were covered with a red textured paper; large colored lithographs were hung in ornate gold frames. There were several red leather wing chairs, each by an end table covered with financial investment magazines.

"Can I help you, Miss?"

Behind a small desk sat an older man in a dark blue uniform. His face–and especially his nose–was ruddy.

"Oh, hello," she replied. "I'm looking for the Equality Forum."

"Up them stairs to the second floor, then turn left." He paused. "Left?" Still seated, he attempted to swivel his body, as if he were making the journey in his mind's eye. "Yeah. Left." He smiled.

It was Paul who said, "Well, thank ye kindly," as Amy headed for the wide wooden staircase with its red velvet runner. She thought to him, *Pretty swank for a social service group.*

A social service group run by lawyers, he thought back.

At the second-floor landing, they turned left and began reading the plates on the doors they passed. All of them were for lawyers or law groups, but none said 'Equality Forum.' When they reached the end of the hallway–the window framed the view of the Harrah's Hotel, a piece of the Mississippi, and hazy homes in Algiers Point– Amy said, "About face." They retraced their steps to the stairwell, then explored the other wing.

After passing a few more law offices, Amy read the door plate for The Equality Forum. "Show time," she whispered to Paul, and knocked.

"Who is it?" a high pitched voice responded.

Smiling, Amy shouted through the door, "Detective Clear with NOPD!"

They heard a series of coughs, then "Just a sec." There were footsteps from inside the office, what sounded like a pile of paper falling to the ground, and a muttered "Shit!" A few seconds later the door opened.

Amy was startled to have to look down to see the five-foot-two-inch leader of Equality Forum. He was very thin, accentuated by the oversized blue dress shirt and patterned necktie he was wearing. What remained of his hair was cut short. She saw his light brown eyes, set wide on his narrow face. "Hi," she said. "May I come in?"

"Of course!" he said, surprisingly cheerful compared to what they had heard through the door. He stepped back, holding the door open wide. "I have to pick up some stuff that fell–"

"Yes, I heard that," Amy interrupted. "Can I help?"

The man let out a sigh of relief. "No, that's okay. In fact–" he pointed to a round conference table, "–why don't we sit over there? I'll mess with the mess after you go."

The office was a typical fifteen feet deep, but it was at least thirty feet wide. Beige carpet with a thick nap covered the floor. One wall was a mass of tall filing cabinets, while the others were painted a light rose. Framed certificates hung around the room. Amy guessed the man's desk was at the other end of the room, where paper and manila folders were scattered about. All the furniture matched, stark modern in pale wood.

When Amy sat down she put her clipboard on the adjoining chair so the director wouldn't be right next to her; it would be easier for her to gauge his responses to her questions that way.

Amy began, "Forgive me, but I don't remember your name."

"That happens a lot," he said. "I'm Dakota Phillips. On the phone you said you wanted to ask me about the same-sex wedding at the MCC?"

Amy nodded. She moved her clipboard to the table and clicked open a ballpoint pen. "Were you at the demonstration?"

"No," he said. "Crowds make me nervous. And it was a lesbian wedding, not a gay one; I would have felt out of place." He coughed, swallowed, and erupted in a long series of gross coughs.

"Are you okay?" she asked. Dakota bobbed his head and waved his hands while he continued to cough. It was a full minute before the spasm subsided. "I'm sorry," he said, wiping his mouth with a paper towel. "I'm okay, really."

Amy and Paul exchanged silent *'He's not okay'*s at that; Amy thought, *AIDS? TB? Ebola?*

She shrugged at her own words and then took a few seconds to restore her concentration. Then she asked, "Since you didn't attend, who from your group was at the demonstration? I need to talk with them."

"Gabe, and...I think Parker was there. They're coming in this evening for a wrap-up meeting."

"What time? I may drop in to speak with them."

He shrugged. "Six-thirty, seven. I don't know that we allow outsiders to attend."

"Oh, I don't want to sit in on the meeting. I just want to spend a few minutes with them. Sometimes a witness notices some dumb thing and it turns out to be the last clue we need to ID the perp and get them off the street."

Dakota coughed, a single, controlled cough, then replied, "Yeah, that would probably be all right."

Amy turned the page on the pad in her clipboard. "Good. In the lead-up to the demonstration, did you have contact with the Community Forum or Advantage Trust? The other sponsors?"

The man smiled for the first time. "Sure. I talk to Jess at the Forum all the time. We decided that if we ever both go straight we're going to get married."

Paul snorted and said, "It's good to have a Plan B." Dakota frowned. Paul heard Amy laugh, and he went on, "Aside from seating plans at the reception, what do you two talk about?"

"Community Forum does field work," he answered. "They bail people out of jail, help them pay the NOPSI bill, find a safe place for them to stay. My group goes to court to sue people who violate the rights of GLBTs -- hiring, housing, bullying, that sort of thing. So we coordinate. She tells me about the people she's helping who maybe can use a lawyer. I tell her about cases where one of our plaintiffs needs some immediate help."

Paul took the pen out of their right hand and wrote notes while Amy replied "But if your group is a bunch of lawyers, why were you involved in the demonstration?"

"There are two answers," Dakota said, wiggling his fingers in excitement over getting to use a statement he had prepared. "The first answer is, 'Why not? It's not illegal or anything. And a lot of our volunteers care about the issue.'" He smiled and added, "The other reason is that Louisiana passed a dumb law that those ladies ignored, those women who got married. They just might need a lawyer."

Huh? Paul thought. Amy thought back, *Isn't that cute? Dakota thought of a lawyerly answer.*

She took the lead, and took the pen back into their right hand. "How about the pastor who performed the wedding? That's the person who broke the law."

"I'm not a lawyer myself," he said. "Is that the pastor who got killed?"

Amy shook their head. "The one who planned to do the ceremony was murdered. An associate took over for her."

When the man didn't respond, she said, "I want to back up a moment. We talked about Community Forum. What about Advancement Trust NOLA?"

His body sagged as if someone let the air out of his body. "I'm not one of those queens who hates women, really," Dakota said, "But that Sam bitch gives all of us a bad name. Didn't Jess tell you about the flyer?"

"Please. I'd like to hear you tell me."

He put both hands on the seat of the chair and repositioned himself. "When the preacher who got killed began to publicize her plans in the GLBT world, Sam called me, and I know she called Jess, and she volunteered to help. Since she said she represented an organization, we stupidly looked at her as an equal." He coughed again, then looked down and swallowed carefully a few times before going on. "We discussed a flyer design; I made a mock-up and sent it out. Jess and I both got emails and tweets and IMs from her, must have been twenty, twenty-five of them. Some of her ideas were crazy, like she was doing ecstasy or something, really, really far out. Jess sent an email saying the flyer was completed, thanks for your help, which meant, 'stop pestering us.' Sam blew up." He smirked. "It's funny now, but it was a nightmare to go through."

"Did you ever meet her face-to-face?"

"Oh, God," he moaned, and then broke into another prolonged cough. Amy reached one hand toward him on the table, but the man shook his head as he gasped for breath. Gradually the attack passed.

"What is wrong with you?" Paul asked, bluntly. "This doesn't sound like allergies. Shouldn't you be in a hospital?"

"I'm seeing a doctor about it. It's a fibrosis. It's not AIDS and it's not contagious. What did you ask me?"

"Sam Atkins. Did you–"

"Oh, right," Dakota said. He gave a little cough. "Once. She came here right after Sam threw her out of the Equality office." Shaking his head, he recalled, "She was wearing an old lady skirt, those long and loose things? Her hair was a mess, and she had this dazed look in her eyes. When I opened the office door she was smoking a cigarette and barged right in. I told her no smoking, but she acted like she didn't hear me. Then I tried to grab the cigarette out of her mouth and she hit me." He shivered at the thought, and gave a little cough. "At least she left."

"Sounds like she's a piece of work," Paul said.

"More like bad news," Dakota replied.

"Did you ever hear her talk about the preachers at the MCC?"

"Nah. Or if she did, I was tuning her out. Even her voice is obnoxious."

Amy nodded at the man, even as she thought to Paul, *He reinforces what I've heard but nothing new. You want to ask him anything?*

Amy shook her head, which made no sense to Dakota. He saw her stand up and heard her say, "I'll be back this evening to talk to those people who were at the demonstration. You said six-thirty?"

At her example, he stood up. "Yeah. Six-thirty, seven, something like that."

"I'll give the official police knock," and she used their right hand to beat the cadence as she chanted, "Shave and a haircut, two bits." Amy smiled. "You'll know it's me."

As they left the parking deck, Amy jumped to lead so she could yell, "Hey! Hey! I need a receipt!" to the attendant.

"You should have asked for it before you paid me," the woman in the kiosk said.

"Well, I'm asking for it now. I need a receipt!"

The woman shook her head. "Sorry, sister, but the machine won't do it now."

Paul could feel their body's blood pressure spiking. *Let me do this,* he thought to Amy, then said to the attendant, "I've got a pen and a pad. Write me up a receipt." He handed their clipboard through the car window.

The attendant began a torrent of muttered curses.

Maybe she's illiterate, Amy thought.

He opened their eyes wide in recognition, then said, "Tell you what: give me back the clipboard. I'll write it up and you can sign it. Okay?"

"I don't know," the clerk said, but she thrust the clipboard at them.

Two cars behind them began honking; a man in the Lexus inches from their back bumper was shouting. Paul wrote up the receipt and handed it back to the woman. "Just put your X on it so I can get reimbursed," he coaxed. The woman did exactly that, then handed it back.

The honking was rattling Amy. *Can we go now?* she thought. Paul's answer was loud clanking and what passed for rapid acceleration in the old diesel Benz.

"Thanks for fixing that," Amy said aloud as Paul drove. He was retracing their earlier route from the Community Coalition, with the destination even farther north and east, in Bywater. "I'm pissed off that it cost eleven dollars to park there for an hour. Then I was fixing to be even more pissed if I couldn't get reimbursed."

"We'll see if Commander Ramirez will take a hand-written receipt. Especially my handwriting."

"Eleven bucks. He'd better."

Paul rolled down the window and propped their left arm up on the sill. It was a warm day, and he enjoyed the feel of the moving air. He drove up Rampart to a red light at Esplanade and said, "Now what?"

Amy picked up the clipboard with their right hand and leafed through to the details she'd gotten from Jess Rodgers at the Community Coalition. "Sam is on Desire Street. Go up to St. Claude."

Once past Faubourg Marigny, the view along St. Claude Avenue was of renewal and renovation. Both private homes and offices showed fresh coats of paint and new styling; the few empty lots were well greened, often serving as an area's vegetable garden. To their right was one of the few small sections of New Orleans above sea level, which had escaped the worst of the devastations of Katrina, Rodrigo, Bianca, and all the other hurricanes, floods, and catastrophes of the last forty years. To some, this part of Bywater was the poor man's French Quarter, an as-yet-affordable neighborhood of young, hip, artistic types.

When Amy saw the ugly stone block of the Rosenthal Center, and the pink of the taller St. Margaret's Daughters nursing home behind it, she said, "Desire is coming up. Turn left there." She felt him nod their head.

Once they were headed north on Desire Street, there was an increase in peeling paint, graffiti, boarded-up windows and abandoned lots, still punctuated by other homes with cheerful paint jobs and new siding. As they passed the walled cemetery Paul asked, "How far up are we going?"

"Two thousand something," she answered. "I think it's almost to Florida Avenue."

"Please tell me she's not in the Desire Project. I don't want to go to the Desire Project. I don't want to think about the Desire Project."

Amy waved their right hand and said, "As your fairy God-dyad, I free you from all worry and concern about the Desire Project. No, we're staying this side of Florida." As Paul drove on, Amy added, "They've cleaned it up, you know. They tore everything down before you came to me."

"I heard about the Desire Project when I still lived in West Virginia. A crime cesspool built in a swamp."

"Yes, it was that. Mom told me about the Black Panther shootouts there when she was still in school. Glad I wasn't a cop then."

The closer they got to the dreaded Florida Avenue, the more houses were dilapidated, boarded up, or disappeared, leaving behind cinderbrick footprints or nascent jungle. "It should be on the right," Amy said, "number 2023. There! Pull over."

"Gotcha," Paul replied. He parked at the curb in front of a blue shotgun house with badly faded siding. The roof was missing shingles on the right side of the center peak, and the right-hand door on the porch was boarded up. Amy picked up her clipboard and walked to the closed chain link fence. Through her skirt she pushed the thigh holster with her pistol back so the butt was not making a little tent. As she opened the gate she thought to Paul, *Let's see if Sam Atkins is as bad as everyone says.*

When Amy knocked, a gravelly female voice behind the door called, "Who's there?"

"Detective Amy Clear, NOPD," she returned. "Is this Sam?"

They heard a bolt turned back, and heard the chain keep the woman from opening her door more than two inches. "Where's your uniform?" she growled.

Amy fished her badge case from under her skirt as she said, "Plainclothes detective. Here's my ID." She held it up for the woman to examine, and she did more closely than anyone ever had before.

"Awright. Wait." The door closed, they heard the chain drop, and the door reopened. "Get in here fast," she said, looking up and down the deserted stretch of Desire Street.

As soon as they were inside, the woman locked the door and replaced the chain. "It's a shitty neighborhood," she explained in her rough voice. "I've been here five months and people broke in twice."

Three things immediately struck Amy. First was the overwhelming smell of cigarette smoke. Second was the Ché Guevera poster on the wall. Third was the absence of furniture, unless the status of milk crates has been upgraded. There were a few overstuffed pillows around the room, and a flat-screen TV was propped up on some crates, against the front wall where it could not be seen through the windows.

The woman said, "Hey, for a cop you're damn cute. Want some wine?"

Amy and Paul thought, *What in hell?* to each other. Aloud, Amy said, "Miss Atkins, I'm investigating the death of Reverend Riley Tibbs. I'm hoping you can help me."

Sam Atkins was in her mid-forties. She was about six feet tall and about a hundred and fifty pounds, giving her a six-inch and forty-pound advantage over Amy. Her unkempt black hair looked as if it had started out in a beehive and then gave in to gravity and Louisiana humidity. Paul thought she had been attractive in her day, but the bags under her eyes, the wrinkles around her nose and mouth, and the hint of a wattle below her chin spoke of alcohol and tobacco, if not worse. He thought to Amy, *Rode hard and put up wet.*

"We can talk about whatever you like, Honey," Sam said. She kicked a blue pillow to land beside a green one. "Have a seat," she said, as she dropped herself in the green one.

I'm not used to suspects being so friendly, Amy thought to Paul. She put a foot on the blue pillow and slid it maybe eighteen inches away from Sam, then sat down carefully to keep the police paraphernalia under her knee-length skirt concealed. "Thank you," she replied to Atkins, and put the clipboard in her lap. "Tell me about–"

"Are you sure you won't have some wine?" Sam interrupted. "A beer? Some pot?"

Amy frowned when she heard Paul silently shout, *Yes!* "I'm on duty," she told the woman. "Do us both a favor and do not bring out marijuana in front of me."

"Oh! Of course. I'm such a ditz. Sure I can't get you anything?" The woman was beaming.

Amy looked down at the clipboard. "Tell me about Advantage Trust," she said, then looked back up at Sam. The woman was staring back at her, mouth open. Amy heard Paul think, *Uh-oh. She's got the hots for us.*

"It's a gay rights social services organization. It's based in Maryland. What do you want to know, Sweetie?"

"I want to know why Advantage Trust, which is based in San Francisco, thinks they don't have a branch in Louisiana."

"Some kind of fuck-up," Sam said, and scooted her pillow a little closer. "I talked with a man in Baltimore who set me up. Maybe he hasn't been in touch with the San Francisco people. Look, Honey, does this matter?"

"Miss Atkins, my name is Detective Clear. I'm trying to solve a murder; I'm not interested in fraud right now. Were you at the demonstration yesterday?

"Please, call me Sam," she smiled, and placed a hand on Amy's exposed knee. "We don't have to be formal."

Paul reacted first. Using just the thumb and index finger of their left hand, he gently pinched Sam's wrist, moved her hand off their body, and dropped it. Amy spoke: "Yes, we do. This is a police investigation." Thinking to make the woman's familiarity cease by ignoring it, she added, "Were you at the demonstration at the church?"

"You're no fun," the woman pouted. But she put her hands in her lap and answered, "Yes, I was there."

"Did you see anything there that you thought was dangerous?"

"Those creepazoids in camouflage with the ugly signs. The soul brothers with the sunglasses." She took a squished cigarette package out of a pocket and looked to find a smoke that wasn't broken, then stuck it in her mouth. "I didn't like the anti-gay posters and chants, but I wasn't worried about any of those people hitting me." She flicked a blue Bic lighter and inhaled, then slowly released two nostrils' worth of thick white smoke.

Amy made a note on her clipboard. "Did you go into the church at any time?"

Sam leaned forward. "Yeah. There was a side door. I used the ladies' room a couple of times. Didn't seem to be a problem."

Amy slid her pillow, trying to escape the cigarette smoke. She followed up, "Did you see anyone when you did that?"

"Ummm." She scooted her pillow towards Amy. "There was a woman outside, I recognized her from the archdiocese group. She was sitting out there both times. She looked a little green around the edges." She let out another stream of smoke. "Oh, and some really fat woman in a robe was in there one time, doing something at the sink. We just nodded, you know."

To escape the fumes, Amy started to stand up. "I've got some pictures I want to show you." She slid the one of Riley Tibbs out of a folder on the clipboard and asked, "Did you ever see this woman?"

Barely looking, she said, "No, never," and stood up.

"How about this woman?" as she held out a photo of Drew Malone.

"Huh! That's who was washing up the second time I borrowed their bathroom."

It was Paul who asked, "Did you ever talk to anyone at the church? Telephone? Email?" He started to put the photographs back in their folder.

"No." Sam dropped her cigarette on the wooden floor and rubbed it out with her foot. "Look, I think you and me got off wrong." Paul was leading; he looked up at her while dealing with the pictures. "You are so pretty! And it's not like I've done anything wrong–I'm not a suspect or anything. I'd like to, you know, get to know you." She stepped toward them, and Paul involuntarily stepped back until they bumped into the wall. "Are you sure I can't get you some wine?" She placed her hands on the wall, on either side of Amy's head. "Anything? Anything at all?"

Amy was thinking to Paul, *We have got to get out of here. She's going–"* when Sam bent her elbows, thrusting her body against theirs. "Anything at all?" she whispered in their ear, then kissed their cheek and started to work her way to their mouth.

Paul barked, "Stop!" but when he did Sam put her mouth on theirs and licked their teeth. She moved her hands to hold and caress them. Paul pushed against her, but the woman was bigger than they were and did not yield. Internally Amy took the lead. As she did, she felt Sam slide a leg between her thighs, pushing her against the wall. The hands were wandering.

We're trapped, Paul thought.

Silently, Amy replied, *I've got an idea.*

She let herself fall to the floor, sliding out from Sam's grasp; when she was sitting on the floor, back to the wall, she swept her right leg around and knocked the woman's feet out from under her.

As Sam fell on her back, Amy shouted, "I'm a police detective and I order you to stop!" She started to stand back up by using their bent legs like a car jack, slowly straightening their knees to raise their body. She was panting from exertion.

"You little tease," Sam growled, smiling. "You're breathing heavy for me." She got back up and threw herself at Amy. "You know you want it." She was kissing Amy's neck, hands on her breasts, rubbing and kneading and using her size to hold Amy against the wall.

This is so creepy! Paul thought to Sam. It didn't seem to faze her that she heard the words in her head and in Paul's male voice; she smiled, and said, "No, you'll like it fine." She resumed working her mouth on Amy's skin. She moved one hand to Amy's knee, and started to slide it up her leg. But when she reached the thigh holster with Amy's pistol, she stopped, confused.

Amy used the moment to push Sam away, and when the woman attempted to resume her attack, Amy kicked her squarely in the left kneecap.

Paul smiled inside when he heard the woman's piercing scream. *Well done,* he thought to Amy.

Sam lay on her side, holding her left leg close to her body. If the cigarette she discarded was not entirely out, it would soon be burning her pants leg.

Standing against the wall, Amy smoothed her skirt. "I've heard from several people that you talked about how the death of someone involved in the marriage would create a martyr for the movement. Who all did you say this to?"

Panting in pain, Sam said, "You fucking bitch. I'll file a brutality report." Even with tears on her face and pain in her leg, she lifted her head and spit in Amy's direction.

"I've got it," Paul said aloud, which prompted Atkins to squint back. Paul bent over to retrieve their clipboard, then stepped to where Sam was whimpering in pain. Using their foot, Paul rolled her onto her back, then sat themself down on the woman's stomach. Ceremoniously clicking the pen in their left hand, Paul asked, "To whom did you express this idea?"

"Get off me!" Sam roared. Smiling, Paul bounced on the woman's belly. "You fucking Nazi, I'll see you in jail!" Paul bounced again, and said, "And I'll file rape charges against you. Who do you think anyone's going to believe?" He heard Amy laughing silently and think, *Nicely done.*

"You may not have noticed, Sam," Paul said from their perch, "but you are not the most popular activist in the New Orleans gay rights movement."

"Misogynist fuckwads," she gasped in shallow breaths.

"Oh, sure. It's them. Never your fault. Look, several people have told me you talked about the need for a dead martyr in your movement. Did you kill Riley Tibbs?"

"No! Oooh."

Paul wrote it down. "Did you enter into a conspiracy with anyone to have them kill Riley Tibbs?"

"No," weaker, the woman was running out of lung capacity. "Can you get off me? Please?"

"Since you asked nicely, okay." Paul made one last bounce, and stood up over Atkins. He tensed their body in case the woman tried to resume her attack, but she rolled onto her side, panting, and held her injured leg again.

Amy took the lead and said, "I trust we have settled our little disagreement among ourselves. If you file a complaint, I will charge you with assault." She waited, but all Atkins did was groan. "Okay, then. I have two more questions. First, who did you talk to about the need for a dead martyr?"

"No one," she panted. "I don't remember. I never did."

Paul thought, 'I didn't do it, nobody saw me, you can't prove a thing.'

Amy wrote the woman's answer on the clipboard. "Sure. And second, why on earth do you live in this half-wrecked shack that's spitting distance from the Desire Project?"

Still feeling the pain from her leg, Atkins forced out a disjointed answer: "I. Can. Afford it."

Now that her threat was neutralized, Amy felt some sympathy for the woman she had kicked. She stood over Atkins and said, "Are you going to be all right? Can I get you anything?"

Sam looked up. "Why. Are you. Commando?"

It took a moment for Amy to understand what the woman meant. She laughed and stepped back, then said, "Thigh holsters with gun and gear. I got tired of ripping perfectly good underwear every time I went to the bathroom. Sorry, I didn't mean to excite you."

"Are you. Done. With me. Yet?"

"Yes, I believe so."

Still clutching her leg, the woman said, "Go away. Leave. Please."

Smirking, Amy said, "Don't leave town, Miss Atkins," and she let themself out.

Paul cranked the engine and turned on the air conditioner. Amy said, "Wait," and locked the car doors. She put the gear shift in neutral and just sat there.

Paul asked, "Are we allowed to use mace when a subject tries to rape us?"

"I'm allowed to break their kneecap if I have to," she answered. She shivered and added, "I've got to take a shower before we meet Christine. God, my skin is crawling where that beastighouli touched me."

"It's nice to know there are limits to my appreciation of female attention," he said. "I had no idea women ever did that."

"Civilized ones don't. Brrr!"

Paul put the car in gear. He made a three-point u-turn and headed back toward the river and home. "Let me call Christine," he said. "She should be home; she took off from work today." At a stop sign Paul retrieved Amy's phone from one of the thigh holsters, and punched in his lover's number.

"Paulette, are you and Amy okay?" Christine sounded worried.

"We're doing fine now," he answered. "We've been interviewing people about the murder, and she has to be at a meeting around 6:30. Want to come?"

"And see you work? You know I love doing that."

Paul asked how her day had gone. She admitted she lay in Amy's bed until noon, then drove home and went back to her own bed. "No structure, no Paulette, nothing for me to do," she said.

"I thought real estate agents always were on the clock."

"When there's a conflict between work and a vacation day, I let vacation win. Otherwise, what's the point of vacation?"

"I like your reasoning," he laughed. "We're going to stop at the house to grab some things. Then we'll be at your place around five. Will that work?"

"Yay!" Christine shouted. "See you soon. I love you, Paulette. You too, Amy," and she was gone.

He dropped the phone on the seat next to them. "Now that's a woman I want to have touch me," he said.

"I'm going to lead now," Amy said, and she traded internal places with Paul. "I need to check in with Cranston." When she heard the lieutenant growl "Yeah?" she said, "Just want to check in, boss. What have you found?"

"Yeah, Queenie. Those guys you pegged as muscle? Well done. They're out of LA. I think they got some drug connections. They agree with me about that kind of marriage."

"Did they kill the pastor?"

"I don't know. They say they didn't, but prison is full of thugs who say they're innocent. Tomorrow morning, let's you and I visit them again. I want your take. Did you find anything interesting today?"

"Sam Atkins," Amy replied, "the gal from Advancement Trust NOLA. I think she's less popular than Hurricane Roberta last year. Nobody has anything good to say about her, and that includes me."

"Detective, you need to keep an open mind this early in an investigation."

"I tried, Duke, but the bitch slammed it shut when she attacked me."

Cranston chuckled and said, "Maybe I should come with you and we visit her again?"

"Oh, sure," she teased, "you just want to see an old-fashioned cat fight. I smashed her knee, so I don't think she'll be putting up much of a fuss anymore." Now that she was upriver from Canal Street, Amy turned onto Magazine, heading for her Carrollton section. "Did the *Times-Picayune* come up with any pictures for us?"

"Yeah, but the photo guy says he didn't get their names because they were only in the background. I'm hoping our tech guys can sharpen the images, maybe give us something to go on."

They were silent for a few moments, and then Amy asked, "How'd that thing in Tremé go?"

"Huh! A bunch of dopers beat the shit out of each other. No guns, no knives, just a baseball bat and some chains. Ugly, man, ugly."

"You get the perp?"

"I got eight of 'em. I'll let the DA figure out who's the giver and who's the getter."

"Good work. I'm meeting with some folks at Equality Forum in a little while, so I'll let you go. See you in the morning?"

"Yeah. By eight o'clock. See you, Queenie."

As soon as Amy locked her front door behind them she started ditching articles of clothing, headed for the shower. "I'm afraid I'll never get the stink of her cigarettes off me!" she shouted while she worked a soapy washcloth.

Paul said, "Can we brush our teeth with bleach? That animal stuck her tongue in our mouth."

"There's a wire brush in the shed," Amy offered.

Later she decided against thigh holsters and went for blue jeans; she pulled a white ribbed poorboy over their head. "I still smell her," Paul said. "Do you have any perfume?"

"As a matter of fact, I don't. Oh, wait. Christine gave you that little thing of patchouli oil for Christmas. Where did I put it?" She slapped the cluttered top of her bureau, then looked in the drawer where she kept unmatched socks, old boyfriends' underwear, her passport, and similar treasures. "There it is." She shook the bottle, then unscrewed the top and put an index finger over the opening. One more shake, and she stared at the yellow-orange splotch on her finger.

"Anywhere," Paul said. "Under our nose? In our hair?"

Amy wiped the oil onto the skin where their collar bones didn't quite meet. "Whew! That's strong stuff," she said. "A little goes a long way."

Trading one stink for another, but I like this stink better. So does Christine.

"She likes it," Amy said as she threw the next day's clothes into a bugout bag, "because it hides the odor of her damn pot."

Paul led to drive the familiar way to Christine's triplex in West End. He wound down the driver's window to let the breeze dry their hair. "Do we have time to eat before you talk to those people at Equality Forum?"

He felt her smile inside. *If I ate half as much as you want, I'd weigh two hundred pounds. Maybe you had a hollow leg, but I don't.*

"Okay. But after you interview them?"

Aloud, she answered, "We'll see."

Paul put Amy's old yellow Benz next to Christine's Smart car in the little parking area behind her house. Then he let Amy lead to grab her overnight bag and a wine bottle and walk to the little porch and the door beyond. When Christine let them in, Amy said, "Thank God. I need a hug!" and embraced the woman.

It startled Christine, who—somehow—always knew which of them was leading. "Amy? Are you okay?" She patted Amy's back tentatively; she was always careful to save her amorous or intense physical contact for Paulette, so as not to break any boundaries with his dyad.

"I had to interview a woman who tried to rape me," Amy said over Christine's shoulder as she hugged her. "I must replace that with a woman I like."

Christine allowed herself to return fully the embrace, and rub Amy's back. "You poor thing," she said. "Paulette, how bad was it?"

He replied, "I used to think I liked a woman's touch. Now I know I just like your touch." Christine gave a little "Squee!" Paul went on, "She tried to make a pass at us, Amy tried to ignore it, and finally the wretched witch went into grope mode. Ugh."

Christine relaxed her hug and leaned back so she could see their face. "Amy? Did she–I mean, she didn't–"

"She tried to lick our teeth!" Paul said. Then Amy added, "Well, yes, she did. She felt me up and was trying to get under my skirt."

"What?" Her mouth was hanging open. "Oh, Amy, what did you do?"

"I'm pretty sure I broke her kneecap. She screamed and hit the floor and that was that."

Christine gaped. "Uh, Paulette?"

"Yep, that's about it. Amy knows all sorts of ninja tricks."

"So–I mean, Amy arrested her, right?"

Amy let go of Christine and picked up her bag and wine. "No. I'm pretty sure she learned her lesson."

"But–but, do I have to go over there and beat her up?"

They coughed, the sound of both people trying to talk at once. Finally Amy said, "Umm–if she acts up again, sure."

"How awful," Christine said as she followed her Paulette and Amy into the kitchen. Amy put the wine on the counter by the sink. "Oh, I'll get the corkscrew."

"No, please," Amy said. "I have to talk to two people about the murder in a little while."

"Do you think they did it?"

Amy leaned her back against the countertop and smiled at her friend. "I doubt it. With luck, though, they may have seen whoever did it."

"Paulette?"

"I'm here, Honey," he said as he stepped to her and put their left hand on her shoulder. "I am so glad to see you." He moved their hands to hold Christine's face, and started a long, serious kiss.

After awhile Christine rested her head on their chest, still holding them. "I worry about you," she said softly. "You and Amy, you do great things but it's dangerous. I–I worry that you'll get hurt."

"We've been hurt before," he said, letting their fingers trail up and down his lover's back. "We always end up okay. You take great care of us. Besides, I'm nowhere near done with you."

"Me neither. That's why I worry. I don't ever want to lose you."

Paul smiled and held the woman. He was a happy man.

"I have to get going," Amy announced. "I need to be back at Equality Forum by six-thirty. Paul wants to eat afterwards."

"Okay," Christine said, stepping back from the body that her lover no longer was leading. "I'm meeting a Chinese family in Westwego tomorrow to show them some houses. Can we have Chinese food?"

"Uh, I guess. Sure. Why?"

"I want to be on the client's wavelength," Christine said.

Amy thought to Paul, *I've never known anyone quite like her;* he thought back, *Me neither. God, I am so in love.*

Christine offered to drive to Equality Forum, and Paul argued with Amy to let her. *But I know where we're going,* Amy thought.

Great. You can navigate.

But it'll be more efficient if I drive.

Paul thought, *It'll make Christine happy to help us.*

Much to Christine's surprise, as she did not hear their internal exchange, was the sight of Amy rolling her eyes, throwing her hands in the air, and barking, "Oh, whatever!"

"Paulette? What was that about? Is Amy okay?"

Paul said, "She's fine. It's great that you'll drive. Amy knows the way, so she'll navigate."

"Arrrgh!"

"Amy?"

Paul answered, saying, "We might just leave Amy here while you and I drive out."

Christine stared. "Wait. You can't do that. Uh, can you?"

"If we could," Amy said, "I'd kick him out and you could have him." She turned in a tight little circle and added, "Let me grab my clipboard. Then I guess we should go."

He thought to Christine, *She's pissed. It's good for her.*

"That's mean, Paulette."

"Yup."

"'Yup,'" Amy mocked. "I don't know what you see in him, Christine. He's a self-centered, egotistical jerk, a flaming asshole, a real, a real–"

She heard Paul think, *You left out trashmouth.*

"–Yes, a trashmouth! Garbagemouth! And, and–"

And a bodyless succubus.

"–And a bodyless–a what?"

And a West by-damn Virginia hillbilly.

Amy started to laugh. She continued to laugh, and sat heavily in one of Christine's kitchen chairs. She rested their head on the table, laughing, and pounded the tabletop with her right fist.

Christine was relieved to see Amy laughing, but because she hadn't heard Paul's internal prompting, she did not know what provoked it. "Paulette? Is everything okay?"

Before he could answer her, Amy lifted her head and shouted, "Succubus!" She shrieked and put her head back down to continue laughing.

He thought back to his lover, *In the words of Paulette, 'yup.' Everything's fine. When Amy calms down you can drive us to that meeting.*

Sitting in Christine's tiny car, Amy said, "You've said you get along great with your mother. But when you were still at home in St. Louis, didn't you ever just want to scream at her?"

"Want to? I did scream at her. Yeah. I'm not exactly proud of that."

"Don't be ashamed, either," Amy responded. "You live in close quarters with somebody, you're bound to get on each other's nerves sometimes. And Paul and I use the same nerves. Oh, make a left up there on Audubon Street." Dutifully, Christine turned and headed north. "I love the man, you know that. And he loves me. But there are times when I tell him to sleep on the sofa. He's been known– hold on, I'm trying to tell her!–he's threatened to pack up his stuff and move out."

"So you fight a lot?" She looked at Amy for a moment, then aimed her eyes back at the road.

"Not a lot. Not even often." She thought about it. "I guess things build up, and we'll go a week where we're fussing at each other. Then we're okay for months."

Paul spoke up, "Amy and I have talked about it. Speaking for myself, it's been years since I felt like I was stuck with Amy, but the truth is Amy and I are forever. We try to put up with each other because staying friends is way more important than how I squeeze the toothpaste. Yeah, you did so," he responded to Amy silent objection, "you said I'd do better with a handful of baking soda."

Christine was giggling. "I swear, sometimes you two are like an old married couple."

Paul chuckled. "An old, still-married couple."

They drove in silence for a minute, until Amy said, "That's Claiborne up ahead. Make a right."

Christine did so. Softly, she asked, "Amy? Will I always have to compete with you for Paulette?"

While Paul thought, *No!* directly to Christine, Amy paused. "You have to share him with me," she said carefully, "but it's not a competition."

"Okay," Christine said, nodding, "because I can't compete with you. You're prettier than I am and you're smarter and you do such exciting things like catch murderers."

Amy thought to Paul, *Please reassure her. I don't know what to say.*

"I love both of you," he said; Christine, as always, knew which of them was speaking. "I love Amy because the universe sneezed and I became a part of her. And I love you because you make me happy."

He heard Amy think, *I don't make you happy?*

Uh-oh, he thought back. *Maybe I should walk home, let you and Christine settle this without me getting in the way.*

"Okay," Christine said, tentatively. "So, does that mean we're a threesome?"

"Would you like that?" Paul replied.

"I used to think so, but now I just want you, Paulette."

He kissed her on the side of her face. He did not hear Amy think to the woman, *I understand, Christine. But I'm part of this deal, too.*

"Oh, I love you too, Amy," she said. "You're the sister I should have had. And you put up with me, and you like me, and you tell me what's going on in your life." She sneaked a quick look at them in the passenger seat. "I love you, too. I love you both."

Amy said, "Good." She thought to Paul, *And you, my succubus buddy, are staying right here with me.*

It's a deal, he thought back.

Amy directed Christine to the same parking deck she had used earlier in the day. Christine saw the sign and shouted, "Eleven bucks! Amy, are you crazy?"

Amy took some bills out of her wallet. "Just make sure you ask for a receipt before you pay."

As they walked to the Equality Forum building, Paul was taken by the contradiction of the lights and noise coming from the hotels and businesses along Poydras Street and the dim silence from the warehouses and office buildings that were closer to the river. New Orleans was a lively city, an exciting city, but with a dark streak that could leave a clergyman dead in her office.

Amy briefed Christine on what she hoped to accomplish with the looming interviews. "Maybe they saw someone or something suspicious. I need help getting a handle on this case."

"Who do you think did it?" Christine asked.

Amy shook their head. "I don't have any evidence yet. I'd love it if that Sam woman turns out to be the killer, but that's only because of what she tried to do to me."

"So, you and Paulette have to be careful about who you suspect?"

"That's right." Then Paul took the lead and grasped Christine's hand as they walked. "You know I don't like cops. But as long as I sort-of am one, I ought to be fair. I'd love to kick that Sam woman all the way to Mississippi, but that doesn't mean she's a killer."

"I guess you're nicer than I am," Christine said.

The concierge desk was vacant, so Amy led toward the stairs. Christine's head swiveled to take in the opulent wallpaper and lobby furniture. "This place is nice," she said. "Do you think they'd mind if I moved in here?"

Paul said, "They might have a problem if you camped out here." Thinking about it, he added, "The guard today didn't know his left from his right. Maybe you could take his job. Make them let you move in as a fringe benefit."

Laughing, Christine said, "Except that I have a job. I'm liking being an agent. I get to travel all over town, and I meet nice people, like that Chinese family."

It was Amy who asked, "Making any money?"

"Finally!" Christine cried. "If I sell four houses this year, I'll make as much as I used to when I was the receptionist."

Amy led to the right when they reached the second floor. At the door to Equality Forum she beat the shave-and-a-haircut tattoo. From inside they heard Dakota's high-pitched voice calling, "That's for me!" There was another voice, but they couldn't understand what it said.

When the door opened, Amy and Christine were facing a tall man in a tweed business suit. With a soft English accent he said, "Can I help you?" He had planted one foot that prevented the door from opening any further.

"I'm looking for Dakota Phillips," Amy said. "He's expecting me."

"I'm Evelyn Holder-Pfann," the man said. "I am the Secretary for Equality Forum, and I am not expecting you." Behind him, Dakota coughed.

Christine began to cringe and slowly moved behind her Paulette. Amy opened her badge case and said, "Detective Amy Clear, New Orleans Police. This–" she motioned to her right and then saw empty space; she turned until she found Christine, then continued, "–and this is Deputy Hodges. May we come in?"

"What is this about?" His cold, dark blue eyes gave away nothing.

"I'm investigating the murder of a clergywoman yesterday while a demonstration was going on at her church. I understand two of your members or volunteers who are supposed to be here tonight were at the demonstration. I'd like to ask them some questions. I hope they can help us with our inquiries."

Holder-Pfann stared at Amy for a few seconds. "Do you suspect my people of murder?"

"Not yet." It was Paul

The man opened the door wide and said, "I will sit with them while you question them."

"Sure," Amy said, while she heard Paul think, *Suit yourself, jerkwad.*

Once inside, Amy greeted Dakota and asked if his cough was any better. He answered, "I live on Hall's and Luden's." Glancing at the Secretary, he whispered, "I hope this is okay. I didn't know–"

"It's okay," she interrupted. "You didn't know."

"To whom do you want to speak?" Holder-Pfann asked.

Amy peeled back a few pages on her clipboard and said, "Gabe and Peyton." She looked up and asked, "Who are they?" as she handed the clipboard and legal pad to Christine.

Dakota said, "Gabriella Santiago and Peyton Long. I'll get them." But as he turned to find them, Holder-Pfann put a hand on his shoulder and said, "The little conference room."

"Yes, sir," Dakota mumbled as he started off, coughing.

"Why them?" the Secretary asked as he walked them toward what apparently was the little conference room, a small corner office with a round table and half-a-dozen chairs.

"I was told they attended the demonstration."

"Who told you that?"

Amy smiled. "It's a beautiful evening."

"I asked you something," said Holder-Pfann, abruptly standing still. "You will answer my question."

"No, Mister Holder-Pfann, I will not. This is a police homicide investigation. You can read about it in the *Times-Picayune* like everyone else."

"This is private property, Detective," he countered. "You are in our suite at my sufferance. You will–"

"Deputy Hodges," Amy interrupted, "Please indicate in your notes that the Secretary is threatening a sworn officer's access to material witnesses." Then, to Holder-Pfann, "I'm sorry. You were saying?"

"Very well." He resumed their walk to the corner office. Along the way Dakota joined them with the people Amy had asked to interview.

"He doesn't want us here," Christine whispered to Paul; he thought back, *You're right, but you saw how Amy handled him.*

As everyone circled to find seats at the round table, the Secretary said, "Thank you, Dakota. You can start the follow-up meeting. I'll be along in a few minutes." Phillips looked to be surprised by his dismissal, but he turned and left the room with a series of coughs.

Holder-Pfann sat back with his arms folded in front of his chest. After a few seconds of silence Amy began: "I am Detective Clear with NOPD, and Deputy Hodges will be taking notes. I understand you two were at the demonstration yesterday at the Metropolitan Community Church on St. Charles Avenue." She paused as the man and woman across from her exchanged looks and nodded. "I'm sure you heard the news today, that a pastor at the church was found murdered there while the demonstration was going on. NOPD is hoping you may have seen something, anything, that will help us solve this case."

Gabe and Peyton, both appearing to be in their mid-to-late twenties, nodded silently. Amy heard Paul think, *They're not going to volunteer, are they?*

Silently she replied, *Nope*. Then, to prod the two who, she hoped, had valuable information, she asked, "The archdiocese and the black clergy were on the Henry Clay Avenue side of the walkway, and the pro-marriage people seemed to be on the Calhoun Street side. Where did you hang out on the church grounds?"

"I volunteer for the Equality Forum," the woman said. "Of course I was on the pro-marriage side." Then she corrected herself, "The pro-marriage choice side." She was wearing a white sleeveless blouse that showed off a small fortune in tattoo parlor fees: a Mexican day-of-the-dead cartoon skeleton down her right arm, and an intricate rosebush entwined around a cross and a dagger on the left.

While Christine took notes, Amy turned to Peyton. "You?"

"I know some people on the anti-side," he said, apologetically. "They're wrong on this issue, but they aren't mean or evil." Holder-Pfann snorted but did not speak. Peyton pushed his blonde hair off his face and went on, "So I spent time everywhere."

"Did either of you see anyone, maybe, sneaking in the side door? It's on the Henry Clay side, back along the side of the church."

Gabe shook her head, but Peyton said, "I saw a woman back there; she was sitting on a tree stump, I think. A couple of times she got up and went in the side door."

"And came out of it, I suppose," Amy mused. "What did she look like?"

He thought for a moment, eyes aimed at the ceiling. "Dark hair. Longer on one side of her face. I think she was wearing jeans. Uh, blue pants, at least. I was too far away to see her face."

"A couple of times?"

"Yeah. I was talking to a neighbor who was with the archdiocese people, so I was there maybe half an hour."

Paul thought to Amy and Christine, *Who goes to the restroom twice in thirty minutes? Someone who's ill.* Christine made a note on the legal pad, while Amy softly said, "Good point."

Holder-Pfann went, "Hmmm? What's a good point?"

"Your volunteer acknowledging he was too far away to make out the woman's face," Amy ad-libbed. The secretary leaned back in his chair, as Amy asked, "Have either of you been to that church before?"

"We met there two years ago," Gabe said, "and then marched up to the Catholic church at the Loyola campus to protest. I think the archdiocese had issued a statement about not ordaining women as priests."

"When was this?" asked Peyton.

"You remember. It was sweltering hot. Everyone was sweating buckets."

He shook his head, "That must have been before I volunteered."

"Really? I thought you were there."

Amy asked, "Did you go inside? Did you meet–"

Gabe shook her head. "They just let us meet on their grounds. A bunch of people from their congregation came with us."

"Riley Tibbs," Amy said. "Did you meet her? She was the pastor."

Head shake; then, to Peyton, "Are you sure you weren't there?"

Amy tapped the table to get their attention. "What part of town do you live in?"

Holder-Pfann began, "I don't believe that's relevant," but Peyton answered, "Algiers. Old Aurora."

"Both of you?"

Peyton laughed abruptly while Gabe pursed her mouth into a frown. "Yeah," she said. "We don't, you know, live together."

The extreme difference in their responses piqued Paul. "Is there a joke that I'm missing?"

"Yes," said Holder-Pfann in his soft English accent. "Any more questions?"

She glanced at the notes Christine was still writing. "Not for now," Amy answered. As everyone but Christine stood up–she was scribbling as fast as she could–Amy handed out her NOPD business card and said, "If you think of anything that might help us solve this crime, call me. Sometimes little things build on other things we know and open doors for us." She reached out to shake Peyton's hand, and then Gabe's.

As they began the walk to the suite's entrance, Gabe said, "You know, Peyton and me drove in yesterday. We saw some of the wrong protesters before we got to the church."

Amy stopped, and Christine, still writing on the clipboard, walked into her. For the first time Holder-Pfann laughed.

The 'wrong' protesters? Amy heard Paul think, *Lone gunmen.*

"You know, the ones that didn't want those ladies to get married. When we got off the Huey Long bridge, we got caught at a traffic light, and we saw something."

Christine was scribbling faster as Amy raised an eyebrow and prompted, "What did you see?"

"It was a little strange–" she began, but Peyton interrupted, "Nah, it was very strange. It was a big pickup truck, the kind with a double back axle. There were these five guys standing around, they all had on camouflage clothes, and they were loading stuff in the truck. One of the things was a picket sign."

"It was so gross," Gabe said. "The sign said 'AIDS cures fags.' I honked my horn and Peyton flipped them a bird, but they just laughed at us."

Excited, Paul jumped to lead and asked, "Did you see any of them at the demonstration?"

Gabe shook her head, but Peyton said, "Come to think of it, yeah. One or two of them."

"You did?" Gabe asked, incredulous. "I know I didn't."

"You were with all the people from our side," he replied. "I was on the anti-side with my neighbor, that's when I saw them. Same picket sign."

Amy had taken back the lead. "Did you see all of them? Were they together?"

"Two of them, I think," Peyton said. "And now that you mention it–no, they were not together. It was like they didn't know each other." He snorted. "Even though they were dressed the same."

"This is helpful information," Amy said. "Do you remember anything about their truck? Color? Make? License tag? Bumper sticker?" Christine was watching them, hand with pen poised over the clipboard.

"M-O-L," Gabe said. "It was a sticker in the back window. What does it mean?"

Paul answered, sounding like Amy, "They were in camouflage, maybe it was Marine On Line, a veterans' website. That's great. Anything else? What color was their truck?"

"Tan." "Gray." "Are you sure–" "–Don't you remember?"

"If you don't mind, detective," the Secretary said, "I believe this interview has come to a natural conclusion." Hands on their backs on either side of him, he began walking Amy and Christine toward the door. Gabe and Peyton stayed put and continued to bicker at one another.

Amy heard a long series of coughs getting louder. She turned to see Dakota Phillips coming toward them. "You're supposed to be leading the group," Holder-Pfann barked, but the man finished walking up to Amy. "I hope you got what you need," he said. "Sorry there was any problem."

"That's enough, Dakota!" the Secretary said. "I want you to–"

"Here's my card," Amy said, handing one to the young man. "If anyone tells you anything that might help us, call me. Okay?"

He examined the card and nodded, while Holder-Pfann used his suit-jacket clad forearm to push the man back toward the recap group. "I'll talk to you later," he muttered to him. Then he turned back to Amy and Christine with a cold and insincere smile: "Have a good evening, officer."

Christine said, "Detective," as they left the suite.

Paul thought to Christine, *Were you okay with taking notes?* as they walked down the stairs.

"I don't know that I did a good job," she replied, aloud, which startled Amy, "but it's exciting to help." Seeing Amy's reaction, Christine explained Paul's silent question. "Did I do okay?" she asked.

"I'm sure you did great," Amy answered. "I appreciate you letting me draft you for the job."

"Did you find out anything important? Can you solve it yet?"

"Not yet," Amy smiled, "but soon."

"Here, let me," Paul said; he took the lead to open the front door and let them outside. Then he said, "Peyton corroborates what

Sam said, about a woman sitting near the side door and going in and out of the church. Who do you think it is?"

"Who's Sam?" Christine asked.

"That woman who tried to rape me," Amy answered, then went on, "No clue yet who she was. If she went in and out several times, she may have seen something useful."

"Wait," Christine said as they walked down Lafayette toward the parking deck. "Why do you pay any attention to someone who tried to hurt you?"

Paul answered, "That's why I said 'corroborate.' Amy?"

"Paul's right," she said. "If I've got a reason to doubt someone, I look for corroboration from a less questionable source. Just because Sam is a female rapist doesn't mean she lies about everything, but Peyton Long strikes me as a more reliable witness."

"That must be hard to do. I don't know if I could listen to someone who had hurt me like that."

"I understand," Amy said. "Years ago another detective helped me get past the defensiveness. He must have told me a dozen times to get over myself, that the only thing that mattered was catching the killer."

Paul said, "Riordan. I remember that guy. He wasn't very gentle about teaching us."

"You mean there is a nice way to say 'get over your damn self'?"

Christine clicked her key fob to unlock her Smart car. "Are we ready for dinner yet?" she asked.

"I'm in," came from Paul.

"Sure," said Amy, "but I have to check in with Lieutenant Duke."

Christine backed out of the parking space, saying, "Paulette, how about that Chinese place on Filmore? We've been there before."

As Amy was fumbling for her phone to call the Lieutenant, Paul thought back, *Funky dive, but the lo mein is good. Sure.* He laughed and went on, *As bad as it looks from the outside, it's worse on the inside.* Meanwhile, Amy heard Cranston's "Hello," and started to brief him on her findings.

"Would you rather we go somewhere else?" She was third in line at the cashier's kiosk.

Absolutely not! he thought to her. *Really, I like their lo mein.*

"Does Amy?"

When she heard her name she glanced at Christine, and she heard Cranston say, "Who is talking to you like you're someone else?"

"Friends in the car. We're going to dinner. Look, I got a bite at Equality Forum." She felt Christine move up to second in line, and she added, "Oh, wait a minute!" Lowering the phone, Amy said, "Ask for a receipt before you pay." Then, "Sorry, trying to make sure I get reimbursed."

"Yeah, Queenie," he said in his slow, deep voice. "Anything useful?"

"Advancement Trust seems to be a one-woman scam. Two people noticed a woman sitting outside the side door of the church yesterday, over some period of time. I'm guessing she was sick. And it looks like all the Lone Gunmen were together, even though they seemed separate at the demonstration. What are the odds they're ex-military and use Marine On Line?"

"Say what?"

"Someone spotted a window sticker on their truck, M-O-L. Any idea what it means?" Duke started to answer but Amy went on, "More or less? Mount Olympus lovers? Meat or legumes? Midgets over linguini? My own lunch? Uh–"

"Please stop," he said. He was not laughing, although Christine was. "We've had some run-ins with the Militia of Louisiana. I didn't know they were advertising."

Paul heard that, of course, sharing ears with Amy as he did. *Ah-ha!* he thought to her.

"We'll work on it tomorrow," Cranston said. "And I want you to come with me when I stop in on my pals from the African-American clergy. Did I tell you this? You were right about them being muscle. See you in the morning."

"Good night, Duke," she said quietly and folded her phone. *I don't think he likes me,* she thought to Paul.

"He doesn't have to," he said out loud, startling Christine. "He only has to respect you."

"I don't know what that was about," Christine chimed in, "but, Amy, he's bound to respect you. I mean, how can he not?" Then, "Who are we talking about?"

"My current partner in crime fighting," she sighed. "Duke Cranston. I understand he's a great cop, but I seem to rub him the wrong way." She felt Paul use their left hand to pat her on the leg. "It's another example of why I left the force," she continued. "I really don't fit in over there. Either I'm too weird or they're too normal, and I can't tell which."

Christine said, "You don't have to worry about it now. Think dinner." She swiveled her eyes to glance at Amy and her Paulette, then looked back at the road. The large Marquis Apartments complex was on the right, three klunky buildings, each five stories of red and white stone built in what passed for modern architecture when they had been erected twenty years earlier. It was the landmark that said, 'Poydras is ending, go left or right on Broad Avenue.' Christine turned right.

"Dinner, yes," Amy replied. Then to Paul she thought, *It's just sinking in on me what happened with Sam. What kind of a life am I leading?*

He took the lead to say, "I need to talk to Amy for a bit, okay?" It was not the first time Christine had heard those words, and they did not disturb her.

"Sure. Can I interrupt when we get to the restaurant?"

"Yeah," and he kissed her cheek. He loved the exaggerated smile she wore when he did that.

So, existential crisis? he thought to Amy.

When Sam got out of line I was too busy dealing with her to think about it. A touch of fear, a double-dose of adrenalin, and it was over. That's good. But now it's sinking in. Paul, she tried to rape me!

She tried to rape us, he corrected, while Christine put her right hand on their left thigh. *It happened too fast for me to be any use. You handled it great. Dropping down to get out of her grasp, that was brilliant.*

She smiled at the compliment, and truth be known, she was pleased with herself for thinking of that maneuver. *No harm done,* she thought back, as Christine removed her hand. *Well, only to her kneecap, and she deserved it.*

It's not the first time we've been attacked, he thought. Christine returned her hand to their leg. *It's not even the first time someone tried to rape us. What's different today?*

There was a long pause before Amy said aloud, "I'm not sure." Christine let go of their leg. Silently, Amy said, *She is the most considerate person in the world. I don't know how she can tell which one of us is leading, but she wants to touch you, not me. She's told me she doesn't want to make me uncomfortable by being physical.*

Yeah, he laughed silently. *That does make things easier for you, doesn't it?*

Yes, it does. She's a thoughtful woman. Then, *I don't know why this deal with Sam is making me feel vulnerable. I think that's what it is. She could have hurt me. She's taller and heavier and she really could have messed me over.*

Are you looking for suggestions? he thought to her, *Or some sympathy?*

Years ago, the first few times Paul had asked those questions, Amy had exploded in anger; defensively, she had assumed Paul was making a value judgment about which was worth more. Eventually she let him explain that he asked so he could be supportive. "Sometimes people want ideas on how to cope with things," he had said, "and sometimes they want someone to say 'poor baby.' I don't want to guess wrong and piss you off." Now, after more than twenty years of sharing her head with Paul, she had learned to accept his questions at face value. *Mostly sympathy,* she finally thought back. *But any ideas of why this is bothering me would be appreciated.*

She felt Paul nod their head

"We're here!" Christine called as she parked her Smart car in one of the spaces in front of the Chinese Tea Garden. It was in a strip shopping center, wedged between a caterer and a dry cleaner. "Do you need me to wait until you're finished talking?"

Amy placed their hand on the woman's. "I'm good. We're good. Maybe you can help me."

"Like taking notes?" Christine replied. "Sure. You know I like to help you, Amy."

"I need you and Paul to help me figure out why I'm upset about that fight I had today."

Christine's eyes went wide. "You said she tried to rape you. I'd be upset, too."

It was Paul who said, "Me for some shrimp lo mein. We can talk about it over some beer."

As they got out of the little yellow car Paul said, "I just remembered, they don't have Dixie Beer here."

Christine took their hand and said, "One Abita won't kill you."

Amy squeezed Christine's hand as she took the lead, so the woman couldn't let go. "The Assorted Vegetable Delight might do him in. What are you having?"

She knew her lover's heart's desire. "Me for some shrimp lo mein. Paulette, I'll share."

The restaurant specialized in fast take-out. There were only seven dining tables: mismatched, aged, but spotlessly clean. One couple was seated at a corner table, and another three people were waiting for their to-go orders, seated at a large table piled with week-old newspapers and months-old magazines. The restaurant was brightly lit, uncomfortably so; the light revealed every cracked and chipped plastic floor tile, every peeling table top, and a wall calendar displaying June 2032 as if it were still unfolding.

The menus were on plain paper, spit out by a black-and-white inkjet printer and heavily stained from coffee cups and soy sauce bottles. Many of the prices were crossed out, with new charges written in with ballpoint.

"Oh, Assorted Vegetable Delight," Amy crooned, "how do I love thee? Let me count the ways."

Paul said, "What? No meat? Again?"

"There's plenty of protein in snow peas and broccoli," she answered, smiling.

When the waitress appeared–short, skinny, young, and oriental, with a smattering of English–Amy and Christine placed their orders.

The waitress confirmed they still didn't carry Dixie, so Christine asked for a Tsing Tao and Amy ordered a Corona.

"We could have split a Heineken," he said after the waitress was gone.

Amy said, "You know I like sweet beers. The Corona will be fine."

Feeling sorry for her Paulette, Christine said, "You can have some of my lo mein."

"Thanks, honey. I need meat. I'm a growing boy."

"If I ate the way you'd like," Amy said, "we'd be growing wider."

"Tell me how you're upset, Amy," Christine said. She reached across the table to hold their hand for a moment.

"I'm a detective. I deal with bad people. Sometimes I get scared, but I go ahead and do what I need to do. I've been shot, stabbed, half-strangled, and dumped in a bayou." She shook their head. "That part is not much fun, but it doesn't slow me down. Until now."

Christine sat back and stared, open-mouthed. Paul thought she had never heard Amy express any doubts about what she did; he hadn't heard many himself.

"Slow you down. How?" Paul asked.

Amy saw the waitress coming with their beers, so she forced a smile and said nothing. Christine thanked the woman, then said, "She could be part of that family I'll meet tomorrow. I hope they buy a house from me."

When Amy took a long mouthful of the Corona, she heard Paul think, *Hey! That's not bad.*

"I'm glad you approve," she said softly. Then she went on, "Slow me down, like–like I'm scared."

"You have a dangerous job," Christine said. "Being scared seems natural. Smart, even."

"Yes, I guess so. But why is this different?" Amy asked, looking glum. "For me, fear is situational and brief. But I think of Sam nuzzling my ear and–Whuh!" She flinched, and shook their head.

"Have we ever been attacked by a woman before?"

A young man, silently smiling, brought a big tray over and moved plates of entrees and rice to the table. Christine said "Thank you," and he nodded like a bobble-head doll with a loose spring. Even though there were two beers on the table, he also off-loaded a teapot and cups and saucers.

There was silence at the table for a good long while. Amy poked at her Assorted Vegetable Delight, while Christine pushed some of her pork lo mein onto a saucer for Paulette.

Finally Amy began, "I like women. Uh–not like you do, Christine–" they both laughed "–but, you know, I like them. I trust them. You. My sister Kaylee. Florence, who I hardly ever see anymore. Mom, MeMaw." She pursed her lips, thinking for a moment. "I think that's it. I trust women won't hurt me. They won't start a fist fight. And then–" suddenly looking very sad "–and then Sam tried to hurt me."

"Oh, Amy," Christine said, and took her hand again. "That girl blew up a whole lifetime of expectations. Is that what's getting to you?"

Christine heard Paul think, *You are brilliant, do you know that? To figure that out? Wow.* Then, to Amy, he thought, *I can feel how disappointed you are. Is there anything I can do?*

His words made her smile just a bit. Then she looked down at her Assorted Vegetable Delight; she did not feel delighted.

Christine got up and moved to the chair next to Amy. She held her arms out, and Amy leaned against her. "Thanks," she said.

"I'm here," Christine said. "Paulette's here. We're here for you."

There was a faint nod. "Yes."

Christine could feel it when Paul took the lead and said out loud, "Some things are worth feeling sad about. I love you, Amy."

She hugged their body, knowing Paul was leading. "And I love you, too, Amy. You know that."

Amy relaxed. Sam was a thug, but Christine was the other sister Amy never had. And Paul was there, using their left hand– 'his' hand–to rub their right arm; and he was in her head, telling her she was smart and that he'd help her as much as he could to put this part of her life back together. She allowed herself to accept the love that Paul and Christine were surrounding her with.

It felt anti-climactic after a few minutes when she said, "I'm not hungry. Christine, do you want some of my veggies? They're good."

Christine patted them on the shoulder, then returned to her own chair. "Paulette? Please have some of my lo mein. I know you like it."

Can I? he thought to Amy. He heard her laugh inside and think back, *Yes. Not too much, though. I'm really not hungry anymore.*

Out loud he said, "I'll make up for you." He smiled at his lover across the table and stuck a fork into the pork lo mein he liked so much.

☙ TUESDAY, August 15, 2034 ❧

Christine's alarm clock went off at six-fifteen. Instantly she was wide awake and cheerful; so was Paul. He rolled over to hug his lover, whispering, "I love the mornings when I wake up with you."

This was followed by an enormous yawn. Amy wasn't asleep anymore, but she wasn't exactly awake either. Paul said, "Kiss me quick, before Amy returns to the land of the living." They hugged; they kissed; they petted; and at last he held her close, inhaling the scent of her hair.

"God, what time is it?" Amy said aloud. Immediately Christine let go of her Paulette because she could tell he wasn't leading anymore. "It's twenty after six," the woman said. "Good morning, Amy. When do you have to leave?"

Another yawn. "Duke wants me at the station by eight-thirty. Can I hit your snooze alarm?"

Before Christine could answer, Paul said, "C'mon, Amy. A shower will wake you right up."

"I don't want to wake right up," but even as she was saying it she was pushing their body to a sitting position, and thinking about telling their legs to stand up.

"When do you meet that Chinese family?" Paul asked his lover.

"Not 'til ten," she said, flashing a smile that showed off her crooked front tooth. "But I want to go in to the office and pick up some paperwork. I have to bring a contract in case they want to buy one of the houses we look at." She stood, and reached down to take Paulette's hand and help them stand "We can shower together. Tell Amy I'll behave."

"I can hear you," Amy said, smiling. She took Christine's hand and stood up. "Thanks."

As Christine gathered up things to bring to the bathroom, she asked, "Are you doing better now? Do you have to interview more women today?"

"I don't know how I'm doing yet. I'm going to talk to three topless activists, and two college lesbians who look like models from a Laura Ashley catalog." She thought a moment. "I'll wear slacks today."

As they drove to the Rampart Street station, Paul asked, "Are you still shook up about Sam?"

In the privacy of the car, Amy and Paul both spoke out loud. "A little," Amy admitted. "That's why I'm wearing pants. Suddenly the idea of a skirt makes me feel vulnerable." Paul did not share his thought, that from the first time Amy wore a skirt after he came to her, he had felt the same way. She went on, "And with all my gear on a belt, it's easier to get to anything I need." She laughed, "When I'm dealing with a total stranger it's weird to reach under my skirt to pull out my badge and ID."

"I'm glad it's not just me," he replied.

Paul was leading to drive. He took the old Benz down the driveway to the officers' lot and parked next to a black-and-white with its hood raised, belching smoke and steam from its radiator. "Hey, Sergeant," Amy called to the officer staring at the exposed engine.

"Morning, Detective," he responded. "You better hope whatever's wrong with my cruiser isn't catching."

"Oh, I blow off steam just like that every time I go to the Mexican buffet. It'll pass." She locked her car and headed to the station's back door.

When Amy got to the uniformed officers' bullpen, roll call and orders of the day were still going on. She leaned against the door frame and thought to Paul, *We have different reasons, but you're not the only one who's glad I didn't become a uniformed cop.*

You know I hate cops, he thought back. *What's your excuse?*

Regimentation. Stand at attention while a sergeant barks and yells. I'd fall asleep standing up if I had to go through this every day.

They watched the sergeant issue instructions to the various officers. When he called "Cranston!" Duke said, "Sir! Continuing murder investigation of Riley Tibbs." The sergeant nodded and made a note on his clipboard before moving to the next officer on his list.

This is so boring! Amy thought to Paul. She sat in a nearby chair and began to consider what she'd have for lunch.

When the roll call was done, the officers walked to this group and that to exchange greetings or gossip, then left the bullpen to get to work. Cranston stood towering over Amy, looming until she noticed the room seemed to have gone dim. When she looked up, he said, "You're on time. That's good. Let's get moving."

"Hey, good morning," she said as she got out of the chair and began to walk with the lieutenant. "Tell me about the muscle we're going to visit."

"You pegged them right, Queenie." He led them down the hallway, then down the concrete stairs to the parking level. "J'waun Simmons, the small one. Juvenile record in Chicago for jacking cars and selling dope. Moved to L.A. two years ago, hooked up with SEIU as a union enforcer. Somehow stayed clean." He opened the door to the parking area and let Amy go through first. "The big guy is Calvin X, although his mama named him Calvin Brocious Jackson. Born in L.A. No priors. Converted to Nation of Islam under Louis Farrakhan in 2012 and now heads the Fruit of Islam security forces–that's the bow-tie thing." Cranston opened the passenger door to his cruiser to let Amy in. "His tie is red because he's the boss."

When Cranston was fastening his seat belt Amy asked, "How did they hook up?"

"You're going to help me find out," he said. "The two of us can question them apart and then compare their stories."

Amy thought to Paul, *Big guys, but they don't scare me. I'll be okay.*

As the lieutenant backed out of the parking space, Amy asked, "Where are they?"

She heard the officer chuckle. "They're at the Midtown Motel on Tulane. I want to surprise them before check-out time."

"Why does that sound familiar?" Amy mused.

"What, the Midtown? Not a total dive, but we know there's a lot of prostitution and drug activity there." He turned to look at her for a moment. "It's mentioned in a lot of crime articles."

She heard Paul think, *I guess the Times-Picayune has a satellite office there.*

"Hey, Queenie, what's so funny?"

"Part of me is thinking about the newspaper having a reporter permanently stationed there. I mean, they have a police beat reporter, so why not?"

He frowned. "'Part of me is thinking'? Jesus, Queenie, get serious! Now, here's my plan on handling these muscle guys. You okay with that?"

He doesn't want to play, Amy silently cried to Paul. Then, aloud: "Sure. What's the plan, boss?"

"I talked to them yesterday. They're on the same page I am about this queer stuff. But the important thing is, they claim the woman from Advancement Trust tried to talk them into killing the pastor. Since you've interviewed that woman, I want you to get a description from Muscle 1 and Muscle 2. You know, make sure they actually met her."

"I heard she was putting out feelers," Amy replied. "A couple of folks I'm sure are innocent said Sam was talking about how the pro-same-sex marriage side needed a martyr. What did our muscle say they did? Since I'm guessing they claim they did not kill Riley Tibbs."

"Good guess, Queenie. They said they went to Reverend Rutter, and I asked her about it. She said Calvin told her about it on Saturday. She also said she trusts Calvin."

Silently, Amy conferred with Paul, *So, the question is, did the muscle kill Tibbs anyway?* He thought back, *That's how I see it.* To the lieutenant she said, "Do you? Do we?"

"You're going to help me find out." He flicked on the siren to run a red light as he turned onto Tulane Avenue. "If they can't describe the real person, then maybe they're lying and they're killers."

She thought about it. "Do we do 'good cop/bad cop' with them?" she asked. "Oh, please! Let me be the bad cop, okay?"

"What is wrong with you?" he barked. "The big guy is as big as me and the little one is twice your size. Why would you want to be the asshole?"

"Hey! I can be a great asshole. You haven't seen me go all asshole yet." She heard Paul think, *Have you become suicidal?* but she went on, "Look up asshole and my picture is in the dictionary."

A smile crept onto Cranston's face. "It won't hurt my career if my partner gets eaten alive by a suspect. If you really want to be the bad cop, sure. Uh, the safety word is 'banana.'"

She thought to Paul, *What's a safety word?* Amy heard him laugh inside and silently explain, *It's for bondage and rough sex. Say the safety word and you partner stops whatever they were doing to you. Assuming they hear you.*

"How do you know this stuff?" she asked aloud.

The lieutenant broke up laughing. "Oh, Queenie, you don't want to know!"

Cranston parked his cruiser half on the sidewalk in front of the Midtown Motel. "They're in room 128," he said as he locked the doors. "Let's go see the desk clerk."

The reception area was small, and the older, morbidly obese clerk looked as if he were wedged behind the counter. Three oscillating fans were aimed in his general direction, but he was drenched in sweat. His radio was broadcasting a weather alert that Tropical Storm Olaf could come ashore by Friday, anywhere between Tamaulipas in Mexico and the west coast of Florida; wherever it landed, it would be a full-fledged hurricane. "Morning, Harvey," the lieutenant called.

"Duke! Hah! What brings you back so soon?"

Amy heard Paul think, *Why does this place look familiar?*

Cranston leaned over the counter. "Have our friends in 128 checked out yet?

Harvey pulled the registration book closer. "Nah. Still here. They've got 'til eleven, you know. Hah!"

"Good, good. I'm sure they'll be along soon." He straightened up and turned, pushing Amy toward the door. "See you soon, my man."

"I'm sure they're planning on leaving town," he explained as they walked around the registration office and into the parking lot. "They don't know that I checked them out with LAPD." A few steps later he added, "I told them I want them to meet you."

"And I'm sure they're thrilled at the opportunity," Amy laughed. "This is going to be enjoyable."

"Cool it, Queenie," the lieutenant said, shaking his head. "This ain't no game. These guys are tough fuckers, and Calvin is as big as me."

I swear I've been here before, Paul thought to Amy as they walked down the parking lot, checking the room numbers as they went.

Amy answered silently, *Did you meet a hooker here while I was asleep? I've never been anywhere near this place.*

"Here." Cranston stopped. He unsnapped the security strap over his pistol, then tugged at his utility belt. "You ready?"

Amy took their baton from its holster and slowly tapped it against their left palm. When she nodded, the lieutenant banged on the door twice with his fist as he shouted, "Police!" He tried the doorknob, but when he found it was locked he stepped back and kicked the door just under the knob. The door burst in to the dimly lit room. "I hope I'm not interrupting anything," he said.

The big man cried, "What the fuck?" as he turned to face the door. He was reaching for something under his vest until he was able to see the huge cop from the day before in the room, along with some cute white chick with a nightstick. Slowly, he raised both his hands in the air. "What the fuck?" he repeated.

"Where's J'waun?" the officer demanded, while Amy walked toward Calvin. She was still tapping the baton in her palm.

"He's in the crapper." Calvin answered. He was eyeing Amy warily as she stood in front of him, staring up at him, tap-tap-tapping the baton against her hand.

Cranston went to the room's bathroom door. With back to the wall beside it, he beat on the door with his elbow and shouted, "Front and center, J'waun!"

A muffled, "Gimmie a minute" came through the door, along with the sound of running water.

"Now!"

"Is it okay with you if I wipe my fucking ass?" The voice got louder as the man got closer to the door, and he finally opened it. "Like, what the fuck?"

Cranston flipped a light switch. Suitcases were open on each of the beds, partially full of dirty laundry and some folded clothes. "Are y'all going somewhere?" he asked, rhetorically.

"Can I put my hands down?" Calvin asked, turning his head toward the lieutenant.

Amy said, "No." Slowly he looked back at her. She was still tapping the furled baton against her palm.

"The fuck you say!" As he lowered his hands, Amy flicked the baton to extend it to its full twenty-four inches, and continued to tap it against her hand. Calvin raised his arms again.

"Yesterday," Duke began, "we talked about the run-up to the Sunday demonstration. I told you I'd be back with my detective. You fuckers hurt my feelings by trying to pack up and leave before we got here. Do I have bad breath or something?" He was grinning.

Amy was nodding to what he said, even as she continued to stare at Calvin and slap the baton. She heard Paul ask, *What are you doing? This guy can cream us.*

She thought back, *I'm being the bad cop. I'm enjoying this. Uh, so far.*

The lieutenant said, "J'waun, you and me are going to have a pow-wow in that bathroom you just stank up, while Detective Clear and Calvin will discuss the nature of reality in here. C'mon," and he took the smaller man by the upper arm and shoved him at the bathroom; he did not close the door.

Amy hadn't stopped staring at Calvin or tapping the baton. After fifteen seconds of silence he said, "So what you want, bitch?"

"That's 'Detective Bitch' to you." She delivered a light touch of the baton to his right knee, then resumed tapping it. "So, what's my name?"

"You're fucking crazy."

This baton touch was heavier, against his left knee. The man barked and then let his arms drop.

"I said, 'what's my name?'"

"Keep up this shit and your name is Mud."

The tip of the baton landed on the back of his right hand.

He was breathing heavily, trying not to let the pain show in his face. "You put that thing down, we'll see how brave you are."

Amy broke into a broad smile. She tossed the baton over her shoulder; they heard it hit the side of a bed and drop to the floor. She jumped forward about six inches, and Calvin stepped back. They were locked in eye contact. Paul thought to Amy, *Today is not a good day to die!*

Nobody's dying, she thought back. *Let's see if this works.* She made a feint to her left, and when Calvin flinched she unloosed a roundhouse open palm slap on his face. She was counting on the man feeling it as an insult, to be slapped by a woman.

"You wouldn't be so tough if your chaperone wasn't in the next room," he growled. The way he was flexing his right hand told her the baton strike had left its message of pain.

"Calvin, you misunderstand. Lieutenant Cranston is here for your protection, not mine." She smiled again. "If he weren't here, I'd have you hogtied on the floor by now." Then, forcefully, "So, tell me, what is my name?" Her smile was gone.

They stared at one another until Amy said, "Do not make me ask you again. What. Is. My. Name?"

"Yeah. You're Detective Something."

"Very good, Calvin. Clear, I'm Detective Clear. You know, I think we're going to get along fine. Don't you?" She stepped back, then motioned to the nearer bed, "You can sit down. It's easier to talk when we're comfortable." Slowly, uncertainly, he took the few steps and sat by the open suitcase. Amy took a desk chair and placed it two feet away but directly in front of the man. She laughed when she heard Paul think, *I am in awe. By all rights we should have a dozen broken bones.*

She leaned forward and said, "Just between you and me, I don't think you did anything wrong. You're too smart to do anything that dumb. But if I'm to make a case against somebody else I need to know about their interactions with you." Paul saw the man's impassive face and added, "You hear what I'm saying?" Finally the big man nodded.

"Lieutenant Cranston tells me a woman came to you and J'waun to ask you to kill the pastor at that church." She paused to let him nod again, then went on, "And that pastor indeed got killed at that church during the Sunday demonstration."

"Are you accusing me of something?"

"Oh, relax," she said, waving one hand. "What I want to know is, who was the woman that tried to solicit you to murder?"

"Sam something," he said. "Only reason I remember is 'cause she had a man's name."

"Was she with any organization?"

"Yeah. I don't remember what it was." He thought for a moment. "She said it was one of the groups that was sponsoring the demonstration, but I don't remember what."

Amy nodded and prompted, "Equality Forum?"

He shrugged. She noticed he was still flexing his right hand. She thought to Paul, *I love my baton.*

"Community Coalition?"

Another shrug.

"Advancement Trust NOLA?"

His eyes lit up. "Yeah. Something with 'NOLA' in the name. Yeah, that's it."

"Okay, Calvin. Where did she make this offer?"

"It was here. Uh, the coffee shop in the motel."

While Amy leaned forward to retrieve a notepad from their back pocket, Paul–sounding exactly like Amy–asked, "How did that happen? She just bump into you and J'waun around the corner or what?"

"Nah." The big man ran his left hand over his shaved head. "Reverend Rutter called me, said this Sam girl was with the protest and that she wanted to talk security. She gave me her number. I called her, and we met up here."

"What did she look like?" Paul thought to Amy, *The $64,000 question.* She thought back a quick, *Huh? Is that like 'one meellyon dollars?'*

"A big girl," Calvin said. "Not as big as me, but, shit, she could have squished you like a bug." He thought. "Maybe six feet, maybe a hundred and sixty pounds?"

Paul was still angry that Sam Atkins had attempted to rape them. He asked, "Hair?"

"Dark. Like an old fashioned beehive that was collapsing." He snickered at the memory.

"Scars? Piercings? Tattoos? Missing body parts?"

"Nah," shaking his head. "I don't know what it was, but she looked tough. Not like a trouble-maker, but ... you know, like she had a hard life." He thought some more. "I'll tell you, though, she was smoking cigarettes like a holy roller going through a Bible. And her voice was rough. Like she drank a lot of whiskey."

It's Sam Atkins, Paul thought to Amy.

She thought back, *Unless they met and now he's trying to frame her for the murder.*

Aloud, Amy asked, "What did the woman offer to do the killing?"

Calvin's face was a combination of a little smile and puzzled eyes. "The bitch said she'd pay for the coffee." Shaking his huge shaved head, he added, "Amateur."

Paul led to ask, "You said you told Reverend Rutter. What did she tell you?"

"Don't do it."

"Uh–were you considering it?"

A laugh. "No way. Minister Farrakhan taught that taking a life is wrong, even if it's a dhimmi. Besides, she was such a loser! I thought sure it was a sting. J'waun, he had some problems in the past. I needed to protect him. And then I saw her at the demonstration."

"What happened there?" she prompted.

"The clergy group we were with was doing a silent protest thing, and the bitch walks up and says, 'Hey Calvin, change your mind yet?' I told her to get lost. I didn't want J'waun to see her or he'd go all schoolboy on her."

Amy thought, *That woman at Community Coalition, Jess–she said Sam was in ultrayellow.* Out loud, she asked, "What did she look like then?"

A frown. "Like a fucking daffodil."

Idly, Amy leaned over to retrieve her baton from where it had rolled part way under the bed. She jammed the extension into the carpet to furl it. "I want to get me one of them," Calvin said. "You know what my job is, right?"

Even though Duke had told her, she said, "No, I don't. Tell me," as she sat back up in the chair.

"I'd a thought the lieutenant would of told you. I lead the L.A. branch of the Fruit of Islam. It's the NOI security division. We protect Minister Ishmael Muhammad, and make sure no bad shit comes down at any of our events." His eyes were on Amy's baton as she slipped it into its holster. "I could use me one of them."

Smiling, she said, "Well, maybe Santa will put you on the good boy list." She stood up and shouted, "Duke! Ready to trade?"

The lieutenant came out of the other room, still holding J'waun by the upper arm. "Did Calvin here behave himself?" he asked.

"Oh, Calvin and me, we're great buddies now. What's up with J'waun?

"Don't try to beat sense into him; his head is too damn hard." Then he leaned to her and whispered, "I had you in the medicine cabinet mirror, me and J'waun saw you. You do asshole good."

Amy smiled and said, "Thanks. I told you." As they swapped persons of interest, Amy held her arm out to the nearby bed and said, "J'waun, make yourself comfortable. I need to ask you a few things."

The only way one could describe J'waun Simmons as 'smaller' was to stand him next to Calvin X or Lieutenant Cranston. He was five-eleven, north of two hundred pounds, with close-cropped hair. There were scars on his face from his careers as a juvenile thug and union goon. He was wearing a white collarless shirt buttoned to the neck, and gray slacks held up by red suspenders.

"Are you gonna work me over like you did Calvin?" he asked.

She took a step closer to where he sat on the bed. Paul balled their left hand into a fist and rubbed it with their right hand and said, "Do I need to?"

"Shee-it, no!" He leaned back on the bed, away from Amy, with a look of surprise on his face.

"Good. I'm watching my weight, and it makes me so hungry to go all psycho on people." She sat in the desk chair opposite J'waun, then pushed it to one side so she was not confronting the man. "You and Calvin had some dealing with people in our sights, so I'm trying to get enough information to make a case against them. What's the story on this? Somebody wanted the two of you to kill the pastor at that church?"

"Yeah. That crazy bitch. Calvin called her and we met her at the snack joint in the motel. She smoked the place up with her Marlboros and talked crazy trash about making a martyr for the cause."

"For the cause? What cause?"

Laughing, J'waun said, "I told you she's a crazy bitch. She didn't realize she and us are on different teams."

Amy heard Paul think, *She really is a dim-bulb.*

"What team is she on?" Amy asked, notebook open in her lap.

"Them queers. She thinks girls should marry girls and men should marry men." He shook his head. "She thinks different from me, I get that. But why did she want help from us?"

Paul thought, *Whoa. Maybe her idea was to get the bad guys to do the killing. Maybe she's not so dumb after all.*

"No telling, J'waun. I've given up trying to understand how people think. What exactly did she ask you and Calvin to do?"

"She said somebody needed to shoot that pastor dead. She told Calvin, 'You big. You could do it.'"

"And what did he tell her?"

The man laughed. "He called her a bunch of names and said, 'No.' He asked her why he shouldn't tell the cops. She say, 'Oh I'm just teasing.' I tell you, that one crazy mother fucking bitch right there."

Amy tried not to laugh. She asked, "So, what did this woman look like? Was she–"

"She look good, if you like white women–uh, excuse me. She had a pile of black hair on top of her head, but it was coming down some, not tidy. What–" trying to remember, "–some old hippie shirt with ruffles and shit, showed off her rack–uh, excuse me." He smiled like a little boy caught doing something wrong. "I'm just saying."

"What did she sound like?"

"Like an old guy," he said, "like she been smoking and boozing a lot." He pitched his voice down and tried to imitate what he remembered; "Like this," deep and raspy.

She asked, "How did the meeting end?"

"Calvin said no, she said she was kidding, and Calvin said was there anything else she wanted to talk about and she said no." J'waun scratched his head. "I asked her where she was staying. Calvin's all religious and shit, but she looked good to me and I was lonely, you know what I mean? Then the bitch said," he thought carefully, "she said she might see me around. Crazy damn bitch."

Amy stood up and stepped to the open rest room door. "I'm done, Duke."

The lieutenant stepped into the main room and pointed at J'waun. "You. Go keep your friend company in there."

He muttered, "Aw, shit, I don't wanna..." but he got up off the bed and joined Calvin. He closed the door behind him.

"What'd you get, Queenie?"

"They both described Sam Atkins, and they both told the same story. Except J'waun wanted to knock boots with her. But they both think she's crazy, and I pretty much agree."

"Do you think they killed the pastor? That's what–"

Through the closed door they heard Calvin shout, "No! I ain't gonna give you the bitch's phone number. She's poison, my man. Poison!" They heard J'waun's higher voice but couldn't make out his words.

"Sorry, Duke," Amy said, "I have no idea if they did it. They both say they didn't. All we know for sure is that Sam was trying to get them to kill Pastor Tibbs. She dropped hints with some of the other people I interviewed." Amy let Paul scribble some notes and close her notebook. "We need more to go on to guess who stuck the knife, but it looks like it was at Sam's direction."

Calvin's voice boomed, "I don't give a shit what you do back in L.A., but you're getting on that fucking plane with me today. We got cops visiting us daily, why you want to stay here?" They heard J'waun say something, and Calvin's response: "A white woman with big tits and you're in love? Man, we get home I'll turn you loose in Holmby Hills, we'll see what kind of action you get."

Amy and Duke laughed out loud. He knocked on the door and called, "Everything all right in there? Do you need a cop or something?"

J'waun opened the door, mumbling, "It ain't none of your business, you know?" Behind him, the big man was frowning. "If you want to join the Fruit of Islam, it is my business."

Paul spoke, "When's your plane leave?"

"Two fifteen," said Calvin, "and J'waun's going to be on it if I have to nail him in a crate and call him baggage."

"Well, don't let us get in your way," the lieutenant responded. "Thanks for your time, even if you were trying to duck out on me."

As they opened the door to the outside, Amy took her beloved baton from its holster. "Calvin! Catch!" and she tossed it to the big man.

Grabbing it in his right hand, he looked at her with a puzzled smile. "Uh, Detective. How you open it?"

"Just flick your wrist," she said, making the motion with their right hand. "It takes a few tries to get used to it." Meanwhile, Cranston rested his hand on the butt of his holstered pistol. "What the hell are you doing, Queenie?" he muttered from the side of his mouth.

"And to close it?"

"Just jam it straight into something solid."

Calvin experimented. He nearly dropped the baton when it suddenly opened. Then he pushed the tip against the wall a few times until it collapsed. "You all right, Detective," he beamed. Two golden crowns glittered in his wide mouth.

"Yeah, yeah, I'm all that. Look–" she fished out a business card and held it out to him, "–let me know how it goes."

He looked at the card, and the baton, and back again. "Uh–yeah. Sure."

"Merry Christmas," she said as they left the muscle behind.

In the parking lot Cranston grasped Amy by the left shoulder and marched her to his squad car. "What's the deal?" she asked, but he was silent until he opened the passenger door. "Get in," he ordered as he pushed her at the opening. She was fastening her seat belt when the lieutenant got behind the wheel and locked all the doors.

"What were you thinking?" he shouted. "You gave a weapon to a person of interest! He could have wailed on you. He could have wasted both of us."

Amy smiled. "But he didn't, did he?" She heard Paul think, *What's this about?*

"For a detective with a good track record, you don't make any sense. You want to get yourself killed, be my guest, but I don't want to be collateral damage."

"You said you saw me deal with Calvin," she protested. "I tamed him. He mentioned that he could use a baton in his job. So I squandered thirty-five dollars of NOPD gear by giving it to him, and he'll be on our side in the future."

"It's not the dollars, Queenie. He'll be on our side in Los Angeles. It may be LA, but it ain't Louisiana."

I'm going ballistic, she thought.

Take a deep breath, Paul thought back. *I want to hear why you did this, too.*

Amy shook their head and said, "Don't think geography. Think demography. Calvin runs security for the Nation of Islam. Do we have Muslims in New Orleans? Will we ever have a problem with perps or suspects that happen to be Muslims? Will a call from Calvin X de-escalate a situation?"

Duke held the steering wheel and stared ahead, down Tulane Avenue. "Oh." In her head she heard Paul think the same thing.

"I think a baton is cheap for buying that kind of help. Think of it as insurance."

"Yeah." He turned to look at Amy. "Some of the guys at Rampart Street warned me you don't think normally. No–" he held up a hand when she started to protest "–I mean, you don't think the way other cops do." When Amy nodded he went on, "I go by the book. You don't. It seems to work, the way you bullied Calvin, even though it was ballsy dangerous. I have trouble with it."

Amy beamed. "Trust me, Duke. I spent three years on the force. Really, I know what I'm doing." When Cranston finally cranked the engine, Paul asked, "If what I did to Calvin didn't work, you'd have saved me, right?"

"What?"

"I said, 'you'd have saved me, right?'"

He stared at her. "I guess so."

Amy rolled her eyes. "Oh, Lieutenant! You sure know how to sweet-talk a woman."

"It's that kind of shit!" he barked. "Can't you just be normal?"

"No!" she shouted, and then thought directly to him, silently but loud, *There's nothing normal about me!* Duke cut the engine and leaned against the driver's door, away from the Amy he had never before seen angry. "You have to put up with me," out loud. She took a few deep breaths to regain control of herself, then continued with an indoor voice. "Just like I put up with your 'queer' and 'faggot' crap. I'm not asking you to be someone you're not, Duke. Can you please give me the same God damned slack?" She and the lieutenant stared at each other. Until, that is, she heard Paul silently singing one of those Jurassic-era songs he knew from before he came to her: *I don't tell you what to say, I don't tell you what to do...*[5] Amy looked down and smiled despite herself. *Shush,* she thought back to Paul, laughing inside.

"Whu-what did you just do?" Cranston asked. He looked confused.

"I just demonstrated. I'm not normal. Can you deal with me?"

"I'll work on it. Queenie," Cranston finally said, "but I'm not promising anything."

She nodded. "It's all a work in progress. Thanks."

He started the squad car again and pulled out onto Tulane Avenue. After a few blocks of silence he said, "Really. What you did awhile ago? How?" He glanced at her, then back at the crowded street.

"It's something I can do, Duke. I don't know how; I just do it." She touched his right arm for a moment and said, "This is our little secret, okay?"

He made some strange noise. "Well, I guess. Who would believe me if I said Detective Clear can think into my head? It would kill my career." He shook his head. "What's that called? Telemetry?"

"Telepathy," Amy corrected. "It's saved my life before. It might save yours." The lieutenant did not respond, so she asked, "Are we good?"

"I don't know what we are, Queenie. I hope it's good." Stopping for a red light, he turned to her. There was a half-smile on his face. "But if you can do that, I'll learn to get used to the rest of your shit."

She heard Paul think, *I do believe you've won him over.*

"I'm supposed to work a smash-and-grab in the Garden District now," Cranston said. What's on your plate?"

"A man called Sunchild, three topless lesbians, a fake gay couple, and two very earnest lesbians. Just another day."

Duke dropped Amy off in front of the Rampart Street station and made a three-point turn to head uptown to the Garden District and his smash-and-grab.

She stood on the sidewalk, soaking up the hazy sun. *I hope Duke and I get along now,* she thought to Paul.

Sounds like it, he thought back. *That was brave, thinking to him. What did you say to him?* When either of them aimed a thought to a third person, the other didn't hear it.

"That I'm not normal."

Succinct.

"I'm thinking Duke responds best to simple, short, declarative sentences." She walked up the three steps to the main entrance, where the air conditioning chilled them. "And now I have to set up appointments with the stars of 'News Weirdos: New Orleans'." She waved her ID at the uniformed officer in the Plexiglas reception kiosk and headed for the stairs and the detectives' work room.

Her first call was to Sunchild. The man answered his cellphone with, "Carpe Byte–Uh, I mean, it's Larry."

Amy introduced herself and asked if she could visit him at work–at Carpe Byte–to ask a few questions about the marriage demonstration.

"I'll be here until six," he said, and dictated the address out Tulane Avenue.

"I have to make some other stops," she explained. "Can I give you a call maybe half an hour ahead?"

"If you want. But I love surprises, so just drop in any ol' time."

Paul pulled a clean leaf from Amy's legal pad and wrote, "Larry << 6PM CBD"

"Sharpie Girl is next," she announced to the empty room as she dialed the number she had been able to squeeze out of the television News Director. On the second ring there was a loud noise and an over-modulated, sleepy "Hello."

"This is Detective Clear with Orleans Parish Police. I'm looking for Kelly Overton."

"Ummm."

"Excuse me, are you Miss Overton?"

"Ummm. Uh, yeah. Who is this again?" The voice was beginning to sound awake.

"Detective Clear, NOPD. I want to–"

"My God, what's wrong?" the woman interrupted. "It's what, eleven o'clock? Is Morgan okay?" The voice became more awake and more agitated.

"As far as I know, everything is okay. No one is in trouble. I'm sorry if I woke you."

"I work at the Seven Seas bar," Kelly said, calmer. "I got off work at four and–" a very loud yawn "–didn't get to bed until seven or so."

Paul thought to Amy, *May as well blunder on.* When she didn't respond, he led to say, "I saw you and some friends on the TV news Sunday night. I–"

"Oh, yeah," a drowsy laugh. "Me and Hayden and Morgan."

"I'd like to talk to you about the demonstration. We're looking for any information about a death at the church."

"What, now?"

Paul laughed and answered, "When do you usually get up? I can stop at your place then."

"Oh, let me think. I've got stuff to do before work. Is three o'clock okay?"

Cradling the telephone handset between ear and shoulder, Paul used a ballpoint to write '3 PM – Kelly' on the inside of their right wrist. "Anything I need to know about getting to your place?" He read to her the address Amy had gotten for her.

"Don't park on the wrong side of the street or you'll get a ticket." She laughed at her own words. "I guess you don't have to worry about that. Three o'clock. I'm going back to sleep now."

On a legal pad, Amy added to her schedule. So far it was Larry before six, and Kelly at three.

Her next call was to one of the men who may or may not have been part of a gay couple, but did an excellent job of playing one on the TV newscast. She heard the outgoing message: "This is Taylor, I'm a junior in the college, majoring in beer, girls, and disorganized crime. Leave a God damned message." At the beep she said, "Taylor Grice, I am Detective Clear with the Orleans Parish police. I would like to ask you some questions about Sunday's demonstration at the MCC. I hope you can help us in our inquiries." She dictated her cell phone number and rang off.

"We may not get to them until tomorrow," Paul said aloud in the empty room.

"His message said he's majoring in girls? Another hint that the gay pose may have been an act."

He thought to her, *I remember your college days. Hell, I remember my college days. Fun times, but a lot of it stays in college days–if we're lucky.*

For a moment each of them was thinking about being on opposite sides of panty raids that took place some forty years apart. Amy shuddered and said out loud, "If we're lucky."

"So, who's left?"

"Parker and Kendall. Mom would love the way they were dressed on the newscast. Did you see they both were wearing pearls? Maybe I ought to wear the pearls Dad gave me, maybe they'll make a difference."

She heard Paul laugh silently and think, *I do not understand your taste in women. But, then, you don't understand mine.*

Quiet, you, she thought with a smile as she dialed the number the women shared.

There was a whispered, "Hello?" on the line. In the background Amy heard a droning male voice. Without thinking, she responded in the same whisper, "Parker? Kendall?"

"It's Kendall," the whisper replied. The background voice was getting fainter. Amy heard something like a door slamming, and the woman went on in a normal voice, "You caught me in class. Who's this?"

Amy introduced herself. "I'm interviewing some people who were at the church demonstration on Sunday," she went on. "There was a, umm, an incident and we're looking for information that might help us."

"I heard about that pastor. I don't think I saw her, though."

"You may have seen something that points us in the right direction. When can we meet?"

Paul doodled on the legal pad while the woman made some quiet noises, as if she were thinking. "This class will be over in another half hour...I'll be back at the dorm by noon. Parker, too." She explained where the new Sophie Newcomb housing was. "There's no parking, though. Not unless you buy a permit."

Paul laughed. Sounding like Amy, he said, "Police badge. I don't need no stinkin' permit."

Amy took the lead to say, "See you shortly."

Paul left off the doodling and wrote 'Parker and Kendall–noon' on the pad. Then he added to the notes on their right wrist. "Do we have time for lunch first?" he asked aloud.

"What a glutton you are," she replied. A yeoman in the hallway walking past the work room heard her and stuck his head in the door. He looked around the otherwise vacant room and said, "Detective, who are you talking to?"

His voice startled them. "Oh, uh, uh, just talking to myself. Part of me wants a whole shrimp loaf for lunch." She shook her head. "That's no way to keep this petite little body in good shape, you know?"

The man held up one hand as if to say he had heard enough, and walked on. As he did, Amy heard Paul think, *Shrimp po-boy? I'm on board.*

Damn, she thought back. *Half a loaf. And soup, not fries. Bastard.*

"Call me whatever you like, but feed me." In mock zombiespeak he thought, *FEEEEEEED MEEEEE!*

Amy gathered up her notes and slipped them into her clipboard. "Uptown on Claiborne and a left on Broadway Street," she announced to the empty room. "I'm sure we'll find a po-boy emporium somewhere along the way."

Claiborne Avenue–North above Canal Street and South upriver from there–is one of the main surface street corridors in New Orleans. It runs alongside and underneath the elevated interstate until I-10 turns west at Gravier and Poydras. Beyond the Superdome the street runs past light industrial buildings, vacant lots, fast food chain stores, and even more vacant lots. Things change abruptly at Napoleon Avenue, where the shopping options increase and the residential housing becomes larger and grander; there are more trees, and the empty lots are farther apart.

When they could see Tulane University's baseball stadium on the left, Amy turned to the right and pulled into a parking space outside Crumb's Sandwich and Seafood. It was a local place with garish, faux-fifties neon outside. Inside it was tiny, with no more than eight tables. The teenaged boy behind the counter asked, "What'll ya have, what'll ya have, what'll ya have?"

Paul jumped to the lead. Sounding just like Amy he said, "Gimme half a shrimp loaf and a side of jambalaya." While the boy nodded and wrote on an order pad, Paul thought to Amy, *Can we have a beer?*

Paul! she shouted silently. *It's not even noon!* Then out loud she said, "And a Barq's to drink." She hummed idly while the boy assembled her meal, then walked the tray to the vacant table with the least number of crumpled ketchup packets and straw wrappers. As she sat she thought, *We drink a lot.*

Beer good, Paul thought back.

Wine, too, she added silently. *And when we meet Christine at Sappho Rising, it's Margaritas or Daiquiris. We're turning into a couple of alkies.* She took a bite of the po-boy and said, aloud, "You're going to love this sandwich." After she swallowed, Paul led to take a bite. "You're not kidding!" he enthused. "Can we upgrade to a full loaf?"

She smiled inside; Paul was her best friend and she enjoyed his sense of humor. *No, we can't,* she thought. *And we can't wash it down with a Dixie. And I'm thinking it would be good for us to go, I don't know, a week without any alcohol.*

He stopped in mid-chew. *I'll die,* he thought to her. *My mind is fueled by alcohol.*

"Collateral damage, it can't be helped. But I'll have a big memorial service for you. My parents will come, and Christine will cry, and I'll play a bunch of those ancient songs you seem to like."

Amy heard him laugh silently. *I could have picked anyone in that hospital to get splashed into. But no, I had to pick the little girl who wants to put me on the wagon.*

They took turns with the sandwich and jambalaya so each of them had a chance to enjoy the full taste, and get a sense of appetite satiation.

After awhile Amy thought, *Really. I think we should drink less. We'll be healthier. I want to live with you for a long time.*

Paul took a sip of root beer and made a face. *But we'll be sober. Soberer. Is that too high a price for being healthy?*

She gathered up the debris from the meal–styrofoam plate and bowl, plastic sporks or foons, wadded-up napkins–and slid them into the trash receptacle. "Let's go visit the well-dressed lesbians," she muttered.

Paul led to drive. He made a left at the second light and headed south on Broadway Street, past bungalows with neatly trimmed lawns and larger houses that had been converted to quadruplex apartments thirty years before, if not earlier. As they neared the river, more residences had tall, thick hedges and spiked wrought iron fences. Amy said, "We're near Tulane, so Sophie Newcomb has to be here somewhere."

Almost immediately they came up on a large lawn with big brick buildings on three sides. "Quadrangle," Amy said. Paul thought back, *Trirangle. Is this it?*

"Turn left," she said. "Kendall said this is the Newcomb Lawn." As Paul turned left on Zimple, Amy added, "It's that building over there. Damn, we passed it. Turn around, okay?"

Paul made a three-point turn and stopped at Broadway. "Now what?"

"Let me drive," she said. She made a right and passed the quad–uh, trirangle–then turned into the campus on Plum. "They're in this building. Will you look at all these no parking signs?" Amy pulled her yellow Benz to the side of the street, with the right wheels up on the curb. She heard Paul think, laughing, *That's some wiregrass that'll never recover.*

Amy slapped the cardboard 'NOPD OFFICIAL BUSINESS' sign on the dashboard, and set the emergency blinkers going. "Come on, I want some fashion tips about wearing pearls."

The Josephine Louise House, named after benefactor Josephine Louise Newcomb, was a three story red brick building. It was a cross between Greek Revival and Federal, looking reliable, solid, and old. Amy went up the back steps and through the red schoolhouse doors to the lobby. At the reception desk sat a woman in her early sixties, with gray hair tinted blue. She looked like everyone's grandmother–well, not like Amy's MeMaw, but like everyone else's granny. Before Amy got to the desk the woman said, "Your car will be booted, young lady. I've already called the campus police." So much for grandmotherly.

Paul said, "Did you tell them it's Detective Clear with New Orleans Police?" He pulled Amy's ID case out of a back pocket and unfurled it for the woman. "I'm here on business. Where will I find Kendall Bourgeois or Parker Frye?"

"Surely they haven't done anything wrong!" the woman exclaimed. The laminated sign in front of her said 'Desk Service Coordinator.'

Amy smiled. "Where can I find them?"

"But–but–" the woman stammered, "I can't believe those girls are in trouble! What did they do?"

"Please, Ms. Coordinator," Amy frowned. "This is a police matter. Where can I find them?"

"Let me call up there!" and she reached for the phone. Paul thought, *I take it this is the most excitement this woman has had in quite a while.*

Silently, Amy thought back, *It's easier to let her call Parker or Kendall than to keep asking where they are.*

"Parker! There's a woman here who says she is a police detective and–" Ms. Coordinator listened, "You're expecting her? Parker, what have you done?" Amy couldn't hear the short response, but the desk lady went on, "But–but–huh!" She held out the handset and looked at it while it played a dial tone. "Well, I never!" she muttered.

"Thank you," Paul said, "NOPD always appreciates a citizen's help." Amy turned so her sudden grin wouldn't insult the woman.

Parker bounded down the stairs, wearing jeans, a denim workshirt, and pearls. She was calling to the coordinator, "Maxine! Where is the detective?" when she arrived at the desk.

Amy held out their right hand, saying, "Hi. I'm Detective Amy Clear with NOPD. You're Parker Frye?" Even as she did so, Paul took the lead.

Reflexively the woman shook their hand. She was a few inches shorter than Amy, looking up to meet Amy's gaze that was really Paul's. He thought to Amy, *Now, what do we have here?* Aloud, he said, "Is Kendall here? I'd like to talk to both of you."

"She's not back," shaking her head, "but she called me to say you were coming. We can talk in the lobby," as she held an arm out toward the old waiting room.

"This is a police matter," Amy said, while silently giving a raspberry to Paul, "we need some privacy."

"Sure." She turned back to the stairs and said, "My room is on the second floor. Come on!"

As they climbed the stairs Amy thought to Paul, *Bad boy! I'll tell Christine you were ogling her.*

Just because I'm on a diet, he thought back, *doesn't mean I can't look at the menu.*

Parker led down the hallway to where her dorm room door was standing open. "It's not much, but it's home," she said.

Amy took in the typical college decor that reminded her of her own dormitory life at the University of New Orleans Lakefront more than a decade earlier. The big difference was how tidy everything was.

The woman took some textbooks off a chair at a desk, then sat in the one catty-corner. "Did that pastor have any family?" she asked.

"I don't know," Amy said, shaking her head. "I'm grateful somebody else has to break the news to any relatives."

"So how can I help you?"

Paul was taken with how alert and engaged the woman was. Sparkly blue eyes over a nose as small as Amy's, a serious expression on her face. She pushed a few stray strands of her shoulder-length blonde hair behind her ear.

Before Amy could begin, Paul took the lead. "I saw you on the TV news Sunday. I am a fan of Captain Reynolds and all who know him."

A grin broke the woman's face. "It's all shiny on Serenity," she laughed. "We're all Browncoats now."

"Libertarian?"

"Absolutely. Just leave me alone."

Amy shouted Paul's name silently. *Quit making a pass at her! I've got work to do.* He withdrew and let Amy begin the serious interview.

"Did you notice anything unusual or troubling at the demonstration?"

Parker laughed, a long, deep laugh. "Did you see the fellow with the fairy wings? The naked drum circle? Everything there was unusual."

"Let me rephrase that," Amy laughed. "Did you see anything that struck you as out of place, or dangerous, or intimidating?"

"A couple of things." From her closed hand she stuck out an index finger and said, "Some of the people demonstrating against the wedding. There were some ugly signs." She stuck out a second finger and went on, "Some of the people supporting the wedding. Some of them had signs or chanted slogans about homosexuality being better than heterosexuality. They made me even more uncomfortable."

But she was in favor of the wedding, Paul mused to Amy. *I don't get it.*

Parker seemed not to notice Amy nodding at Paul's silent comment. Amy said, "But I saw you on TV. We thought you were quite eloquent defending Gina and Shawna. I guess I assumed you and Kendall were, you know–"

"Oh, we are. But when I talked to the reporter I was defending individual rights, not gay or lesbian or LGBT rights. Individuals are more important than groups. I'm attracted to who I'm attracted to, but that does not define who I am."

"This woman is wonderful," Paul whispered...out loud.

"What?"

"What?"

Parker stood up and stepped away. "Please explain yourself," she said. Her voice was not harsh, but her arms were folded in front of her chest.

You got me into this, Amy thought to Paul. *Get me out of it.*

As Paul took the lead, he got up from the chair to match Parker's position. "I am sorry," he said. "I talk to myself a lot. Usually I keep our mouth shut."

The two women stared at each other. Paul sighed and added, "I am impressed with your reasoning. I'm a Libertarian, too. Let's just say there's not a lot of support for our views in a police station." He noticed the beginning of a smile on Parker's face. "What I said out loud was unprofessional. I am sorry if I offended you."

"So, you're not hitting on me?"

He felt their face flush. "Not really," Paul said. "I, uh, I'm in a relationship. But I'm impressed with you."

Her smile grew. Parker let her arms down and said, "Apology accepted." Still standing, her mouth fell open. "Wait! You–you're the one who made the archbishop apologize!"

4All yours, Paul thought to Amy and retreated. Unprepared, she ad-libbed, "Uh, I was, umm, off-duty that day."

Parker took her seat again, and Amy followed suit. "So, why were you there? You can't be a cop if you're a lesbian, can you?"

"I'm friends with the bride and the bride," Amy replied. "I was trying to protect them from the worst of the demonstrators when the church dwarf spat on Shawna."

"Kendall said it was the bravest thing she'd ever seen."

Amy nodded, looking down. She was embarrassed by the praise because it was Paul who had challenged the archbishop. Then she went back to her interview. "Did you or your friend go into the church?"

"Not that day. I've been to worship there before, so I know where the side door is. We were on the Calhoun Street side of the walkway."

"Was there anything that you now think was suspicious? Dangerous? Out of place?"

Parker rested her head in her hand, rubbing the sides of her chin as she thought. "You know–this is going to sound silly–when Kendall and I first got there, we overshot the church and came up St. Charles from the Henry Clay Avenue side. There was a woman down the side of the church, near the door. She was retching into some bushes. Is that any help?"

"Actually, yes," Amy said as she opened her notebook. "You're not the first person to mention her, but you're the first to confirm that she was sick." She made a note. "Anything else?"

"Some woman in an atomic yellow dress. She made me wish I had my sunglasses. I overheard her talking to some people about someone getting killed, I thought it was a joke."

Paul thought, *Sam Atkins.*

Amy thought back, *How would Sam have known that Tibbs was dead? Unless maybe she's the one who killed her?*

Paul thought, *I want to ask her something. A serious question.*

Don't be crude, Amy replied silently, and stepped back internally.

"The other people that the TV crew showed. Did you see them?"

Laughing, she said, "Wasn't Sunchild great? I mean, he's an obvious goofball, but that was brave. Can you imagine doing something like that–damn near naked, with wings glued to your back, waving a home-made magic wand? My parents know my preference, but I'd die if they saw me behaving like that." She shook her head. "Actually, he was kind of sweet when we talked later."

Paul jotted down notes. The woman's smile turned into a curious frown. "You can write with both hands?"

Her question startled him so much he dropped their pen. As he bent over to retrieve it he said, "Uh, yeah. It's convenient. You ought to try it."

"Shiny."

You're blowing our cover, Amy thought to him. *I'm taking over.* Internally she pushed Paul back, but continued his line of questioning. "How about the angry, topless women?"

"I only saw them on the newscast. They were embarrassing."

Amy lifted one eyebrow. "How so?"

"They behaved like being lesbians is who they are. I think it's sad. There is so much more to life than who you sleep with."

Amy thought, *You want to write that one down?*

Sure. Don't want to fuck up our cover any worse. He scribbled in Amy's notepad.

Trashmouth, she thought, but she was smiling. Out loud, she asked, "What about those two men? Were they–"

"Mooks!" she called. "They were boorish college boys putting on a show for the camera. If they're gay then so is Captain Reynolds. Jerks."

Amy laughed. "That's what the News Director said about them. He only kept them in the broadcast because he thought they played the part so well."

They sat silently for a few moments. Finally Parker said, "I'm sorry Kendall hasn't come home yet. Is there anything else?"

Amy closed her notebook and stood up. "Just one thing, it's not police business." She saw the woman tense up, as if she were expecting Amy to make another pass at her. "When I graduated from college my dad gave me a string of pearls. I think I've worn them twice. On the newscast I noticed you and Kendall both wearing pearls, and you've got them on now. Do you always wear them?"

The woman stood with her arms folded in front of her. "Well, not in the shower, or when I play lacrosse. But, other than that, yes."

"It's classy," Amy said. "Do you think I can carry them off?"

Amy half expected the woman to laugh, but instead she let her arms fall and she seemed to be examining Amy's looks–black loafers, creased black slacks, and a starched blue dress shirt. Parker considered it, then said, "Not while you're wearing half a hardware store on your belt."

Amy looked down at her duty belt. Pistol, baton, handcuffs, flashlight, mace, phone, card case, and badge, all in separate holsters attached to her 2-1/4 inch black nylon duty belt. Disappointed, she looked back at Parker and said, hopefully, "Sometimes I wear a long skirt with all this gear in thigh holsters."

"Yes. Pearls would work with that."

Paul felt Amy take a deep breath and experience a mixture of relief and gratitude. She nodded and said, "Thank you. Oh–" she fished a business card out of that particular holster "–if you think of anything else that might help us, please call me."

"Let me get you back to the stairs," she offered, and followed Amy out the door and down the hall. "Would you tell Maxine I'm not under arrest or anything? She's a great desk sergeant, but she likes to worry about all of us in JL House."

"Sure. Thanks for your time." Amy waved, then headed down the stairs. *She thought you were flirting with her* she thought to Paul. *You nearly made her too defensive to interview.*

I was flirting, he thought back, sheepishly. *She's a pretty woman, but that's not the big deal. She was so alert! So involved in the world! And she's a Firefly fan. All that's more appealing to me than just a pretty face or a hot body.*

Next time, keep my mouth shut when you have those thoughts, okay?

Back to the main level of the dormitory, Amy returned to the reception desk. Before the older woman behind the counter could speak, Amy said, "Parker and Kendall are not under arrest. They were witnesses at a crime scene, and I wanted to find out if they noticed anything that might help our inquiries."

"You could have told me that," the woman huffed. "Here I was so worried about them. We expect Sophie Newcomb women to behave better than that."

"Better than what? Most witnesses have no idea a crime is about to be committed."

"Like I say, you could have told me."

Amy thought, *I want to pistolwhip this granny,* and she heard Paul counter with, *Ooh, can I hold the gun when we do it?*

"Sorry, Maxine, but now you know."

The woman smiled, but it was not appealing. "They're booting your car," she gloated. "I told you you shouldn't park like that."

Amy pivoted to look out the door toward her old Benz. A campus guard was still crouched by her right front tire. "Hey!" she called as she ran out to the sidewalk. "Hey! Police! Stop!"

The guard looked around for the voice. Amy's hands were on her pistol and baton to keep them from bouncing as she ran. "What are you doing?" she shouted.

Wearily, the guard stood up to deal with another pissed-off student who probably thought her daddy would raise a stink with the school over a parking violation. As Amy reached him, he said, "I'm booting an illegally parked car. You got a problem with that?" He was six inches taller than Amy, maybe twenty-five years old, in a blue uniform with a tin badge that read "Campus Security."

She pulled her badge case from its holster and held it up in front of the man. "Official NOPD business," she said.

He swiveled his eyes from the ID to her face and back. "I'm, uh, I'm not allowed to take a boot off without collecting eighty dollars. Otherwise my boss'll kill me."

Paul was even angrier than Amy and jumped to lead. "You son-of-a-bitch. Interfering with a police investigation is a felony. Is your boss going to stand trial in your place?"

He heard Amy think, *Well done. Make him think his choices are getting fired or going to jail. Poor bastard.*

"I've got my instructions," he said stiffly, and bent down to finish installing the boot.

"Hold out your hands," Paul said, sounding like Amy. He was holding her handcuffs.

"No, wait!" the guard said, standing back up. "This is my job and–"

"I said, hold out your hands." Paul was pulling on each cuff, noisily testing the short chain that connected them.

"No, wait!" The guard parked his hands in his armpits. "You don't understand!"

"I understand you are disobeying police instructions and resisting arrest. Hold. Out. Your. Hands."

When it looked as if the guard might start crying, Amy thought, *Let me take it from here.*

"Sir," she said, "if you remove that boot, your boss will never know. But if you leave it, he might notice that you're in a holding cell at the Rampart Street station." She looked up at him, head tilted and eyebrows raised to prompt a response. She folded the cuffs back into their holster.

Silently he dropped to his knees and took the device off her car. Amy patted him on the shoulder and said, "Thank you, sir. I appreciate your flexibility."

Paul added, "Why don't you explain to Maxine over there what happened?"

"Who's Maxine?" He was looking at the ground.

"The desk sergeant in JL House."

"Oh, Mrs. Lacobee. She's the one who phoned security."

"So she said." Amy waved and opened the driver's door. "Thanks." In her rearview mirror she saw the guard, still holding the bright yellow boot, walking toward the dormitory's rear entrance.

Paul looked at their right wrist, where he had written Amy's interview schedule. "Kelly the topless Sharpie girl at three o'clock. It's only one-thirty. Now what?" He turned on the glow plugs, counted to eight, and mashed the starter button. The engine cranked with its typical erratic mixture of pops, booms, and purrs.

"We're near the church," Amy said aloud. "Let's see how Associate Pastor Drew Malone is doing."

The houses and apartments got bigger and nicer as they drove down Broadway Street. The enormous Baptist church complex on the left was the landmark for St. Charles Avenue, and Paul made the left turn to head for the Metropolitan Community Church, just two days earlier the site of Shawna and Gina's wedding, of the demonstration, and of the murder of Pastor Riley Tibbs. They passed the top of Audubon Park, with its long, flat expanse of grass bleaching yellow in the summer sun; opposite was the elaborate wrought iron 'Audubon Place' arch and two guard houses protecting the entrance to the millionaires' row of homes shared by Tulane and Sophie Newcomb, with a few privately owned mansions to boot.

"I hope she's doing okay," Paul said. "She was brave to go ahead with the wedding after seeing the other pastor dead."

"If anybody can handle dead people, you'd expect it to be preachers," Amy replied. Then, thinking of how her father had inured her to gore and death, she added, "Or a doctor's daughter."

Paul turned down Henry Clay and pulled the right wheels up on the curb between a pair of 'No Parking, No Stopping, No Standing' signs. He withdrew to let Amy slap her police business sign on the dashboard and set the emergency blinkers. "Duke said that Drew was being cooperative, but that she wasn't any help. Let's see what kind of mess she's in."

She walked back to St. Charles to enter the front door of the church, but it was locked. *That's not very welcoming,* she thought to Paul, then tugged at the door again to be sure.

Tuesday is for AA meetings, he thought back, remembering his younger years in West Virginia, *but not for church, I guess.*

"I'll try the back door," she said out loud, and walked down the side of the building. She kept a wide berth of the bushes where, according to Parker Frye, a mystery woman had been spewing two days earlier. Amy held her breath until she was able to open the side door.

"Hello?" she called out. The hallway was brightly lit but silent. Remembering her path to Pastor Tibbs' office, she went to the stairwell and walked up the one flight.

Someone must be here, Paul thought as they entered the upstairs hall. *Otherwise the side door would be locked, too.*

Nodding, Amy walked down the hall toward the scene of the crime, the place where Pastor Tibbs had breathed her last. "Hello?" she called ahead, "Drew? Somebody? Anybody?" When she turned a corner she was surprised to see a pile of trash blocking the hall. Paul thought, *That open door–that's the pastor's office, isn't it?* As they approached it, a book flew out and hit the wall opposite before falling onto the trash pile.

"Hello?" she said, as a purple and green dream catcher hit her in the arm. "Hey!" Paul shouted in surprise and anger, "What the hell?"

The chubby face of Drew Malone stuck out the doorway. "I didn't know anyone was there," the associate pastor said. "Can I help you?" and she came out into the hallway.

It was Paul who said, "I was hoping you could help me out. I'm a single mom with two toddlers and they're hungry." He heard Amy think, *What?*

"Bless you," Malone said, "but you can get the best relief for that at the Union Mission or at the parish foodstamps office." The woman, with her absurdly short crewcut, tilted her head and stared. "Wait. I know you. You're, you're–"

Amy kicked her left ankle with her right foot as she took back the lead. "I'm Detective Clear with NOPD. I was here on Sunday."

"Yes! That's it! Do you really have two kids?"

"No," Amy said, staring at the carpet. "That was a very bad idea of a joke." She looked back up and went on, "How are you doing? It's been an awful few days."

"Ah. Well, the congregation is in shock, as you can imagine. I hope we get a good turnout for supper tomorrow night. I plan on leading grief and comfort worship."

Without her liturgical robe, the Associate Pastor was wearing civvies–black and red plaid shorts that went to her knees, and a white polo shirt that emphasized her girth. Apart from her obesity, Malone looked entirely unremarkable. She fished a Tic-Tac container out of the right front pocket of her shorts and spilled a few of the pills into her palm.

"What's with all this stuff?" Amy asked, motioning toward the trash in the hall.

She sighed. "I'm cleaning out Riley's office." She ducked her head and wiped at her eyes. "The Elders met yesterday and asked me to serve as interim pastor while they put a search committee together. The MCC is all about committees." She leaned her head back and poured more of the candy mints into her mouth.

"You're throwing out books?" Amy bent over and picked up the one she'd seen bounce off the wall a few moments earlier: *Biblical Theology of the New Testament* by Charles Ryrie. She lifted the cover and it fell open to a well-worn page with someone's hand-written notes in the margin. "'Beyond all question, the Gospel of Matthew exerts a major influence simply because it stands first in the New Testament[1],' Amy read aloud. "In my family we give books away, but we don't trash them."

"Are you kidding?" Drew answered. "That's obsolete. It's from the '50s. Theology is all about new ideas and proving the previous generation of commentary wrong."

It was Paul who said, "I didn't realize they were adding new books to the Bible."

The Pastor stood with hands on hips. "Riley was a great leader, but she went to seminary in the '80s. Some of her concepts were a bit fuddy-duddy. It's time to get with the twenty-first century."

Amy dropped the book back onto the pile of debris. "Donate it to an orphanage?" Paul suggested.

"I won't be responsible for warping the religious prejudices of the next generation," Malone replied as she stepped back into the office and resumed her triage of its contents. "Besides, most of this–" she pointed back at the midden in the hallway "–is personal stuff that Riley's partner didn't want."

Amy followed her into the office. "So, what's going to happen to this room?"

"As soon as I clean it out to the point that I can vacuum it, it's my office. And I've got a sermon to write for Sunday."

Amy heard Paul think, *That's cold. Two days later and she's moving in?*

"I guess life goes on," Amy replied, but aloud.

"Whether we want it to or not," said Drew. "Somebody's got to preach and lead communion." She tossed a stack of *Preaching Magazines* out the door.

"When's the funeral?" Amy asked.

"Memorial service this Sunday," she replied while examining another pile of magazines. "Her partner said Riley wanted to be cremated."

Amy scratched her head, then smoothed her hair back in place. "I guess you're doing okay, then. I was concerned about you."

"Bless you," Drew said, looking up from her cleaning. "I'm broken up about it. Riley was a mentor to me." She sighed. "I've lost my parents and a sister," she went on. "You learn to cope."

Paul thought to Amy, *I've lost my own body. I guess I've learned to cope with that.*

"Look, Drew," Amy began, "about Sunday. Did you notice any outsiders in the church? Aside from in the sanctuary for the wedding."

"I don't think so," she said, returning to surveying and evaluating the clutter. "The shock of seeing Riley may have pushed everything else out of my head."

That don't smell right, Paul thought.

Hush, Amy thought back. Then, to the Associate–no, the *Interim* Pastor–she said, "I meant to ask you. Have you spoken to anyone from a gay rights group called Advancement Trust NOLA?"

"I've never heard of them," Drew said. She crouched in front of a set of shelves to declutter the bottom shelf. "They're good guys?"

"Yes," Amy answered, watching the pastor's enormous back. "How about a woman named Sam Atkins?"

"Holy mother of Jesus!" Malone exclaimed and jumped up. "We've got mice down there!" She looked around for a tool or a weapon, then grabbed a rattan flyswatter from a higher shelf. "Shoo! Shoo! You vermin!" she shouted, slapping at the bottom shelf with the swatter.

Amy stepped back, not being much of an animal lover. "Did they bite you?" she asked.

Still staring down at the bottom shelf, the pastor said, "No. Just scared me." She turned to look at Amy and said, apologetically,

"They're all God's little friends, but rodents spread disease. Plague." She shuddered.

Paul took the lead to say, "Sam Atkins. Did you speak to her?"

There was a noticeable pause before she answered, "Who? I don't think so."

"A woman in a screaming yellow dress. She said she saw you in the rest room on Sunday."

Shaking her head, Drew said, "I don't remember seeing anybody."

All things being equal, Paul thought, *I'll believe Drew over Sam.*

Amy kept the lead. "Well, I'm glad you seem to be doing okay. If you think of anything that might help us, call me or Lieutenant Cranston." She dropped a card on the corner of the desk. "Like, if you remember seeing anyone who didn't belong in the, uh, the non-public part of the church."

"Sure. Thank you for checking on me, Detective. And may the love of our risen Lord–"

Amy held up their hand to stop her. "Please. Twelve years of Catholic school. Spare me."

"Whatever. You'll excuse me if I don't see you out, but I'm kind of up to my elbows in this cleaning." She flashed a smile, then tossed a coffee mug into the hallway; the handle broke off when it bounced off the book.

Going down the stairs and walking back to the car, Paul thought, *She never asked about the investigation. That's weird.*

You're right! Amy thought back. *That didn't register on me, but you're right. Most people, the first thing they say is, 'Have you caught the killer?'*

So, we've got another suspect, Paul thought as Amy unlocked the Benz and turned off the flashers. *But what motive could Drew possibly have?*

It was Amy who mashed the glow plug button. "She said Riley had some fuddy-duddy ideas."

"So fuddy-duddy that she was ready to conduct a same-sex wedding ceremony and defy state law. Besides, Drew called her her mentor."

Paul cranked the noisy diesel engine, then drove them back onto Henry Clay Avenue. "So, are we ready to visit Sharpie girl?"

Sharpie girl Kelly Overton lived in part of Esplanade Ridge, in a duplex she shared with two other women. Paul drove them up Rampart, past the station house, and turned left onto Esplanade Avenue. They passed empty lots, typical two-story houses probably carved into triplexes, and more empty lots. They drove under I-10, across Claiborne, and emerged in a strikingly better neighborhood. On the right was the Baldwin house, a two-story Greek Revival Italianate mansion from the eighteen-hundreds, now used as a religious retreat. Beyond it were more huge structures, still stately on the outside although subdivided internally to quadruplexes and more.

A yellow brick hole-in-the-wall, with balcony for living quarters on the second floor, was the landmark to turn right down Galvez. Before they reached Kerlerec they saw gated homes with landscaped lawns on the left, while on the right were smaller houses still recovering from hurricanes in 2029 and 2030, although each was surrounded by what looked like new chain-link fence.

Kerlerec Street between Galvez and Johnson was filled with common duplexes, houses with different street numbers for each apartment. Paul parked in front of 2014 and set the blinkers.

It was a double shotgun cottage. One story tall, each side had a door and floor-to-ceiling window on the raised brick foundation. They were so common that Amy knew before she got out of the car what she would find: a parlor with an office or spare bedroom on the right; the living room; the narrow kitchen, with a door to the only bathroom; beyond the kitchen, one more bedroom. If it was a rare, fancy cottage, there might be yet another bedroom, but the absence of a front porch suggested the additional sleeping quarters were not likely

Paul held their right hand up so Amy had to see their wrist, with the schedule he had written there. "Sharpie girl 3 PM," it said, and it was ten minutes before the hour.

"Thank you, mister appointments secretary," she said with a laugh. "If you're lucky, she's still topless."

"I'll behave," he thought to her. "I'm dying to know if her tits are pixilated, or if that was just something they did in post-production."

Amy straightened her duty belt, then crouched for a moment to loosen her underwear. *You see my boobs all the time,* she thought. *Are they pixilated?*

"God, no. Just freckled."

Just so. She went up the half dozen brick steps to number 2014 and rang the after-market doorbell. She was holding the door shutter open.

She heard movement, and a female voice calling, "Who's there?"

"Detective Clear, NOPD," she shouted back.

A moment later there were bolts thrown, and a door chain dropped, and a dead bolt turned. A dark-haired woman Amy's height opened the door; she was wearing a low-cut sleeveless blouse over yellow athletic shorts. As ashes dropped from the cigarette between her lips she opened the door inward and stepped back to let Amy in. "I was washing dishes," she said. "Come sit with me and we can talk."

The woman led the way through the living room and into the kitchen, and motioned to a bar stool in front of the stove. A bright red tea kettle was whistling over a high flame.

"Want some tea?" the woman asked. "I'm still waking up."

Amy shook her head and said, "Thanks, but no. I'm on duty. Are you Kelly Overton?"

"That's me!" she said, pouring boiling water over two tea bags in a 'Seven Seas Bar NOLA' mug. "You didn't recognize me?"

It was Paul who blurted out, "Not with your clothes on, no." He heard Amy scream silently at him.

"That's rather judgmental," Overton said, her posture stiffening.

"Just descriptive," Amy defended themself. "I'm sure you've heard by now that the preacher at that church was killed while the demonstration was going on. I'm talking to some people who were there on Sunday. I hope you can help us identify a suspect."

"Not me," she said. She blew on the tea and took a careful little sip. The temperature or the taste made her wince. She opened the cabinet below the sink and retrieved a pint bottle of rum. "I was busy giving the finger to the patriarchy. Wasn't it great that those women got married? And–oh–" she looked up at Amy while she spiked her tea "–maybe a cop doesn't agree."

"Actually, I'm friends with the brides. Did you go inside the church on Sunday?"

Shaking her head, she said, "Against my religion to go in any church." Cigarette ashes splashed onto her tea. She stirred them in.

Paul took out Amy's notebook to take notes while Amy continued, "Okay. Did you see anyone go in the church?"

She took a long sip of tea, then topped the mug off with some more rum. "Sure. Fifty, a hundred, I don't know. Lots and lots of people went in to see the wedding." She turned on water in the sink and went back to washing dishes.

Amy spoke louder to be heard over the running water. "How about the side door? Did you see anyone using it?"

"There's a side door?"

Paul thought to Amy, *Not the most observant witness.*

"How about, did you see anyone who seemed out of place at the demonstration? Creepy? Dangerous? Intimidating?"

"All those religious assholes," Kelly answered, cigarette wagging as she spoke around it. "Patriarchal ball-busters. They think all a woman is good for is cooking and making babies. They probably think you're going to hell because you're a cop and you work for a living."

"Do you have any male friends?" Paul asked. Amy rolled her inside eyes and thought, *Don't mess this up.* He thought back, *How can I ruin it? It's not going anywhere.*

"Sure. I know lots of the gay boys who were there. They're as marginalized as women are." She put a clean plate in the drainboard and turned off the water. When she tried to take her smoke in her fingers she cried, "Fuck!" and dropped the butt into the sink. "And that's my last ciggie." She turned to Amy and said, "I'll bet you're a regular girl scout, but do you have any cigarettes? Can I bum one?"

"Sorry."

"Gimmie a minute. Maybe Hayden left some when she went to work." Kelly disappeared into the hallway and the bedroom beyond.

They heard the woman cursing and commenting on her search. *She's a little out of control,* Amy thought. *Rum in the middle of the afternoon? What kind of life do you think she leads?*

She paid more attention to the Women's Studies teacher than we did, Paul answered silently. *I start to itch when I hear people use the word 'patriarchy'.*

"No! Virginia Slims? Virginia fucking Slims? Hayden, you are such a tool!" Kelly reappeared with a long, skinny cigarette. "And it's menthol! These are the most–the most–the most–" She turned on a stove burner and leaned over to light the smoke in the blue flame, then rocked back to make sure it was lit by taking a deep drag. Immediately she coughed; her eyes watered and she smacked her lips, trying to find and oust a strand of stray tobacco that likely wasn't there, considering the cigarette was filtered. "A man had to have invented menthol," she finally said. "As soon as we're done I'm going over to Rosie's to get a pack of real cigarettes instead of this shit." She took another puff, a little more cautiously.

Amy was trying not to smile. Not only was she amused by Kelly's performance, but she was hearing Paul laughing inside, silent to everybody but her. "Are you okay?" she finally said, and pretended to scratch her nose while she really was hiding her smile from Kelly.

"Yeah. I can't believe my roommate smokes this shit." She held the long, skinny thing out, watching white smoke curl off the burning ember. "So now I smoke this shit. Kill me, will you?" She parked the cigarette between her lips and said, "What were you asking me?"

"Was there anything at the demonstration that struck you as out of place? Dangerous, even. Anything?"

"When Hayden and Morgan and me took off our shirts, the men on the anti-side went crazy. They were calling us sluts and whores, but I swear I could feel their eyeballs rubbing up against my tits."

Paul began, "A friend of mine was wonder–"

"And Hayden took a marker and wrote 'Make your own fucking sandwich' across my stomach. That wound 'em up even more."

He tried again. "So, were there a lot of people without–"

"Even the news guy who put us on camera was a Neanderthal. I was so pissed by the time they talked to us that I just ranted–" she waved her hands, scattering cigarette ash across the kitchen "–and raved about how heterosexual intercourse is a way men control women and hold us down, and that..." Kelly trailed off, smiling as she was remembering. "I had a blast," she said. "That was so much fun. Hayden and Morgan and me came back here and fucked for hours, we were so turned on."

Amy heard Paul still laughing and now hooting inside. She was shaken by the different parts of her own response–embarrassment that a stranger was so open about any sexual activity; surprise that anyone could be sexually excited by anger; sadness that Kelly was driven by hatred of men; and anger that the woman seemed to be so willfully contrary. She shook her head and got back to her earlier question: "But did you see anything that made you worry about an imminent danger? Anyone who looked like a murderer?"

"Nah. The hippies were fun, and the anti-people were all pussies. I didn't see any trouble. Otherwise I wouldn't have had to make some."

Paul wrote in the notebook with their left hand, even though he was still snickering silently. "What do you do?" Amy asked her. "Three of you here?"

"Yup." She picked up her nearly forgotten mug of rum tea and drained it. "I'm a bartender in the Quarter, at the Seven Seas. Usually I work seven at night to four AM, but tonight I'm the night manager, got to be in at five-thirty."

"And your roomies? Are they–"

"Hayden's a waitress at an Italian restaurant, and she's taking some medical classes at Blue Cliff. And Morgan has a four-to-one shift at a cat house on Dumaine Street. Oh–" the woman laughed, "I guess you didn't hear me say that."

"I don't work vice. What kind of rent do you pay? This is a nice place."

"It's a grand a month, and that includes utilities. I don't know how any one person could afford it, but it's easy for the three of us." She took a last drag off her scavenged cigarette and flicked it into the sink. They heard the hiss of hot coal meeting wet porcelain.

Amy pulled some business cards out of her belt as she stood up. "Thanks for talking to me, Kelly. Talk to your roomies. If anyone saw anyone going in the side door at the church, call me. If anything made their spidey sense tingle, call me. Okay?"

"Yeah, I'll tell Hayden. I, uh, I might not tell Morgan that a cop was here, though."

"If it makes you feel better, I'm a detective, not a beat cop. She doesn't have to worry about me."

Kelly walked Amy to the doorway. When Paul said, "You know, I'm dying to know–" Amy feared the worst, so she tried to speak. Since both of them could not talk out loud at the same time, the result was a cough; and since Paul kept trying to talk and Amy kept trying to block him, they coughed for a long time.

Kelly said, "It must be the menthol. I'm sorry I did that to you."

In the parked Benz on Kerlerec Street, with the doors locked and the windows rolled up, Amy shouted, "What were you trying to do?" She was twirling some hair around her right index finger. "You were going to ask–"

Since he couldn't speak while Amy was yelling, Paul thought to her, *I was going to ask her how she did that thing with her tits on TV. You know, obscuring them.*

"Better than I feared, but only marginally. Damn it, Paul, I'm a detective. I have to behave around suspects and witnesses. And that means YOU have to behave around them."

Is that a trick all women can do? Like, stick your thumb in your mouth and blow, and your nipples go all Renoir?

"Do what?" Amy said. "No! You idiot! No, all women can not do that." Paul's silliness was starting to win her over, as it often did.

"So, I want to know, could she do it? Can you?"

"Of course not!" she barked, but she was smiling.

"But you can do so many amazing things no one else can," Paul protested. "Have you ever tried to blur your boobs?"

"They're not as big as I'd like," she said. "If I blur them, they might disappear."

"Nah, that would be a violation of the Law of Conservation of Tits. You can look it up."

She shook her head, laughing. "Well, let me see," and she looked in the car's mirrors and craned their neck to see down the street. There were no pedestrians. Amy tilted the rear view mirror toward her and down. She undid the top several buttons of her shirt, then slid their hands inside and behind her to unclasp her bra. Another quick look in the side mirrors, and she let her bra drop. "Put my thumb in my mouth and blow?" she asked, and heard Paul silently say, *I hear that's how it works.*

She put their right thumb, 'her' thumb, in their mouth. She took a deep breath, then blew against it; since their mouth was closed, their cheeks and eyes bugged out, and her head began to spin.

Yes! Paul thought to her. *It works! Look!*

She did. *I don't see any difference.*

Ah. Freckles. My mistake. He was laughing inside.

Amy ended the experiment, holding her saliva-drenched thumb out while she tried to button her shirt back up. "Crap. I need my thumbs to do this." She left a wet splotch on the placket near the fourth button down.

About the time she finished a car was approaching on Kerlerec. Even though she had gotten all her buttons done, Amy held their folded arms in front of her chest until the vehicle had passed behind her.

"Let's you and me play tonight," Paul said.

Not if we're with your girlfriend, she thought back. Then, aloud, "Really. You can't talk to the people I interview like you do to me." She wiggled to let her bra fall to a less annoying place, then mashed the glow plug button. "My sense of humor is too weird for NOPD, that's why I quit the force. But yours makes mine look like that joke book I memorized when I was eleven."

"Ah. 'I can tell you like me, your tail is wagging.' Yeah, I remember some of them."

Hands on the steering wheel, she dropped their head into their arms to laugh. "Thanks," she said. "Most murder investigations are not this much fun." She looked ahead and pulled into the street for her appointment with Sunchild.

Paul led to drive, a task he relished. He traced around some side streets and finally headed northwest on Esplanade. A garish Tastee Restaurant on the right and a dull gray block of a rent- to-own place on the left were the landmarks for Broad Street. He had to make a right at the intersection and make a U-turn across the neutral ground, then head down Broad the way he really wanted to go. This is known as a New Orleans left turn.

As he drove, Amy used the luxury of the privacy of the car to talk out loud. "She wasn't any help. I hope Sunchild saw something."

"What did pearl girl say about her? That her and her friends were embarrassing because they came across as professional lesbians?"

"I do not have a dog in that fight," Amy answered. "Considering Christine, maybe you do."

He shrugged their shoulders as they passed storefronts, warehouses, and the occasional house that had been grandfathered when zoning was changed. Amy said, "Pull in at that Popeye's." As he drove into the parking lot he said, "Are you hungry again? I told you we should have gotten the full po-boy."

Silly boy, she thought. *I need the rest room to put my bra back on.*

When they resumed their drive, Paul said, "Kelly seemed scattered. Who drinks rum and tea an hour after waking up?"

"She said I was being judgmental."

"You were. You've got a brain, you should be judgmental." He stopped for a red light behind one of those creepy electric cars that don't make any noise. "People can live however they want, but they have to accept the consequences of their choices. If they're happy, fine. If they bitch, it's their problem." He let out the clutch. "And then it's your right to decide if they made bad choices."

Amy smiled inside; it was a conversation they had had many times before. "That's not very understanding of your fellow man."

He snorted. "The older I get, the more I miss my cat. You run out of patience with stupidity."

"So, you're saying Kelly is stupid?"

He thought. *Nah, not really. Now, if her goals are the same as mine–a long life free of drama–then she's making stupid choices, smoking and drinking. She may be intelligent, but she's not using it the way I would.*

"And if her goals are different from yours?" Amy wished more people would talk to her about interesting things the way Paul did. "Then what?"

"Say she wants to have a good time getting drunk all the time. As long as she doesn't go 'oh woe is me' when the doc tells her that she's destroyed her liver and she's only got six months to live. She lived the way she wanted and it was her choice. But if she moans about how unfair life is, fuck her."

"Trashmouth," Amy said, but she was giggling.

The familiar complex of parish and city courthouses was the landmark for Tulane Avenue, where Paul turned right. In the three years Amy served as a detective with the parish police, they spent many a day in the waiting rooms, standing by to be called as a prosecution witness. With his antipathy toward most things police, Paul hated being inside those oppressive buildings, with their mashup of Greek neoclassical and Art Deco Minimalist styles. The only way he liked to see them was like this, disappearing in the rear view mirror.

When they were three miles down Tulane Amy said, "Sunchild's job is this side of I-10, but just barely. And he said–"

Paul interrupted, *Do we bear left or right?*

"Right! Right!" she shouted. Paul did as he was told, and she added, "We almost ended up in Kenner." They had managed to avoid the Airline Highway ramp.

He slowed until Amy recognized a street number, 4213. If the building hadn't been fifty years old it would have been called modern architecture, but what appeared to be steel board-and-batten construction was rusted and weather stained. There were no windows on the front face.

To their left were dark recesses beneath the Airline Highway ramp and the elevated portion of the interstate highway. Piles of trash were in the street. Amy saw two private homes at the end of the block with brightly painted burglar bars. "Oh God, don't park here," she said. "Didn't we pass some shopping center?"

Paul made a three-point turn and made their way back to the mostly deserted retail center one block over; a Nike factory outlet was the anchor store. He parked the old yellow Benz near the side street that separated the lot from the block where Sunchild's office was. Amy put the NOPD Business sign on the dashboard and set the blinkers before getting out and locking the car. She straightened the hardware hanging from her duty belt. "The pistol's on your side," she said, so Paul rested their left hand–'his' hand–on the gun butt. "It's a pretty day for a walk in the neighborhood."

For a walk in a war zone, Paul thought back as they moved toward the building that housed Carpe Byte. *Trash in the streets. If you're poor, you've got less stuff, so why is their trash over there?*

"Maybe the garbage man is afraid to come here. If it weren't for you and Rosckette, I would be."

Feh! he thought back. *It's broad daylight. And if Sunchild can come and go without being murdered twice a week, it ought to be safe enough for you and me.*

There was a small brass plaque next to the door. '4213 - Carpe Byte – Ring' it said, in fancy engraved calligraphy.

Ring what? Paul thought.

Amy tried to run her fingertips across the lettering, to feel the engraving, and was startled when the plate sank under her touch. "What the hell?"

A moment later the door opened three inches on a stout chain. The man she saw in the gap said, "What's the password?"

Amy said, "Password?" Immediately, Paul led to say, "Oh, no, you don't, sir. I shall never be tricked into telling it. It's a secret."[2]

The piece of visible face said, "A name would be a help."

Amy held up her badge case. "Detective Clear, New Orleans police. I'm here to see Sunch-uh, Larry Weisblatt."

"Weisberg," the slice corrected. The door closed, the chain dropped, and the door opened wide. "You may have noticed the neighborhood," he added. He was taller than Amy, musclebound, with a swarm of tattoos visible on arms and neck where his shirt ended.

As she entered, it was Paul who said, "You look like you wouldn't be frightened by a bad section of town."

When he closed the door he turned the bolt and replaced the chain. "I can take care of myself, but I don't look for trouble," he said. "It's smart to know when you're in a place where trouble looks for you. Follow me." He led her to a skeletal metal staircase. As they got about twelve feet off the ground, they could see down into the huge undivided space below. It was empty but for some tables standing on end in a corner.

"I don't get it," Amy said. "Why is Carpe Byte here? A crappy area, unnecessary square footage–it doesn't make sense."

"Ask the boss," her guide answered. "I just work here."

They alit on the second floor, at the beginning of a carpeted hallway. She could see doorways, seven or eight on each side. In the blue-tinged fluorescent lighting she got a better look at Mister Tattoo: at least six feet tall, muscles rippling under his shirt, short, wide neck, and a Mohawk haircut–as well as skin art–disappearing into the neck of his polo shirt. To Paul she thought, *Part-time job at the circus as the tattooed man?*

She heard Paul reply, *Wouldn't it be funny if his only tattoos are the ones we can see? And the rest of him is hairless pink?*

She considered it and winced.

"Larry's the third office on the left," their guide said. "I've got to get back to work." He went back down the stairs.

Amy knocked on the frame of the open door before what she was seeing registered on her. Sunchild was hunched over a keyboard, engrossed in whatever he was working on.

He was wearing a shiny blue evening gown. It was an ornate off-the-shoulder job with spaghetti straps.

A second look showed the straps were a home-made after-market addition of blue insulated wire with alligator clips on both ends, holding up a bodice that his natural anatomy could not.

The man turned his head toward the knock; she saw the confusion as he changed his focus from the nearby computer screen to the more distant doorway. "C–can I help you?" he asked, distracted.

Amy ignored Paul's silent laughter. "Larry? I'm Detective Clear. We talked this morning?"

It took a few seconds for recognition to cross his face. "Oh, right!" He looked around his office. "Dump that stuff off that chair," he pointed, "and drag it over here. Do you mind if I work while we talk?"

While Amy tilted the chair to drop a huge stack of greenbar onto the floor, Paul said, "I really would like your attention for this. It's a murder investigation." He lifted the chair and sat it alongside Larry, but facing him.

"Well, give me a minute then. I'm just about ready to let this compile."

While he worked, Amy made herself comfortable and opened her notebook. *You want to take notes?* she thought; she heard Paul's silent assent.

With a dramatic flourish the man hammered the Enter key and sat back, satisfied to see the compiler going to work on his code. He kicked his chair back on its casters, but when he pivoted to face Amy, one of the wheels caught in his skirt. "Oh, poo," he blurted. "That's the tenth time today that's happened." He lifted himself out of the chair with his knees bent, like a horseback rider posting, so he could free the hem of his gown. He sat back down and lifted the skirt to examine it, exposing a hairy leg and more.

He's as good in person as he was on TV, Paul thought to Amy, chuckling.

"If I had a sewing kit I'd let you borrow it," Amy said, helpfully.

"Oh, I've got one here somewhere," he said. "I just don't have the right color thread here. This is Royal Blue. Isn't it a pretty color?"

Paul led to say, "It looks very striking on you. The whole ensemble." Somehow he kept from laughing out loud.

"Oh, thanks!" Sunchild beamed.

"I saw you on the news on Sunday," Amy began. "I'm sure you've heard by now that a pastor was killed at the church. I'm hoping you can help us solve it."

"That was so sad," Sunchild said, looking as if he was about to cry. "It was such a pretty day, and there were all those pretty people there, and we all were having such a pretty time. It was–it was–" and, by damn, he began to weep.

Paul closed his inside eyes, annoyed by the effeminate dress, speech, and tears. Amy was moved by his sadness, but she wanted answers to some questions. She tried distraction: "Tell me about what you saw at the demonstration."

The tears stopped and he broke into a smile. "Oh, lots and lots of my friends were there. Vick brought a boombox and was dancing, and Jayden had a gallon of soap and was blowing the best bubbles, and Avery–well, Avery was just Avery. It was so neat."

"Did you go inside the church?" Even though it was Amy who asked, Paul was twirling a pen through the fingers of their left hand.

"Oh, sure! I figured if a bathroom was going to be safe, it was one at a church."

"How did you–"

"I had to run an absolute gauntlet of all those bad anti-gay people because the door was on their side. People were saying ugly things to me. I waved my magic wand at them but they didn't go away."

"So you went inside. Did you see anything, ooh, suspicious? Unusual?"

"Oh, I liked that it was so quiet in there. I saw a couple of people in long black robes, and a lady in a yellow dress, and they smiled when they saw me so I waved my wand at them. And the bathroom smelled good." Larry glanced at his computer monitor to make sure the compiler was still at work.

Paul held up their left index finger as if to tell Sunchild to wait while he thought to Amy, *The people in robes had to be Riley and Drew. And Sam was in a yellow dress that day. But Sam said she never talked to Tibbs or Malone. And Drew said she didn't see Sam or anybody in the non-public areas. You'd expect even a lesbian preacher would notice a nearly naked man with a magic wand and wings taped to his back.*

You would, Amy agreed silently. To Larry she said, "Did they say anything to you? Or did you speak to them?"

"Oh, no. They all seemed happy, and I was happy, and there wasn't anything needed to be said."

"What did they look like?"

He thought. "The yellow lady was really tall. The ladies in the robes, one of them had white hair, like my grammy." He thought more. "The other one was fat. I mean, really, really fat."

Amy coughed because she and Paul both attempted to say "Drew" at the same time. Finally Amy was able to say, "During the demonstration, did you see anyone that was suspicious looking? Dangerous?"

"Oh, yeah. There were all those people who were so serious, and they were dressed like for a funeral, and they looked like they were not happy. That can make you sick, you know."

It occurred to Amy that she was not likely to learn anything else from Larry. *What do I expect from someone who calls himself 'Sunchild'?* she thought to Paul. After a bit of silence she asked, "What do you do here?"

"Oh, I'm a programmer. I know a bunch of obsolete languages that sometimes come up. If you ever have to modify Autocode or Fortran or Pascal or Cobol, I'm your girl. And I know the current ones like Ruby and Python and XML. Last week I read about a new one called GOOfly that I want to play with." His eyes were shining with excitement. "I love doing this stuff. And they tell me I'm pretty good at it."

"And they don't mind you dressed like this?"

Sunchild laughed. "When I interviewed I wore a bridal gown and veil!"

"That's great," Amy offered. "A lot of places might have a problem with, well, you know."

"Oh, don't I know it. I lost my last job when I came out and tried wearing heels. How do women do that, anyway?"

"Very carefully," she answered. "I'm not so good at it myself." She heard Paul silently comment, *We damn near broke our ankles at your sister's wedding.*

"I'll let you get back to your work, Larr–uh, which do you prefer, Larry or Sunchild?"

"Oh, I made up Sunchild for the TV man, but I really like it, don't you? But you can call me whichever you like, it doesn't matter." His smile took up half his face.

Paul said, "Okay then, Whichever You Like, it was good to meet you." While Amy was thinking, *Shush! Shush!* Larry's smile faded into confusion. Then, "Oh, I get it. I told you to call me whichever you like." The smile began to return. "That's very clever. You're smart."

"Ain't I though?" Paul answered, then retreated behind Amy's internal pushing. She continued, "I appreciate your help. If you think of anything that might help us identify the killer, call me." She handed him a business card. Then, head tilted, she examined him. "You know, pearls would really make that outfit."

"Really?" Larry was beaming again. "I never thought of that. Oh, thanks!"

Walking up the little stub of Tulane Avenue back to the shopping center parking lot, Amy said, "I think he's from another planet. It's not just the clothes–like New Orleans hasn't been drag queen headquarters for a million years. I think he really believes that baton he had on the newscast was a magic wand."

If I were being kind, Paul thought back, *I'd call him childlike. But I'm not, so I'll call him a Looney Toon.*

Amy smiled and said, "So, Sunchild's a friend of your hero, Bugs Bunny?"

Aaaah! he shouted silently. *Get the bleach! I have to wash that image out of my brain!*

"Well, I think he's harmless. And sweet. And he gave me an important clue: he saw Riley and Drew with Sam Atkins."

"Granted, I'm not a preacher at a gay church, but I'm afraid I will never forget having seen Sunchild."

"Are you talking to me?" A frail black man lying in a pile of trash was looking up at Amy. There was a nearly empty pint bottle of Black Eagle bourbon by his hand.

Amy and Paul had been talking out loud because they thought they were unobserved; the man's question disoriented her for a moment. In the breech Paul took the lead. He stopped walking, faced the man, and jumped up and down in place. "Of course she's not my wife!" he shouted.

The only reason the man did not step back was that he was lying down. His creased face was clouded with confusion. When Paul saw him reach for his liquor bottle, he continued their walk to the car. "What were you saying?" he said out loud.

Silently Amy said, *Paul Owens, there are times when you are not a very nice person.*

"No one ever accused me of being perky."

Back in the privacy of Amy's car, Paul mashed the glow plug button and said, "Where to, boss?"

She looked at the car clock: it was four-fifteen. "Home, I guess. I want to call Duke to check in. And I think I want to make an appointment to visit Sam again tomorrow. People said she was dropping hints about killing someone on the pro-side to make a martyr."

Before Paul got out of the parking lot, Amy's phone rang. "It's Christine," she said, and let Paul take the lead to talk to his girlfriend.

"I sold it! I did it, Paulette! I sold it!"

"Honey, that's great! They wrote a check?"

"I'm looking at it now. It's the escrow money. They signed the contract. I'm so excited! My first house!"

"We should celebrate," Paul said. "Let's go get a steak."

"Not tonight," she said. "This Chinese family is as excited as I am and they're taking me to dinner."

Amy interrupted to say, "Christine, it's—"

"Hi, Amy!" Somehow, even on the phone, Christine always knew which one of them was leading. "I was just telling Paulette that I sold the house."

"I heard. Congratulations! All that studying for the real estate license was worth it."

"You two, come over tomorrow night and I'll cook that Mama Mia spaghetti Paulette taught me to make."

"Mama Rienzi," he corrected. "Sure. Amy and I will bring the Chianti. I'm so happy for you, Christine. And I'm proud of you."

"I love you, Paulette. See you tomorrow night."

He put the phone back in its holster. "Looks like it's you and me tonight," he said aloud. "Any thoughts?"

She sold a house. Crap. Now I'll never talk her into working for me.

"Amy!" he barked. "Can you at least pretend to be happy for her? This is a big deal to her."

"I know," she said as she let their shoulders slump. "And I am happy for her. Trouble is, I'm not happy for me." She fastened the seatbelt.

Sorry, Amy. We've got voice mail, you know. It's not like you need a real person to answer the business phone line.

"No. I mean, yes, you're right, I don't need a receptionist. But I want one. And Christine would be ideal."

"Ain't gonna happen," he said. "Shall we go home now?"

He felt Amy smile. "We can see if you have more luck than I did with that boob blurring thing. After all, they're your boobs, too."

Paul put the Benz in gear and went to the exit they used to enter the shopping center. He wound through the little neighborhood to get past the one-way streets, then made another right and headed south, toward the river and toward their house in the East Carrollton neighborhood. As they rode, he said, "We can stop at Rouses and get some wine."

Amy wrinkled their nose. "I was serious," she said. "We drink too much. It's messing up my complexion and it can't be good for my liver."

"But–but–but–"

Since Paul was using their mouth to stammer, Amy thought to him, *For real. I wake up with bags under my eyes, don't you see them? I'm thirty-four, I can't get away with what I did when I was twenty-four.*

"But–but–but–"

"Did you have a drinking problem when you had your own body?"

He said, "No. I drank, but if it had been a problem, Mary Pat would have let me know."

Amy thought, *I never asked you this. Did Mary Pat drink?*

"Of course she did. Everybody drinks. I don't think she had bags under her eyes, and she was in her fifties."

She was startled to feel Paul's defensiveness, but said, "You don't notice the bags under my eyes, either. I'm glad you won't notice when I'm an old hag, but crap and a half, I don't want to look like an old hag." If he hadn't been driving she would have folded their arms across their chest and tapped their foot.

"What! No, wait! What?" he sputtered. She felt anger join his defensiveness. "You'll never be an old hag. I'll always be forty-seven years older than you."

"Pull over!" she commanded.

"What? No, wa–"

PULL OVER! she screamed silently. If Paul weren't using their body to drive she would be twirling her hair around an index finger.

He swerved into the parking lot of a strip shopping center and pulled in next to a beat-up pickup truck with three Hispanic men in the cab and half-a-dozen more in the bed. Its engine was running noisily as they seemed to wait for someone.

He turned the Benz engine off and sat back. "What?" he spat out.

"We will not have anything to drink for the next seven days." Her anger was so strong that he could feel it. "Do you have anything to say about it?"

"Yes!" he shouted. "Your imagination is running away with you about beer and wine doing bad things to you, and it's not true!"

"Paul Owens," she said–a sure sign she was exasperated with him–"I am not talking about alcohol."

"You're not?" Then he shouted, "What the fuck <u>are</u> you talking about?" beating their hands against the steering wheel.

"Mister Trashmouth, I'm talking about I am in charge of this body!" Now Amy was slapping the steering wheel. She was rocking back and forth, shouting, "I said this body is not going to have any alcohol for a week! If you–Oh–" she reached for the rear view mirror and swiveled it so both of them could see their eyes "–Look! Look at these bags under my eyes. Are you looking at them?" She was waving their hands in the air.

Neither of them noticed that the men in the pickup truck were elbowing each other, watching with big smiles on their faces.

Sullenly he thought, *I see the same thing you see.*

"I don't want you to see them, I want you to look at them!" She placed their right index finger under their right eye and tugged the lower lid down. "Do you see this? What color is that, hmm? Is that the same lovely young pale skin of the rest of my face? Well, is it?" She leaned closer to the mirror to make the region of their eye even larger. "Well?"

I–I never noticed that before, he admitted softly.

"What? I didn't hear that, what did you say?"

There was a long pause as Amy stared at the Paul that she knew was behind their eyes in the mirror, and as he focused on the slightly puffy, slightly reddish area under their finger.

"I said I'm sorry."

"We're sorry, are we?" She let go of their lower eyelid, and finally did fold their arms in front of their chest. She was tensing all her muscles to prevent Paul from doing anything.

He thought to her, *So, this is what we've been arguing about? That I haven't noticed our eyes?*

"Kind of," she said, "but not entirely."

After some silence he said, "Give me a clue. Can I buy a vowel or something?"

"You want a clue? I'll give you a clue: who does this body belong to?" She straightened the rearview mirror while she waited for Paul's response.

You and me, he thought to her.

"You're half right," she corrected, out loud. "Want to try again?"

Oh, I get it. Yes, this body belongs to you.

"That's right, it belongs to me. You get to use it when I let you. And you know I'm willing to share. I don't think I'm unreasonable." She paused, waiting for a response.

Not at all, he thought, although a bit snarky. *You are generous and accommodating, fair and wise. You are the best master a slave ever had.*

"Damn right," she said, and laughed. "You could have been in your body when it died, but I took you in." Smiling, she looked around and saw the men in the pickup truck watching. She waved, and they looked away.

Her laugh allowed Paul to let go of his anger and resentment; he knew everything with Amy was going to be okay. He said, "Do we really have to have this fight over and over?"

"No. As soon as you realize I'm the boss of this body, we'll stop arguing."

He tried to nod, and Amy allowed him to move their head. "You'd think I'd have realized it by now. Okay, no booze for a week. But I promised Christine we'd bring Chianti tomorrow."

"Sure. We'll stop and get a bottle on the way to her place so there's no danger of us sampling it." She relaxed and added, "You want to get us home?"

His answer was to light the glow plugs, count to ten, and start the engine.

Once they were in the house, Amy sat on the sofa and called Duke Cranston. After swapping pleasantries, she said, "I talked to most of the entertainment from the newscast. Calvin and J'waun said Sam Atkins with Advancement Trust NOLA was at the demonstration. Sunchild said he saw Atkins inside the church with both pastors. All of that made me go back to talk to the Associate Pastor again–excuse me, she's been promoted, she's now the Interim Pastor. I heard something I don't like from her."

"She's nice enough," the lieutenant said, "but she hasn't been much help. I don't know if she's stupid or just not particularly observant."

"Or maybe hiding something. When I talked to her today she never asked how the investigation was going."

"That's a red flag," he said back. "Everybody, that's the first thing they ask."

"Exactly. Were you able to work on it today?"

"A little. I had to go back to that smash-and grab in the Garden District, seems it's part of a series. But I went through our files on the Militia of Louisiana. I got ten, twelve names of guys in the area that we think are members. You want them?"

"Absolutely. What's the worst that can happen. I interview them and they kill me. It's happened before."

Cranston said, "If you want me to talk to them, Queenie, you can just say so."

Amy said, "We can split them. Give me the ones in Orleans and St. Tammany Parish."

She heard him shuffling through papers. "Five, six, uh–six names. I'll have them for you in the morning."

"Thanks, Duke. Anything else?"

"Nah. We good, Queenie, we good."

When Amy closed her phone, she thought to Paul, "No Christine. No wine. Whatever will we do with ourselves tonight?"

"I think we should investigate a hypothesis of boob blurrage that tests the validity of the Law of Conservation of Tits."

"Lead me to the laboratory, doctor."

When Amy's alarm clock blared at six–fifteen, their thumbs were chapped, and she and Paul both were in excellent moods.

Amy got to the uniformed officers' bullpen while the duty officer was still taking roll and making assignments. When he called Duke Cranston's name, the lieutenant said, "Garden District street robberies. And MCC pastor homicide." A nod, a checkmark, and the next patrolman's name rang out.

"Good morning, Duke," she said, holding out a large Styrofoam cup of chicory coffee.

"How'd you know I'd need that?" he smiled, taking the coffee. "Thanks, Queenie."

As the bullpen emptied out, the two of them took a desk with computer. The lieutenant inserted a jump drive, then opened a file and sent it to the printer. "You take the guys above the line," he offered, "and I'll try to get to the long distance ones. I should have time this afternoon to go out to Jefferson Parish, at least."

Then he dropped a manila folder on the desk. "These are the pictures we got from the *Times-Picayune*. Even if you decide these people weren't involved, it'll be a help to the department if you can match names to faces." He stared at the first photo of an angry-looking man in camouflage, mouth twisted open in mid-shout.

Amy cleared the bullpen printer. "Remy Besson, Papite Dardar, Jacques Griffin, Lionel Melançon, Sebastion Pierce, and Armand Terrebonne. Any priors?"

"Dardar–Fish and Wildlife got him for poaching. He took three gators out of season." Cranston shook the page he was reading from. "He pled out, probation, no jail time, finished supervision 2029. The others are clean."

Amy heard Paul think, *How did the police get their names? And numbers?* Dutifully she relayed the question.

"Come on, Queenie!" Duke laughed. "We're not allowed to surveil without probable cause, but we hear about what they do. They have a day at the pistol range, the next day we ask the rangemaster for their names. Or maybe a fireman goes to some meeting and tells his police buddy what he saw."

Paul let to say, "Wait. I know there are lots of things police can do that citizens can't. You mean civilians can do things we can't?"

"Bingo. We can say 'thank you' when a civilian gives us the information we're not allowed to get on our own."

"That's a little bit crazy," Paul said.

"We don't make the rules, we only use 'em and stretch 'em. Queenie, you know this stuff!"

Amy took the lead. "Yes. But I have a friend who likes to go on about the Fourth Amendment."

"Shee-it. They repealed that long ago. Or may as well have."

She heard Paul silently moan, *And you wonder why I hate cops.*

"I have to get going," the officer said. "Me and Flores are researching those street robberies up Magazine. I'll call you this afternoon; you can tell me what you're up to."

With the lieutenant gone, Amy leafed through her clipboard until she found the page with Sam Atkins' phone number. As she punched the woman's numbers into her phone she heard Paul say, "So that's why you wore slacks again. I was wondering why you didn't go for skirt and pearls."

I don't trust that fiend, she thought back. *Never again will there be nothing but air between her and my, uh, our private parts.*

On the third ring there was a click and a gravelly 'hello.'

"Ms. Atkins, this is Detective Clear with Orleans Parish Police. I have more questions—"

"Oh, God, not you!"

"Yes, Ms. Atkins, me. I have more questions for you in our investigation. I'd like—"

Sam swore. "I don't want you in my house. I'm using crutches, you stormtrooper."

Paul laughed silently, then startled Amy by saying aloud, "And I'm wearing underpants and slacks, you pervert."

Amy waved him back internally and went on, "I'd rather meet you in some public place. There's that chicken wing place down Desire, I think it's at Galvez. When can you be there?"

More swearing. "I can't. I don't have a car and I'm not walking that far on crutches."

"I'll pick you up," she said. "I'll take you there, and then I'll drive you back." She looked at her wristwatch. "Thirty minutes. I'll honk when I get there. Don't make me wait."

"Hold on!" Sam cried; it stopped Amy from closing her phone. "What?"

"That's too much trouble. Just fucking come in."

Amy thought to Paul, *No way I want to be alone with her in her house.* Aloud, she countered, "Put some chairs on your porch, we'll talk there." She ended the call before the woman could object.

She took a look at the top page on the clipboard. *May as well start on these guys,* she thought. *Armand Terrebonne, Metairie.* She dialed his number and waited.

There was an abrupt female "Hello?" accompanied by the sound of squalling children. Amy introduced herself and asked for Armand.

"He's at work," the woman answered. "At least, that's what he said. Be quiet, Sharona, mommy's on the phone!"

"How can I reach him?"

"What did he do this time? Sharona, I said hush!"

"We think he was a witness where something took place," Amy answered. "We hope he can help us figure out what happened."

"Well, Okay. He–Sharona!" There was a loud 'thwak!' and a louder child's wail. "He works at the Dick's Sporting Goods, the one near us. You want his cell phone number?"

Amy wrote down the number the woman dictated, then hurried to end the call. "I'm not crazy about my sister's kids," she said, "but did you hear her hit hers? Whoa!"

Amy grabbed her clipboard and her coffee and went back to the employee parking area behind the building. *I know you want to drive,* she thought to Paul, and ceremoniously moved the car keys from their right hand to their left.

Up Desire but not as far as Florida, he thought back as he unlocked the vehicle. *Please keep your seat backs and tray tables in the upright and locked position.*

When they reached Sam Atkins' dilapidated half of a shotgun, they saw the woman sitting on the porch in a rattan chair; alongside it was a brown metal folding chair. Sun glinted off her silver colored crutch.

She hasn't given up, Paul thought. *She put your chair right next to hers.*

Well, that's not going to happen. She straightened the half-a-hardware store on her belt and walked up the cracked and worn steps. "Thanks for meeting me, Ms. Atkins," she said aloud. Sam nodded but did not speak.

When she reached the porch, Amy slid the vacant chair sideways, to give her some distance from Sam and to allow her to face the woman. As she sat down, Sam said, "Don't know if that part of the porch'll hold you up." Immediately Amy stood back up, but she heard Paul think, *If we can stand on it we can sit on it. She's yanking our chain.*

Amy sat again. "I appreciate your concern."

"So, what do you want now, you fascist thug?" Sam's arms were folded across her chest.

"I want a day where no one tries to rape me," Paul answered. He heard Amy laugh, and then she led to ask, "Were you at the demonstration on Sunday?" Paul paged through their legal pad to a fresh page.

"I told you last time."

"Okay. Tell me again."

"Yeah, I was there."

"Last time I asked you if you ever spoke to the pastors at the church–"

"And I told you I didn't."

"So you did, so you did. But it turns out we have a witness who says you were in the church talking to the late Riley Tibbs and the live-and-breathing Drew Malone." Paul held their pen, poised to transcribe the woman's response.

"They're wrong. They made it up. They're trying to get me in trouble."

Paul said, "Ms. Atkins, you don't seem to need any help getting in trouble. And your dress that day couldn't have been more distinctive if it blinked 'My name is Sam' in neon. Yellow neon."

No reply.

"Then there was a different witness who overheard you talking to someone–" she leafed back in the legal pad to her notes from interviewing Parker Frye "–and telling them that someone had been killed. If that's so, the only people who would have known were Pastor Tibbs and her killer."

Squirming in her chair, Atkins said, "Bullshit. You're making this up to try to make me confess to something I didn't do." There was a defiant frown on her face.

"Two types of people say things like that," Paul said slowly. "Guilty people, and, uh, guilty people. Which are you, Ms. Atkins?"

"Are you accusing me of murder?"

Amy took back the lead with the standard police rebuttal. "You're the only person talking about accusations and murder. Why is that, I wonder?" Amy let the woman's silence last for a long twenty or thirty seconds before she went on. "Several different people have said you talked about how a martyr's death would help the cause. They all said that you claimed it was a joke when they challenged you. Now, I have a peculiar sense of humor, but I don't hear a joke in any of this. Do you?"

"Not a joke," she began to protest, "a, uh, what is it, a hypochondriac."

Paul in Amy blinked. "That makes no sense."

"You know, like a guess, or a what-if, a, a—"

"A hypothetical? You were hypothesizing that the death of a gay rights pastor would benefit the gay rights movement?"

"Well, uh–yeah."

"Ms. Atkins, can I ask you what medication you take?"

"No, you can't!" Sam attempted to stand up, but without her crutch she fell back into the rattan seat.

Amy said, "I want to know who you shared this hypothetical with. In all the citizen review boards that cropped up after that scandal with King Henry II and the Archbishop of Canterbury, we tend to think of the person soliciting murder to be as guilty as the one doing the deed. Now, I'm not a prosecuting attorney so I cannot make any offers or promises, but things might go easier on you if you steer me to the person who thought you were being serious."

"It was just a joke!"

Paul thought to Amy, *So how come we're not laughing?*

Amy stood up. "Ms. Atkins, you are not the only person of interest in this case. But I advise you not to leave New Orleans, and maybe you ought to talk to a lawyer. Commander Ramirez was very clear that he doesn't like preachers getting killed on his watch."

"Fuck you. It's all a joke." Sam glared at her from her chair. Amy backed away toward the stair, keeping an eye on the woman as she said, "Thank you for your time, Ms. Atkins. I'll be back in touch, believe me." Without waiting for a response Amy took the steps two at a time to return to the sanctuary of her old yellow Benz.

"She didn't try to touch us," Paul said, "but I still want to take a shower."

"It's the sleaze," Amy countered. "It's like excrement; it sticks to everything it touches." She lit the glow plugs and waited to start the engine.

"Where are we going now? Metairie for that lone gunman?"

She shook their head. "I'm going to drive. You just stay awake. Talk to me, okay?" She started the car and headed south—uptown in this part of the city; the definition of 'up' in New Orleans is upstream of the Mississippi River, which meanders with contempt for mere human concepts like the compass.

When Amy parked outside the archdiocese complex, Amy thought to Paul, *Are you awake? Do you know where we are?*

I'm sorry, I'm sorry, I'm sorry! he replied silently. *I promise I will not say fuck in front of the receptionist.*

"Good boy, my foul-mouthed friend. Let us check in with Father Johnson. And What's-Her-Name at the desk."

The lobby guard pointed her toward the archdiocese administrative office. *You are going to watch your mouth,* Amy thought as they walked down the hallway. *Our mouth.*

Amy presented herself to Receptionist Grace, hoping the woman didn't recognize her. No such luck; Grace looked up and blurted out, "Not you again!"

"I hear that a lot," Paul said out loud. Amy took over and said, "I'd like a few minutes of Father Johnson's time, please."

"Do you have an appointment?"

Paul stared at the woman for a moment. He thought to Amy, *Mine.* He took a step back and shouted, "Father Johnson!"

The priest burst out of his office. "What's wrong?" he cried, "Is everyone all right?"

She thought to Paul, *Effective, but next time let's try a little finesse.* Then she waved and called, "How nice to see you, Father."

He was no more than ten feet away from her. The worry her shout had caused passed from the prelate's face, replaced by annoyance, and then a smile. "I was about to telephone you," he said, holding out his hand. "There's someone in my office I want to introduce you to."

She heard Paul think, *Uh-oh,* but she shook the archdiocese public relations officer's hand. "My mother tells me I need to be in the market for a husband," she said, following him back to his office. "Non-smoker, likes dogs, has a job."

"I'm married to God," he grinned. "And we haven't changed our position on same-sex marriage since Sunday, so I'm afraid you'll have to keep looking." In his office, he held his arm out to a seated young woman. "Detective, this is Angel Villanueva, one of the archdiocese volunteers."

Amy held out her hand. "Nice to meet you, Angel. I'm Detective Amy Clear with New Orleans police." The woman stood up while shaking hands, struggling with her free hand to keep the sweater that had been on her lap from falling to the carpet.

Angel was a stocky woman, a little shorter than Amy and a good bit heavier. She had a trendy hair style; her brown hair fell to her left shoulder, but stopped at her right jaw. Maybe twenty years old, she was wearing a gray dress with a shorter hemline than might be considered appropriate for the archdiocese office. She said, "The good father was talking about you. It's like an angel told you to come here."

Johnson pointed Amy to a chair, then pulled his own from behind his desk to join the women. "Angel was at the demonstration on Sunday," he explained, "and she may have some information to help you." He looked at the volunteer expectantly.

"I ate something bad," she finally said, looking intently at the carpet. "Every ten minutes I needed a bathroom, so I finally sat down by the side door of the church." She carefully spread her sweater over her lap and knees.

"Several people mentioned seeing you," Amy offered. "Was it awful?"

"Yeah." She smiled a little, but still looked down. "So, anyway, a couple of times I went in there I saw some women. Some of them were in church robes. They didn't talk to me or bother me. I just—I just used the bathroom a lot."

Paul thought, *Tibbs and Malone and who?* Amy nodded, and asked aloud, "The women you saw—what did they look like?"

"One was in a pretty dress, it was bright yellow and looked happy. The ones wearing vestments—one had kind of short hair—" she looked up at the priest "—longer than his but short for a woman. And it was all white. Another lady had hair shorter than Father Johnson, and she was—"

"Yes?" Amy prompted.

"I don't like to use the word." She was still looking down.

What the hell? thought Paul. *Lesbian? Dyke? Butch? What's her—*

"Fat," Angel whispered.

Paul thought, *What?*

"You don't have to say it again," Amy soothed. "But what's the problem with that word?"

She waved a hand in the direction of the priest, who leaned forward to grasp it. "I'm—I'm that word," she said softly. "And I hate it when people call me that word. It makes me feel bad." Face still aimed at the floor, the woman inhaled noisily. Amy patted her pockets for tissue but she didn't have any.

"Oh."

Paul said, "It's okay. You weren't calling her names. You were just describing her appearance, and you did well. We're pretty sure we know who you mean."

Angel Villanueva nodded a few times. She released the priest's hand, quickly glanced at him to smile and say, "Thank you," then took the sweater from her lap to wipe her eyes. It left a small black smear of mascara on her cheek, and probably on the sweater.

She took a few deep breaths, then finally met Amy's eyes. "I saw them a few times. Then I went in and the, uh, the last woman was by herself in the restroom. She was rinsing the sleeve of her robe. I'd have asked her about it–it was a black robe, I didn't see anything on it–but I needed the toilet again. When I left she was still scrubbing. By then I felt too lousy to want to talk to anyone."

Paul thought to Amy, *Ding! Ding! Ding!*

"Do you have any idea what time that was?"

"Actually, yeah, I do," she replied. "I looked at my phone because I was supposed to take another dose of Pepto Bismal at eleven thirty. It was ten after." After a moment she added, "As soon as I got outside I took the dose anyway." She shrugged. "For all the good it did the bushes I threw up in."

Amy thought, *Jermaine said time of death was eleven o'clock.* Then, aloud, "Did you see any of the women again?"

Shaking her head, Angel said, "Next time I tried to use the bathroom there was a policeman at the door and he said I couldn't go in. I told him I was about to vomit, but he pointed me to the bushes." She looked up at Amy. "I'm sorry."

"Are you feeling better, my child?" Father Johnson asked.

"Yeah. I felt a lot better on Monday. I finally felt like checking in with everyone today."

It's Drew! Paul shouted silently. *She must have been working with Sam Atkins!*

Maybe, Amy thought back. To Angel she said, "You've got nothing to be sorry about. You've been a tremendous help to this investigation. Can I get you contact information? There may come a time when I might need you in a courtroom."

"Oh, I couldn't do that!" she said, turning a luminous red. "I don't like public speaking or anything."

"Well, maybe a deposition, then." Then she asked, "What do you do, Angel? Are you in school? Or–"

She shook her head. "I take care of the little ones at some parish churches. A lot of part time jobs and volunteer stuff." She looked up at Amy. "I love the kids. I want to have a dozen of 'em."

"I'll sell you my sister's. That's three right there."

Angel squinted at her, confusion on her face.

"Family squabble," Amy went on. "If there weren't women like you, the human race would die out in a generation."

Father Johnson stood by Angel with a hand on her shoulder. "I'm glad you're feeling better," he said. "I was worried about you on Sunday, but His Grace was keeping me busy."

"Thank you," she said, looking up at the young, handsome priest. "I appreciate it. You've been such a rock for me."

Amy stood up while Paul was thinking, *Are we done here? Let's go find that lone gunman.*

"This was a lucky accident," Amy said to Angel. "I thought I was going to catch up with Father Johnson, but talking with you has been a bonus. You've been a big help, Angel." She held out her hand. "It was a pleasure to meet you."

When Amy left the PR director's office, Paul led them by the receptionist's desk. "Have a good day!" he called to the woman, and winked. She frowned and went back to her work.

Sitting in her yellow Benz, Amy placed her call to Armand Terrebonne; it was the number she had been given by the woman who answered when she called from the station house.

"Eh, bonjou," dropping the final 'r' as Cajuns will.

"Bonjour, Monsieur Terrebonne. This is Detective Clear with the Orleans Parish police."

"Oh, shit. Is Sharona okay? My Denise? What's wrong?"

"Nothing is wrong, Mister Terrebonne. I'm sorry if I alarmed you." Amy heard Paul think, *His daughter is black-and-blue by now,* but went on, "I'm hoping you can help us with our inquiries. I believe you were at a demonstration on Sunday?"

"Hey! Nothing wrong with that."

"That is correct. I hope you may have seen something that will help us catch a murderer."

There was a long pause. Finally he said, "I'm at work, I can't stay on the phone."

"How late are you there? I'll meet you."

More silence. "I don't know. Da bossman will be on my ass about it."

Smiling, Amy said, "I can take care of that for you." She loved how being official police made interviewing so much easier. "I promise, he doesn't want anyone asking for his insurance certificates."

"Yah. I'm here up to five thirty." He told her the address of the sporting goods store where he worked. "I'm in the hunting and fishing section," he added.

When she ended the call, Paul asked, "What about all the other ones on Duke's list?"

Even as she added notes to her clipboard pad, she thought back, *I want to get a feel for the lone gunmen first. If they seem unstable I may ask Cranston to come with me for the others.*

"Wow!" he exclaimed.

"Hmm?" She pressed the glow plug button.

"I remember when you got pissed at an officer because he insisted on coming with you to interview a murder suspect."

"I don't remember that, but I'll take your word for it," Amy said. "I'll bet it was before suspects started shooting me and stabbing me." She started the engine. When the sound smoothed out she said, "You want to get us to Metairie?"

Their eyes lit up as Paul took the lead to drive. A right on Claiborne, up the ramp, and then bearing right into the asphalt spaghetti that would take them to Interstate 10 westbound.

"I expect our lone gunman will be as bad as Duke," Amy offered.

"Six-six and carrying a pistol?"

"Maybe," she laughed. "I mean his attitude. Considering the signs all of them were holding, he's probably all 'queer' this and 'butch' that."

Paul nodded but kept their eye out for their exit sign.

"This is an interview, not an interrogation," she went on. "So no matter how rancid the man is, I can't argue with him. Can't be judgmental."

"And when it becomes an interrogation?" Paul flicked the signal blinker to change lanes.

"If he's being your kind of trash mouth, I have to out-vulgar him. Have you noticed how that actually makes some bad guys shut up?"

You mean it makes them shut the fuck up?

A smirk. "Something like that. But if he's just spouting troglodyte hate, I'm stuck listening to it. As much as I don't like that kind of talk, it could compromise an investigation if I argue with him."

Exit 228, Paul thought to her, and moved further to the right.

"Already? Okay, go right. He works in Lakeside Shopping Center."

"Lakeside? Lake Pontchartrain must be three miles from here."

She thought to him, *Ever notice roads called 'Pine Tree Lane' don't have any pine trees on them?*

"What a world we live in."

He drove up Causeway Boulevard and got caught at a red light at Veterans' Highway, which marked a corner of the largest shopping mall in the southern part of the state. "Where in this enormous money vacuum is Dick's?" he asked.

As far away as possible, she thought back. *Make a left and a right. It's just above Dillard's.*

He went straight when the light turned green and made a New Orleans left turn across the neutral ground; then south on Causeway back to Veterans, and finally a right. Some of the landmarks looked familiar–Lager's Grill, a big place succinctly named Daiquiris, and, incongruously, an old private house converted into a family dental practice. "Where do we turn into the mall?" he asked.

Not yet. The street up there with the traffic light? Turn right. I think that's Severn.

Paul did as he was told, and they quickly passed satellite malls. When he saw the tall monument sign with 'DICK'S' at the top he signaled to move to the right turn lane.

"No, not yet," Amy said. "We'll get lost in the mall. Go up to the traffic light past the parking deck, that's where we need to go."

He slowed down to make sure he didn't overshoot the entrance. "Why does this all look vaguely familiar?"

"After you helped me buy my first pistol, we came out here for cheap ammo. You really don't remember?"

He saw the store's name on the side of the building and turned in front of it. "Paulzheimer's Disease," he said. "I'm glad your half of our brain still works."

I'll look after you when you don't remember me anymore, she thought, *but the first time you need a diaper, I'm out of here.*

The first section of Dick's Sporting Goods was crowded, with people looking at Saints jerseys, Zephyrs hats, and even some Dallas Stars hockey sticks. Beyond that were what seemed like acres of athletic shoes; some solid black or white, but mostly intense colors that don't show up in a prism. Sweatshirts. Tents. Freeweights. Golf clubs. Treadmills and trampolines. Paul thought, *Can we try out some tennis rackets while we're here?*–it was the one sport they both enjoyed.

Nope, she thought back. *Working. Where do they hide fishing rods?*

"You need some help, hey?" a voice called.

Amy turned to face a store clerk wearing a blue long-sleeve jersey, with his employee ID hanging around his neck like an all-access pass. He was a few inches taller than her, with a thin face and light brown eyes that seemed to be looking next to her instead of at her. His brown hair was wavy and long, unkempt. She thought his forehead was huge. "Uh, yes, as a matter of fact," she answered. "Where's hunting and fishing?"

Even with his eyes averted, he smiled and said, "Which you want? Fly casting rod? Big ol' shotgun? What you want?"

"I want Armand Terrebonne," she said. "I'm–"

"Oh!" Finally his eyes met hers. "You that po-po I talk to, yeah?"

"That's me. Can I–"

"Non! I tell you da bossman don't like this."

Amy touched the man on the arm. "Let's go find him. You won't be in trouble."

"I don' know," he muttered, but he led her from the deserted outdoors section toward the apparel department, with its racks of brightly colored sweatshirts and jackets.

They came up on a thin man, early thirties, in a gold polo shirt, complete with Dick's name tag around his neck. "What are you doing over here, coonass?" he challenged Armand. "Get back over to your bayou shit, you hear me?"

"Excuse me," Paul said, sounding just like Amy. He was holding up her police ID.

"What?" he shouted, waving his arms the way an animal will flex its wings or legs to appear bigger.

"This is official police business," Amy said. "We're investigating a murder at a public gathering. Armand was there, and I hope he has information that will help us take a killer off the street. You should be proud of him; he's being a good citizen." She heard Paul make a silent raspberry.

The supervisor stopped short.

"Really. Armand can make all of us safer by telling me what he may have seen at this event. May I have ten minutes with him?"

Paul thought he saw smoke coming out of the supervisor's ears, but the man succumbed to Amy's appeal. Only the hardest of hardcore jerks could refuse to let an underling talk to police after that buildup, and the supervisor—hardcore jerk though he might be—was not *summa cum laude* in jerkhoodness. "Clock out," he told Armand, then turned to busy himself behind a counter.

"Tell the truth!" Terrebonne said as he led them to the time clock. "I thought non, dat bossman never let me do this. You all right for po-po, yah?"

After Armand did as he was ordered, they stayed off the sales floor so they would not be interrupted by customers. Amy began, "My information is that you were at the Metropolitan Church demonstration on Sunday. Were you really there?"

"Yah. Is that a problem?"

"No. Just if you weren't there, there's no point in us having this conversation."

"Oh, okay. So what you know now?"

Paul thought, *Do what? What did he say?* Amy said, "My Cajun is rusty. What did you just say?"

The man grinned. "So what you know now? You know–" He looked up, thinking "–what do you want to know from me? Uh, find out from me." Smiling at Amy he said, "I have the same problem with da bossman. He a *texian*."

Amy went on, "I think you were there with some friends or colleagues. Is that right?"

"Yah. Me and some–Oh. Yah."

Paul surprised Amy by saying, "Look, I know you're in the Militia of Louisiana. I know who all the people are in the militia. It's okay, that's not against the law and besides, I'm more interested in solving this killing. So I need to know which of your colleagues were there, in case they saw something you didn't."

"You for true! Yah, my people from the militia. We had signs and all."

Taking a small notebook from a back pocket, Amy asked, "Who were they?"

Armand rattled off four names, and helped Amy with the cajun spellings: "Sebastion Besson, Papite Dardar, Jacques Griffin, and Lionel Melançon."

"Did you go inside the church?"

"Non!" He crossed himself. "My priest says it's not allowed."

"Any of your buddies go inside?"

He shook his head.

Did you expect him to say that Old Marcel Ledbetter stabbed the pastor? Paul thought to Amy. Silently she answered, *I guess I hoped so.*

"Did you see anyone or anything at the demonstration that concerned you? Maybe seemed dangerous or unstable?"

"Yah. A *grand sallope*, a big woman, all *jaune*, all yellow. She come up and talk to my *podnas* Lionel and Papite. I see them, I hear them."

"And that was dangerous?" Amy asked, one eyebrow raised.

"What she say!" Armand was agitated, talking as much with his hands as mouth. "She say they look like brave men, real men. That someone should *chué* that holy woman, that–"

"Wait. Do what? Chewy? To who?"

"–that, uh, the priest there, the woman. *Chué*, she say, take her life, because to marry those girls would be a sin. And that Lionel and Papite, they have the *kouraj* to do that, yah."

She heard Paul think, *I knew it was that Sam bitch! I knew it!*

Amy tried to hide the excitement she felt from making progress on the investigation. "Armand. You say you heard that woman in yellow ask your friends to kill the pastor at the church?"

"Spooky, no? Lionel, he say 'non, non, you leaf us be.' But Papite, he been to the *kalabous* before, he say, 'what give you?'" Armand laughed at the memory of a *texian*, a person who didn't understand Cajun. "She stutter, den figure out and say 'you be a hero, that's what you get.' He say, 'non, *couillon galette*, go away.' She just stand there, so Papite, he make to jump at her. She leaf fast, I guarantee."

Amy made some notes in her little booklet. "Tell me what she looked like."

"*Grand*, she tall as me. Big hair. She smoking *sigarét*. She don't look like a nice lady."

Nodding, she added to her notes. Then, even though Duke had given her their addresses, she asked, "How do I get in touch with Lionel and Papete?"

"Lionel, yah sure," and he gave a phone number, adding, "You tell him I give you this. But Papite, he don't like po-po. I tell you, he been in tha *kalabous* afore."

She heard Paul remind her what Duke had said, that one of the lone gunmen did have a police record for poaching. "If I came along, would he meet you somewhere? He may know something about the dead pastor, and I really don't care how many alligators he bagged out of season."

"Non, non," Armand said, shaking his head. "Papite is my podna, I don't want him *en colaire* with me." He took his time card out of the metal caddy and clocked back into work.

"I appreciate you talking with me, Armand," Paul said, sounding like Amy. "You've told us the whereabouts of one of our suspects." Then Amy took the lead and brought out the newspaper photographs Lieutenant Cranston had gotten from the *Times-Picayune*. "Can you help me put names on these faces?"

She held up the first on her clipboard and said, "That's you. Who's that?" pointing at the image of a man with a dark, messy beard.

"Hey," he smiled, "that be Jacques Griffin."

She changed photos. "How about these men?"

"That be Sebastion Besson, he got that *petit* beard. And --" Terrebonne laughed and pointed "-- Lionel Melançon,"

"And here?"

"That be Papite." He smiled and added, "Nice picture, yah?"

She took another look. The man, Papite, was standing on the 'anti' side of the walkway, smiling across the path at two women who seemed frozen in mid-argument with him. The bottom of his picket sign was in the photograph, just the word "Queers".

"Well," Amy offered, "at least he's smiling."

Armand nodded vigorously. "Da bossman wants me back to work. I got to go."

Amy held out a business card. "If you think of anything..." but by then she was speaking to his departing back.

Damn! she thought to Paul as she walked out onto the sales floor and headed toward the front door. *I feel like he slapped me or something.*

What did I miss? Paul replied silently. *He touched us?*

No, he cut us dead. If Amy the detective had feelings, they'd be hurt.

Paul nodded. *But Amy the person does have feelings.*

Yes. Hurt feelings. She considered it but couldn't bring herself to think the word 'coonass' to her dyad. She settled for *Bastard!*

Sitting in the yellow Benz in the parking lot, Amy reviewed her notes. Out loud she said, "So, Sam is there with a different story. She told Jess at Community Coalition that she wanted a martyr for the gay marriage cause, but Armand heard her tell his militia buddies that a pastor who would perform a same-sex marriage ought not be allowed to live."

Paul replied, "I wonder what her real reason was."

"Doesn't matter," Amy muttered as she leafed through the material on the clipboard, "it's not like there's a good reason to solicit murder. Here–" pointing at the paperwork Duke had given her "–Papite Dardar. I wish he didn't live in Slidell, that town depresses me."

"It does? Why?

"I was six years old when Hurricane Katrina hit, and half of Slidell still looks like Los Angeles after the 2028 earthquake."

So we're going to St. Tammany Parish?

She tapped their right hand against their lips while she thought. "Duke's dossier doesn't say where the man works. I think I need to visit him after work hours. Assuming he works days."

Paul said, "Can Christine come with us?"

Amy snickered, "Oh, sure. She's helped me interview real killers before, not just suspects. I wish you could talk your girlfriend into carrying a gun, though."

"We took her to the range once. She dropped our pistol and held her hands over her ear protection. The noise freaked her out."

"I remember. She put a dent in the slide."

Amy pushed the glow plug button and said, "You want to drive us home?"

"Please don't throw me in that briar patch," he replied, and took the lead to crank the engine and drive back to town.

While waiting for a traffic light to change, Paul said, "Want to stop at Rouses to get some wine?"

Amy decided not to act on her burst of anger; instead, she replied calmly, "No. Seven days without alcohol, remember?"

"Argh! I'm sorry. I forgot."

"I can't stop thinking about it." Annoyed, she turned on the radio. Some peppy pop song ended, and the DJ said, "The latest from the National Weather Center is that Olaf will be a hurricane when it comes ashore on Friday, somewhere between Galveston and Pensacola. Make sure you have enough milk and–"

"I'm tired of hearing about it!" Amy exclaimed as she turned the radio off. They drove in silence for several blocks before Amy added, "Have you ever talked to anyone about Alcoholics Anonymous? I mean, what it's like in their meetings?"

Even though they were in the privacy of Amy's car, Paul wanted to protect their privacy on the subject. He thought to her, *Nope. Just stuff I've read about Bill W.*

She sighed. "I think it's a lot like going to church."

"I don't know. We can look it up." Then, silently, *Do you really think we're alcoholics?*

Her silence was all the answer he needed. He felt his–their–someone's–stomach drop. *Really? Shit.*

"Pull over," she said, and he parked at the curb along South Carrolton Avenue, under a live oak in front of the green expanse of Palmer Park. Paul could feel Amy's fear, but he waited for her to speak or think to him.

Abruptly she said, "No. I will go home. I will take a run around the block. I will take a shower."

"Home? Okay," and he returned to traffic. "Later, can we go to Christine's?"

"Yes. She may not want to keep us company when we go to Slidell, you know."

"She's not shy anymore," Paul said. "She'll tell me if she'd rather stay at home. We can still visit after your interview."

Once home, Amy changed clothes and took a run around the block. She rested for a few minutes in front of her house, then ran around the block a second time. *Trouble is,* she thought to Paul, *I still want some wine.*

As she ran, Paul thought back, *Even if you weren't drying us out, you wouldn't drink before you interviewed a person of interest. Uh, would you?*

"Today I would. But no, I've never done that. It would be unprofessional."

Paul responded silently, *So it's not like we're hopeless winos.*

He felt her run faster. *Not yet,* he heard her think.

After Amy showered and dressed, Paul called Christine. "Did everyone at work high-five you for selling that house?" he asked.

"Lowell didn't, but he feels bad because he hasn't moved any inventory in five or six months. Everybody else was real nice to me. When I got in this morning there were flowers on my desk from the sales manager!"

"I'm so proud of you," Paul said, a huge smile on their face. "A year ago you were answering the phones, and now you're selling houses."

Softly, she said, "Stop, I'm blushing."

"So they recognize how valuable you are at–"

"Hi, Amy," she interrupted, demonstrating her uncanny ability to know which of them was leading and speaking. "Yeah, most all of us are mutual fans. How did your investigation go today?"

"As a matter of fact," Amy replied, "I have to drive out to Slidell to interview a man from the Militia of Louisiana about the pastor's murder. Want to ride shotgun?"

"Umm, Paulette? Do you want me to come along?"

"Only if you'd like to keep us company," he said; he knew his lover sometimes needed help saying no when she meant no.

"I was going to cook that super spaghetti you taught me how to make. Why don't you and Amy come over to my place after the interview?"

"Sounds good to me. Let me check with the co-pilot. Amy?"

"You don't have to cook for me, Christine. If it's–"

"Silly Amy. I want to cook for Paulette and you. We're celebrating, remember?"

Amy shook her head with a smile. "Of course we are. Paul can call you when we finish with this person of interest, and we'll be there maybe forty-five minutes later."

"Yay!"

Paul took the lead to add, "But I'm not bringing the Chianti. Amy's decided we should dry out for awhile."

"Really?" They heard Christine laughing. "That's pretty silly, but whatever. You and Amy are what I'm looking forward to, not wine."

After the call, Amy let Paul lead to throw the next day's clothes and some toiletries into a bug-out bag. He heard her think, *We may as well start off for Slidell. Traffic will be nasty on the Twin Span Bridge.*

While they kept a steady eighteen mile-per-hour pace on Interstate 10, Amy moaned, "Has it been a week yet?"

"We have a problem," Paul answered; then, "No. You have a problem. I'd like a Dixie, but I'll be okay without. I'm getting worried about you."

"Me, too."

A moment later she smiled and said, "Papite. I'll get him to give me his background, see if he owns up to the poaching arrests. Ask about the demonstration and hear what he has to say about Sam Atkins."

"Do you think he's the killer?"

She shrugged. "It could be anyone except you and me. But that's what an investigation is for. I'll find the perp."

Rush hour traffic remained miserable as they drove east. When they crossed the Inner Harbor Navigation Canal the huge CSX freight yard spread out on the right, then fell back as the road turned north, then east again. Now there were lakes and bayous among the recent modern housing that had replaced what Hurricane Rodrigo had damaged in 2026 and that Katrina had utterly destroyed twenty-one years before that.

The landscape changed abruptly as they passed the I-510 interchange and the New Orleans East monument sign: swamp in every direction. They drove past three exits that actually went nowhere, left over from the Louisiana Department of Transportation & Development's fantasies about land fill and future growth.

And then there was water. Not as overwhelming as the Lake Pontchartrain Causeway, where seven of its twenty-three miles gave no sight of land in any direction; merely a six-mile trek across the lake, still enough to make some tourists seasick. At least traffic was moving faster.

Land returned as the interstate met the north shore at Eden Isles, a wealthy enclave where every home included a dock on a manmade bayou. Paul took exit 263 and made a left on Old Spanish Trail, passing gas stations, house trailer sales lots, fast food restaurants, single-story motels, mini-storage sites, and car dealership after car dealership after car dealership, all of them named after individuals instead of manufacturers. Low overcast made the trip even more depressing.

"How far up is our man?" Paul asked.

"Next traffic light," Amy answered. There was an Aamco and an appliance parts place on the right, and a deserted strip shopping center on the left. "That's Slidell Avenue."

Paul signaled, then moved into the turn lane. At least Slidell didn't make people take U-turns halfway down the block.

After the down-scale commercial nature of Old Spanish Trail, the turn took them to a pleasant residential street of turn-of-the-century homes surrounded by small trees, trees that didn't take root until after Rodrigo and Katrina had drowned their predecessors.

First right, Amy thought, *Carafe or something.*

"Carollo Lane," Paul read from the street sign as he made the turn.

Houses on the uphill side of Carollo were older and larger, while those on the left were much smaller and of recent vintage. At a low point down the road he saw curb cuts to driveways that went to empty lots. Paul thought, *Why do they bother to rebuild in the low spots?* He heard Amy laugh and answer, *You can say that about all of New Orleans.*

Paul parked in front of 689 Carollo Lane. It was a small house, built after one of the hurricanes that periodically tortured Louisiana. The chain link fence surrounding the property had several gaps, but the overgrown yard was happy to stay where it was, unmolested and unmowed. There was a shiny Ford F-250 in the carport, not more than two years old. They could see the MOL decal on its back window.

"Truck," Paul observed. "Somebody must be home."

Amy stood on the grass verge–there were no sidewalks on this residential street–and rearranged all the hardware hanging from her belt. As she took her badge case from its holder she began walking up the driveway, stepping around the tall weeds sprouting from cracks in the concrete. Two steps up to the front door, and she knocked.

"Go away!" a male voice called from within.

"Oh, great," she moaned softly. She knocked again, this time shouting, "Police!"

She heard sounds of movement, some furniture legs grating on a solid floor, and muttering. Suddenly the door flew open, inward, and she was staring at a short, bare-chested man in bare feet. "What you–Whoa now! You *po-po?*"

Holding her badge aloft, Amy let the accompanying ID cards unfurl in their plastic holders. "Papite? I am Detective Clear with New Orleans Police," she said. "I'm hoping you might have seen something that helps us with a murder investigation."

He examined the ID Amy was holding up. "You real *po-po.* PO-lice," he finished, grinning at having said the word in southern dialect instead of Cajun. "So, what you want, hey?"

"I have some questions," she said. "Is there someplace we can sit down?"

He stepped backwards and made a sweeping gesture for Amy to come inside the little house. She smiled and said "Thank you," even as she heard Paul shout silently, *Ding! Ding! Ding! Don't go in a strange man's house when he might be a damn murderer!*

She thought back, *Since it bothers you, keep your hand on my gun. But I'm not worried about Papite; he's my size.* She felt Paul roll his inside eyes, and she gave him a silent raspberry.

"You better come in my kitchen," he said. "You caught me eating my supper." As she followed, she saw a ladderback chair lying on the floor by the only place setting at the table. He motioned to the chair opposite his meal while he restored his own chair.

She saw red beans and rice with some slices of sausage on his plate, along with some stewed okra and sliced, boiled potatoes. Paul thought, *If Christine weren't cooking dinner, I'd ask Papite to dish us up some chow.*

"Thank you for letting me interrupt your supper," Amy began. "I talked to Armande Terrebonne about the demonstration last weekend. He said you were there as well. I was–"

"Go to bed!" Papite exclaimed, fork full of rice in mid-air. "That's not true. I wasn't there." His fork finally reached his mouth.

Amy shuffled through her clipboard and pulled out the photograph where Armand had identified Papite. Sliding it across the table for the man to see, she said, "Is this you or your evil twin?"

Paul felt their chair vibrate from the way Papite was jiggling his legs. *He's nervous,* he thought to Amy. He heard her silent reply: *Good.*

"Oh. That demonstration. The queer ladies at the church." He put down the fork. "So, what you want?" He was glaring at her.

"You may have heard, a preacher in the church was found st– uh, found murdered. I've been asking people who were at the demonstration if they saw anything suspicious, or dangerous, or just out of place."

"That's nice." He took another forkful of beans and rice. He was still glaring.

If his eyes were lasers, Paul thought to her, *we'd be fried like a bug under a kid's magnifying glass.*

I don't think he likes me, she thought back. Aloud, "So, Papite, when you and your Militia of Louisiana buddies were at the demonstration, did you see anything that made you concerned?"

He chewed his potatoes slowly. Eventually he said, "*Non.* I liked the crazy *filles* what tried to argue with me; they funny." He speared an okra pod and waved it. "That–that–" still holding his fork, he flapped his arms up and down "–that homo with wings was *zeerahb,* but he don't scare me none." The okra finally entered his mouth.

She leaned back in the chair, even as Paul kept their left hand on the butt of their holstered pistol. "How long have you lived out here?" she asked the man.

A shrug. More beans and rice.

"Are you married?"

"*Non.* Not no more."

"Do you own guns?"

"You *texian,* what part of 'militia' you not understand?"

Amy forced a smile. "Parabellum? Seven-six-two? Twenty-two? Nine millimeter Makarov?"

"This gumbo is good good," he replied. "Too bad you can't have none."

Paul thought, *Can I try?*

May as well, she replied silently. *I'm not getting anywhere.*

He took the lead, and leaned forward. "Papite, tell me about the time Fish & Wildlife busted you for killing alligators out of season."

The man put his fork down, and carefully wiped his lips with the paper towel that served as his napkin.

"You don't know nothing," he announced. "It was in season." Paul raised an eyebrow, and Papite laughed. "I only have two tags, but I have three gators. I tell the *po-po* he can have one, but I can tell, the man don't like me, he say *non.*"

Nodding, Paul prodded, "Did you do any hard time?"

A guffaw. "I spend the night in a *petit* cell, they feed me good, and next day my *podna* Jerome, he bail me out. I go to court, but not back to jail." He shook his head, "I never, never go back to jail."

"Tell me about the woman in yellow," Paul said.

"What woman in yellow?"

"Sam Atkins. We have witnesses that saw you talking to her at the demonstration."

"Ah." He took another mouthful of beans and rice, and chewed slowly. Paul thought he was giving himself time to come up with an answer. Finally Papite said, "The *grand sallope.* I remember now. I told her to get fu–uh, *pic kee toi.* She go away."

Armand having told Amy about the confrontation, Paul egged Papite on. "What did she do to make you tell her to get lost?"

"I tell her *pic kee toi* because she want someone *tuer* someone. Papite a good man, he don't *tuer* nothing on two legs."

Paul nodded and said to Amy, but out loud, "That matches what we heard before."

Papite slammed his fist down, which made a salt shaker jump and fall over, scattering little white grains across the table top. "So, this just a, a, a, test? Like a schoolboy exam? You already know what I say?"

"Easy, Papite," Amy tried to soothe. "It's just basic police work."

"It's *barboter,* my time worth more," he growled, and stood up. "I no like *po-po.* I no like you. Outside you *belle fille* but inside, you bad." He made a twirling motion with his index finger at the side of his head. "*Couillon galette. Pic kee toi.*"

Paul thought to Amy, *I don't know what he just said, but I don't like it.* She thought back, *So what? Let him have his temper tantrum.*

Sage advice but ignored. Paul stood up sharply, knocking their chair backwards. "Talk American, coonass!" he shouted. Amy thought, *Oh, no.*

"Who you call coonass, you *galette?*"

As Paul leapt at the man, Amy shouted out loud, "Not the face! It's the only one I've got and I need it." She would feel the blows from a fist fight, of course, but not nearly as much as Paul would– like with their drinking and eating and sex, whichever of them was leading got the more intense sensation, be it pleasure or pain. But the black and blue marks, they would be hers.

Paul, with Amy's body as his tool, grappled with the short but strong Papite. They muttered and swore at each other as they flailed, slapping and pulling hair. Paul felt pain in their left hand when he punched the man's head. It was enough to convince Papite that this woman did not deserve his chivalry, and he hauled off and planted a roundhouse right to their neck.

They had trouble breathing. Amy began to panic when Papite rolled toward them for his next attack. But when she felt Paul start to reach for their pistol she froze their left arm. *You started this,* she shouted silently, *you can't use my gun now.*

Unable to access their handgun, Paul shifted gears. He had a man's body for 58 years, and even now, after living in Amy for twenty years, he hated what he was about to do. Still struggling to breathe as Papite grabbed their arms, he jerked up their knee and made contact between the man's legs. There was a gurgle, then a series of low moans.

Both lay still, waiting for their various pains to subside and for their breathing to return to normal. Amy thought to Paul, *My neck is killing me and I probably just lost my job. What set you off?*

Sheepishly, he thought back, *Pissing contest. Sorry. Damn, it really hurts.*

Aloud, Amy could only whisper. "Can we stop this now? Papite, are you okay?"

"*Non*," he gasped. Both of them lay on their backs, trying to breathe. Shortly he went on, "What you do? What happened?"

"I'm possessed by a demon," Amy answered in short breaths.

He responded, "I guarantee that."

"I hope he didn't hurt you. I–I mean, I'm sorry." To Paul she thought, *You're the one who should be apologizing,*

To you, yeah. To him, never.

Amy poked herself in the neck to prod Paul with a pinch of pain. *You'll be apologizing to me for months over this. I expect flowers every day.*

"I be alright," Papite wheezed. "You? I never hit a *peeshwank* before."

Amy felt Paul tense from hearing a foreign word. *Get over it,* she thought to him in a growl, then said out loud, "What's a *peeshwank*?"

"You. A little girl, that's a *peeshwank*." He took a few breaths. "You *texian*."

"What's that?" Amy was twisting her head, trying to loosen up her neck.

"*Texian*. You don't talk my language."

"So, those other things you called me," she croaked, "what did they mean?"

"Oh." He lay quietly, breathing deeper as the pain in his groin began to subside. "They bad. I was *en colaire*."

I knew it, Paul thought to her. *He was disrespecting us.*

And that's why you got me in a fist fight? she thought back. *After all this time with me, how could you be such a, such a, such a testosteroney man?*

It's the rules of the schoolyard, Paul thought. *You've got to be the strong horse. Otherwise–*

Painfully she interrupted by croaking, "Otherwise, you need to get a grip." She started to sit up, lifting themself on their fallen chair.

"I got a grip on my *bibitte*," Papite gasped.

"I wasn't talking to you," Amy answered. She held out their right hand as she stood up, "Here, I'll help you."

Papite took their hand and pulled himself up to his knees. "Ho, that hurts," he muttered. Then, "Who you talking to?"

"That damned demon. Look, can we start over?" Her voice was hoarse and croaky, and it hurt to speak and swallow.

"Give me a minute." He let go of her hand, still on his knees, now his hands on the sides of his thighs. He was taking slow, deep breaths.

Amy righted the chair Paul had knocked over, and also the one Papite had been using while eating his supper. She dropped themself into his chair, closed their eyes, and rubbed their neck gingerly. "That was some punch," she rasped. "You're a good fighter."

"You're not as tough as some 'gators I've fought, but you not bad," he said. He was still staring at the floor.

Paul thought, *So we're all friends now?*

"Not you," she whispered. Then, louder, "That wasn't to you."

"Demon?" He looked up.

Amy nodded, and held a hand out to help the man regain his feet. He crouched several times, legs spread wide, trying to let his anatomy return to its normal position.

"You *bracque*, you know that?" He grinned for a moment, still working his knees and hips.

"What's *bracque*?" she asked.

Papite wound his right index finger alongside his head, and the grin returned. "Cuckoo. Loco."

Still rubbing their neck, Amy said, "Yes. That's me. I'm the queen of crazy."

The man reached for a chair and gingerly, slowly, sat himself down. He looked at the remains of his dinner and said, "I no hungry anymore." There was a pause, and he added, "I need a drink. You want?"

Before Amy could respond, Paul blurted, "God, yes. What do you have?" She thought to herself, *Seven days,* but didn't protest to her dyad.

"Under the sink," Papite said, but made no move to stand up.

Amy noticed. "Oh, okay. I'll get it." One hand on their neck, she used the other to open the cabinet under the kitchen sink. Along with bleach, Windex, PineSol and bug spray was a bottle of Everclear. Her eyes got big as she thought to Paul, *Isn't this stuff, like, three hundred proof?*

Something like that. It'll make our throat burn so much we won't notice our neck hurts.

Amy put the bottle on the table in front of Papite. "Glasses?"

The man twisted off the cap and took a slug directly from the bottle. He winced; he pulled his head into his shoulders and waited for the burn to dissipate. "You need a glass?" he finally asked, handing the bottle to her. His eyes were tearing.

She took the bottle and eyed it cautiously. She heard Paul think, *I haven't had Everclear since I went rafting with some buddies on the Greenbrier River before you were born. Can I lead?*

"Be my guest," she mumbled.

"Ah. Demon," Papite nodded.

Paul wiped the open neck of the bottle with their hand. He sniffed the opening, enjoying the medicinal odor of almost pure ethanol. Holding it in their left hand, he lifted the neck to their lips and leaned back to let the nectar he remembered come into their mouth.

He coughed. He sneezed. Tears burst from their eyes as flame scorched their tongue, their mouth, their throat, their stomach. He heard Amy scream silently.

He dropped into their chair. "Damn, that's good!" he told Papite, and handed the bottle back to him. "That's pappy's corn squeezings right there."

"*Oui.* Nothing burn like Everclear." He was grinning again.

"Look, I'm, uh, I'm sorry I kneed you in the nuts. I was afraid you were going to kill me."

"*Non!* We were just playing, right?"

Paul nodded. The liquor's warmth was numbing the pain from their neck. He heard Amy think, *That's like drinking a firecracker!* Laughing, he said, "Yep, sure is."

"Demon?"

"What? No. Uh, actually, uh, I'm the demon. Let me get Amy for you. Detective Clear, front and center."

"Thank you, my dear demon," Amy said. Then, to Papite, "Queen of crazy."

"*Bracque*," he smiled. He took another pull on the liquor bottle, then passed it to Amy. Paul bobbed their head. Without bothering to wipe the bottle's neck, he took another drink. It was as incendiary as the first had been.

They sat quietly, both grateful for the anesthetizing effects of the potent grain alcohol. Finally, Amy croaked, "So, did you kill the pastor?"

"*Non.*"

"Do you know who did?"

"*Non.* That *sallope*, she evil. Maybe she done it."

It was Paul, feeling more of the alcohol than Amy, who asked, "What's *sallope*?"

"Umm...pig." He made a snorting sound to illustrate. "Maybe whore. Sloppy. Not nice. You not *sallope*."

"Well, thank you," Paul said. "And you're not a coonass."

Papite smiled. "Yah, I am, but you okay."

"If I can interrupt this love fest," Amy said, and she took back the lead. "At the demonstration, did you see the *sallope* talk to anyone else?"

He laughed, "Demon." Then, with an exaggerated nod, "Yah. Two gorillas. Big, big men. Loud jackets. They wear sunshades. I don't hear what anyone say, but it look like the men, they don't say much."

"Did you ever go inside the church?"

"Non!" He lifted the bottle and took another swallow. He coughed, his eyes bugged out and watered, but he held the bottle out for Amy. It was Paul who took it greedily, ignoring Amy's silent complaints. Papite went on, "Father St. Pierre, he say I go to hell if I go in someone else's church." He crossed himself.

"My condolences," Amy said. "I had twelve years of Catholic school." She coughed from the burn that Paul's gulp left in their throat.

Papite giggled. "Hey, *peeshwank*, you want some of my gumbo?"

"Christine's making dinner," Paul said. "Uh, I'm expected back in NOLA. A friend is cooking." He turned their head to look at Amy's watch, and their neck reminded him of Papite's punch. "Yeah, we gotta go."

Amy thought to him, *Stop saying 'we.'*

"Am I saying 'we'? I mean, us gotta go."

"*Peeshwank*, you want a drink for the road?"

Even as he heard Amy silently shout *No!* Paul smiled and said, "*Peeshwank* like. Thanks." He ignored Amy's protests and took a long pull on the bottle.

"Oh, it burns!" Amy cried out loud. Paul felt like he had just gargled broken glass. It took several seconds before the astringent pain dissolved into warm numbness. Paul shook their head and slurred, "Hmm, Thanks, Pap-Pap-Papittey."

The man laughed and said, "Hey, you okay to drive down the bayou?"

"The demon will not be driving," Amy said. The alcohol would have only a little impact on her since she had not led to drink; it was Paul who was racing towards liquor joy, liquor exhaustion, and liquor hangover. Amy smirked to start thinking of names to call him the next day.

Papite stood up slowly, and bounced gently on the balls of his bare feet. "For *po-po*, you okay, hey? *Bracque*, but okay." He held out his hand.

"Thanks for your help," she said. "Oh, wait–" she fumbled for her business cards "–Here. Call me if you remember anything that might help us. And, uh, I'm sorry about, well, you know." She shook his proffered hand.

"You think of me when you see that *bleue* tomorrow, yah?"

As soon as they were out of Papite's house Amy began scolding Paul. *You couldn't help me go a week without a drink. Day two and you're guzzling that legal moonshine. What do you have to say for yourself?*

"Medicine," he slurred, aloud. "It's not hooch, it's medicine."

She snorted. "Medicine! If you hadn't attacked Papite you wouldn't have needed a pain killer." She unlocked the door to her yellow Benz and threw it open. "I swear, if I could manage it I'd throw you in the trunk and leave you there for a week."

She heard him silently singing one of his Jurassic era rock songs, something about *'drinking wine spo-de-oh-dee.*[6]*'*

Amy lit the glow plugs, and when they were warm she started the engine and made a three point turn to head back toward I-10. "I want you to shut up," she hissed. "Stop that singing! Do you hear me?"

"Yeah, I, uh... what?"

"Shut up, shut up, shut up!" she screamed. "You are in the dog house, mister."

"Aw, what's wrong, *peeshwank?*"

"You are what's wrong, geezer! Old fart! You provoked that man into punching me in the neck. It hurts like hell and probably looks like Aunt Peggy's goiter. I bet I look like I was in a boxing match. You just had to jump him?" She kept a watch out for the signs pointing to the interstate.

Wine, wine, wine, keep your head stoned all the time[7], he sang silently.

"So, Papite can complain to NOPD and get Internal Affairs to fire me, and I'll never get another consulting job with them. My PI business, such as it is, will completely dry up. God in heaven, is this national sharp-stick-in-the-eye day?"

"Whiskey on my breath, trouble on my mind[8]," he sang.

"Listen to me!" she shouted aloud. "I can't trust you? Paul, we need to be able to trust each other. You agreed to help me not drink, and then you poured that lava down my throat. Why?"

Skinny girl made it clear that she only came here for the beer[9].

"Earth to Paul," she turned onto the entrance ramp to I-10, "If I lose my job, we're going to starve. And if we starve, I will make sure you starve first."

"Christine's making dinner," he slurred, then sang, "Oh show me the way to the next whiskey bar, oh don't ask why...[10]"

She tried to close her inside ears (not nearly as easy as closing her inside eyes) to concentrate on the murder of Pastor Tibbs. Papite said he hadn't been inside the Metropolitan Community Church. Armand Terrbonne had said the same thing; as a survivor of the St. Giles Academy she believed them, that their priest had convinced them it would be a sin to enter a house of worship for a different faith. And only someone inside the church could have planted that knife in the back of Riley Tibbs.

Who did that leave? Just thinking the name Sam Atkins made alarm bells go off in her head, almost drowning out Paul silently singing something about one scotch, one bourbon, and one beer[11]. That woman asked the Partnership of African-American Clergy muscle to kill Tibbs, and she tried to solicit the Militia of Louisiana cajuns to do the job. And Angel Villanueva put Atkins inside the church, talking to both Tibbs and Drew Malone. *I wonder if Walter has a gizmo I can put on Sam that'll show me where she goes and what she does. Particularly if it has the 'what she did last week' module.*

Next issue was getting to Christine's duplex in West End. Without realizing it she had made it to the I-10 twin span bridge, and was driving up the steep bulge of the bascule section. Traffic was sparse, but the sun was long set; driving New Orleans' long bridges could be nerve-wracking at the best of times, let alone at night when a drunk dyad was singing strange songs about having some madeira, my dear[12].

She fumbled for her phone and speed dialed Christine. The woman picked up on the second ring. "Paulette?" she said, tentatively, "Where are you? Dinner's been ready for an hour."

"It's Amy. Sorry we're running late, there was an, uh, an issue with the guy I interviewed."

"Are you okay? Is Paulette okay?"

"Your obnoxious boyfriend is drunk!" Amy shouted. "He got me into a fight, then passed a peace-pipe of Everclear again and again and again."

"Oh, no. Paulette, how could you?"

Christine's voice finally registered on Paul, and he spoke while Amy held the phone. "Christine! I love you! Do you know that? That I love you? I love you this much. No–" attempting to move Amy's other hand, which was on the steering wheel "–this much."

"I love you too, Paulette," she said. "Hurry over, I've got dinner waiting." A moment later she added, "I guess I'll put the wine away."

Amy said, "I don't know what to do with him. I begged him to help me not drink for a week, and now he's loaded."

"Uh, Amy? Did you drink anything?"

"No! I was arguing with him and–"

"So you still haven't had anything to drink. Right?"

In the several seconds of silence as she considered Christine's point, Amy heard Paul's sloppy singing, *Wastin' away again in Margaritaville, searching for my lost shaker of salt..*[13].*"* Finally she said, "You are a genius. Did you know that? Paul's the alkie, not me. Thank you!"

"Glad to help," the woman responded. "Where are you? When will you get here?"

"I'm on I-10, I think I'm coming up on the industrial canal."

"You'll be here in twenty minutes. That's great."

"If your boyfriend doesn't stop singing I may just drive into Bayou St. John to shut him up."

"Don't do that, Amy," Christine said, sounding as if she thought Amy were serious. "I'd miss you, and I'm not done with my Paulette."

Despite herself, despite Paul's annoying singing, Amy laughed. "Only because you asked me," she said. "I'm headed for I-610 and Paris Avenue. See you soon, my sane sister." She heard Christine laughing as she ended the call.

Wake up late honey put on your clothes and take your credit card to the liquor store...

Enjoy yourself, my friend, she thought to Paul. *Your girlfriend is going to whip your butt when we get there.*

"She can do anything she wants to me," he slurred, then went back to singing, "I'll be loaded like a freight train, flyin' like an aeroplane...[14]"

How was she going to bring down Sam Atkins? The woman had pulled a 'will no one rid me of this meddlesome priest' deniable request of people at the social service agencies that someone kill Riley Tibbs. So far, everyone had a believable story that, no, they didn't kill the woman. But Atkins was seen inside the private working areas of the church just before the murder. How? How? How?

"Amy! What is that? What happened to you? Is Paulette okay?"

"Paul is still singing these ancient songs," she answered, standing in the doorway of Christine's triplex. "Maybe he's making them up; I wouldn't know. If you want to talk to him, do it fast, because I expect him to pass out in no time."

"Well, come inside. I want to look at you two. You–you do know your neck is swollen, right?"

Amy pushed past her to stand before a mirror on her dining room wall. Indeed, she saw the goiter her Aunt Peggy had, only it was an iridescent yellow. "He punched me!" she called. "Paul, wake up. See what you've done."

"Hah? What? Where's Christine? What–oh, wow, what is that?" Delicately he touched the swollen tissue between their chest and their chin. "Wow. I've never seen anything like this. What is it?"

Amy closed her eyes and said, "It is your doing. It is the end result of you jumping Papite Dardar and provoking him into a fight. Are you happy?"

He tried poking the mass and said, "Ouch. That hurts!"

"I'm glad you feel pain. It's the consequences of your acts. Unfortunately, I'm the one everyone will laugh at."

Christine said, "How serious is that thing? Is it going to get worse?"

"I hope not," Amy groaned. "The militiaman I interviewed punched me in the neck. I can–"

"He attacked you?" Christine's face was frozen with alarm.

"No," Amy replied. "He defended himself. It was Paul who threw the first punch–yes, you did! I was there!"

"Paulette! Is that true? You started a fight?"

"Had to," he slurred. "He insulted Amy's honor. I had to defend her. The strong horse."

Amy responded, "The law of the schoolyard." She tried to shake their head, but the neck pain made her stop. Looking in the mirror, she said, "I can still breathe and swallow, so I don't think I'm going to die from this. Oh, God, I look deformed."

Christine took Amy's hand and led her to a seat at the dining room table. "Paulette? What did you do?"

When he took the lead, their eyes became red and bleary. "Ah, my better half," he said, sounding like a slurring Amy. "It's so good to see you." He leaned forward to kiss her on the cheek, then rested their head on her shoulder. "Did you ever drink Everclear? Ha ha– ever drink Everclear, that's funny. You smell good."

"I smell like tomato and garlic," she said. She wrapped her arms around her lover in Amy's body. "Were you bad to Amy today?"

"What? No way!" He attempted to sit up straight but abandoned it and rested against her shoulder. "That coonass, he dissed Amy. I defended her honor." He giggled. "I kicked him in the balls."

"He did, too," Amy added. "At least that made Papite stop."

Christine said, "Paulette? Did you really have to do that?" Knowing her lover was taking the lead, she patted their face.

"I didn't want to," he slurred. "I used to have balls. I know what it's like to have them stomped. But I had to do it. Amy wouldn't let me shoot him."

"Euuuww. Good." Then, "Amy? What is Everclear?"

"It's a mixture of rat poison and napalm in a bottle. Paul said it's three hundred proof."

"Oh. Paulette, how much did you have?"

There was no answer.

"Paulette?"

Amy thought to him, *Your girlfriend is calling you.* After a few seconds she announced, "I think he passed out. That's how much he had." Since she had taken the lead, Amy was able to sit up. "How do you put up with him?" she asked while she patted her swollen neck. "I mean, I love him, too, but today he was so exasperating."

Christine stood up and said, "Do you want dinner? I'm starving and I've been smelling food for hours."

Amy waved, "No, I'm not hungry. Besides, it hurts to swallow." She looked up at the woman, with her hair of various lengths and various shades of blonde, with that one blue streak. "I'm sorry he ruined everything. This is supposed to be congratulations for selling that house yesterday. You deserve better than my misery."

"Nothing is ruined," she said with a quivering lower lip. "You and I will celebrate, and if Paulette sleeps through it, well, that's her hard luck." She disappeared into the kitchen to fetch a plate of noodles and sauce. "Sure I can't get you anything?" she called back to Amy.

"I want a Dixie," she shouted back. "Can you bring me a glass of water instead?"

Once Christine was seated with a plate full of spaghetti and sauce, she paused between bites to say, "I've never noticed you worried about drinking before. What's going on?"

"My skin is getting slack. My face is puffy the next morning. Even before this," as she touched her swollen neck. "I tried to explain to Paul, I'm thirty-four and I just don't rebound like I used to from beer and wine. Let alone Everclear."

"You know I'm your friend," Christine began. "I love Paulette, she's so good to me and for me, and I'm glad you're a package deal with her." She smiled, then slurped a noodle off her fork. "You're right. I've noticed it but I haven't said anything because, well, it's none of my business. But you sort of asked."

"Yes," Amy moaned. "Me and my big mouth."

"Paulette doesn't agree with you? Or does she not care?"

"Mostly he doesn't see it, and from his male perspective he says he doesn't care." She took a painful sip of water from her glass. "Mind you, we had a good talk about it, and he agreed to help me go a week without drinking. Today was day two." She made a frog face, a frown with both lips sticking out beyond her little nose.

"If Paulette is passed out, she can't hear us. Tell me what you're thinking that you don't want her to know."

Amy shook her head slowly so her neck wouldn't throb. "Believe me, I've told him all this stuff. I'm–" she dropped her eyes from Christine's and examined the tablecloth in front of her "–I'm worried that I've turned into an alcoholic."

"But Paulette is the one who drank today, not you."

Amy traced her finger around an embossed pattern in the tablecloth. "Yes. But my skin doesn't care which one of us drinks, it's going to be puffy tomorrow."

"Oh." Christine took another forkful of pasta and chewed it carefully. "I paid attention when Paulette showed us how to make this sauce. She's missing a great dinner, if I say so myself." Another bite. "Paulette loves you," she went on. "I used to be jealous that she wants me because she can't have you. She wouldn't do anything to hurt you."

"Oh." A deep breath. "You're a clever woman. Yes, he and I love each other. I'm sure it's not a secret that we wish we could kiss each other. And if we could do that, well–yes. But he is absolutely in love with you, Christine. Every now and then he asks if I'll let him ask you to marry him, like Shawna and Gina." She sighed. "I'm just not ready to give up on men yet. But it's what he'd like." Smiling at the woman, she said, "Can you forgive me?"

Christine frowned. "It's getting harder. I'm older than you. My mom asks me if I'm ever going to settle down." She took another forkful of noodles. "If Paulette asks me, I'll say 'yes', you know."

Amy nodded. "Yes, I know."

After a long silence, Christine said, "Stay here tonight, okay? I want to be with Paulette if she wakes up during the night."

Another nod. "I understand." She looked at the woman that Paul found irresistibly cute. "Besides, I'm not used to being alone, and he's off my grid. I'll be glad for your company. You really are my best friend."

Christine smiled but tried to hide her face. "I'm glad," she finally said. "I love my Paulette, and you're part of her, so I love you, too. The sister I never had."

Amy felt a jolt of fear, anxiety, guilt. With Paul unconscious, she felt like she was being unfaithful for staying over with his girlfriend, even though it would be an innocent and platonic thing; she felt as if she were cheating on someone–on Paul? On Christine? When she shook her head at the familiar black humor of her emotions, her neck barked with pain. "Do you have an icepack I can use?"

That night Amy propped her pillow against the wall that served as headboard, and lay back against it with the icepack resting on her bruised neck. Christine was undressing and telling her about the flowers her boss left at her desk that morning for having sold her first house. "He doesn't do that kind of thing," she said. "A lot of the agents are scared of him because he yells about quotas and how we're all sending him to the poorhouse." She laughed. "And then he sends me flowers."

"I'm glad he's not a total bozo," Amy offered. "I'm sure this is just the first of your first thousand houses, and maybe he understands that."

"Yeah. Thanks." Her voice was muffled as she slipped a flannel nightgown over her head, and then shimmied to let it fall in place. The woman sat on the side of her mattress on the floor and took a jewelry box off the nearby bookshelf. "If I sell one house every three months, I'll be ahead of when I was the receptionist." She opened the box and carefully spilled a small amount of marijuana into a small, worn wooden pipe. "Do you want some?" she asked.

"Uh, no," Amy said. "I always say no. I'm a cop, you know." She was smiling.

"It would be rude not to ask," Christine said. "I'm glad you forget you're a cop when I do this."

"If I were the one passed out and you offered it to Paul, he'd–"

"Oh, she always says yes when that happens." Christine flicked the little butane lighter and took a long drag on the pipe, then held her breath. In an odd voice–trying not to exhale–she went on, "She coughs and says you don't know what you're missing."

Amy's jaw dropped. "I was going to ask you not to let him do that. Huh. Guess that boat sailed."

Still speaking strangely, Christine said, "Yeah, Paulette said you'd be pissed if you knew."

When Christine was done with her evening self-medication, Amy said, "I forgot to check in with Lieutenant Cranston. He's going to rag on me when he sees my neck in the morning."

Christine fluffed her pillow, then lay back. "Tell him it's none of his beeswax."

"What I'll tell him is I think the lone gunmen are in the clear. I'm convinced that woman who tried to rape me is the killer. Or at least, the one who set the killing in motion."

"Be careful, Amy. It scares me to see Paulette and you get hurt from your job."

"Oh, I'll be careful. That woman was on crutches last time I saw her. I think I need to visit her again. Something about her being inside the church with both the pastors just–" Amy shook her head, careful to keep the icepack pressed in place "–it just doesn't fit. I mean, she couldn't kill Riley with Malone right there, but she lied and said she'd never even been inside the church."

There was a yawn. "Can I turn off the light now?"

"Good night, Christine. Congratulations on selling the house."

The woman turned off the lamp next to the bed. "Good night, Amy. If you talk to Paulette before I do, tell her I love her." Amy felt a sisterly peck on her cheek, then heard the noises of Christine settling in on her side of the bed. Somebody said, "Sweet dreams."

Why does our neck hurt?

The alarm clock had just gone off. As Christine groaned and grumbled to push in the little button that would shut off the obnoxious buzzing, Amy heard her dyad think to her.

Our neck hurts? she thought, crossly. *Are you sure?*

She felt Paul raise their left hand to their neck and poke. "Ow! Yeah, I'm sure. What happened?"

"Paulette?" Christine asked, hesitantly.

"Christine!" he cried out loud, and rolled toward her. "What a great way to wake up." He kissed her, and the woman returned his embrace.

"Are you all right?" she asked between kisses. "I was worried about you."

"Worried? Why?"

It was Amy who said, out loud, "Because a certain someone got into a fist fight last night, basted his innards with sulfuric acid, and passed out halfway through a sentence. Sound familiar?"

"Oh. Oh, shit! Papite! Are we okay?" He turned their head and felt the pain again. "Is that why our neck hurts?"

Christine started to laugh.

"What?"

"Yes, my dear dyad. That is why our neck hurts."

Paul sensed he was in trouble, and probably why. "Everclear?"

"Christine, isn't he so smart? I understand why you love him."

"Don't be too mean to her," Christine said as she pulled her nightgown up and off before heading for the shower. "She did bad, but I'm sure she didn't mean to."

With Christine gone from the room, Amy sat up on the mattress and said, "You are so far up Shit Creek I may never forgive you. This may be the day I get fired because of you."

"I remember the fight with Papite. We ended up friends because of it."

"Yes. Well, that's one of the two hundred and ninety-three things about men that I will never understand. Do you remember sealing your friendship?"

She felt their eyes open wide as he said, "Oh, yeah. With a drink. That's what men do, you know."

"How many drinks do men share to confirm their new bosom-buddyness?"

"At least two. More if there are lots of people."

Amy stood up, letting the sheets fall to the floor bed. "It was just the three of us, and you drank so much that you passed out while you were talking to your sweetheart."

There was a pause until Paul said, "I don't remember that."

She fished clean clothes out of the drawer that was reserved for Paulette. She was planning on seeing Sam Atkins again, so she picked out clean slacks. "And do you remember your promise to help me not drink for a week? Hmmm? For seven little days?"

"Uh. Oh. Yeah."

She carried clothes and towels to the bathroom, arriving as a clean but wet Christine was wrapping a towel around her hair. Amy went on, out loud, "And your lover girl says she's noticed how our alcohol is ruining my looks, but she was too polite to mention it until I asked. I am afraid to look in the mirror this morning."

Christine interrupted to say, "Your neck's not so swollen. It's a funny color, though."

Amy closed her eyes and said, "Can I borrow a scarf?"

"I'm sorry, I'm sorry, I'm sorry!" Paul said.

Amy exclaimed, "You're like an abusive husband. You're full of apology, but that doesn't keep you from starting a fight and probably getting me fired."

Christine, working a towel on her legs, said, "That's a little harsh, Amy."

It was Paul who said, "Christine, Honey? It's embarrassing to have this spat in front of you. Can you give us a few minutes? I promise there will be no bloodshed."

"Don't be too sure," Amy hissed.

"My, oh my, aren't the walls perpendicular," Christine said as she grabbed her gear and escaped to the safety and sanity of her bedroom.

Alone, Paul said aloud, "I fucked up. I'm sorry. What can I do?"

"Well, you can–you can–" Amy was thrown off track by his concession, just when her mouth and her brain had been prepared to exact verbal vengeance. She stopped, then said, softly, "You can not do that again."

"Yeah. I was bad."

"And you have to help me stop drinking."

"Yeah. I was bad."

"And you have to quit giving in, because I was all ready to go so ballistic on you."

"Yeah. I–Oh. What were you going to say?"

Amy dropped her shift and started the shower. "I don't know. Something about you being a charming sociopath who would choose a bottle of Dixie over saving your grandmother." The water felt good against their skin, and seemed to soothe the dull ache on their neck. "And that you would promise me anything but do what you want anyway."

There was a pause while she worked shampoo through their hair. Then, in a silent, contrite voice, Paul thought, *Is that really how I behave?*

"Not a lot. But often enough."

Shit. Paul knew he wasn't perfect, but he wasn't prepared to believe he was that despicable, not anymore. When he was a young man in and out of college, of course he said anything that he thought would make a woman open her arms and legs, but that was long before his happy marriage to Mary Pat, and long before the bizarre medical accident that wed his mind to Amy Clear. *Am I really that awful?* he asked. He was afraid to hear the answer.

"Not usually," Amy said, moving a washcloth up and down their legs. "And, really, not that often. But you sure were yesterday."

When he did not respond, Amy stood in the shower stream and looked up–not for any reason but that both Amy and Paul sometime did so when thinking or talking to the other–and said, "I need your help. Please, don't drink. Don't let me drink. Please." There was still no answer. She worked at rinsing the soap from their body and added, gruffly, "And don't get me into any more punch-ups, okay?"

"I am sorry I let you down. I remember your mom once saying, 'We're all sinners.' All I can say is, I'll try to do better."

"I suppose I can't ask for more than that. But Paul Dominic Owens, you <u>will</u> do better. Am I understood?" She turned off the shower and stepped out onto the wet mat. "Hmmm?"

"I hear you. I wish I didn't, but I hear you."

When they joined Christine in the kitchen, the woman asked, concerned, "Is everything okay now, Paulette?"

Amy answered, "It better be," and laughed. Then Paul said, "I hope so. Amy read me the riot act. We're giving up alcohol for Lent."

"But it's August."

"We're getting a running start."

Christine always could tell which one of them was leading or speaking, so she understood it was Amy who added, "And physical confrontation will be confined to police matters, thank you very much."

"So, you're friends again?" She was pouring milk into two bowls of Cheerios.

Paul said, "We are, right?"

Amy answered, *Yes. But don't blow it.*

"The consensus," Paul announced, "is that we are friends again. And speaking for myself, I apologize for ruining your celebration dinner last night. You did great, selling that house."

A smile spread across Christine's face. She stepped toward their chair and hugged them from the side, burying her head in the uninjured side of their neck. "I need you two to be friends," she said. "I'd be lost without both of you. Oh, Paulette, I–" she moved to kiss her lover. Then she stood up, and in mock sternness said, "Don't be bad to Amy; she loves you. And so do I."

Paul was smiling until Amy took the lead to say, "I have to get moving. Duke wants to see me right after muster." Then, "I'm sure Paul will listen to you. He doesn't always pay attention to what I tell him."

"I have a class tonight," Christine said as she began to work on her bowl of cereal. "I can bring leftover spaghetti tomorrow night. That way, you and Amy can help me celebrate my house sale."

"I'm on my own tonight?" Paul said. "Amy'll keep me out of trouble. I'm looking forward to you coming over tomorrow, though. I'll make up for last night."

Muster was just finishing when Amy got to the uniformed officers' bullpen, breathing heavily from having run up the stairs from the parking area. She kept tugging at the raspberry colored scarf around her neck, making sure the unfamiliar article of clothing was remaining in place and hiding the bruise left from Papite's attack.

"I was afraid you gave up, Queenie" Duke Cranston said as he approached her. "You didn't call me last night."

"Got back late from Slidell," she said. "I talked to a couple of the lone gunmen yesterday. I think they're in the clear."

He pressed close to Amy to allow another officer to pass behind him, then moved to the far end of the bullpen table and pulled out two chairs. Amy sat next to him and placed her clipboard on the table top.

"I talked to Armand Terrebonne. He ID'ed his militia *podnas* in the pictures you got from the *Times-Picayune*." She passed the three photos to him. "He says he didn't go in the church–that none of his pals went in–and I believe him."

Cranston was examining the photographs. "Why would you take his word for it?"

"First off, nobody says they saw any of them inside. Plus, Papite Dardar said the same thing and gave the same reason: their priest told them they'd go to hell if they went into somebody else's church."

"And you believe that?" Cranston looked up at her.

"Twelve years of Catholic school," Amy sighed. "They told me that'll happen, and I'm not even Catholic." When Duke continued to stare, she went on, "Best I can tell, these men are, umm, honorable. They weren't lying about that."

"Did you talk to the guy with the prior?" The lieutenant turned back to the photos.

"Papite Dardar," Amy pointed to the picture where Papite was smiling at the women haranguing him. "He owned up, but said the problem was three gators and only two tags, but in season." When she stopped, Paul added, "He said he offered the third one to the ranger. I suppose he's lucky bribery wasn't one of the charges."

"He tries to bribe a Fish and Wildlife agent and you think he's honorable?" Duke was still staring.

"Yes. It may not make sense, but yes."

He broke his gaze to pull at the paperwork on Amy's clipboard. "There are more names on the list I gave you. What about them?"

"Terrebonne named the militia members at the demonstration. The other three are–" she leafed through her notes on the clipboard, "–Sebastion Besson, Jacques Griffin, and, and, oh! Lionel Melançon."

"You ought to talk to them," Cranston said. "Make sure their stories match what you got yesterday."

"Umm–Duke, can you work them in? I want to bring in Sam Atkins. I'm just about ready to arrest her for murder by hire, or at least solicitation of it."

The lieutenant raised his eyebrows, "You got enough to charge her?"

"Nothing forensic, but I've got three witnesses that put her inside the church just before the pastor was killed. And you heard Calvin and J'waun say she tried to talk them into a killing. I've got, what–" another flip through the notes on the clipboard "–three other people saying she solicited them. And all she says to defend herself is that it was a joke."

She watched Cranston tapping his fingers on the tabletop as he considered what she said. "Nice work, Queenie. You want help making the pop?"

"Thanks, but it's okay. I trained Sam even better than Calvin. No worries." She turned in the chair and the raspberry scarf abruptly succumbed to the seductive lure of gravity. It landed in her lap.

""Damn, woman," Cranston grinned, "that's one hell of a hickey!"

Instantly their whole head turned a bright red, which merely emphasized the yellow-and-purple bruise. Amy, at a loss, fumbled with the piece of cloth. It was Paul who said, "I walked into a door. Fucking sue me."

The lieutenant laughed louder. "Whatever you say, Queenie. Whoo-wee!"

Mortified and angry, Amy retied the scarf. "Can we get back to business, Lieutenant Cranston?"

"Okay." He shook his head and took a moment to stop laughing. Then, fighting to keep a grin from returning to his face, he said, "You bring her in, and I'll interview the rest of the militia guys. Let me have the pictures, okay?" Amy nodded, and he went on, "See you back here this afternoon."

"We cool?"

"We cool, Queenie, we cool. But don't walk into any more doors."

Amy responded by sticking out their tongue and blowing, "Pttthhhhhh!"

Walking down the stairs to the parking area, Amy fumed silently, *I'm finally getting some respect from Duke and pow! Now he thinks I'm some kind of, of–*

Paul interrupted to think back, *Now he thinks you're some kind of normal person with a sex life. I think we handled it pretty well. Uh, considering.*

"Oh!" she shouted in frustration. Then, to Paul, *I've been trying not to be so totally Amy when I'm with him, and then the scarf falls off and I blow it.* They reached the parking level, and Amy headed toward her old yellow Benz.

Yeah. I know you feel shitty about it, but I'll bet Cranston's already forgotten it. He's a pro. I'm sure all he cares about is collaring Sam.

"I hope so." As she unlocked the driver's door she added, "I will be mortified if this scarf goes AWOL while I'm arresting her. Horrified. Humiliated. Do you think I can paperclip it? Staple it?"

"What? Are you crazy? It'll hurt if you staple that to our neck!"

As Amy pushed the glow plug button she was laughing. That had been Paul's goal.

It was an uncharacteristically cool day, with heavy overcast and typical New Orleans humidity. "Radio said Olaf might get us. It's going to land between Port Arthur and Mobile," Amy commented. "We haven't had a hurricane in four years."

"When I was a stupid jerk in West Virginia," Paul said aloud, "I used to think it would be fun to ride out a hurricane. Rodrigo cured me of that notion. I had no idea what a hurricane smells like after the water goes down." He was leading to drive them to Sam Atkins' dilapidated double-shotgun on Desire Street.

"*Eau de* dead things," she responded.

The thick cloud cover muted the sun and removed any vibrancy from what restorations or repairs had been made in upper Desire Street. When Paul parked, Amy looked up at the porch and said, "Something's wrong."

"What? Isn't this Sam's place?"

"The door is open. Sam was spooked by having been burgled twice. She wouldn't leave her door unlocked, let alone standing open. We'd better check." Amy hurried out of the car. She drew her pistol before she opened the chain link gate, then took the four steps to the porch. "Police!" she shouted, pausing alongside the doorway. As she took a few deep breaths she thought to Paul, "I'll look straight ahead, you do the peripheral vision. Warn me if you see anything." When she heard him think, *Gotcha*, she spun into a crouch, gun pointed inside the house.

There were two large pillows in what appeared to be an otherwise empty front room. She hopped forward, holding her shooting stance, and swung both her eyes and her gun left and right. In the front corner, hidden from a view through the windows, was Sam's precious large-screen TV. "Good Morning New Orleans" was playing, with the sound turned off.

So much for robbery, Paul thought.

Slowly, Amy walked toward the closed door that led to the kitchen, bath, and bedroom; the barrel of her Ruger pointed the way. *I hate this,* she heard Paul think. *Can't you just send three slugs through the door instead of waiting to open it?*

"Shhh," she said aloud, then silently, *Sam might be waiting with a bow around her naked waist. Horrible as that sounds, it's not grounds for shooting her.*

She stood alongside the doorway to consider the next step. An inside hall door isn't likely to have a lock. She saw it wasn't latched, just resting against the door jamb. Amy crouched in a shooting stance, with their right foot forward. *Same deal, okay?* she thought to Paul, then kicked the door open. But she hit it too hard; it bounced off the hallway wall with a crash and swung closed with a thud, this time latching.

Aw, shit, Paul thought. *So much for the element of surprise.*

Shush, Amy thought, *I'm listening.* She hoped for an audio clue as to who, if anyone, was on the other side of the door, in the back two-thirds of the house. All she heard was the faint static of her tinnitus, and the percussion of their adrenalin-charged heart thumping, THUMPing, THUMPing in their ears.

She thought to Paul, *I need your help. The door knob is on the right, and I want to be hiding behind the wall when I open it. You hold the Ruger. When I push the door open, be ready for anything. Okay?* Paul was left-handed, so he would be a better shot from this particular cover if a boogieman was waiting for them.

She took a deep breath. Crouching behind the wall, she used their right hand to turn the knob. This time she pushed gently. The door swung and stayed open. *All clear,* she heard Paul think. THUMPing.

Still crouching, Amy scuttled into the hallway. She turned to the right at the bathroom door, Paul still holding her pistol, and found the room empty. THUMPing.

The door to the kitchen was standing open. She could see a small coffee percolator on the stove, but no flame underneath it. She strained to hear any sound that might give her some warning or advantage over a hidden assailant. THUMPing. Amy inched forward, until she could see the entire kitchen. Empty. THUMPing.

There was one more closed door ahead, the one that led to the bedroom. Silently Paul thought, *I'll pick door number three, Monty.*
What?

Now's not the time to explain. I keep forgetting how young you are. Just take my word for it– that was funny.

Put it on my tombstone–'Killed in action, but it was funny.'
THUMPing. *Knob on the right, but there's no room to hide next to the doorway. You open the door, I'll hold Roscette.* She took the pistol into their right hand. Crouching again to offer the smallest possible target, Amy took another deep breath and felt Paul rest their left hand on the knob. THUMPing. THUMPing. THUMPing.

He turned the knob and pushed the door open. As Amy hopped into the bedroom, her fears were answered by the smell.

She stood up and used an elbow to flip the light switch up.

"Damn it!" she shouted. "I am so tired of finding bodies everywhere." The color of Sam Atkins' face and the large dull red stain under her meant there was no need to feel for a pulse. What appeared to be a snapped off knife blade was stuck in the side of her neck.

Released from fear, Amy leaned their back against a wall and let themself drop to sit on the floor. Their heart was still THUMPing, but she was feeling giddy from survival. "Can you believe some people like being terrified?" she asked out loud.

"It's the only explanation for sky diving and zip-lines," he answered.

As she fumbled for her phone she mumbled, "I could use a beer."

NO! Paul shouted silently. *This is day one.*

He felt her smile come across their face. *It wasn't exactly a test,* she thought back, *but you get an A-plus.*

Amy speed-dialed Duke, but got voice mail. "Can I arrest a dead person?" she said to the recorder. "It's Amy. From the smell I'd say Sam Atkins has been dead two days. I'll call Rampart Street for a meat wagon, but I wanted you to know."

Next she called the Rampart Street station and asked for Sergeant Francks. When he picked up his extension, Amy said, "Walter! It's Sugar! How the hell are you, anyway?"

"If I was any better they'd pass a law against it," he said. "I heard a rumor that you've been in the station house every day this week, but I haven't seen you since Monday. What gives? Are we not an item anymore?"

"Walter, I live to hear the water cooler stories about us making out in the evidence locker. I'll stop by next time to make up for how I've been neglecting you."

"Oh, Sugar, no one can push my buttons like you do. Rrrrrrawr."

"Down, boy. I was all ready to arrest a suspect, but someone arrested her vital signs first. I need a meat wagon and Doctor Tallant."

"Doctor who?"

It was Paul who said, "Precisely." Walter didn't know why the same voice said, "Hush, you," then said, "You know, Jermaine."

"Why didn't you say so? Give me the address, I'll let him know."

Amy dictated Sam Atkins' last known address, 2023 Desire Street.

"Is that in the Project?"

"God, no," Paul said, sounding exactly like Amy. "We don't go to the Desire Project unless there's an entire regiment with us."

"I worry about you, Sugar," the Sergeant said. "I'm going to Jermaine's dungeon right this second. Come see me when you get in, okay?"

When she closed her phone, Paul said, "He's so funny. What do you think he'd do if you made a pass at him?"

"Not going to happen," she snickered. *I don't think Walter's the kind of man who scares away that easily.*

After a minute, Amy mused, "Sam is the only woman I ever was afraid of. That day she tried to rape me–when we were at the restaurant with Christine, I realized I was frightened. Bummed me out." Then, "Huh. I guess I'm not afraid of her anymore."

They sat in silence until Paul said, "Can we wait in the living room or something? The smell is getting to me."

She stood up, saying, "When dad brought me to his ER, the dead people were fresh–and I threw up anyway. I'll wait for Doctor

Tallant to get here before I examine the bedroom." She closed the bedroom door behind them and returned to the front room. She kicked a pillow to where she'd be able to ignore the TV set; she knew not to turn it off without a forensic examination. But instead of sitting, she stepped out onto the deteriorating porch. *Let's see what we see,* she thought to Paul.

Atkins' side of the porch did not have gaping holes in its floor, although the part in front of the companion, boarded-up dwelling did. Flecks of black paint remained on the worn wooden decking. There was a flowerpot with cigarette butts instead of flowers in it. One stray butt on the floor looked weatherbeaten, but you never can tell–she pulled a neon orange post-it from a pocket, put a big "1" on it with a ball-point pen, and dropped it by the lone fag-end.

Amy began a search of the living room. She began circling at the baseboards, and gradually worked their way to the center of the room. The black paint on the wooden floor was worn but in better condition than on the porch. The cinder blocks and pillows looked the same as she remembered from her previous visit.

The kitchen was tidy. A drinking glass and a coffee mug were in the sink. Amy tapped the side of the coffeepot and felt liquid rippling inside, but she did not want to risk ruining possible evidence by grabbing the handle or removing the lid.

Bathroom, she thought. *I could stand to use it but I'll wait for Jermaine to get here.* She flipped on the overhead light to see an old, chipped claw-foot tub. Several towels were in it, and appeared to be wet. Paul bent over and touched their left index finger to one– damp. "I wonder if Sam took a bath just before–before, you know," he asked aloud.

"Or if her killer washed up afterwards," Amy answered.

She looked in the little trash pail by the sink. "What's that thing?" she asked. Rather than reach into the can she held it close to their face to examine. Something plastic. She shook the pail to coax the item into showing another side of itself. And again.

"Well, what have we here?" she said, excited. She pulled out her phone to take a photo of a plastic case for Tic-Tacs. Strawberry Fields. "What interim pastor do we know who eats these things like candy?"

"Wait," Paul said. "They are candy. And if our interim pastor was the only person who ate that flavor, Tic-Tac would have cancelled it long ago."

Paul's words knocked her excitement down to a more pragmatic degree of hope. "Thank you, Mister Bringdown," she said, smiling. "I never saw Sam use these things. Let's–"

There was a commotion at the front door. Voices, some loud knocks, and Doctor Jermaine Tallant's cry of, "Hello? Hello? Police."

Amy stepped out of the bathroom to see the medical examiner, a photographer, and a pair of EMT specialists coming in the house. "Doctor Tallant!" she called, always glad to see her favorite person on the force.

"Really, Miss Clear," he returned, "it's Jermaine. Haven't you learned that yet?"

"I guess not, Doc. And it's good to see you, too."

"This is Hortense," he said, arm out to usher in the young photographer. "Hortense, this is Detective Clear. She's quite the legend at Rampart Street Station."

Amy smiled at the very young woman, who seemed overwhelmed by the large camera around her neck.

"Where is the body?" Jermaine asked. "The sooner you and I process the crime scene, the sooner Johnson and Baker here can get to work."

While the EMT workers stayed in the living room, Amy led Jermaine and Hortense to the bedroom. "It smells pretty rank," she said, "but it's not overpowering yet."

"Oh, dear," Tallant exclaimed as he put on latex gloves. "That's a big knife. She's very dead."

"Really most sincerely dead," Paul chimed in. Amy frowned, not recognizing his quote, and asked the medical examiner, "Time of death?"

He crouched by the bed where Sam's head was face down. As Amy had noticed, the woman's face was a dark purple. Jermaine poked a cheek with a gloved finger. "Livor is permanent, so at least eight hours." Then he reached under the stained sheet covering the body and pressed a palm against the back. "I can't be positive, but I'm guessing room temperature. That puts it to ten hours or longer."

Finally, he attempted to bend the body's left arm. "Rigor still present, so it's less than thirty hours." He stood up to let Hortense begin photographing the room and the body. "No significant insect activity, which can happen pretty quickly in a Louisiana summer. I'll know more after I do the autopsy, but I estimate time of death between ten and sixteen hours."

Paul looked at their watch and did quick math in their head. "So, as late as 11:30 last night, or as early as 5:30 yesterday afternoon."

"I'll get an accurate body temperature from her liver in the autopsy. And I may discover maggots when I open her up." He noticed Amy's frown and added, "Oh, I guess you don't need to hear all the details."

"While she's taking her pictures, let me show you something I found," Amy said. She led him into the hallway, then reached into the bathroom to grab the wastepaper basket. "This may be a big deal. I don't know that Sam Atkins used this candy, and I have in mind someone who does."

"They still make Tic-Tacs?" Jermaine gushed. "I used to love these things. They had a tangerine flavor that was more tangerine-y than any clementine you've ever eaten. God, I loved them."

"The associate pastor at the church says she lives on this flavor. Is there any way you can, I don't know, dust it for prints or something?"

"Giving our killer credit for possessing more than three functional brain cells, I imagine he, she, or it was wearing gloves," Tallant said. "But when I gobbled these things, I'd swing that hinge back and hold the container against my mouth. Perhaps our he, she, or it only had four working brain cells."

He held up an index finger, then ducked back into the bedroom and returned with his medical bag. Opening it, he removed a clunky electronic gizmo. "My Polilight," he said as he plugged it into the wall outlet by the bathroom sink. "Let me show you magic. First, Detective, will you secure our potential evidence?"

"You bet, Mister Wizard," Amy said. "Goll-ee, is today when you show me how to blow up the world?" She heard Paul laugh inside as she took blue nitrile gloves from a belt pocket and stretched them on.

Smiling, Tallant shook his head. "Maybe just the lower ninth ward for starters. No one will miss it." He was fiddling with dials on his Polilight. "Open up a bindle, put the clean inside of it facing up." Amy took one of the simple evidence wrappers, a bindle, from a belt holster; she undid the tape, unfolded it, and placed it on the bathroom sink as Jermaine instructed. "Now use a business card or something to put that Tic-Tac box on the paper."

"I don't need no stinking business card," she said with a smile. Amy always enjoyed Doctor Tallant's real-world teaching examples. She tipped the trash can on its side and shook it until the little plastic box was near the opening, then carefully coaxed it onto the opened bindle.

"Excellent, my dear young lady. Now–" he turned the big dial on the front of his machine "–we set the Polilight to regular white light, but shine it at a sharp angle." Paul said, "Ouch," and shut their eyes when the very bright light came on. "Then, we look for ridges." Amy and the medical examiner bumped heads as both tried to look at the Tic-Tac box from the same place.

"Either it's a mirror and your gizmo blinds me," Amy offered, "or it's dark and I don't see anything."

Nodding, he said, "Turn the box over. Perhaps we'll find something on the other side."

Amy carefully lifted a corner of the opened bindle until the candy box turned over. Jermaine repeated the exercise. "Still nothing," she said. "Either a mirror or nothing."

"I'll show you what we're looking for," he said. He opened the medicine cabinet and removed a glass shelf, letting containers of band-aids, mercurochrome, and vaseline fall into the sink. He wiped both sides of the shelf on his trousers, then rested it on the lip of the sink, next to the bindle with the Tic-Tac box. He said, "May I?" as he grasped Amy's left hand and rolled her index finger against the glass. When he was done, Paul held the finger up to their eyes to examine it. "My print is still on it," he said.

"Oh, dear. We may have to abandon our entire philosophy of fingerprint identification," Jermaine said dryly. He turned the bright light on again, at a low angle, and said, "Now look straight down at the glass."

"Well, what do you know!" Amy exclaimed. Their print stood out plainly.

"If we had found a print on the box I'd have been able to photograph it. I like my Polilight. If I get another dog I may name it Polilight."

"He'll have problems at the dog park," Amy said. "'Fido, this is Polilight.'" She shook their head. "I can hear all the dogs laughing now. Fistfights in the playground, dog wedgies, graffiti on his locker–you might want to rethink that. At least give him a doggie middle name like 'Spike' to use with strangers."

"I never considered the psycho-canine ramifications of nomenclature," he said. "You are a delight, Miss Clear. It's a wonder you ended up as a police detective. Anyway," turning back to the machine of which he was so fond, "for saliva we set the Polilight to four hundred fifty nanometers, and–"

"What is a nanometer?" Amy interrupted.

"A very, very small part of a meter. We used to identify light wavelength by hertz or cycles per second, but somehow that went out of fashion. Four-hundred-fifty nanometers is on the purple side of blue," and he flicked the machine on. Light the color of a Milk of Magnesia bottle spilled out of the display. "And we put on the right goggles–here, hold this," he ordered, handing Amy the cloth bag containing a dozen sets of delicate and expensive colored lenses. "Orange, orange, or–ah, here!" he said, retrieving two sets of lenses from the bag. "Put these on, please," he said as he handed one to her, then donned the other set himself.

"Whoa, that's trippy," Paul said. The combination of the colors of the lenses and the light gave things a surreal monochromatic wash.

"As you say, Miss, trippy. Now, look at this–" he was holding a pen, pointing at a thick white line on the side of the Tic-Tac container, near the hinged opening "–and tell me what you think it is."

"It's not there under normal light without these glasses," Amy said, and looked up at him. "What is it?"

"Saliva trace," he said smugly. "Our he-she-it sweets lover obtained candy the same way I did back in the day." Looking at Amy he said, "Wrap this in a bindle. It'll be easy to do a tape lift and DNA test back at the station house. If our candy gobbler has had any legal run-ins, I'll find them in the database."

Paul exclaimed, "That's amazing. What did police do before to find saliva?"

Jermaine turned off his beloved Polilight while Amy fished another bindle from its holster and began to prepare the Tic-Tac package as evidence. "We used something called the Phadebas method. It's effective, but it involves water and specially prepared paper and maybe an hour out of your life. It works fine, but this is faster."

"Doctor Jermaine?" the photographer called. "I'm done in here for now." Hortense stood in the hallway outside the bathroom where he had been working with Amy.

"Notice anything in particular?"

"Stabbed in the neck. I'll bet it hurt." She was changing lenses on the camera. "When you move the body I'll take the rest of the pictures."

"If you don't mind helping me, Detective..."

Grinning, Amy followed the man back to the crime scene. "Doctor Tallant, when will you ever learn my name is Amy?"

"What? Maybe when you learn mine is Jermaine. Were the lights on when you got here?" he asked.

She shook their head. "I flipped it on with my elbow, through my shirt sleeve."

"We may be able to find a print." Then he bent to the mortal remains of Samantha Atkins, sprawled across her bed, face down, head hanging off the side of the mattress. He pulled back the bed clothes to expose the bare body.

"Hortense, if you would." He pointed to the wide tattoo of a disturbingly realistic pair of bloodshot blue eyes across the corpse's lower back. The photographer clicked several shots with her digital SLR camera.

"When you find a murder victim nude," he began, "you must consider sexual assault."

Paul spoke, "I thought you always consider that no matter how the body is dressed."

"Well, yes, I suppose so." He was plugging his beloved Polilight into a wall outlet beside the bed. "But especially when this much skin is available." Fiddling with the device dial, he went on, "Four hundred and fifteen nanometers. What did you do with the bag of viewing lenses?"

"Uh, I put it in the bathroom sink. No, wait–the toilet lid. I'll get it."

"Very good." He looked at the settings on his Polilight, and changed the bandwidth filter to 40 nanometers for the next scan.

"The blue lenses this time," the medical examiner said; "No, the light blue ones." She handed him a set and slipped the elastic on the other one around their head, popping the blue goggles over their eyes.

The man picked up the light-emitting wand and held it out to Amy. "Start in the obvious places, but cover the entire body, top and bottom."

When she began at Sam's neck and shoulders, Jermaine said, "Like this," and took her hand in his. "Aim straight down, not at an angle."

"Okay. Thanks," she said. Then she heard Paul think, *Can I do it?* She placed the wand in their left hand, and Paul took the lead.

"What are we looking for?" he asked.

"Fluorescence," said the medical examiner. "It'll be bright blue. Whoa–like that." Paul was shining the violet light from the wand halfway down the body's back. There were long blue streaks, pale in the middle but with very bright edges.

Paul in Amy looked up at Jermaine. "So what does this mean?"

"Occam's Razor suggests our perpetrator was a male who rather enjoyed himself while he was sending Miss Atkins into eternity."

"No," Paul said. "This can't be." He was hearing Amy silently object to the doctor's diagnosis. "We're pretty sure who the killer is, but he's a she."

A shrug. "I suppose it's possible a dozen Hooters' hostesses brought the one male cook with them when they killed her. You realize, of course, that when facts interfere with a theory, it's wiser to change the theory than to explain away the facts."

Amy pushed to lead. "Not to get too gross, Doc, but a cat? A croc? A tarantula?"

Jermaine took the wand from Amy and continued the examination of Sam's body. "Cogent," he offered. "My Polilight does not know the difference between human and animal semen. However–" he returned the light beam to the body's lower and middle back "–the volume seems to indicate something more virile than a hamster."

"So, who else?" Paul asked Amy, aloud. "Calvin and J'waun left days ago."

"Armand Terrebonne?" she remarked. "Papite Dardar? But why would they want Sam dead?"

Amused, Jermaine asked, "Is this a private conversation, or may anyone contribute?"

"What? Oh–uh, sure, Doctor Tallant. Please, fire away."

"There is always the possibility that Miss Atkins' demise is not related to the church murder you are investigating. This is a particularly nasty area of the parish."

Amy thought, then shook her head. "You're right about that, but I'm not a big believer in coincidence. It doesn't look like anything was stolen–" She heard Paul think, *How would we know? All she had was that TV.*

"See, the TV is still here," she answered aloud. "The door was standing open when I got here and no one took it."

"I think I follow you, Miss. Do you always converse with yourself like this?"

"What? No, no–uh, yes. I talk to myself all the time, so it's me and me. Or me and myself. And sometimes I."

She heard Paul silently say, *Sometimes I? Are you a vowel?* "Shush," she hissed.

"It appears you listen to yourself, too. Someday, Detective, I would love to have your fascinating brain on my laboratory bench."

"Sorry, Doctor Tallant, I'm not done with it yet."

"And first I have to hire a hunchbacked assistant named Igor."

Amy smiled, more from Paul's silent laughter than from the medical examiner's reference to ancient Boris Karloff movies she had never watched. She said, "Back to evidence. You said you can get DNA from the Tic-Tac box. From the ejaculate on the body?"

"Of course. And from our deceased friend as a comparison. You do realize she may have liked Tic-Tacs as much as I used to."

Paul blurted out, "How can I get a sample from Drew Malone?" Amy took the lead in mid-laugh and said, "You think she's the source of the semen?"

Tallant was marking notes on a diagram of Sam's body, noting the tattoo, the biological stain, and the knife wound. "Excuse me," he said, "I was getting whiplash from watching you talk to yourself. Give me a minute and then help me turn the body, okay?"

I want a beer, Amy thought to Paul.

Me, too, he thought back. *But no.*

Meanie.

It's not even lunch time and you really want a drink?

Time compression goes along with smelling dead bodies, she thought. *It feels like it's already five o'clock.*

"Now, Detective?"

"Oh. Sure. I'll take the feet."

"That would be most kind." Jermaine waited until Amy was at the foot of the bed, hands on Sam's ankles. "When we lift, you'll bring up her left leg and pull it to the right." They both nodded. He counted, "One, two, three!" and they managed to flip the stiff body. There was an ugly sound as the bottom sheet, stuck to the corpse's chest by the dried blood, pulled free.

"What an odd place for a tattoo," he observed. "Miss Clear, do you have a tattoo over your bottom left rib?"

"I didn't this morning," she said. "Do you need me to check again now?"

"Ah, perhaps when you get home you can look and let me know. I believe that is a cow. Who on earth gets a tattoo of a cow?"

Amy asked, "Are you going to use your light gizmo thingee on her front?" The medical examiner handed the light wand to her, and she carefully ran the violet light over Sam's face and then the rest of her body. There was no more fluorescence.

"I believe I am done," Jermaine said as he unplugged the Polilight. "I'll get the EMT people to package Miss Atkins for her trip to my autopsy table."

Amy said, "When they're done I want to examine the bed and the room. Maybe there's another clue waiting for us."

Johnson and Baker wheeled their portable gurney into the bedroom. A black plastic body bag lay on top, unzipped open. Baker asked, "Are you ready?" and Johnson nodded to her. They efficiently moved the body, zipped the bag, and wheeled their gurney out.

"Do you need anything else from me?" Jermaine asked. He was removing the bedsheets and stowing them in a large evidence bag.

"Wet towels in the bathtub," Amy replied. "Maybe Sam took a bath before she got killed, or maybe the perp washed up afterwards."

"I will process them. Anything else?"

"Answers," Amy replied. "I hope you have some for me tomorrow."

Alone in the death house, Amy stared at the large, dark stain on the mattress where Sam Atkins had breathed her last. Out loud she said, "Nobody much liked her, but I don't know who would have wanted her dead."

As Amy systematically examined the bedroom floor, Paul offered, "Maybe one of the men she pulled that bothersome priest routine on did the killing and was afraid Sam would rat them out."

"Or, maybe one of the men she tried to get to kill Tibbs didn't do the killing but was afraid Sam would say they did."

"Great. So every man Sam ever talked to is a suspect."

"Oh, not at all," Amy said, eyes aimed at the painted wooden floor. "Just the ones she talked to in the last two weeks or so."

She was processing the cigarette butt she'd found on the porch when her phone rang.

"Hey, Duke," she said, "how's it going?"

"Your suspect is dead?"

"I had a great night, thanks for asking. And I spotted something at Crate & Barrel that just might end up in your Christmas stocking. Do you prefer blue or green?"

"Cut the crap, Queenie, I'm in a hurry. Dead?"

"Yes. Dead. As the proverbial doornail." Paul added, "Shuffled off this mortal coil, run down the curtain, and joined the choir invisible."

There was static on the line, until the lieutenant said, in measured tones, "Please. I asked you to cut the crap. Just tell me what happened."

Even as Paul laughed inside, Amy hissed silently, *Shush! I want to make him respect me again.* Then, aloud, "Jermaine says time of death was yesterday between, like, five-thirty in the afternoon and eleven-thirty at night. Knife to the side of the neck. Body nude in bed. No signs of robbery. We'll have DNA from saliva and semen."

"Any leads?"

"We'll see when Jermaine finishes the DNA analysis and comparison. I am upset that my main suspect is physically incapable of leaving a souvenir of spent sperm."

"What? Christ almighty, Detective, can you please speak normal English?"

It was Paul who said, "Sure. My next biggest suspect is female. Pearl necklace not likely. Got it?"

"Oh. Well, shit. Who else is on your radar screen?"

"Doctor Tallant points out this killing may not be related to the church murder," Amy said, thinking out loud. "Theoretically he's right–this place is so far up Desire I can throw a rock into the project–but that would be more coincidence than I can accept. Did you talk to those other militia people?"

"Besson and Melançon, yeah. Each of them told the same story–they were there, some woman approached them and asked about killing someone, and they chased her away. And they couldn't go in the church or their priest would kill them. I'm meeting Jacques Griffin in two hours, that'll finish up the militia angle."

"I don't know," Amy mused. "Any suggestions?"

"Wait on Jermaine to tell you what he finds," the lieutenant said. "Me, I've got a pile of reports to go over and then my patrol shift."

Paul thought to Amy, *Can we sleep in tomorrow?* Duke didn't know why she laughed, but then she said, "No reason for me to come in when you muster. Let me drive in after the sun is up and I'll meet with the doc."

"Yeah. Okay, Queenie. Don't be walking into any more doors, you hear?" He laughed and hung up.

"'Duke's a pro,' you said. 'He's probably forgotten it by now,' you said. But no! He's still making fun of me." She put her phone back into its holster.

Paul asked, "Am I back in the doghouse?"

"What makes you think I ever let you out?"

He hung his inside head. *Tell me what you want me to do,* he thought to her, *and I'll do it. Grovel? Hari-Kari? Push-ups? Clean the bathroom with a toothbrush?*

"I haven't decided yet." Paul thought–he hoped–he felt the trace of a smile on their face.

Amy finished processing the stray cigarette butt into a bindle. "I have to bring this to Jermaine. And the towels he forgot to take." She considered that task, and headed to the kitchen. "I need a plastic bag from Rouses for the towels. I don't have any plastic evidence containers with me."

Amy opened and closed kitchen drawers until she found the one every kitchen has, with the thin plastic bags crammed beyond capacity. Paul thought, "So we go to the station house. Then what? Christine is busy tonight; we're on our own."

"The radio says Olaf will be a hurricane before it makes landfall. It can hit anywhere between Port Arthur and Mobile. I want to stock up on supplies." She squeezed one towel into a bag, then went back to the kitchen for more bags. She took a handful back to the bathroom to continue work.

"Supplies?" Paul mused. "Toilet paper. Cans of soup. Sterno. A frozen blueberry pie. Maybe a jeroboam of Shiraz, or a twelve-pack of Dixie. You know what they say, any port in a storm–"

"No beer!" she shouted, "No wine!" Each of the three remaining towels in the tub got its own plastic bag. "This is day one, remember?"

"Ah. Right. This has been a test. This was only a test. Had it been an actual request for booze, I'd have removed our wallet and driven us to Big Man's Discount Liquor Emporium. This was only a test."

"Thank you," she said. "Don't let the sarcasm drip on you."

Sitting in Amy's Benz, with the wet towel evidence seeping through the flimsy grocery store bags into the back seat cushions, Paul said, "What do we do about Sam's apartment? We can't lock the door because we don't have a key. Her stuff is going to get ripped off."

"You know, that's always bothered me," she replied. "We like to say 'Protect and serve,' but police aren't a security company." She looked down the deserted rainy street. "When I give the evidence to Jermaine, I'll look up the property owner and alert them. It's not like Sam needs that big screen TV anymore."

"Wow," Paul said. "Too bad you bought a big TV last year. Otherwise we could, uh, take Sam's. For safe-keeping, of course."

"You've admitted you weren't always a pillar of society when you had your own body. Exactly how bad were you?"

"I've told you before; I was good bad, but not evil."

She pressed the button for the glow plugs. "I can guess evil, but what is good bad?"

"Oh look. It's raining outside."

She shook her head as she started the diesel engine, and began the drive back to the Rampart Street station.

"You forgot the towels," she admonished the medical examiner as she dropped the three bags of wet evidence on his desk. The front of her shirt was dark with the water that had leaked out of the plastic grocery bags. "And I've got this–" she retrieved the bindle with the cigarette butt from her back pocket "–it was on the porch. Maybe it's useful."

"I thank you for provoking me into washing my desk," he said with a smile. "I had a feeling there was something I'd forgotten." He was wearing a stained but clean lab coat over his clothing.

"I thought of something," she said as she sat on one of the wheeled stools in his outer office. "Has there been another case like this in Louisiana? Do preachers get murdered in church very often?"

"None that rings a bell. Shall I look into it for you?"

She smiled broadly, but it was Paul who said, "That would be swell."

"'Swell'? How could I say no?"

Amy took back the lead. "Is Olaf going to nail New Orleans?"

"I keep an ark in my basement for just such occasions. But I fear the answer is yes."

"Crap. Depending on what you find out from the DNA, I may need to arrest someone tomorrow."

"Take water wings with you," he said. "The courts say it's our fault if a person in custody drowns."

"Hey! What if *I* drown?"

"Oh, that's just workers' compensation. Although you'd make more money if you lost one finger and one eye."

"Did you know that you are my very favorite person in this building?" Amy laughed. "But I probably ought to hit Rouses before all the bread and milk is gone. I hope I see you tomorrow."

"The good Lord willing and the bayou don't rise."

Amy stopped in the detectives' office and pulled up the Orleans Parish property tax digest. She entered the address of Sam Atkins' duplex and was rewarded with the name and contact information of the property owner. It was listed to an Alveric White in Mount Hermon, Louisiana. Amy punched the number on the office phone keypad and waited through three rings before a peculiar outgoing message played. She rolled her eyes, and at the beep said, "Alveric, this is Detective Clear with Orleans Parish Police. Your tenant at 2023 Desire Street in New Orleans was found murdered today. We have no way of securing your property, so you might want to, I don't know, change the locks, maybe call ServiceMaster to get the blood out of the bedroom. NOPD is not responsible for your property. I'm just saying. Thank you."

When she hung up the phone, Paul thought to her, *What a creepy message to have to leave.*

"At least notifying next of kin is not my problem. That's a job that would creep me out."

The Rouses Market #29 on North Carrollton Avenue was in a huge building with an even larger parking lot. Paul led to drive Amy's yellow Benz up and down the lanes until he finally saw a dark red SUV turn on its lights and back out of a parking place. It was only a little after three o'clock, but the heavy overcast and rain allowed all the illumination of an evening.

Amy found her travel umbrella on the floor of the back seat. "Let's see how wet we get anyway," she muttered as she opened the car door to dash for the store. The rain was heavy and chilly, with gusting winds warning of the approach of Hurricane Olaf.

Three steps away from the car the umbrella was blown inside out. As she swore, Paul thought to her, *Hang on to it. Maybe we can turn it right side out.* But before she could answer him, a gust blew it out of her grasp and down the parking lane, leaving it wedged underneath someone's pickup truck.

It was a relief to reach the store, to be protected from wind and rain and cold. Instead they faced a crowded and humid store full of wet, worried, and annoyed people. All the bascarts were in use, so Amy settled for one of the dark brown baskets. She heard Paul think, *It's so small—we need three of these. And it's a long walk back to the car.*

"I guess we'll have to limit ourselves to what fits in one," she said. The people around her were preoccupied with their own inconvenience and did not notice the slim, wet woman talking gibberish to herself. "If there's any toilet paper left." She elbowed her way into the slow-moving crowd choking the aisles. *It's like Mardi Gras,* Paul thought. *Lift up your feet and let the crowd take you wherever.*

Three lone rolls of the house brand single-ply tissue were all that remained on the long, empty shelf. She dropped one of them in their basket. *Can we hide in the restroom when they close and stay here all night?* Paul thought. *There's stuff to eat here.*

"Tempting," she said aloud. Her next stop was the pharmacy aisle for aspirin and vitamin C.

Their search for double-A batteries led them through the liquor department. Paul said, "Wine? Beer? Vodka?"

Amy stopped; some people behind her bumped into her, but then went around her without a word. "Is this day seven?" she asked aloud.

Uh, no. But–but–but by day seven we might still be marooned. We need something for just in case.

"I recommend rat poison," she replied. "We need batteries, they're down here somewhere," and she went down a side aisle to escape the alcohol section that was a temptation to both of them.

They spent twenty frustrating minutes in line while the frantic cashier with the red-and-black checked snood was scanning and bagging groceries like an eight-armed Hindu goddess. The shoppers in front of and behind them were complaining non-stop: about Olaf, about Rouses, about the Army Corps of Engineers and the likelihood of levees breeching and drainage canals overflowing. When it was their turn, Paul said, "You are doing an incredible job. When do you get to go home?"

"I don't. I expect to drown while I'm ringing up rotisserie chicken and twelve-packs of Dixie beer." Mechanically, she was scanning their purchases. "If you see my husband, tell him to get the kids to higher ground."

Amy squinted at the woman's name tag. "Uh, Tanya. Sure thing." By the time she collected the two plastic bags of her purchase, the cashier was halfway through processing the next customer's supplies.

It was a cold, wet walk back to Amy's Benz, made worse by both of them having forgotten which lane they had parked in. "There's our umbrella!" Paul cried.

"Change in course," Amy replied aloud, and squeezed them between parked cars to get closer. A few vehicles nearer the store was her car. The driver's side window was down about two inches. "Oh, crap and a half!" she shouted, then thought to Paul, *A little bit of Lake Pontchartrain right there in my car. Double crap!*

Indeed, the driver's seat was very wet. "No standing water on the floor, though," Paul observed. "You know, I was hoping we were going to find Nemo."

"If I do, I'm going to fillet him and eat him." She tossed her purchases onto the back seat, and laid the plastic bags over her seat. Even so, she felt the cold dampness when she sat. Annoyed, she said, "Paul, why don't you get us home?"

"Aye, aye!" His smile burst across their face; he so loved to drive. He went through the ritual of glow plugs and started the engine. He also rolled up the window, and turned up the heat on the old car's climate control. "Next stop, Carrollton," he said. "Please keep your hands and feet inside the vehicle at all times."

I'm glad one of us is having a good time, she thought, but Paul could feel her inside smile.

When they were safe inside Amy's house, she changed out of their wet clothes. Paul said, "Let's invite Christine to stay with us. She's between Bayou St. John and the London Avenue Canal, not exactly high ground." As he speed-dialed his lover's phone, he heard Amy musing, "Weird, but the closer to the river, the higher the land. We'll use Tchoupitoulas or Magazine to get to the cop shop tomorrow."

Paul always enjoyed hearing Christine's outgoing message: "This is Christine Hodges' phone. You know how it works, so leave me a message. And Paulette, I love you!" At the beep he said, "Hey, Honey. I know you're in that calligraphy class right now, but I'm inviting you to bunk with Amy and me. We're on higher ground than you are. If you have any worries about the storm, come on over! I love you." Before he could end the call Amy added, "It's Amy. We can light a fire in the middle of the living room floor and roast marshmallows. It'll be great. Be safe."

"We've got marshmallows?" Paul asked.

"Actually, no, we don't. I lied to your girlfriend. Can you ever forgive me?"

"I like how you're as crazy as I am."

Amy smiled. "Of course I am. You're the one who taught me."

℘ FRIDAY, August 18, 2034 ℞

On Friday morning Amy turned on TV to find local coverage about the pending landfall of Hurricane Olaf, now expected somewhere between Port Arthur and Gulfport. The talking weather heads on all the channels agreed that New Orleans was in for a pounding even if landfall were at the edges of the projected landing cone. The CBS affiliate predicted Olaf would come ashore between three and four in the afternoon.

She peeked out the bedroom window to see more rain, and wide puddles in the patio. "I think it's time to close the shutters," she said, and began fiddling with a yellow rain slicker she hadn't used since Hurricane Rodrigo several years earlier.

In many parts of America, house shutters are decorative rather than functional; nailed uselessly in place, they merely make a residence look complete. But in New Orleans and other coastal communities, working shutters are a vital necessity to survive hurricanes. Without them, hurricane-force winds lead to broken windows and water damage. The homeowner who battens down strong shutters before serious storms goes a long way toward protecting everything. Well, everything but the roof. You do what you can.

Despite the yellow slicker, Amy needed to change into dry clothes afterwards. "Today's the day," she informed Paul, and found the string of pearls her father had given her more than fifteen years earlier. With difficulty, she fixed the clasp on the back of their neck, over a dark blue blouse. Then she strapped on her thigh holsters for pistol, baton, handcuffs, phone, and badge. Finally she wiggled her way into a long blue skirt that went halfway between knees and ankles.

"Not bad," she said as she stood before the full-length mirror on the inside of her closet door, examining her reflection as she turned this way and that. "I think Parker was right–the pearls work with a skirt."

"You look very preppy," Paul offered. "Trust me, that is a very good thing."

She made a final twirl in front of the mirror. Only then did she notice her cellphone blinking its alert about a missed call. "It's Christine," Paul said, "I'm sure of it." He called through to Amy's voicemail to hear his lover say, "My class just ended and I got your message. I don't think it's bad enough to abandon ship yet, so I'm going home. But I'll be over tomorrow after work. Or sooner, if the boss closes the brokerage early. Amy? Marshmallows are great, but do you really want to burn down your living room? That's a strange way to shelter from a hurricane."

Amy and Paul laughed–one out loud, the other inside. "Sometimes she's so literal," Amy said. "What a dear."

"I love her, I love her, I love her. Can I marry her yet? Please? Pretty please? With no booze on top?"

"While you were passed out the other night," Amy answered, "she told me she'll say yes if you ask."

"And you're surprised?" Paul said. "So can I? Can we? Can– you know."

She did not tell him Christine indicated the wait was wearing her patience. "I'm not ready yet. We'll see. And I've got to get to the station house to talk to Jermaine."

The day was dim and chilly, with rain that pulsed between steady and extreme. She was grateful there was no standing water on Magazine Street as she drove a longer route to the Rampart Street police station to keep to what little high ground there was. She said to Paul, "If I let you drive our usual way through the Central Business District we'd probably be stalled in a flood by now." The area known to locals as the CBD included the business hub surrounding the Superdome; like much of New Orleans, it was below sea level and vulnerable to storms.

"Good morning, Detective," Jermaine said, when she entered his office. Behind him, the door to his work area was open. Amy could see a heap of God-knows-what on the work bench and a large puddle of blood on the floor underneath it.

"Hey, Doctor Tallant," she said. "Did it take you long to swim to work this morning?"

"Ah. Not as long as it will take to swim home this evening, I fear."

It was Paul who led to ask, "Anything yet on the Atkins murder?"

"As a matter of fact, yes, yes, not yet, and yes."

"Oh, Mister Wizard," Amy smiled, "you make my little head explode. What do you have?"

He picked up his clipboard and tapped his pen on the table top as if calling a meeting to order. "The things going in and coming out are from the same person."

Amy tilted their head and squinted as she heard Paul silently say, *Huh?*

"The DNA from the Tic-Tac container and the semen on the body match," he clarified. "Needless to say, they are not from the deceased."

Paul popped their eyes wide. "So, what's the 'not yet' part?"

"It'll be this afternoon before I know if the DNA matches anything in the FBI's CODIS database."

Paul whistled. "You can turn a search around that fast?"

"It used to take weeks," he said, finally sitting on one of the many stools on casters in his outer office. "But the problem is the local database is incomplete. Do you know for more than ten years after Katrina there wasn't a DNA laboratory in New Orleans? It was something like 2020 or 2021 before the new building went up, but that's a lot of DNA that never made it to the database. Anyway," he went on, "There is one more 'yes' to relate."

Amy bent both arms and held their hands palms up. "Sorry, my head exploded. What?"

"You asked if there have been any other murders of religious leaders. It turns out, there was one in 2026 that was similar."

"Similar? Tell me!" She pulled her notebook from a back pocket and opened it to a fresh page. She heard Paul think, *How similar?*

Jermaine glanced at his clipboard to get the details correct. "Summer Grove. It's near Shreveport. A Baptist preacher was found stabbed to death in the parking lot of his church. The trail of blood indicates he was wounded in his office, then somehow made it down a flight of stairs and out the back door before he died."

"Perp?" She was writing notes.

"Well, that's the thing. Eight years later, it's still an open case."

Amy stood up. "What's the church? Who were the employees then? Volunteers? Anyone–"

"Harley Malone," he interrupted. "Junior pastor at Second Baptist Church of Summer Grove. He was considered the prime suspect, especially after he disappeared."

Paul led to say, "I'm going to let you tell me the whole story. I'm tired of saying 'What? What?'" They sat back down.

"Very good, then. The murder weapon was a hunting knife; it was found in the preacher's office, and his prints were the only ones on it. Seems Pastor Butch Normand was able to pull it out of his back and get down the stairs before he expired from exsanguination."

Amy said, "From exsan-what?"

"Blood loss. Bleeding out. Now, Assistant Pastor Harley Malone was interviewed during the police response, but he must have been a fast talker, because he wasn't taken into custody. When Caddo Parish police went to his house the next day Harley was gone. His name disappeared from the Southern Baptist Convention register. Even the IRS claims it's never heard from him again. Disappeared."

"So, maybe Harley is related to Drew?" Amy mused aloud. "Brother and sister? Cousins? Parent and kid?" She twirled the stool she was on, and when she was facing Jermaine again she said, "I'm going to call Caddo Parish. I want their photo of this man."

Jermaine said, "I will let you know if there is a match on CODIS."

"Yes. Thank you, Doctor Tallant."

As she stood to leave, the medical examiner said, "If you don't mind me saying so, Detective, you look different today."

She smiled proudly. "Pearls," she said. "I think I've learned how to wear them."

He nodded. "Very classy. Well done, Miss."

In the detectives' workroom Amy found the number for the Caddo Parish Sheriff's office, which handles law enforcement outside the parish seat of Shreveport.

The switchboard relayed her call to the records division, where a Sergeant Meriwether picked up. After Amy identified herself, she said, "I'm looking for whatever information Caddo Parish has on a cold case from 2026. The murder victim was a pastor Butch Normand, and the prime suspect was a Harley Malone."

Amy heard the woman go "Ummm," and the click-clack-clacking of her typing at a keyboard. "Okay," the sergeant finally said, "April 19, 2026, in Summer Grove. Yeah, I've got it."

"Great!" Amy responded. "We're working a church murder in New Orleans, and we have a person of interest named Malone. Can you email me scans of what you have?"

"Uh... Actually, how about I fax it to you?"

It was Paul who said, aloud, "I remember fax machines. I thought the last one in captivity died in a museum of obsolete technology in 2016."

After a short silence the sergeant said, "Do you want it or not?"

"Yes, yes," Amy said. "Do you have a picture of your suspect?"

"Yeah, that's part of the package."

Amy looked at the office directory to see the fax number she had never been asked to give before, and dictated it to the officer. "If we find a link to your case, I'll let you know," she added.

After the call, Amy fidgeted as she waited for the ancient Brother machine in the corner of the office to awaken. Trying to make the time pass, she thought, *You're right about faxes being obsolete. I remember how bad they make a photo look.*

Paul said, "Caddo Parish is stuck in the 1980s."

After college, my old boyfriend Timmy was based up there, in Shreveport. Last time I was there was to see him in a rodeo. I think he came in second in bull riding.

The ancient fax machine began to clatter. The second page was a blurry half-tone of a man in his twenties or early thirties; short haircut, full smiling face, and widely spaced brown eyes. Paul thought to her, *Holy fuck! The eyes are just like Drew's.*

"Family resemblance," Amy murmured aloud. "I'm thinking brother, not husband."

Yeah, Paul thought. *For some reason I can't picture Drew married.*

She shrugged as she watched the noisy machine churn out another thirteen pages–the blurry recap of the Shreveport murder. As Amy scanned the documents, she mused, "Like Jermaine said, only the preacher's prints on the knife, but they didn't think it was suicide." She flipped a few pages. "Huh! Attempt at follow-up interview with Harley found his house empty. No furniture, and...uh...–" she laughed, "–not even a refrigerator."

Let me check something, Paul thought, and Amy let him lead to sit in front of one of the office computers. He clicked away, then leaned back. *Zabasearch says there are 27 Harley Malones. Did Caddo Parish offer a middle name?*

Amy leafed through a few pages of the fax. "No, but an initial. D. Harley D. Malone."

Paul thought, *I wonder if the D stands for Drew.* He revised his web search and got no hits.

After a long silence, Amy thought back, *You just made my head explode again. No. No way. No way in hell.* She stood up with the printout. "Time to visit the real Drew. If she bothered to row to the church today."

The constant rain and the threat of Hurricane Olaf's landfall kept many people off the roads. Even so, Paul drove slowly and carefully past backed up storm sewers. Of course, it took longer than on a normal, sunny day to get to the Metropolitan Community Church on St. Charles Avenue. As usual, he parked on the side street, Henry Clay, with their right wheels on the curb and blinkers flashing. Amy led to put her 'NOPD Official Business' sign on the dashboard. She grabbed the wet yellow slicker from the back seat and tried to cover themself.

It works! she thought as she stepped out into the rainwater river flowing over the street. *We're dry. Above the ankles, anyway.*

She scurried to the side door of the church and found it unlocked. *So, what are we asking Drew today?* Paul thought. *Are we arresting her? Accusing her of murder?*

I'm going to ask her who Harley is, she thought back. She shook the slicker off and let it fall to the floor by the doorway, then headed for the stairwell.

Associate–no, *interim*–pastor Drew Malone was at the desk in her office, looking like a fat drowned rat. Her short, wet hair was stuck to her head in peculiar patterns, and the shoulders of her shirt were dark and spotted from rain. Amy knocked at the open doorframe and said, "You look like you walked to work. Are you okay?"

The woman looked up in surprise, then smiled. "Vespa," she said. "Not a good day for it."

Amy stepped inside. "Don't you have towels or something? You'll catch cold."

"Too late," Drew sniffed, "but this sermon will not write itself."

"I need to ask you something. Did you ever live in Shreveport?"

It seemed to Amy that the woman blanched, but the pastor said, "I don't think so. No. I'm from Iowa."

"Okay. Are you kin to anyone named Harley Malone?" Amy and Paul both stared intently through their one pair of eyes, looking for any quiver or tremor that might be a clue to Drew's honesty.

"Truly I tell you, I am not a relative of anyone with that name." She frowned. "What's this all about?" She put down her pencil and looked up at Amy.

"Something, uh, something happened in, uh, in Shreveport a long time ago," Amy stammered. "Someone had the same last name as you, but I guess it's not rare or anything."

Ouch, Paul thought. *What do you talk about now?*

Silence hung in the room. Finally Amy said, "I didn't get breakfast. I'm going to swim across the street to Loyola for their food court. Can I bring you back anything?" She thought Drew smirked at her. She turned around and went back down the stairs.

As Amy donned the yellow slicker Paul thought, *Breakfast. Did you know it's one of my three favorite meals? What are we having? Omelet? Steak and eggs? Or maybe–*

"Shhh!" Amy hissed to stop him, then thought back, *We're on stake-out.*

Not the steak I hoped for.

She pulled up the plastic knob that tightened the hat's string under their chin, and stepped outside. The rain was heavier than before. "I told Drew I'd be busy for the next little while. I want to hide and watch my car. See if she's up to anything, you know?" She was walking, then walking faster, and finally running, prodded by the chill of the rain and the drumming sound it made as it fell against her slicker hat.

I hope you've reserved some dry, warm place for us to hide, Paul thought. *T'aint a fit night out for man nor beast.*

When she got to the side street where she was parked, Amy crossed over Henry Clay Avenue and trotted to the front of an antique shop, where there was a red-and-white striped awning. The store was locked and dark; the owner had not made the investment of a trip to work in the face of Hurricane Olaf. "At least we won't get rained on here," she said aloud.

If we lean in that corner, Paul thought, pointing, *we can see our car. Damn that wind, though.*

"I wish my raincoat wasn't screaming yellow. If Drew does try something, I don't want her to see me."

They waited.

Amy shifted their weight back and forth from one foot to the other, trying to keep warm. She heard Paul think, *If I freeze to death, I just want you to know it's been an honor knowing you.*

She thought back, *Come on, it's not all that–Whoa! Drew!*

They saw the interim pastor, wearing a brown raincoat and some floppy hat, come through the bushes that edged the church property. She was holding what looked like a shoebox. Drew looked up and down Henry Clay, then began moving toward the yellow Benz with the flashing blinkers.

Amy and Paul watched as the woman splashed through the river of rain to touch the box she was holding to the car. The dome light came on and the running lights blinked; the horn made the same noise as when Amy used her key-fob.

What the fuck? Paul thought, as they saw Drew open the driver's door and bend to peer inside. There was a mechanical thunk muffled by the heavy rain, and they saw the hood pop up an inch or two. *What?* he went on, *Is she going to pull the wires?*

"Shush," Amy whispered. "Let's see what she does."

Drew splashed to the front of the parked car and opened the hood, propping it up with the internal metal rod. Paul remembered a song lyric about "rainwater blowing all under my hood[15]," but he thought, *If she gets the motor all wet we'll never get home.*

"Shush."

They watched Drew open the front of her raincoat and take something blue and cylindrical from an inside pocket. Then she leaned forward, but all they could see were her arms moving, not what the hands were doing.

"Okay," Amy whispered, "I've waited long enough." She walked into the heavy rain and into the street, coming up behind Drew. "Thanks for the tune-up," Amy said. "Do you think the timing belt needs any work?"

When she jumped at the surprise of Amy's voice, Drew hit the back of her head on the underside of the hood. Paul recognized what the woman had been working on–a blue canister of propane designed for a blowtorch, wrapped in a dozen loops of PrimaCord. If it were wired into the car's ignition it could leave a small crater and splatter bloody chunks of Amy over half the block.

Before he could tell Amy about the attempt to put a bomb in her car, Drew stepped back out from under the hood of the car and ran toward Amy. Between the rain, the yellow slicker, and the long skirt, Amy could not get to her pistol. The two women began to wrestle in the street, finally falling into the lake that was gathering in the street.

"You are under arrest," Amy bellowed, while trying to push the obese pastor up and off of her.

Drew raised herself to arm's length, then dropped her head to deliver a brutal head-butt to Amy. Involuntarily, Amy's hands went to the pain; Drew laughed and jumped up, and disappeared back into the bushes.

"Fuck!" Paul shouted out loud, "That hurts!"

"Yes," Amy muttered, "yes, it does. And this branch of the Mississippi River that's flooding my back is no help." She lay in the street, wet and dazed, until the stars she thought were circling her head faded. She grabbed the side of her car to hoist themself up to their feet.

I want to kill that dyke bitch! Paul shouted silently.

"Please," aloud, "it's hard enough to put up with that from Duke. Don't you go all bigot on me."

"Do you see this?" he pointed into the open engine compartment, at the propane tank. "Detonator fuse around propane. And see–" he leaned in and grabbed a blue wire that Drew had slipped into the starter relay "–this wire? She was planting a fucking bomb." He pulled the wire out and threw it into the rain torrent rushing downhill in the gutter.

An unpredictable aspect of their dyad existence was that the two of them didn't necessarily have the same experience of sensation. The pain from Drew's head-butt had largely passed for Paul while it lingered for Amy. Still, she saw what Paul was pointing out; she understood what he was saying. After a long, wet pause, she heard him shout out loud, "She is trying to kill us!"

As her head cleared, Amy's confusion and disorientation resolved into anger. "Yes. Yes, she is," she said out loud. "Now I can arrest her."

She tossed the propane tank into the back of her car. She slammed down the hood, then used her key fob to lock the Benz. Only then did she stumble through the bushes where Drew had escaped, and found themself not twenty feet from the office door of the church. It was standing open.

The discomfort of the windy and cold humid rain overcame her concern of being ambushed. She let themself inside. *Okay, no head-butt waiting for us,* Paul thought. Amy kicked off her shoes and dropped her slicker to the floor. All of her clothes were wet. She retrieved her phone from its thigh holster, but the display was black. "Insurance doesn't cover water damage," she muttered to Paul, while, mindlessly, she put it back in its holster. Then she drew her pistol.

We'll have to clean it good tonight, Paul thought. *Water and guns don't mix, but at least it's not an instantaneous problem like the phone.*

Careful to keep her finger outside the trigger guard, Amy shook the sidearm. Water flew out the barrel and drained from where the magazine fit into the handle. In bare, wet feet she went up the stairs.

The light was shining through the window from Drew's office to the hall, but the door was locked. Amy crouched below the window sill, then poked her head up to try to look inside the room. There was no movement. She stood up again and bellowed, "Drew! Drew Malone!"

There was noise around the corner. Paul led to drop into a shooting crouch, gun in their left hand. They heard a male voice getting louder, "Pastor Malone? Are you all right?" until a clean-cut man in his mid-twenties appeared. He froze when he saw the gun trained on him, and some unintelligible syllables came from his mouth.

"Who are you?" Amy challenged, while Paul kept a bead on the man.

"Juh–Juh–Jordan Finch," he stammered, hands in the air, "the sexton. Wh-Wh-Who are you?"

Paul let down the hammer of the Ruger while Amy said, "Underneath all this water I'm Detective Clear with New Orleans Police. Is Drew Malone here?" She stood up to return the gun to its holster, which involved hoisting up her maxi-skirt in a somewhat unladylike way. The sexton's mouth dropped open, and he turned his head.

"Well? Is she here?"

"She was in her office half an hour ago," the man said to the floor, his eyes still averted.

Paul laughed and said, "It's okay, son, I'm dressed now. Her door is locked. Let me in, okay?"

Jordan reached into a pocket to get the keys, and walked up to the door. "Where did she go?" he asked. "Really, she was just here."

"I know," Amy said as she walked around the man and through the now-open doorway, "I was here a little while ago. But she's gone now." As she looked into corners and behind chairs, she heard Paul think, *Careful. She may be hiding.* Her last effort at exploration was opening the only closet in the room, but Drew was conspicuous in her absence.

"You're the sexton," Amy turned to Jordan. "I don't see a cemetery for you to be digging graves, so what exactly do you do here?"

"Fix what I can," he answered, "and know which contractors to call for what I can't. And even more important, I make the weekly bulletin." He was an inch or two taller than Amy, with jet black hair that was just a little too long–which she found appealing. He was dressed in khakis and a blue dress shirt that showed the top of his undershirt at the open neck. "Are you sure you're a police officer?"

"Detective. Yes, I'm pretty sure of it, or else I wouldn't have come out in weather like this." Paul, sounding exactly like Amy, continued, "Look, son, your preacher–"

"Damn it!" Jordan exclaimed. "Pastor Malone calls me 'my child,' and you call me 'son'–I'm an adult, you know." He was staring at her. "I'm twenty-four. Call me Jordan, for Christ's sake."

Paul was taken aback, but Amy remembered the day, age eleven, when she told her parents not to call her 'Pumpkin' anymore. "Jordan. I apologize, you are absolutely right. But I'm soaking wet and feeling pretty cranky, and I need to have a heart-to-heart with your preacher for trying to plant a bomb in my car. Where does she live?"

"A bomb? Reverend Malone?"

"Yes. Bomb. Malone. Jordan, tell me where she lives."

They saw all sorts of confusion pass across the man's face: disbelief, loyalty, shock, fear. "Come on to my office," he finally said, and led them down the hall and around the corner.

A radio was playing WWL, broadcasting ongoing updates on the approach of Olaf. "We are definitely in for a pounding," the announcer was saying, "but the National Weather Service says the eye will come across at Beaumont or Lake Charles around four o'clock."

Once Jordan was at his desk, he became businesslike. He opened a drawer and withdrew the employee and volunteer roster sheet. "Uh, can I get you not to drip on the rug?"

"Sorry, but no," Amy said. "I'm very drippy right now. And I'll probably be wetter next time I see your boss. The address?"

As Jordan began to recite, Amy fished under her skirt for her notebook. Wet pieces of it came apart in her hand. "Oh, fuck a damn duck," Paul cried. He continued with what Amy liked to call his indoor voice, "Can I get something to write on? Maybe more water resistant than this?" and he dropped the pasty mass of ruined paper on his desk.

The sexton opened another drawer and pulled out a three-by-five index card. "This is the best I can do," he said.

"I'll make it work," Amy replied. "You got a Sharpie pen?"

Another drawer, and he held out a blue felt-tip pen.

"You're very organized," she said. "I'm not. So, what's her address?"

She wrote it as he dictated. "1020 France Street." Paul looked up and thought, *Isn't that in Bywater?*

"Yes," Amy answered out loud. "Not the highest ground, but we should be able to get there before it floods."

"Oh, please, no," Jordan said. "Don't make me come with you."

"What? Of course not. Why on earth did you think that?"

"You said 'we'."

"Oh. Yes, I do that. I mean, uh, we mean that we do that. Sorry. Look, my phone is trashed. Can I call my lieutenant? I want him to meet me at Malone's place."

"Uh, okay," Jordan said, and he pushed his chair back. Amy missed the invitation; she just reached took the telephone handset from the customer side of the desk. From memory she dialed Duke's cell number.

"Duke, it's Amy," she began. "Where are you and how bad is it?"

"I'm working an assault in Broadmoor," he barked back. "You'd think a thug would know enough to stay indoors on a day like this. I'm soaking wet. Kind of makes me want to hand out some justice, you know what I mean?"

"Save some of that justice. When can you meet me in Bywater? That pastor tried to plant a bomb in my car, she head-butted me, and now I'm going to where she lives so I can feed her twelve loops of, what is it?–" Paul thought *PrimaCord* "–yes, PrimaCord. When can you meet me?"

"You got head-slammed by a woman? I didn't think it was possible."

"Duke, I'm as wet as you are and just as cranky. When can you meet me?" She dictated the street address.

"Shit, Queenie, I don't know. I have to rough up this perp a little, and then I'm gonna tie him to my back bumper and drag him to a holding cell–Damn right, asshole," he shouted away from his phone, "I'm talking about you!" Then, "Let me get moving. All I can tell you is, I'll be there as soon as I can."

"Soon would be great. Thanks, Duke." She put the phone back in the cradle on Jordan's desk.

Amy smiled at the sexton and said, "Thanks." Then, to Paul, but out loud, "Where are my shoes?"

"You left them inside the back door," Paul answered aloud. "Along with our slicker."

Still seated, Jordan asked, "You're really a cop?"

"Detective," she corrected.

"You–do you know you talk to yourself? It's kind of weird."

It was Paul who answered, "Yep. And it's not kind of weird, it's extremely damn weird. Stay dry, kid." By the time the sexton began protesting the diminutive, Amy was down the stairs and sticking their feet into very wet shoes.

"The rain is getting worse," Amy said. "You can drive–go down to Magazine and we'll make a left there. It's higher ground than St. Charles." Paul nodded. He was always glad to drive, even in a hurricane downpour. Considering the weather, and the fact that Drew had opened the hood to expose the engine to the elements,

Paul was grateful that the glow plugs indeed did glow, and that the engine started.

"Why her house?" he asked. "Why do you think she's going there?"

"Drew said she's from Iowa. I'd like to go there; I don't think they get hurricanes. Short of that, she could be anywhere. I'm betting she wants to have a change of underwear with her when she goes underground. So: her house."

The only vehicles they encountered were some National Guard trucks and the occasional civilian car that had waded into puddles that were deeper than the driver had thought. Paul kept Amy's Benz in the middle of the street, where the domed pavement was always highest. Some storm sewers on the landward side of Magazine, away from the river levee's higher ground, already had given up any effort of draining the deluge. By now roads in the Central Business District would be impassable.

Amy turned on the car radio, and swiveled the dial from her soft rock station to WWL. The weatherman–with an annoying, squeaky voice–was explaining that the expected landfall near the Louisiana-Texas state line was a boon for New Orleans. "The cyclonic pattern of hurricane winds in our hemisphere is counter-clockwise," he said. "That means those seventy-mile-per-hour winds will be coming south across Lake Pontchartrain. Now, that means trouble for Lakeshore, Gentilly, New Orleans East, and North Kenner and Metairie. But it also means the winds will not be driving the Gulf of Mexico north to flood the Mississippi River."

When Paul turned onto Camp Street, they found most traffic lights were dark; the few with power were blinking red in all directions. When the road reemerged after going under Pontchartrain Expressway, the dark roads were deserted. No sane person was out-of-doors. The squeaky-voiced weatherman said landfall was expected near Lake Charles in two hours.

At Canal, Camp Street turned into Chartres. Even the tourists had abandoned the French Quarter, now entertaining fantasies of making claims on their trip insurance because Olaf was keeping them from beignets at Café du Monde.

"If you had a siren, I'd turn it on," Paul moaned.

"If I had a siren, you'd always turn it on," she answered. "Get us up to Bywater without killing us, okay?"

The rain was playing a drum solo on the roof of the Benz. Visibility was so limited that the quaint buildings of the Vieux Carré were just a dim, wet background of closed shutters. At the north end of the French Quarter, Esplanade Avenue, the streets suddenly were clear. The area, known as the Esplanade Ridge, is the highest ground in the parish. The rain was as fierce as before, but there were no pools on the pavement or struggling storm sewers. A few traffic lights even seemed to be working, although the increased number of civilian cars were paying no attention to them.

Paul rubbed at the fog that kept forming on the inside of the windshield faster than the car's defroster could remove. "Where do we turn?" he asked, as he kept driving down-river, parallel to the Mississippi.

"Here, I think," Amy said. "No, no–" Paul jerked the wheel straight "–over there. Or–"

A huge barricade was in front of them. "I'm turning here," he said, driving up Poland Avenue alongside the closed naval base that had become a local political football after ownership was transferred to the city of New Orleans twenty years earlier.

"Stop!" Amy barked, and Paul applied the brakes in the middle of the street. "Let me drive," she said, and she took the lead. "Drew's place is around a corner or two," she said as she let out the clutch.

A left on St. Claude, and another left on France Street. The rain was even more intense, and the thick cloud cover made the chilly afternoon feel like dusk. Amy parked across the street from number 1020. Behind the padlocked grill to the adjoining alleyway, she saw a dirty, wet, red motor scooter.

The dwelling was a typical shotgun, with four concrete steps up to a tiny landing. The window shutters were secured, but the front door was standing open. With their hand on the car's inside door release, Amy said, "I guess I barge in on her."

She heard Paul think back, *With gun in hand.*

In her side mirror, Amy saw a taxicab slowly coming down France Street, the driver clearly searching for a house number through the heavy rain. She jumped out of the Benz and ran up to the cab as it stopped in front of Drew's house.

The driver rolled down his window. Amy said, "You're here for Malone, right? Number 1020?"

He nodded, and prepared to get out to help her get in his car.

Amy said, "Look, I don't know how to tell you this, but I don't need a cab anymore. I'm sorry I wasted your time."

The driver sat back. "Say what? In this hurricane? You don't–"

"I feel real bad about it," she interrupted, and reached through her slicker to the pocket where she kept her wallet. "Let me give you this for your trouble." Paul heard her scream silently, *Oh, crap!* She handed the cabbie a twenty, her smallest bill.

Suddenly the driver was all smiles; after all, he could go back to the garage now instead of to wherever some insane fare wanted to go in the midst of Hurricane Olaf. "Stay dry," he offered as he drove away.

Amy retreated to the Benz to get out of the downpour. "I can go inside and find out if she's holding a shotgun," she mused, "or I can pretend I'm the taxi. This'll work." She honked her horn twice.

"Give me a minute!" Drew's voice boomed through her open door.

"Bingo," Amy said, and she got out of the car and into the rain. Paul thought to her, *Damn. I never would have thought of that. You're good.*

She smiled at the praise, but thought back, *I'll bet you say that to all your dyads.* She stood about twenty feet away from Drew's door, in front of a lot that had been empty since Rodrigo, if not an earlier hurricane. She fished her baton out from under her skirt and flicked it open. Then, standing in the chilly deluge, she waited.

"I'm on the way! Don't drive off!"

Paul thought, *Shouldn't we have our gun out?*

I suppose it can't get any wetter, but I don't need it now, Amy thought back. *Drew won't be holding a weapon when she thinks she's meeting the taxi that's not there.* She tapped the baton in their free hand. *This will be enough.*

"Here I come!" Drew shouted. Wearing the same brown raincoat and floppy hat, she dragged a wheeled suitcase onto the little stoop behind her, holding a startling pink travel umbrella. When the woman didn't see a taxi, she bumped her luggage down the four steps and looked around.

Amy ran towards her and tapped the tip of her baton against Drew's left knee. The pastor squealed in pain; the umbrella rolled into the street and was blown down the block, while the woman fell backwards.

Drew was wearing a cassock under the raincoat, revealing the physical equipment more typically associated with 'him' than 'her'. *Hey,* Paul thought to Amy, *those balls aren't mine.*

Amy said aloud, "Well, what do you know? Harley, I've got a bone to pick with you." She ignored Paul's silent, laughing comment, *And it ain't between your legs.*

"Fuck you!" Drew–uh, Harley–shouted. She–uh, he–stood up, just a bit shakily, and even with a little limp from Amy's baton strike, ran through the rain at her.

Amy braced themself to wield her baton, but Harley Malone grabbed her wrist and twisted. It deflected the attack and made Amy drop the weapon with a yelp. Before she could retrieve it, Harley grabbed the fumbled baton. He didn't know the best way to employ it; he just swung it like a stick against Amy as he charged. The aluminum stem–not the dangerous button–crashed against the right side of Amy's neck. On top of the barely healed punch from Papite Dardar, the blow dropped her to the ground; painful tingles left their entire right arm and hand numb. Harley stood over her and raised the baton over his head to deliver another blow.

As he brought the weapon down, the wet aluminum slipped and spun out of his hand, dropping into a nearby puddle. He started to reach for it when a flashing blue light strobed over the street.

Malone retreated back to his house and slammed the door shut.

"Detective! Hang in there!" Duke Cunningham's shout sliced through the downpour as he ran to where Amy lay on the wet sidewalk. "I saw the preacher run back inside," he said as he knelt beside her in a puddle. "Where'd she get you?"

She tried to say, "On top of the hickey," but it wasn't just her arm that wouldn't work. A few grunts were all that escaped her mouth. Instead she thought to him, *He hit me in the neck with my own baton.*

For a moment Duke stared, startled, even as rain dripped off his nose and forehead. "Yeah," he finally said. "That 'not normal' thing."

She nodded, and thought, *I can't talk.*

"I hear you," he said, and slid a strong, wet arm under her shoulders to lift her into a sitting position. "You're breathing okay?" he asked, and she nodded. "You're not going to die on me, right?"

She managed a wan smile and thought, *You're not getting rid of me that easy.*

Neither of them saw Harley standing on his front stoop; he was behind the lieutenant, and the officer blocked Amy's view. They could not see him flick his wrist to open a six-inch stiletto blade.

When Duke hoisted Amy up onto her feet, she was able to see Harley coming up behind the officer. *Behind you!* she thought to him. Amy fell to her knees when Duke let go of her to turn to the pastor. Harley's wicked blade sliced through the lieutenant's uniform and into his left shoulder. There was a sudden spurt of blood, quickly diluted by the unrelenting rain.

Right-handed, Duke seized Harley by the wrist and twisted until the knife fell. The pastor responded by punching the officer's wound.

Get up, get up, get up, Amy thought to herself and to Paul. She hobbled to the fence surrounding the vacant property next to Harley's house, then straightened themself up. Amy's pistol was in a thigh holster on the inside of their right leg. Paul used their left arm, 'his' arm, to try to get to it, under the slicker and the soggy skirt and the various other holsters there. *Almost got it,* he thought to her. He took the lead to bend forward, which gave him the extra few inches he needed to reach the gun.

She saw Duke and Harley in a fist fight. The officer was holding his own, considering how he was bleeding from the knife wound, but he was between Amy and the pastor. Paul couldn't dare try to shoot. The deluge became thicker, more like a wall of water instead of drops of rain.

Suddenly Duke dropped. Amy hadn't seen Harley's action, but Paul thought, *I'm guessing a kick in the 'nads. Poor guy!*

Duke crawled toward his squad car, the blood from his knife wound dripping into the wet street. Harley was standing between Amy and the lieutenant, so Paul couldn't safely take a shot at the evil preacher. Smirking, Harley picked up his fallen knife. He shook water from it, then turned to Amy.

"You had to keep poking," he said. "You couldn't blame that bitch Sam Atkins and let it go." He held the knife up in his right hand, and tested the point with his left thumb. "So I have to take care of you, and your cop friend." Despite the heavy rain dripping from his brown hat, he was smiling broadly.

"Why?" Amy croaked. She was backed against the fence and could not retreat.

"Same reason I did Butch in. I wanted his job. I wanted Riley's job. Associate pastor doesn't pay very well." He waved the knife in front of Amy's face. "And I wanted to be the one to do that first new gay wedding. I could make money on a lecture circuit."

Paul thought, *Duke is at his car, but it's right behind Harley. If I shoot him the bullet might hit Duke.*

So we're defenseless, she thought back. *I can't move my right arm and you don't want to show our gun until you can shoot. Great.*

"You said you didn't have a relative named Harley," Amy said in her broken voice. "That's because you are Harley."

The man smiled broadly, "You're not half dumb." He flipped the knife from right hand to left, and then back again.

"So, why call yourself Drew? Why pretend to be a woman?"

Still tossing the knife back and forth, Harley said, "I had to disappear after Shreveport." He waved the knife in front of Amy's face, and she closed her eyes tightly. "My sister Drew was killed in a car wreck in high school, so I just took over her identity." Another feint, another flinch.

"So, did Sam put you up to this?" Her voice broke like a twelve-year-old boy's, and her neck was throbbing.

"I've been planning this for months," Drew said, his gaze boring into their eyes even as he flipped the blade from one hand to another. "When she showed up, I figured she could take the blame."

A grin–no, it was a leer. "That was my mistake in Shreveport, I didn't have a patsy set up."

"Are you even a pastor?" Paul asked, in the same barely understandable voice; their neck still ached and their right arm was so numb that it didn't feel the rain anymore. "Do you really care about gays?"

He held the knife in his left hand, and held it under Amy's chin, point up. "I'm ordained Baptist and Methodist," he said, "and I took those stupid MCC classes. Yep, I am a man of the cloth." He held the knife against Amy's right cheek, and pressed the blade until drops of blood oozed out before getting washed away in the Hurricane Olaf rain. "And yeah, I care about gays. I'm bi myself." He shook his head. "Sam didn't understand. And–did you see those eyes on her back? What kind of person gets eyeballs tattooed on their back?"

Amy's gaze was glued to Harley. Even though they used the same eyes, Paul noticed movement behind the pastor; Duke seemed to be climbing in to his cruiser, head first. Paul thought to Amy, *Tell Duke to move so I can shoot this creepazoid. If I think to him he'll freak out from my male voice.*

Drool was dripping from Harley's smiling mouth, mixing with the rain. He tossed the knife to his other hand, and held it against Amy's left cheek. She was frightened, but she took Paul's advice. *Duke,* she thought to the lieutenant. *If I shoot him, I'll hit you. Can you move five feet left or right? Then holler at the preacher. I'll take it from there.*

Paul, paying attention to their peripheral vision, saw Duke let himself back out of the prowl car and sit in the flooding street. He leaned to his left and crawled a few feet. The torn left sleeve of his uniform was dull red from bleeding.

Harley pressed the knife against her ear and sliced down. Her eyes went wide with the sudden pain. The pastor was grinning as he said, "That's just the start."

Amy heard Paul think, *It's only our ear, we're going to be okay.* The preacher held the knife a few inches in front of her face, pointing the tip of the stiletto first at one eye, then the other.

Amy thought, *Gun?*

"Hey, Preacher!" Duke bellowed.

When Harley turned to the voice, Paul brought Amy's Ruger up and fired twice. The smile on the pastor's face collapsed into an open mouth of surprise, and he took two steps back. He held the knife with both hands, and took a step toward her.

One more shot rang out, from Duke's service pistol. Harley spun around; the knife flew away, and the man fell on his side in the rushing water of the hurricane's flood.

Amy poked at the fallen man with her foot, provoking a quiet shout from Harley. Satisfied that he was alive but neutralized, she went to Duke where he was sitting in a puddle, leaning against the side of his cruiser. "Lieutenant," she croaked, then thought to him, *Thank God you got here. I'm going to call Rampart Street, and then you and I will take a leisurely Sunday drive to Touro Infirmary. Got it?*

A smile flashed across the man's face. "Queenie. Can't you. Talk normal. For a change?"

Smiling, she thought, *Nothing normal about me.*

Amy leaned into the cruiser and pressed the call button on the radio. "I need two ambulances on France Street southeast of St. Claude," she barked, although her voice didn't behave as she'd like. "Got a uniformed man down, and a wounded perp."

The radio squawked, "Who's this? Is it you, Sugar? You don't sound right."

"Oh, Walter," she answered, as blood dripped from their sliced ear. "I never felt better. It's good to be alive."

It was eight o'clock when Amy and Paul got back to their house in the Carrollton section. "I want to worship at the shrine of Saint Mattress, patron of sleep," Amy said. Christine's little yellow Smart car was parked in front, and they could see light coming through the closed shutters. It was still raining, but the worst of Hurricane Olaf's winds had passed inland, as the downgraded tropical storm worked its way into north Texas, upstate Louisiana, and Arkansas.

Paul said, "We can use some TLC. Christine will take care of us, you just wait." Still wearing their yellow slicker, Paul knocked.

"Uh, who's there?" Christine's voice came through the front door.

"It's me," Paul called. Amy added, "And me!"

They heard the security chain drop and the deadbolt open. "Where have you been?" Christine demanded.

Then she saw the bandage on their ear.

Eyes suddenly wide, she cried, "Paulette! Amy! What happened? I've been so worried. Are you okay?"

"Much better now that I'm seeing you," Paul said, and he kissed the woman on the lips. "Just wait 'til we tell you the story."

Christine stepped aside to let them in. Then she secured the door and stood behind them. "Paulette?"

First they shed the slicker and left it in a wet pile inside the front door. Then Paul turned to look at Christine. He was rewarded with her smile that showed off her twisted front tooth, sparkling blue eyes, and her multi-length, multi-colored hair. "How was your day, honey?" he asked, and threw their arms around her.

Christine somehow always knew which one of them was leading. Since her lover was in charge, she returned the embrace. Paul felt a few tears against their cheek. "I worry about you. You and Amy," she said to the side of their neck.

He felt her warmth chase away the chill of the hurricane weather. He thought to Amy, *Let's enjoy this hug a little longer. Then you can tell her how brave you are.*

Christine stepped back to look at her lover. Her broad smile faltered, and turned into a question mark. "Amy? Are those the pearls your father gave you?"

"What? Oh–" she looked down, then lifted the strand away from her neck so she could see them. "–Yes. When they're not covered in mud they're very pretty."

The smile came back to Christine. "Yeah. They're nice. Classy."

After a long pause Amy said, "I am so glad to see you. Uh, did you bring any wine?"

"I–I thought you were on the wagon. I didn't bring anything. Oh, Amy, I'm so sorry."

Paul said, "Day two? What happened?"

"I'm still alive," Amy answered. "I think that's worth celebrating."

❧ NOTES ❦

[1] *Biblical Theology of the New Testament* by Charles C. Ryrie. ©2005 ECS Ministries; ©1959 Moody Bible Institute; ©1987+1998 Charles C. Ryrie

2 The Firesign Theatre: *The Giant Rat of Sumatra* Columbia KC-32730 © 1974

3 A fried bread pudding po-boy really is on the dessert menu at Ye Olde College Inn. I don't pretend to know how they make it, but here's a basic recipe for the brave and the skinny:
1) Make bread pudding
2) Shape pudding into patties and put in lengthwise sliced French bread
3) Drop in deep fat fryer
4) Remove from fryer, being careful not to cook your fingers
5) Don't forget the vanilla sauce

4 "Drive In Saturday" by David Bowie ©James Music America/Chrysalis Songs/Fleur Music 1973

5 "You Don't Own Me" by John Madara and David White, ©Unichappell Music 1963, as sung by Lesley Gore

6 "Drinking Wine Spo-De-Oh-Dee" by McGhee/Mayo, ©Universal Music 1949, as performed by Stick McGhee & His Buddies

7 "The Wine Song" by Jesse Colin Young (Perry Miller) ©1967 Alley/Trio Music, as performed by The Youngbloods

8 "Hit The Floor" by John Doukas, Robbie Dunbar, Stan Miller ©1976 Tremor Music ASCAP, as performed by Earthquake

9 "Had Me A Real Good Time" by Ron Wood, Rod Stewart, Ronnie Lane ©1971 WB Music ASCAP, as performed by Faces; Paul's favorite line of the song

10 "Alabama Song" by Bertolt Brecht and Kurt Weill ©1927 European American Music; Paul prefers The Doors' version, but he also likes David Bowie's weird recording.

11 "One Bourbon, One Scotch, One Beer" by Rudy Toombs ©1953 Aladdin Music BMI, as performed by Amos Milburn, John Lee Hooker, George Thorogood... Paul only knows Thorogood's version.

12 "Have Some Madiera, My Dear" by Flanders & Swann ©1956 Faber Music PRS/ASCAP, as performed by Flanders & Swann, although Paul remembers his older sister playing it on a Limeliters' album

13 "Margaritaville" by Jimmy Buffet ©Coral Reefer Music BMI; Paul is not a Parrothead

14 "Nightrain" by Slash, Izzy Stradlin, Duff McKagan, Axl Rose ©1987 Guns N' Roses Music BMI, as performed by Guns N' Roses

15 "Maybelline" by Chuck Berry, ©1955 Arc/Isalee Music BMI; Paul loves Chuck Berry's music.